Beautiful Pretender

The Life and Circumstance of Arabella Mina Cordell
Book One

JM Howard

authorHOUSE®

AuthorHouse™
1663 Liberty Drive, Suite 200
Bloomington, IN 47403
www.authorhouse.com
Phone: 1-800-839-8640

© 2008 JM Howard. All rights reserved.

No part of this book may be reproduced, stored in a retrieval system, or transmitted by any means without the written permission of the author.

First published by AuthorHouse 6/16/2008

ISBN: 978-1-4343-8243-6 (sc)
ISBN: 978-1-4343-8242-9 (hc)

Library of Congress Control Number: 2008903828

Printed in the United States of America
Bloomington, Indiana

This book is printed on acid-free paper.

Dedicate To...

I'd like to dedicate this book to the
following people who have given me
a tremendous amount of love, inspiration
and support with my writings and who
encouraged me to take them to the next
step and share them with the world.

Thank you, Angie, Christine, Jewles,
Nhukie, Kimberly and a special
thanks to my wonderful husband and
my patient children. I love you all!

$\mathscr{I}$ntroduction

Dear Readers,

First of all I want to thank you for selecting this book to read. It is a great honor to become a published author and to write stories for people to enjoy. This is the first book in what I hope will be an exciting journey together with you.

I've been a story teller all my life. Telling stories is like breathing, it comes naturally and I must do it to live. It's like listening to well orchestrated music, it stirs the heart and refreshes the soul. For me, writing is an art, yet an art that everyone can understand and enjoy. When I write I get lost in time and my soul stirs with every emotion and sensation that my characters feel.

As the beginning of the series, I wanted this first book to be mostly fun, enchanting and exciting. I hope you enjoy reading this as much as I did writing it and I truly hope that if you enjoyed it, you will share this with your friends. I've already written eight other novels, some to this series and some are independent of it. I'm relying on you to let me know how much you enjoy my work and if this book goes well I will be happy to publish more for your reading pleasures.

You will notice right away that my books are not like any books you have ever read. I try to be unique with each story. First of all this entire series takes place in a somewhat medieval time period. However you will notice that I don't use Old English, I like my grammar to be simple and easy to understand. Also, because this is a fictional world, I took some liberties with the way the people act and also with their daily life styles. You will notice that a few things are more modern, though that is done sparingly. My books are meant to be fun more than historically accurate. However, many things are very appropriate to the time period. I also refrain from using intense descriptions of things. I only describe items, people and surroundings just enough to give you the basic idea and then I let the reader form their own image around that. I personally believe that this makes the stories more charming and fun.

This book signifies the beginning of a series known as The Arminian Series. Both the first story and the last story of the series will have sequels, where each of the stories in-between these, will individually be told in their own book. This first story, The Arabella Trilogy, deals with the life and circumstances with the daughter of a nobleman in the setting of a fictional world. Her name is Arabella Mina Cordell.

Arabella's story will take place in three books, though I might consider doing a fourth later on. After her story is where the real Arminia Series begins, however without Arabella's story, you will miss out on quite a lot of the background to the Arminia Series.

Again, if you enjoy this book I hope you will let me know. I really hope to hear from you all and to be able to provide you with more adventures and romance in the years to come.

Sincerely Yours,

JM Howard

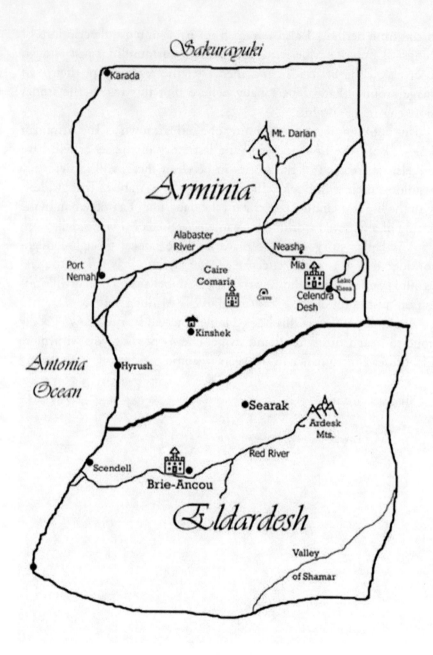

Map of Arminia and Eldardesh

Kendrick & Eric's Father

Sister, Princess Sara
↓
Baron Wallace

First Wife -
↓
Baroness Wallace

Second Wife -
↓
Kendrick & Eric

Kendrick & Eric's Mother

Sister, Princess Cornelia
↓
Baron Aldrich Cordell

Sister, Princess Anna
↓
Lord Peter Evanston

Husband
↓
Kendrick & Eric

Arminia Throne Succession

1. Baron Wallace
2. Lord Wallace
....
6. Baron Cordell

Eldardesh Throne Succession

1. Lord Peter Evanston
2. Baron Cordell

Family Tree and Throne Succession

Part One

$\mathscr{P}$rologue

Aram looked over towards Edmond who stood on the thick limb of a sturdy and old oak tree, opposite his own, on the other side of the rutted dirt road. Currently Edmond's dark eyes were carefully watching the approaching carriage of a noble couple as it made its way towards them. It would still be a short time before it was within range. Edmond's dark black hair matched the simple black mask he wore on his face and the black clothing he was wearing. On their raids, Edmond more then any of the rest of them had to do his best to hide his identity since he too was a nobleman. Edmond was not just any nobleman either but he was also currently second in line to the throne should anything happen to their king and his father. Edmond's father, Baron Wallace, was currently first in line to the throne since their king was only a boy of fourteen and hadn't yet started a family. It wouldn't do at all should any of the nobles of the kingdom discover that this young man of such high esteem was one of the more notorious bandits in the kingdom, who was wanted by law.

Aram laughed softly at his friend's disheveled hair which was not normally quite so messy and this drew Edmond's attention. "What?" Edmond mouthed smiling as his dark eyes glistened in the morning sun.

"Nothing." Aram whispered back with a grin and then he pointed towards the carriage. "It's almost time... Stay alert." Quietly they, along with twelve other friends of theirs, all were wearing black, waited silently in the trees. When the carriage was nearly to the point where it was under them, they all leapt to the ground with their swords drawn. The two horses screamed out in fright as the reared up on their hind hooves and the driver of the gaudy overly decorated enclosed carriage did all he could to calm them down.

"We've come to lighten your master's load." Edmond smiled at the driver. "If you would be so kind as to wait here, we will only be a moment." Edmond never came face to face with the nobles that he and his friends robbed. This was to help hide his identity from those who would most likely recognize him. Even though he wore a mask, it was still possible for them to recognize this popular youth if they had a chance to look at him and hear his voice.

Aram made sure his own black mask was in place along with the black scarf he used to hide his hair. He opened the side carriage door, it as well as the rest of the carriage was red, white and gold. The expense of the gold alone on the carriages exterior could feed a town for nearly a year, in moderation of course. "If you folks would be so kind as to step out of the carriage, we will make this as painless as possible." Aram grinned and reached in to take the older woman's hand to help her from the carriage. A few of his other friends were on the other side of the carriage, 'escorting' the man out. Aram led the woman over to stand by her husband. "We are here to relieve you of the money and possessions that you have on you."

The man of about fifty with nearly completed grey hair on both his head and face spoke in return. "Why should we give you our belongings, young bandit? You boys should find a better pastime that doesn't involve stealing from those who you should be serving."

Aram smiled and brought his sword up to the man's throat. "You seem to forget that your fortune was built due to the blood and the sweat of those whom you look down upon, sir. Not only that but you grievously mistreat those of lower status then you, including your own servants. You dismissed a young woman from your service simply because she had asked for your help in buying medicine for her younger brother who is near the point of death. Since the law fails to protect these people, we, the Black Bandits, are here to bring justice to those that the law has forgotten." He stepped closer causing the blade to

xiv

touch the man's throat. "You will hand over all of your jewels and also your purse. These things are of no matter to someone of your status. They will pay for the medicine that the child needs and will also help to feed, clothe and treat those who can not manage to survive without your charity."

"Why should I have to pay for those lazy common dogs? This is my fortune not theirs…"

"They are the ones you use who make your pockets fat with gold and they get nothing in return for all that they do for you. The least you can do is to be charitable when they are in need. If you had done this on your own, we wouldn't be bothering you right now. Instead, since you failed to do so on your own incentive. Now we are here to encourage you to change your ways." Aram didn't take his eyes from the man as he then addressed his friends. "Boys." That was their queue to remove the jewelry and money from the couple and also to search the carriage.

"You'll be sorry you did this young man." The elderly man warned as his stout wife stood by him as pale as a ghost as the boys carefully removed her jewelry.

Then she spoke softly, "Please, don't take my wedding ring."

Aram looked at the hand she indicated, "Very well. Let her keep her ring." All the boys were very careful from using each others names on the raids so as not to betray their identities. "Such sentiments are the one thing we won't take, milady."

A slight look of relief seemed to ease the tension in the woman's face. "Thank you."

Once the boys were done, Aram told the couple, "You may go now and if I were you, I would try to be a little more charitable to those who are in need of your mercy, especially those who serve in your own home. If you do this, we won't bother you again."

"I'd say not." The man grumbled. "I will personally see to it that the king's men hunt you all down and make all of you pay severely for your crimes." He turned to his wife and ordered her to return to the carriage. Before he got in he addressed Aram one last time. "I won't forget this boy. Next time we meet, be sure I will be ready for you."

Aram bowed humbly, "Then I will look forward to that day sir."

"Impudent fool." The man said hotly and then got into the carriage. Once he was securely inside he yelled at his driver to make haste for home.

Edmond walked over towards Aram. "Looks like you made a new friend." He laughed gently.

Aram placed his sword back into its sheath. "Yes, apparently he wants to play with me the next time we meet. I'm rather looking forward to it." They both laughed knowing that Count Dreskin was a terrible swordsman even though he boasted about his 'skills'.

"Come, we should get these things to a safe place before the authorities come looking for us." Edmond put his arm around Aram's shoulders as they walked. "Did we get much today?"

Aram looked back at their friends and Silas spoke up. "We actually did quite well today. It helps that the Count and his wife like to proudly boast their wealth." All the boys found this to be true and funny. "We should head over to the lake once we're done hiding this stuff." Everyone agreed that a good swim was a just reward for the rich harvest they secured that morning.

"Come on Aram you never want to swim with us." Silas complain as he stared down with blazing blue eyes at Aram who was now lounging in the soft grass under the shade of a rather huge oak tree near the lake they often met at. The warm afternoon breeze rustled in the leaves of the scattered surrounding oaks that lay about the field around them. The water of the lake gently lapped at the dirt shore line in the short distance from where the boys were conversing.

Aram brushed aside some of his light brown hair that had strayed onto his face and then he looked up at Silas with his soft hazel eyes. Then in his young and almost feminine voice he answered, "I'm too tired to swim today." He laid his head back down on his arm which was folded behind his head and closed his eyes.

"Leave him alone, Silas. He doesn't have to swim with us if he doesn't want to. In fact, I'm not really up to it today either." Edmond scolded and then sat down near Aram. "Mind if I join you?" He asked his now lazy companion, compared the fiery youth who had just participated in another successful raid. When it came to sword play and 'pirating', Aram was spit and fire, but when it came to swimming and a few other things, he became lethargic. It was almost as if two different people dwelled inside this young man. Needless to say, Aram was a constant source of amusement for Edmond, which was probably why they got along so well.

"Don't mind if you do." Aram grinned with his eyes still shut. It wasn't the first time they both chose to ignore the others during such occasions and chose instead to sleep the afternoon away under the more then familiar oak tree.

"Is your voice ever going to change?" Edmond laughed softly as he settled down to lie next to his friend. "I swear sometimes you almost sound like a girl."

Aram swung his free arm over and hit Edmond in the chest as hard as he could which caused Edmond to laugh even harder. "It's not my fault that I sound this way." He sighed.

"I know, I know." Edmond's laughter was dying down. He then looked up into the scattered clouds of the midday sky as his black hair gently danced about his face in the soft breeze. "I love days like today." He looked over to where their friends were undressing before heading into the cold dark water of the lake. Some of them had already made it into the water and were roughing around with each other. Their naked bodies betrayed their youth despite the fact that they saw themselves as grown men.

"Yeah." Aram sighed contently still closing his eyes to the harsh light of the afternoon sun and the scenery around him. "There won't be many of these left."

"No." Edmond's voice had a sad sound to it. "I'll be eighteen in a few days and father has talked to me more than once about taking on a man's duties and settling down."

"Sounds familiar. My parents have also been suggesting that I set aside my childish ways and take on more responsibilities." Aram looked over at his friend. "We'll always be friends despite our differences, won't we?"

"It doesn't matter that I'm a noble and you're not. I promise that we will always be friends just as we have been these last several years."

"I'm glad." Aram closed his eyes again. "It would be miserable not having you around anymore. I know things will be different but it's nice to know that you won't let your social status change the person that you are."

"I couldn't bear the thought of abandoning my closest friend. Besides, if I wasn't the way I am, then who would be there for the less fortunate citizen of our kingdom." Edmond yawned and then closed his eyes. Soon they were both asleep as the breeze gently caressed their faces and the sound of splashing water and boys laughing gently filled the air.

Chapter 1

"Arabella!" Jocelyn, her mother called again. "Child, you are going to make us late again. Would you please try to hurry just a little?" She called out once again in a more frantic tone.

Arabella sighed as she looked at herself in the mirror. "I hate these stupid occasions." She grumbled in her thick Eldardesh accent. She watched her attendant do the last adjustments to her soft light brown hair, which had been carefully arranged onto her head in a most modern and stylish fashion. "Can't father and mother go without me? This really is more for them then it is for me."

Her handmaiden, Ida, laughed softly. "Of course not mistress, it really is time for you to at last take your rightful place in society. You certainly have given them more grief then any daughter should with your wild and unrefined ways. Personally I think it was in bad judgment that they allowed you to roam about the kingdom as a boy in the first place. For a future queen, this behavior is simply unthinkable."

"At least I disguised myself so no one knows who I am. They should be thankful for that." She stood up from her stool and adjusted her skirts. "Enough." Arabella told Ida impatiently and pushed her way past the slender hand maiden with golden hair and soft blue eyes and then she headed for the door. "Have my other clothes ready for me for when I return."

"Yes miss." Ida sighed as she slowly shook her head with a gentle smile of amusement.

Arabella made her way down the grand staircase towards the front entry, where her parents patiently waited for her. "Finally." Her mother smiled and walked quickly towards her to meet her daughter at the bottom of the stairs. "Don't you look lovely my dear." She praised as she looked Arabella over. "Come, we're late leaving as it is." Jocelyn reached her hand towards her daughter to encourage her to obey.

"I really hate this, mother." Arabella complained as she finished her decent.

"Please Arabella…" Her mother pleaded.

"Can't you at least call me Ara?" She preferred the shorter name but no one seemed to care and they continued to call her by her full first name. They all knew she was growing a little too comfortable with her alternative persona, Aram. It was beginning to cause them some concern.

"Please child, stop this foolish behavior and act like the young lady you are. If you can't do this for me then I will have to stop allowing you to do as you please when you're not with me. You ought to behave a little more like the bride of a future king and not so much like a penniless urchin."

"Yes mother." She sighed and took the hand her father offered her.

"You do look beautiful my dear." Her father smiled. Aldrich reached forward and gently touched under his daughter's chin with his finger. "Sometimes it's nice to have a daughter instead of a son." He jested with the best intentions. "I don't mind you being Aram from time to time but I do miss my little girl sometimes."

"Let's just hope no one recognizes her alter ego when we present her today at the palace or it will be the worse for us." Jocelyn sighed miserably.

"I'm sure she's been careful about the friends she makes." He assured his wife.

Arabella walked a couple of paces behind her parents and said nothing. Sure, she had initially tried to make friends with only the village boys but befriending Edmond was completely by accident. It happened nearly five years ago. They had moved to Arminia because her father was weary of the status of the government via the royal household in Eldardesh. The queen was nearing her death at the time and the country was on the brink of another needless war to satisfy the selfish desires of Prince Eric, the kingdom's Crowned Prince and heir to his mother's throne.

In Eldardesh, Arabella was forced to play the part of Baron's daughter and she attended the parties of other noble children and dressed in fine clothing. When they made the journey to Arminia she was only eleven years old. When they arrived to the city of Celendra Desh she had noticed some young boys playing with a ball made of pieces of leather roughly sewn together. The sight sent a thrill of excitement through her veins.

After much begging and pleading, her father finally gave in and allowed her to dress in the clothing of a young boy below their station and they tied back her hair into a pony tail that was bound tight in leather strapping. Many young boys would wear their hair tied back this way. She honestly looked no different then the other boys, though her features were a little softer. At the time they didn't have to worry about her chest for she hadn't developed yet, but as she did, she began binding herself to hide her womanly features.

Arabella looked down and knew she wouldn't be able to hide those womanly features much longer. Even now she had to take care to keep her shirt baggy to help conceal her true identity when she dressed as Aram. She would also wear an overcoat or cloak whenever possible to add to her protection to hide anything that her oversized shirts failed to conceal. Unfortunately with it being summer she couldn't wear such heavy garments and so she instead wore a man's suede vest over her shirt. It provided the concealment that she needed but she had to make sure she bound her chest tightly or it wouldn't give her the needed coverage.

She looked over to her father and mother who sat across the carriage from her as they talked about things she didn't care to listen in on. The young king, Kendrick, was having them come to court on this day for a formal introduction to the kingdom's nobles as citizens of Arminia.

Kendrick was ushered in as Arminia's king at the tender age of twelve when his father passed away. Unfortunately, almost immediately a neighboring country declared war to strike at Arminia in her time of weakness and grief. Normally Arabella's father would have been commissioned to go to war but because he wasn't officially a citizen of Arminia yet, he wasn't commissioned to fight on the kingdom's behalf. The law was that they had to live in the kingdom for five years before claiming citizenship and that was why they were now coming before the young king. He was officially welcoming them and better yet he was recognizing their noble blood and allowing them to maintain their noble status.

"Arabella…" Her mother said in a gentle voice.

"Yes mother."

"I want you to do your best to leave a good impression on his majesty. He's only fourteen but in a few more years he may begin to start looking for a bride and you're already a possible candidate for him to consider. After all, his mother was hoping you would marry one of her two sons someday."

"Mother, how disgusting!" She sighed. "I'm two years older then he is. It would be like marrying a child."

"Not necessarily. As you grow older, things like this won't matter as much…"

"Forget it. I'm not going to do it. I'll be pleasant with him but I'm not going to climb any higher in the noble food chain then where I already am. I'm happy with what I have and who I am now. I don't need anything else."

"How repulsive and disagreeable you are." Jocelyn huffed in frustration at her daughter's defiance. "Please Aldrich, do something about her."

Her father took a slow deep breath before he spoke. "Daughter, please try not to upset your mother." He told her gently. "Jocelyn, whomever the king sets his sights on will have no choice in the matter. We will introduce Arabella to him and then the rest is up to Kendrick." He looked over at his daughter. "Child, could it be that another man has caught your interest?"

"Certainly not." She said firmly. "I have no need for such a silly thing as marriage. As long as I have my friends, I don't need a husband. I'm perfectly happy just being the way I am now."

Jocelyn gasped, "You can't be serious. You are one of the most beautiful young women in these parts, not to mention your high social status and the heir to your father's fortune. You're future husband will also stand to inherit all that belongs to my father as well, which includes a vast amount of land in Eldardesh. Any man of noble birth, king or not, would want you for a bride. You are the prize of Arminia and Eldardesh."

"No one in Arminia has even seen me yet…" She reminded her mother. "… well that is, not as a girl."

Beautiful Pretender

"No… that is true." She sighed. "I have them believing that you are busy being groomed to fit your social status and now they are ready for you to make your debut into society."

"Child, it is time you grew up and took your place." Her father agreed. "These silly games must come to an end sooner then later."

"No." She told them firmly. "As long as I can continue hiding my identity, I want to continue to live as I do now. I promise if you let me do this, I will go to any social function you want, but please…" her tears began falling. "Please, don't take me completely away from the life I love and the friends I adore. I beg of you." Now she was crying.

"My dear Arabella." Her father said gently and crossed over to sit near his daughter and then he began to gently wipe away her tears. "If you cry now we won't be able to present you before the king. Please, stop crying, we are nearly there." He did his best to calm her down.

"Let me have this father, please." She begged in a soft voice through her tears.

Her father closed his eyes and sighed as he thought about her request. Then slowly he opened them and looked down at her. "Alright, your terms seem reasonable enough for now but soon you will have to stop dressing like a young man in public. I will give you one more year to be Aram and then you must promise me that you will stop doing it." He kissed the top of her head. "Is that agreeable to you?"

"For now." She gently wiped the tears from her face and eyes and looked up at her father. At least she had one more year and perhaps she could convince him to give her even more time later on. It wasn't that she wanted to be a boy, for she loved being a girl. However, she enjoyed spending time with the boys in the city and now she was very close friends with many of them. They had no clue she was of noble birth, in fact a friend of her father's who served as Celendra Desh's physician allowed her to use his home as her second home. Everyone who knew her as Aram thought she was this man's son. She never said as much but it was the common belief. He wasn't poor by any means, though most physicians were. He came from a wealthy family and had a wife. Together they had five children who ranged in age from two to ten. All of his children treated Arabella, who they were led to believe was a boy, like a big brother. Only their parents were wise to the true identity of young Aram.

The Cordell's carriage pulled into the front palace yard and through the high gates that blocked the palace from the public's view. The carriage moved slowly under the willow trees that made an archway over the road that led to the palace. When the carriage came to a complete stop the doors were opened shortly afterwards by the footmen who assisted them out of it. Arabella had to admit that this palace was something she had never expected. The exterior was a beautiful white stone and it was at least three times the size of the palace in Eldardesh, where they were from. The grounds were immaculate and the gardens were elaborate and filled with every type of flowering plant that was available to this area. Servants were everywhere either attending to them or the gardens or to whatever else needed attention.

Arabella wasn't sure how long she had stood there in simple awe of the entire spectacle but she came to her senses when her father took her gently by the elbow to lead her to the staircase that would bring them up to the palace entry. "A grand sight, isn't it?" He smiled looking down on her in adoration.

"Yes it is." Was all she could manage to answer. They weren't the only nobles arriving at the palace. Many others were showing up in carriages because the king was welcoming in such a prestigious family, cousins from his mother's side. Such occasions called for such an audience.

Once they were in the palace they were escorted to the throne room and to the area reserved for their social status. This area was in front to the right of the throne. This side was for those who were related to Kendrick's mother. The left side was for those who were related to his father. The higher the social status, the closer to the throne the family would stand. This also pertained to family relation. Her father was the nephew of the late queen, which meant he had to take a place further away then a person of a closer relationship would, for instance a sibling of the king, or his aunt or uncle. However, since there were very few that were closer in relation, they stood close to the throne. Kendrick only had one brother and an older sister, but he was the king of the Arminia. His mother hailed from originally, Eldardesh, where his brother Eric currently reined as king.

Arabella's family took their place in the audience and they were given the right to stand on the isle because they were the guests of honor and also because of their social status. Arabella did her best to breathe slowly and evenly as she tried hard to not look at the curious faces that looked her way. She truly hated these royal functions but she knew that she was born into this and would probably die in it. She glanced across the isle at the family of the king's father and wondered how much different they were from the side of the family she stood on. Part of her was curious to know how people would be situated who where related by blood to both the king and queen and she wondered if there were any people there who did have that relation. She looked up for a moment, as that curiosity struck her, at the people who were there. In all the muddle of people filing in and taking their places, one face caught her attention and she gasped in silent fear.

Moving back slightly behind her father, she tried to hide herself from the approaching face but her mother corrected her and made her stand in a more graceful fashion. 'I almost forgot that he was a noble also.' She thought to herself nervously as she tried to hide her face as Edmond walked down the isle towards where she stood. Thankfully his attention was diverted to a friend or family member that he was talking to as he took his place with the other nobles on the other side of the isle. Arabella hoped she would be lucky this day and Edmond wouldn't see her. It helped that he was standing further back in the crowd of people and not right on the isle. Even though technically because of his social status, he should have been on the isle, almost directly across from her. Instead he and the other young man, stood back where they could talk in private with one another.

Edmond was in closer relation to King Kendrick then Arabella's father was, so his position was nearest the throne while hers was nearly four feet further away. Edmond's father was currently first in line to the throne and Edmond was second. Not only was Edmond's father the son of the late king's sister, but Edmond's mother was also Kendrick's older sister from a previous marriage of the late king's. The age difference between Edmond's mother and Kendrick was due to the fifteen years the king remained unmarried in between. Though every nobleman was aware of her status as Kendrick's older sister, no one ever spoke about it because she chose to lower her noble title to baroness.

Trumpets from the back of the room sounded as the people turned to face the isle. They all bowed nearly in unison, Arabella did her best to do as everyone else did. The men bowed humbly at the waist and the women gently bowed with a curtsy. They remained that way until the king had passed and walked up the platform to his throne. Arabella hadn't seen this particular young king yet and she wouldn't until the audience was given permission to raise their gazes from the floor.

The signal to rise was given once the king took his seat and then all eyes turned his way. Arabella couldn't help but to steal a glance in Edmond's direction to see if he might have noticed anything but he didn't seem to have. His gaze was on the king. 'Thank goodness.' She sighed in her thoughts and then she looked towards the king with some relief that Edmond was probably not going to look her way. Kendrick truly was a young king. He was about the same age as some of the boys she hung around with but his gaze was that of a grown man. There was no youth in his stone grey eyes as he sat up straight on the towering throne. She could see some similarities in his features with that of his younger brother, King Eric, whom she had practically grown up with before coming to Arminia.

He began to speak. "As you all are aware, today we have among us a family that you have had a chance to become familiar with over the last five years. My mother's cousin, Baron Aldrich Alphonse Cordell, came to our kingdom from my late mother's kingdom of Eldardesh and has sought to become a citizen of Arminia. Baron Aldrich was a favored nephew of my mother and my father and they had often spoken well of him and also of his wife. Today we will officially welcome them into our kingdom as official citizens along with their daughter, Arabella Mina Cordell. The Baron and his wife will maintain their title and social status. The Baron also is the sixth heir in line to the Arminian throne and the second to the Eldardesh throne, so I expect you to keep this in mind when addressing him."

Kendrick then stood up and descended the stairs. He held out his hand towards Aldrich and that was their cue to begin their journey, as a family, towards the king. The Baron and Baroness walked side by side in front and Arabella followed behind. Once they were just feet from him, they all knelt down before him. Arabella was careful to make sure that she kept her head slightly facing away from Edmond in the hope that he wouldn't discover her. She could feel that her cheeks were flushed with the nervous she felt in the depth of her being. Thankfully, she was sure that everyone would account this to something other then her fear of Edmond recognizing her and instead attribute it to a humbleness of being before a king.

"My dear cousins, I formally recognize you not only as members of my kingdom but also as members of my family. Please rise." They did as he asked. "I personally would like to welcome all of you as official citizens to my beautiful kingdom of Arminia."

"Thank you, your majesty." Baron Aldrich smiled. "May I present my daughter, Arabella Mira Cordell." He and his wife parted ways to allow their daughter to approach the king. Slowly she walked forward and then bowed again before his majesty.

"Your highness." She said gently. "It is an honor to meet you at last."

"Rise child." He waited for her to do so. "It is an honor to meet you as well, dearest cousin. I was told that you were favored by my mother and that she wished for you to become the bride to one of her two sons. Is this so?"

"It is your majesty." Baron Aldrich answered.

"You are truly beautiful, milady." He smiled gently at her and then he looked to his audience. "From this day forth you will address this maiden as Princess Arabella Mina Cordell since she is destined to become a queen in the near future. You will recognize and call her by this title until her title is transferred at the time of marriage. She also shall hold the highest status in my kingdom, second only to my own, in memory of my mother and to honor her wishes concerning this young maiden." He looked back at Arabella. "Thank you for giving my mother joy when you dwelled in her kingdom."

"Yes, sire." She smiled sweetly. Inside she had other feelings. Sure, she liked his mother just fine but it was only because her parents were at the palace all the time. Her father had hoped that the queen would favor her to marry Eric but then they gave that notion up when Prince Eric's (his mother was still living at the time) behavior became questionable. They were worried that even though he would give their daughter a wonderful station in life should they wed, that he wouldn't make a good husband for her. However, this concern was more that of her mother then of her father. Her father had always looked upon Eric more like a son then a king. They had often spent countless hours together, whether concerning matters of the kingdom or spending time doing something recreational.

Eric did seem to like Arabella, well enough that he probably would have married her if they had stayed in Eldardesh. Every now and again he would send a gift to her with a note stating the latest activities in his personal life. Nothing suggesting marriage was ever delivered but the fact that he still remembered her in such a fashion, gave way to the idea that he still might consider her as a marriage candidate. Even though he was already married, he had yet to choose a queen to sit beside him.

The king then handed her father a rolled up parchment that was tied with a ribbon and said, "I will send for you within a fortnight to come to begin your duties in the palace. Until then, may you be well cousin."

"And you as well, my king." Baron Aldrich bowed humbly and then he kissed the king's hand. Then as a family they backed away five paces before turning to resume their place in the audience as the king addressed other matters. Arabella cautiously used this chance to escape and she made her way through the crowd with as little fuss as possible and then she escaped out a side door that had been left open for the servants to use. She then quickly ran through the palace and out the door to where her parent's carriage waited for them. This hadn't been her original plan but she was afraid that Edmond might see her and she was in no hurry for him to learn that his best friend was a girl. She was afraid that if he discovered her secret she would lose the treasured friendship she had with him.

Quickly as possible she made her way to her father's carriage. "Please take me home and inform my parents upon your return that I wasn't feeling well." She addressed the driver before climbing inside.

"Yes, milady." He replied formally and opened the door for her. Quickly she climbed in and soon they were on their way back to the house. She glanced out the back window and was relieved to see that no one had come out searching for her. It didn't take too long for the driver to get her back home since they lived not too far out of town.

Once she was home she immediately ran upstairs to her room and changed into her clothing to become Aram. Her attendant Ida helped tie her hair back with some leather strapping to create the long

Beautiful Pretender

stick like ponytail that was more or less common for boys of a lesser station to wear and soon she looked like the lad she felt so comfortable being. They also folded up her hair to give it the appearance of being shorter. It made the tail thicker when bound but it helped to aid to her deception. "I take it you will be gone for the rest of the day, milady." Ida said.

"Yes." She grinned. "Tell father I'll be home before dark."

"There really is no point in doing so, if I may be so bold as to say so miss."

"Whatever does that mean, Ida?" Arabella looked at her attendant with a scornful look.

"You always say you'll be home before dark but you never are until well after." Ida told her young mistress as she placed her hands firmly on her hips. "What could a young girl like you possible do that would keep you out so late?"

"Not a young girl but a young boy." Arabella reminded her with a grin, using her slightly more boyish Arminian accent, which she now had mastered.

"Yes... I suppose that does explain things." She sighed and then set about picking up the finer clothing that Arabella had on earlier and had been carelessly discarded onto the floor. "Go on then. I'll let your father deal with you later." She watched Arabella run from the room and when she knew it was safe she began to laugh softly. "That child is completely hopeless."

"Where has your daughter gone, Baron Cordell?" Kendrick asked with curiosity as he approached his cousin once the meeting in the throne room had adjourned.

"I'm afraid she was feeling rather poorly today, so she left once the introductions were over." Her father lied. He looked over at his wife and could see she was not happy about Arabella taking off without so much as a word.

"Oh that is disappointing." An older feminine voice said melodically from next to the Baron.

He turned to look at the speaker, "Baroness Wallace, how wonderful it is to see you again." Baron Aldrich smiled charmingly at her.

Kendrick reached out to embrace his older sister. "It's always a pleasure." He whispered to her as she kissed his cheek.

Once she released her brother she spoke to Baron Cordell. "You have met my son before…" She ushered Edmond forward so both the king and Aldrich could see him.

"Indeed I did once a few months back, I believe it was." Baron Aldrich smiled and the king nodded to his older nephew his greeting and he received a nod in return.

"I was hoping to introduce him to your lovely daughter, but it seems we must wait until another day." Her disappointment didn't go unnoticed.

"Mother…" Edmond whispered to her with some impatience.

She sighed with frustration, "Oh very well, go on."

"Sire." Edmond bowed. (He preferred to address Kendrick by his royal title rather than addressing the child as his uncle, which seemed rather awkward for them both.) Then he bowed slightly towards Arabella's father. "Until we meet again, Baron." He then turned and quickly walked out of the throne room.

"It seems unlikely that someone so young could have urgent business that calls him away at a time like this." Aldrich said as he watched the young man walk quickly away.

"I do hope he'll be more responsible in the future. He may be eighteen but he acts like a child still." It was obvious that this youth caused his mother a lot of grief.

"Have you decided on a bride for him yet?" Kendrick asked.

"No, not yet. There are a few families that we are still debating on. All of them are fine candidates and each of them is eager to have him marry their daughter." She turned and then smiled at the baron and his wife. "If Arabella hadn't already been chosen as the wife to one of the two kings, we would have chosen her without hesitation. Your family is truly the cream of the crop not only in Arminia but in Eldardesh as well. It doesn't hurt that your daughter is a rare beauty either."

"I am truly honored by your appraisal, milady." The Baron smiled gratefully as did his wife. "I'm sure we too would have been honored by your proposal. After all, your son comes from a highly esteemed family from our late king's side. Such a marriage would have been ideal for us both."

She then smiled at her younger bother, the king. "Of course his majesty is best suited for such a bride." She humbly bowed, "If you chose her, you will do well sire."

"Thank you, sister." He smiled in return. "I hope to have the chance to get to know the princess a little better in the months to come. However, according to her parents and also due to my mother's wishes, I'm sure she will make a fine queen for whomever she marries."

"King Eric has shown interest in her as well, but being that he is only twelve, he does have other things more pressing on his mind then who will be his queen." The baron suggested.

"Too true." Baroness Wallace agreed. The four continued to converse for sometime before parting ways. However Arabella's mother was personally worried about the impression her daughter was leaving, not that she let on her thoughts on the matter. She was hoping the girl would try a little harder to make a good impression on the Arminian king, especially if she didn't want to marry King Eric. She looked carefully at the handsome young king who was her husband's cousin by blood. In her mind she was sure he would make the better husband to her daughter. It had nothing to do with politics, but with his mannerism. He was known to be gentle and kind compared to Eric who was hot tempered and at times irrational. Arabella wouldn't be happy being married to King Eric but she might find some happiness with King Kendrick should he choose her for a wife.

Arabella, at the moment posing as Aram, laid down in the shade of her favorite oak tree and stuck a blade of grass in her mouth to chew on. She loved this life and lived it to the fullest. While most girls in her station and her age were learning how to become the ideal housewife, she was out here laying in the warm summer breeze under an old oak tree. She sighed contently appreciating her life as it was.

"There you are Aram." Trumpeted Silas as the sound of cheerful voices of some of her guy friends came over the hill just a short ways away from where she was lounging. "We were wondering where you were." Carefully she made sure her jacket assisted in concealing any hint that may have been evident of a female chest, since her bindings were not enough now to totally conceal it anymore.

"Go away, I'm trying to sleep." She said in her best boyish voice that had the usual Arminian accent. She only used her Eldardesh accent when she wasn't pretending to be Aram. It was fairly different and even slightly more romantic then the Arminian sound, at least in her opinion. "Why don't you go and find Edmond to bother?"

"You know he's at the king's court with his parents today. Apparently some noble family from Eldardesh is getting their official citizenship today, and he had to attend. I think they're from the king's mother's side or something."

"Yeah, yeah, I know who they are." Aram said in a sigh. "The Baron Cordell, his wife and daughter Arabella, if I remember correctly. I really don't see what the big deal is."

"Arabella..." Silas said her name to see how it would sound from his own lips. He sat down next to Aram. "Any idea how old she is?" He asked him since Aram who seemed to know more about this family then any of the rest of them did.

"About my age I guess." Aram really wanted to change subjects. He should have just pretended to not know the family, but since he was really the maiden Arabella, he unfortunately knew her better then anyone else did, though he'd never let on.

"Is she ugly or pretty?" Silas continued.

Aram looked up at him in annoyance, "I don't know. She's just a girl, that's all. Leave me alone already."

"You can't seriously tell me you're not yet interested in girls at your age, Aram." Eustace, a rather ordinary boy of seventeen with brown hair and brown eyes, also a friend of Aram's, said with disbelief. "Especially the way you toy with some of the nobles' daughters when we rob them." Memories of how Aram liked to torment them when they wouldn't cooperate by lifting up their skirts with his sword, still struck him as funny. Of course this was when their 'victims' didn't have parents with them.

"I really haven't given them much thought, to be honest. Girl's aren't much fun so I don't ever pay them any mind."

"Get up." Silas told Aram and grabbed his arm to force him to his feet.

"What now?" Aram's annoyed voice wasn't easy to miss.

"Are you going to do what I think you're going to do?" Eustace asked Silas laughing.

"Yep, but don't say anything yet." He grinned.

Beautiful Pretender

"What?" Aram asked confused. "What are you two planning this time?"

"Just come with us." Silas grinned and they practically dragged Aram with them towards town. Normally Aram would try to refrain from going to town because it was too big of a risk of being discovered but he resolved that he would do his best to not get caught and took comfort in knowing that most of the nobles would still be at the king's palace.

"So where are you taking me?" He asked them.

"It's a surprise." Eustace replied. "Don't worry, we'll let Edmond know where we went and he can find us later." Eustace looked at another boy in their group and nodded to him. Immediately the boy ran off to wait where Edmond would find him so he could inform him as to where all of the rest of them had gone. Edmond was the only boy in this group of boys who was born of noble blood. (That is if you didn't include Arabella whom they only knew as Aram. As far as they knew, he was just the same as them in a manner of speaking.)

Aram obediently followed the other boys and was relieved that they headed in the direction of the lower class section of town. Aram's identity was safer here then if they went to the high society part of town. Soon they came to a small house and the noise inside was something Aram had never experienced before. "Where are we?" He asked.

"My house." Silas grinned. "You have never once come to any of our homes you know."

"You made all that fuss just to have me see your house?" Aram sighed in frustration. "You could have just told me…" His jaw dropped open as the front door slammed open and about five girls ran outside. "What the…"

"They're called girls." Eustace laughed and Silas did as well.

"I know what they're called." Aram scolded. "Who are they?"

Silas sighed. "They're my sisters, ten of them to be exact, and all of them ranging between the ages of two to twenty."

"You're parents have been awfully busy, haven't they?" Aram said in disbelief. His comment sent the boys into an uproar of laughter.

"Silas." One of his sisters came up to him. "Who's your friend? He's quite pretty for a boy." Smile smiled sweetly.

"His name is Aram." Silas announced proudly. He knew his

sister would notice Aram and come to meet him. After all she was a notorious flirt when it came to handsome men and she wasn't shy around them either.

The dark blond haired petite girl walked over towards Aram and looked him over. "Pleased to meet you sir." She curtsied. "Will you be staying for the evening meal?"

He was about to answer, 'No thank you,' But he was cut off by Silas in mid sentence.

"Of course he's staying." Silas told her as he threw his arm over Aram's shoulders. "He could never turn down an offer from such a pretty girl as you, Alicia."

"That's wonderful." She ran up and grabbed Aram's arm. Aram was doing his best not to give himself away and play along for his friend's sake.

"Um, thanks…I guess." He muttered.

Alicia dragged him into the house. "I'll be fifteen in the fall." She smiled. "Mother!" Her voice carried above the voices of the other girls. "We will be having some guests over for this evenings meal." Then she looked back over to Aram. "You'll get use to all of us girls in no time. I'm closest to you in age though. The next oldest is Mira but she's eighteen. Silas is right in-between us in age." Aram was wondering if this girl was going to prattle on forever or if there was some way to shut her up.

"Don't worry, once she starts eating she'll stop talking." Silas teased. This made all the boys laugh, but not Alicia. She turned and gave him blue eyes of ice that could quite possibly kill if she chose for them to do so. Silas held up his hands in defense. "Just teasing." He laughed.

"Silas, you're too mean." She pouted and then laid her head on Aram's shoulder. "How can you be friends with someone as mean as my brother."

"He's just mean to girls. I'm alright with that." Aram countered. Again the boys laughed but Alicia chose to ignore them.

"Come with me." She told him and then looked at her brother, "The rest of you stay here."

"Yes princess." Silas mocked and bowed.

"I want to show Aram something. We'll be right back."

"Uh, guys…" Aram tried to ask for their help but they wouldn't

Beautiful Pretender

budge. Instead they sent him off with smiles, waves and the wink of an eye. "Great." Aram said under his breath. She led him out back to where a swing hung from a huge tree on their small property. They walked over to it and she took a seat and began to gently swing it back and forth.

"Do you have a girl you're interested in right now, maybe one that you're courting?" She looked up to him with her innocent eyes.

Aram could feel himself begin to fidget. 'Of course not!' Arabella thought to herself. 'I'm a girl, so why on earth would I want to court one?' Instead 'he' said, "No, I'm not really interested in doing those kinds of things right now."

"You should be." Her voice was gentle, "After all you are about 16 now, right?"

"Yes, but I really don't want to court any girl's at the moment."

She laughed softly. "Don't be ridicules, of course you do. You just have an issue of insecurity, that's all." She stopped the swing to get a better look at him. "I have a little secret I'm going to share with you, but don't tell my brother."

"Alright." Aram said slowly with suspicion.

"I knew you were coming today. Silas had it all planned out."

"That idiot." Aram fumed.

"Don't be mad at him, Aram. He's just trying to be a good friend."

"I told him I wasn't interested…"

"Don't say that. You don't even know me yet." She stood up and walked over to face Aram. "Please, consider courting me. I won't be too pushy about the extent of our relationship and you'd have the perfect excuse not to court other girls. Just consider it." She gave her best puppy eyes to add sweetness to the proposal.

"You really don't know what you're asking. Let me assure you that you don't want me to court you."

"Why ever not?"

"Well…" He took a deep breath, "Just trust me about this one. I won't make a good companion for you or any other girl. I'm just not interested in having that sort of relationship right now." He wasn't sure how else to put it and not give away his secret.

"This is so unfamiliar to me." She whispered sadly in confusion.

"What is?"

"No boy has ever turned me down before." She looked up at him again. "Is it maybe that you're afraid that you might violate me?"

That nearly gave Aram a heart attack, "No, nothing like that." He said with his hands up in self defense.

"I wouldn't mind it at all if you wanted to touch me." She smiled.

"Well I would." He stepped back but she only stepped closer.

"Then is it because you find me unattractive in any way?"

"Not really, you're actually very nice looking but I'm just not…"

"Then I don't see why you should refuse me." She stepped closer again. "I think it's just because you are shy." She reached her hand up and laid it on his shoulder. "Perhaps if I kissed you, you wouldn't feel so uncomfortable anymore."

"No please don't." He tried to move but she pushed him against a tree that was right behind him. "Please don't do this."

"Trust me." She moved closer. "I know what I'm doing." A smile crept across her lips.

"There you are Aram." Edmond said loudly as he quickly walked towards them. "I see Silas introduced you to his lovely sisters."

"Edmond!" Alicia smiled as she turned away from Aram and walked towards one of her former loves. "It's been forever since you have come to visit me." She wrapped her arms about his neck and kissed his cheek.

Carefully he released her from him. "It's wonderful to see you as well." He smiled charmingly. "I see you have a new pursuit." He looked over at Aram whose face was reddened from embarrassment. "You will have to be patient with him my dear. He isn't as easily vexed by your charms as the rest of us."

"Oh don't worry about that." She grinned. "I think I'll enjoy the challenge."

"Why don't you run in and tell Silas that Aram and I will have to cut our visit short, Aram's needed back home."

"Oh no, really?" She said sadly. "Must you leave so soon?"

"I'm afraid so my dear." He smiled tenderly and touched her cheek. "Perhaps we can come again sometime soon."

"I do hope so." She looked over at Aram. "Until next time." She curtsied and then turned to go back to the house.

Beautiful Pretender

"That was close." Aram sighed and walked over to where Edmond stood. "I honestly thought she was going to kiss me."

Edmond laughed, "Would it have been all that bad if she did?"

"Yes. I've never known a girl to behave so..." He sighed. "It just isn't right for a maiden to behave like that."

"No, I suppose not." Edmond laughed. "She doesn't try too hard with me because she knows my parents would never accept her as being qualified as a suitable wife. Her family has neither money nor social status. Those alone are enough but her behavior would null those even if she had them."

"I'd hope so." Aram looked back towards the house and could see her watching them leave. It sent chills down his spine. "I'm never coming here again. I don't care if Silas pleads and begs..."

"If she's serious about you, she'll find a way to see you again." Edmond warned his best friend.

"I'd rather drown in the lake then to court someone like her."

"She's not all that bad." Edmond laughed again at Aram's strange behavior that never ceased to amuse him.

"Then you court her."

"No thanks. I am waiting for that special girl who steals my heart." He placed his hand on his chest and then his face saddened as he lowered his hand. "Actually, more likely then not, my parents will arrange my marriage. They've already been talking with the parents of a few candidates, so it probably won't be long before a decision is made."

"An arranged marriage." Aram thought out loud in a quiet voice. "I wonder if my parents plan to arrange my marriage."

"It's possible though usually that is only done with the higher social classes. Of course your parents aren't poor, so it could possibly happen."

Aram looked up at him for a moment, "Even a better reason for not allowing ourselves to get involved with anyone."

"True." They headed towards their usual spot by the lake. Today they would be alone for a change. It wasn't often they could hang out with each other without the others around. It was something they tried to do on occasion without being discovered. Edmond appreciated Aram's laid back behavior compared to the group's overly active one. As they walked they continued to speak in light conversation.

"It's just the two of us, are you maybe up to going swimming with me today?" Edmond asked once they arrived at the lake.

"Not really." Aram sat back down under his favorite tree.

"Do you not know how to swim or could it be that you do not like being in the water?" He asked in confusion. It was true that in the entire time they had been friends, he had yet to see Aram swim with any of them. He only now finally worked up the nerve to ask about it.

"I actually love swimming but I just don't like doing with other people around. I don't know why, it's just the way I am I guess."

"I see." He sat down by Aram. They sat there for a long time in silence pondering in their thoughts the future that lay before them as they watched the birds come and go from the waters surface and the surrounding shoreline. For Edmond his thoughts drifted off to the plans his parents had for him. For Arabella it was many things, the future marriage, having to give up her life as Aram and so much more. Neither realized that they had drifted off into their own worlds and honestly it didn't really matter. It seemed that no matter what they did, they were always in sync with each other.

Chapter 2

Arabella woke up the next morning, as her attendant who drew open the curtains to her room's windows, allowed the sun to fill the darkness that she had been thoroughly enjoying in the comfort of her large four poster canopied bed. "Close the curtains Ida. I'm much too tired to awake from my sleep yet."

"Come on you lazy girl, wake up." Ida walked over and pulled the covers off of Arabella who immediately moaned with complaint as she unsuccessfully tried to grab them back from her handmaiden. "Your mother is waiting patiently for you downstairs child. You have a visitor."

"I do?" She moaned as she tried to think who would want to visit her in Arminia.

"Yes. Now get yourself out of bed and let me help you get ready for the day." Quickly Ida, her handmaiden, dressed Arabella in the latest medieval fashion complete with the smock, corset, underskirts, farthingale, bum roll, chemise and a gown of green velvet. The gown tied in the front of her bodice, leaving a V at her chest that exposed her chemise underneath and it also tied on her outer sleeves leaving boxes between the strings that allowed the chemise gown to puff through. Her feet adorned the latest fashion in footwear, a pair of black boots that laced up the outer sides. Her hair was put up in a black snood (a circular hairpiece woven in a net fashion made of thick woven thread that was used to hold up the hair up on the back of her head. Many times it had beads or some other decorations to make it even more becoming.)

Arabella's dress and skirts gently swept at the floor as she walked to the stairway that would lead her down to the visiting room, as her parents affectionately called it. It was the room they had especially designed to welcome important guests. Seeing as how they were of royal dissention and that her father was the distant heir to not just one but two thrones, they often had guests of high stature visit them. Today, according to Ida, was no exception. What Arabella couldn't figure out was why she was expected to meet with this guest as well. She had planned on sleeping in longer.

When she approached the entry way, for the doors had been left open, she stopped and looked in. The room was finished in fine polished woods and the décor was the finest her parents could afford. Her mother sat in her usual high back chair and she sipped tea with a man, whose back was currently facing towards the doorway where she stood.

Jocelyn looked up and smiled at her daughter. "Good morning dearest child. Please come in." Both Jocelyn and her guest stood up and they faced the doorway where Arabella was still standing. "Do you remember Lord Burton?" Her mother asked.

Arabella looked closely at the tall thin man of about forty with short dark hair and somewhat dark skin for a moment but she couldn't remember him for the life of her. "I beg your forgiveness sir but I don't recall us meeting before." She bowed humbly with respect.

He laughed softly. "It is only natural for it has been nearly eight years since I last saw you, dearest cousin." He walked over and embraced her tenderly. "My you certainly have become a beautiful young woman." He gave her his arm and escorted her to her seat. "Please sit." He smiled and then returned to his own chair.

"Lord Burton has come on behalf of our cousin, King Eric." Her mother smiled. "He has been concerned about your well being and happiness since we left Eldardesh."

"Yes. Please give me what news you wish the king to hear, milady so I may set his mind to rest." He asked Arabella.

"Oh…" She hadn't realized that it meant all that much to Eric. "You may tell him I'm fairing well and that I am finding suitable friends to keep company with. Mind you, I'm not accepting suitors yet, but I do have friends that I can depend on." A gentle smile lit up her face. To be honest she much preferred Arminia to Eldardesh and she had no plans of ever returning to her former home, even though she had grown up in the palace with the prince after he and his mother left Arminia to return to Eldardesh.

"Have you met with King Kendrick yet?" He asked Jocelyn.

"Only just. We have finally been accepted as citizens."

"Very good." He smiled and then looked back at Arabella. "My King has asked me to send you an open invitation to come back to Eldardesh to visit him. He wishes for you to spend time with him at court."

"Mother…" Arabella felt a panic rise up in her.

"Yes, she would be more then happy to come and visit though at the moment I'm afraid we've already made promises for the next few months to the king and several other noble families. I will try to work out a time that would work well for us all to come and visit him in the near future."

"Of course. I know the King will be pleased to hear this. I have a feeling he is rather fond of your daughter and being one of his advisors, I wouldn't object to such a suitable match. As you may have noticed in the past the king seemed to be happier when she was around."

"Yes, I noticed." She smiled. It was no secret that the Eric was indeed very fond of Arabella. In fact he more likely then not loved the girl very much. It was also true that even though he was hot headed and bad tempered, he usually was fairly calm when Arabella was around him. He tended to dote on her incessantly and even while she was away he continued to think about her.

"I have matters in which I have been entrusted to discuss with your husband, so if you would pardon my short duration, I must leave and tend to these matters as soon as possible so I can be on my way back to Eldardesh without much more delay." Lord Burton informed the Baroness.

"Of course. I will have one of our servants take you to him immediately." Jocelyn smiled warmly.

"You have my deepest gratitude, milady." They all stood up and he bowed before them. Then he gently took Jocelyn's hand to kiss it fondly and then he surprised Arabella by kissing her hand as well. "I look forward to our next meeting, dearest ladies." He smiled humbly.

"As do we sir." Jocelyn walked with him to the hallway but Arabella couldn't move.

Surely this isn't the marriage her parents would have arranged for her. She really didn't like King Eric all that much. Sure she was nice to him because he was family but she really wasn't all that fond of him. Not to mention the fact that the brat was only twelve and she was sixteen. It was even worse then the idea of her marrying Kendrick. At least there was only a two year difference with him, not that she had any intention of marrying either of them. She finally was able to walk to the doorway of the room and there she waited for her mother to return.

Upon her return, Jocelyn reflected to her daughter. "Well at least one of the kings seems to be interested in you." She sighed. "I haven't quite figured out Kendrick yet but I know that Eric has always been infatuated with you."

"Mother, really. I don't need to marry a king. In fact I'm not sure whether I want to get married at all. I like my life the way it is."

Jocelyn reached over and touched her daughter's shoulder. "This foolishness with being Aram has gone on long enough. I think your father is daft to allow you to continue doing this for even another day, let alone a year but he feels that you should be allowed to do this for a while longer before you are forced to live as you should. I personally feel that it should have never been allowed in the first place but you are your father's one weakness." She smiled gently and sighed, "He never could deny you anything, could he?"

"I suppose not." Arabella smiled as well. It was true. Her father adored her with no limitations. In many ways, she was sure, he allowed her to be Aram to make up for the son he never had, yet he also adored his little girl Arabella. She was sure for him it was the best of the two worlds rolled into one pretty little package.

"Come have something to eat before we leave."

"Leave?" She asked surprised. "Where are we going mother?"

"Oh, didn't I tell you? Baroness Wallace has invited us to come to her home for refreshments and entertainment this afternoon."

"Baroness Wallace." Arabella thought about the name for a moment because it sounded familiar. Then fear struck her heart. Was fate trying to be cruel to her by throwing her in the path of Edmond as a girl again? Surely he wouldn't be home during that part of the day. Normally he, like her (as her alter persona Aram), were out with the guys, most likely they were planning another raid since it had been a while since their last one. It was possible that she could do this without being caught but there was no guarantee.

Thankfully she had managed to not go to his house yet as Aram and she was sure, at least for now, that only her feminine self would be going, and hopefully only this once. This being the case, it would be likely that even though Edmond's mother would meet her, she might never know that her beloved son was best friends with a cross dressing girl. It certainly wouldn't do him any good should his parents find out, no matter what her station.

'What a mess I'm getting myself into.' She thought silently. 'If Edmond discovered my secret, he might never forgive me.' He had treated her very much like one of the guys and even shared secrets with her that he would never tell a girl. He had mentioned things that were only suitable in male conversation and slept by her side on the shores of the lake on several occasions during their many midday naps. They even slept side by side under the stars one night. There was also the fact that Edmond, as well as the other boys, never guarded their conduct around Aram. They would dress and undress, relieve themselves and other such things with no inkling that a female was among them. Of course Arabella wouldn't watch when they did things not meant for female eyes. Instead she would nonchalantly conceal her eyes or would turn her head to avoid seeing anything she shouldn't.

If he had known she was a girl, he would have never done anything like that. However, that was what she treasured about their relationship. There was never any need to worry about the boundaries that men and women had to put up in a relationship. There was no need to pretend, well other then the fact that she allowed the others to think she was male. She didn't have to do anything girly to keep him interested in her and he wasn't nervous around her like he was around the other girls.

However, as she grew older she was now facing the fact that she could very well lose her dearest friend and companion. They had promised a lasting relationship that would keep them forever friends but that was only if she continued to deceive him. 'It's impossible.' She thought to herself and sighed audibly.

"Is something bothering you, dearest?"

"Mother, may I ask you a question?"

"Yes."

"This gathering we're going to, it isn't for marriage is it?"

"Oh heavens no, though they couldn't do much better for that handsome son of theirs. The Baroness is well aware that you are most likely are going to be the bride of one of the her brothers. Everyone is aware of that."

"Everyone?" She replied with a shaky voice. "Shouldn't I have some say in this?"

Her mother laughed softly. "Darling, you're the best suited in both kingdoms. It's no secret about Eric's affections but I would prefer it if Kendrick took an interest in you. In fact," She stopped walking and got near her daughter's ear as if this was some big secret. "Your father is arranging for you to have an audience with the king again. It seems your beauty left quite an impression on our cousin Kendrick. Don't be fooled, he is a very busy young man with much more important things on his mind, other then finding a bride, but he did seem impressed by you and word has it that his advisors are trying to convince him to make you his queen."

"I hope you are wrong about that." She sighed miserably.

Her mother backed away and was obviously frustrated with her daughter again. "Do not act so sour about this Arabella. The influence your father has over both kingdoms leaves little room for any other maiden to have any better chance then you. You should be thankful for all your father has done to secure our social status."

"Yes mother."

They waited to leave for Baroness Wallace's home until Arabella's father returned. He had some business to discuss on Kendrick's behalf with Baron Wallace and he thought this would be a good chance to talk to him if he was home.

As they rode together Jocelyn was the first to speak, "For as poorly as the weather this morning had started, it is nice to see that the rain let up."

Baron Cordell looked out at the sky, "Yes, but only just. It looks like it might rain again soon with those dark clouds moving in from the west."

"Indeed." She sighed as she looked out the same window he did.

"Living this close to the coast does tend to bring us rather frequent rains."

"Mother?" Arabella asked.

"Yes dear." Jocelyn looked over at her daughter.

"You don't think Lord Wallace will be there do you?" She was referring to Edmond by his Noble title.

"I'm not really sure. I have been to the Baroness's home before and it seems that he tends to steer clear of the house during her social functions. She told me once that he gets annoyed at how noisy we women get when we're together." She heard her husband laugh at that statement. "Oh hush." She scolded him and then laughed softly as well. Suddenly there was a loud noise and the carriage drew to a halt. They were only about half way to their destination and there were no residences around. "What on earth is going on?" She asked curiously.

"Perhaps I should go and find out." The Baron offered.

Arabella looked out her window and gasped when she saw what was outside. "Oh no." She whispered and quickly drew her hood over her head.

"What is it dearest?" Her mother asked.

"The Black Bandits." Arabella told her. She did her best not to laugh for she hadn't expected her friends to be robbing her own family, not that they knew who they were. "It seems they've caught onto your stinginess father."

"This isn't funny daughter." He scolded nervously. "These are wanted criminals…"

"Oh hush," she laughed softly. "They're just a bunch of boys in masks trying to help the poor."

"You sound like you admire them." He sounded almost angry with her.

"Perhaps I do." She looked up at him but then quickly hid her face when she noticed one of the Black Bandits approaching the carriage door closest to her.

"Good afternoon." The young man's voice said.

Arabella nearly chocked. It was Edmond's voice that addressed them. She knew he was in disguise but he had never been so bold as to actually address the nobles himself. True her family really didn't know him that well but it was still awkward. "How might we help you Sir

Robber?" She asked in a gentle voice.

"Arabella!" Her father scolded.

"Ah, so you are our new princess." His voice betrayed his curiosity. "It is a pleasure to meet you, your highness."

"As it is you, Sir Robber."

"In that case, I will try to make this as quick and as painless as possible."

Arabella reached out her hand towards him, taking great care to keep her face hidden. "Please, help yourself." She offered. On her hand were three rings and two golden bracelets which he indeed helped himself too. "Mother, give them your jewelry."

Jocelyn looked over to the boys who waited near the door she sat by. "I suppose I have no choice." Her voice betrayed her fear.

Once Edmond removed Arabella's jewelry, she retracted her hand and began removing her necklaces. Then she handed them to Edmond. "You are quite accommodating, milady."

"It is for a good cause, sir." Then she said to her father, "Give them your purse."

"Child, how can you be so calm about this?" He reached for his purse and handed it to the boys who had also collected her mother's jewelry.

"Sir Robber?"

"Yes, milady."

"I have one last thing I'd like to give to you, but you mustn't use it for the poor, instead, I wish for you to keep it with you as a token of my appreciation and support for what you do. Should I become queen and if you should come into trouble, use it to gain access to me so I might help you in your time of need." She reached up and removed the broach that adorned where her cape secured at her neck. "This broach is very special to me so I am entrusting it to your keep. It belonged to the very first queen of Arminia and it was given to me by the late queen of Eldardesh."

"You have given me enough, milady." He gently protested. "We never take such valuable keepsakes from those we rob."

She handed it to him. "Please, guard this for me." Edmond could see that her parents were not happy about what she was doing and he hesitantly took the broach from her. She began to withdraw her hand

28

but he quickly took it and brought it to his lips. Arabella gasped as she felt the warmth of his breath and the soft tenderness of his lips on her hand. It was the first time she had ever witnessed him being affectionate with a girl.

When he finished kissing her hand tenderly, he said, "You are indeed worthy to be our queen. I hope that you will help us in our efforts should this happen. Our days of thievery will no longer be necessary if you're to be our queen. I know you will help us to change the way the nobles behave to the less fortunate of our kingdom."

"I will do my best no matter what I become sir." She promised.

"Might I have the honor of looking upon your face before you leave?" He asked.

"Surely not, sir. If I did then it would be awkward should we see each other in public. It is better if we remain unaware of how the other looks for now." Yeah, like she'd let him look at her and discover her secret... not if she could help it. "Now go with my blessing, Sir Robber."

He kissed her hand again, "Then I will bid you ado for now, my princess." Quickly he left and soon the carriage was on its way again.

"I can't believe we were stopped by those bandits." Jocelyn was fanning herself in the hope to relieve her face of the redness she was sure it was boasting because of her nerves.

"What I can't believe is how friendly you were with that bandit, Arabella. How could you encourage him to behave in such a manner?"

Arabella lowered her hood from her head and looked into her father's eyes. "If you weren't so stingy and helped the less fortunate as you should, then this would have never happened. Personally I think what they're doing is very noble. Kendrick is a good king but he is blind to the needs of the less fortunate people in our kingdom. If the king and the nobles ignore these people's needs, who then is left to help them?"

"Her words do have merit, husband." Jocelyn agreed.

"Her words are nonsense." He countered. "I worked hard for my money, why should I give it away to those lazy dogs?"

Arabella sighed, "Because those lazy dogs work themselves nearly to death for you and get almost nothing for it while you grow wealthier without hardly needing to lift a finger."

"Take care who you criticize child. That money pays for your life style and it is responsible for you being sought after by kings. Do not continue to try to make me angry with you over this matter." He warned her.

"Very well father." She looked out her window. "However, don't complain to me should they stop you again to rob you." They all chose not to speak for the remainder of the trip. Once they arrived to the Wallace Estate, Barron Cordell didn't hesitate to leave the carriage immediately to search out Baron Wallace. Arabella and her mother agreed that they wouldn't speak about the robbery since it would only worry the women and frankly, Jocelyn wasn't in the mood to discuss it with them. The fact that she was robbed was beyond humiliating.

Arabella and her mother were escorted into the Baronesses home. Arabella thought it was a splendid residence, much like her own. It seemed that Edmond's family was as well off as her own family was. "Welcome!" The baroness grinned. "You're punctual as usual." She greeted Jocelyn with a warm hug. Despite their set backs, they still managed to make it at the appropriate time. "I see you finally brought your beautiful young daughter. Princess Arabella, welcome to my home." She curtsied. "You are a favorite of both kings it seems and I am honored you have come to grace our humble home."

'Nice... She sees me as a future queen as well.' Arabella did her best to smile and not betray her feelings of frustration. "Your home is lovely. Thank you for inviting me, Baroness."

"I had hoped to introduce you to my son, but he has wandered off again. I'm afraid that boy is hopeless." She laughed softly. "I'm sure he would have been delighted to meet a young lady as lovely as you are my dear."

'If you only knew.' Arabella wished she could laugh as the thought of her and Edmond's most recent encounter came to mind. Instead she said, "It is a shame but I'm sure we'll have another chance to meet him in the future."

This remark made their hostess smile even more as she led them to the room where her other guests waited. "That is precisely why we are gathering today my dear."

Arabella was confused, "You're arranging for me to meet him?"

"Oh no dearest, not exactly. As you may or may not know that every year or so we hold a gathering where we all wear masks and formal dress, we call it a masquerade ball. There will be music, dancing and the best foods our kingdom has to offer. This meeting today is to plan this momentous gathering. Also..." she could barely contain her excitement, "It will be your debut into society. You will be the guest of honor."

"Me?" She pointed to herself in surprise.

"Yes. We will also be celebrating your family's official citizenship in Arminia as well, but you, my dear, will be the center of the celebration this year. It isn't every day that a candidate for the queen is in our midst, not to mention that you will become my future sister-in-law no matter which king marries you. Not only that but you will have the chance to meet all of the eligible young men in our kingdom. I'm sure that if neither one of my brothers end up choosing you, that you won't have to worry about finding a suitable husband. Perhaps even my Edmond might be fitting as an alternative." She giggled femininely as did several of the other women in the room.

"I'm sure one of the kings will decide to marry her." Jocelyn smiled. She knew many of the parents of the young men in the kingdom were hoping that the kings wouldn't choose her daughter so that their sons would have a chance to court her. Her daughter came with not only a high title and wealth, but her husband could very likely inherit her father's place to the throne as an heir. This made her a valuable choice for a future daughter in law. The only man who wouldn't benefit too much from marrying her would be Edmond because he held a place closer to the throne. Only material possessions would be all he could look forward to, not that he lacked them by any means.

"I'm sure I am in no hurry for marriage, dearest baroness." Arabella said kindly. "Though I am extremely honored that you are doing such a wonderful thing for me and my family and that you would consider me to be a worthy bride for your son." Though the thought of being a potential bride for Edmond seemed awkward to her, she tried her best to talk and act like she was expected to.

The talk then turned to the upcoming celebration. Where it would be held, who would be in charge of what and so on and so forth. This also included where each woman planned to have her gown made and where they would purchase their jewelry and other accessories. Arabella found herself standing at the window and staring out into the Baroness's vast estate gardens. Her mother would take care of deciding what she would need for the celebration so there was no point in joining in on the conversation.

Gently she put her finger to the cold distorted glass as the rain ran down it in small streams and she traced one of the streams with her finger. She was so lost in thought that she didn't notice the time that had gone by or the change in conversation. "Well, you're finally home." The Baroness boasted proudly. "Come there is someone I have been wanting for you to meet."

"Could it wait until after I change my clothing? I'm soaked to the bone." The male voice said.

"Of course dear but please make haste. Our guests will need to leave soon."

"Yes mother."

Arabella continued to stare out the window, not even noticing that she was in danger of being discovered by Edmond who was forced to come home early due to the downpour of the rain that had started shortly after she arrived with her parents. "Arabella?" Her mother said gently near her daughter's side. "The Baroness's son just arrived and will come to greet you shortly." Her soft voice barely reached her.

"Hmm?"

"The young master is home and he would like to meet you."

"Young master?" Arabella slowly came back to the reality around her. Then what was just said hit her and she could feel her cheeks grow warm with fear. "You mean Lord Edmond?"

"Of course." She laughed softly. "You really weren't paying attention were you?"

"Mother… It's just that I'm not feeling well." Arabella's hand went up to her head as she began to feel dizzy.

"Oh?" Jocelyn asked in confusion.

"My head is bothering me terribly and it's making me sick. Would it be possible for us to leave now?"

"Before meeting Lord Wallace?" She knew Arabella was prone to severe headaches at times and fevers, though it was worse when she was younger. However she also knew that the Baroness had been wishing for their children to meet.

"Please mother. I feel very sick." She moved her raised hand down to her lips.

"Yes of course." Jocelyn turned to address her hostess. "I'm afraid our meeting with your son will have to wait until another time, my daughter is very ill."

Immediately the Baroness stood up and walked towards them. "Oh dear child, you should have said something earlier." Her voice was sympathetic. Immediately she addressed a servant to have the carriage brought to the doorway and she assisted Jocelyn and her daughter with their capes. They had only made it half way to the door before they heard footsteps hurrying towards them from behind.

"Baroness Cordell, are you and your daughter leaving so soon? I had hoped to meet you both formally." The male voice said gently and soon he was just behind them.

Jocelyn stopped both her and her daughter from walking and she turned to speak with him. "I am truly sorry, Lord Wallace but my daughter is ill and we must return home."

Edmond reached forward and touched Arabella's shoulder from behind. This made her jump and immediately she began running for the door. The servant at the door barely had time to open it before she reached it. "Wait!" Edmond called and ran after her.

'Oh God, what do I do now?' Arabella was really feeling nauseous now. She ran past the carriage and to the some bushes near the property gate and threw up. Her stomach was in knots because of the fear of being discovered by Edmond. If he knew her secret she was sure he would hate her and she couldn't bear the thought of him hating her. Already the rain was trying to soak through her clothing and it caused her clothing to grow heavy about her.

Edmond had grabbed his heavy cloak before running out into the rain and he continued to run after Arabella. He stopped near her as she wretched into the bushes. He brought his cloak over her and up over her head to help keep the rain off of her. "It'll be alright Arabella." He said gently.

"Please, go away." She said as her body began to relax. "Don't look at me."

"I promise I won't but you must allow me to lend you my cloak. You should stay as dry and as warm as possible." He wrapped it around her, allowing it to conceal her to her digression. He placed his arm about her shoulders while assisting her by her elbow through the cloak. "Will you be alright going home? We could put you up in one of our rooms until you feel better, if you'd like."

"No, but thank you just the same." Her voice was soft and feminine when she spoke normally in her Eldardesh accent. "I would feel better sleeping in my own bed."

"I understand the feeling." He said sympathetically. "Perhaps I can call on you in a day or two to see how you're fairing?"

"Again thank you for your concern but there is no need for that. I'm sure this will pass in time." Her heart was racing. The way he spoke to her now, to her as a girl, was far different then the carefree manner that he used when she was a 'boy'. It was even more gentle then their interlude during the robbery. Instead of being rough and teasing as he was when she was Aram, he was gentle and sincere with her as Arabella. "Please tell your mother that I was delighted that she invited me for this gathering and that I apologize for my behavior just now."

"I'm sure she understands." He waited for the carriage door to be opened and then he gently assisted her inside. "Please take care, Arabella." He was still blissfully unaware that she knew he was the one that robbed her. As far as he knew, to her this was the first time they met.

"Thank you, I will." She sat down as her mother entered the carriage from the other side. She listened to the door shut and then her mother's door shut.

"Are you going to be alright?" Her mother asked with concern.

"Yes, I'm sure I'll be fine soon." She replied and then stole a glance that only revealed her eyes out the side window near her. There, in the rain, stood Edmond looking back at her. His features were distorted by the rain but she knew it was him looking back into her eyes. She reached her hand forward and touched the glass of the door and he smiled in return. It seemed he understood her silent gesture of gratitude.

"Mother." Edmond said softly as the carriage took off with a jerk. "Have I met Arabella before?"

"No, not really." His mother replied while holding her cape over her head to protect her from the rain. "You most likely remember seeing her at the king's court the other day."

"Maybe." He really couldn't remember since he didn't pay attention at the time. He was in too big of a hurry to pay his social duty and then leave so he could meet his friends. He continued to stand in the rain as he watched the carriage disappear in the distance. "I must admit that was the most interesting way to meet a girl, if you could call it that." He laughed softly, he had the feeling that they had met before when he robbed her as well, yet he couldn't remember ever actually meeting her. "I think I will pay her a visit anyways. I'd like to get a good look at this maiden that has the attention of two kingdoms and their kings." He stood a moment longer in thought before heading back indoors. "How odd, the first girl I meet that strikes my interest and I haven't even seen her face. Not only that but I've seen her at her worst moment." The thought continued to make him laugh softly.

'That was too close.' Arabella thought to herself. 'I can't take risks like that anymore.' She coughed to clear her burning throat. As they left the Wallace estate her mother had explained to her that her father had gone into town with Baron Wallace earlier to visit Kendrick, so he wouldn't be returning home with them.

"Maybe we should stop and have the physician take a look at you." Her mother suggested. The physician she referred to was the one that everyone believed to be Aram's father.

"It really isn't necessary mother. I'll be fine soon." She tried to assure her. It was true. Her sickness wasn't anything but nerves and fright. Those would quickly pass once she was home safely.

"Well... Alright, but I'm going to have him come by tomorrow to check on you to make sure, if you're not feeling better soon. You're health is too important to take any risks. Which ever king you marry will need you to produce healthy heirs...."

"Please mother!" She scolded.

"Alright, I'll hold my peace for now." Jocelyn picked up a corner of the cloak that Edmond leant to Arabella. "Lord Wallace is a charming young man, isn't he?" Her voice reflected.

"He's alright I guess." Arabella really wasn't in the mood to talk about him with her mother. All it would take was one slip of the tongue and her mother would know that she had mingled with a noble as Aram. That was the one thing she was warned against doing, not that Arabella had known that Edmond was a noble at the time she net him. They had been friends for nearly two years before that fact had been made known to her. By then their friendship was so strong that she wasn't willing to give it up. So instead she allowed it to continue in secret.

"I think he is a fine young man with great promise. I'm sure he would be a wonderful husband to some noble woman in the future." Jocelyn thought out loud.

"I take it that you are not considering him for me?" She said firmly. "I already have enough to deal with."

"Oh heavens no. You're destined to become the wife of a king. Though, if it weren't for that, he would have made a good candidate for consideration. He is second in line to Kendrick's throne after all. That is higher then your father's position."

"Is that all you can think of mother? Is that all that really matters to you, is social standing and money?" She looked over at her mother. "Do my feelings regarding this mean anything at all?"

"Of course your feelings matter but you must trust your father and me when it comes to decisions that are as important as this. Why do you think your father has let you go about as Aram? It was because he wanted you to have some good memories of your childhood before you took on the difficult duties that lay ahead of you. We have known since the birth of the two kings that you would most likely be the bride of one of them, which was also their mother's wish, despite the difference in age."

"I don't want to do it. I don't want to marry them or any other man I don't love." Arabella protested.

Jocelyn sighed as she looked at her daughter. "You look so pale, Arabella. We're nearly home. Why don't you try to rest some until we get there, dearest." That was her way of saying that she didn't wish to discuss that matter any further. Jocelyn knew the heartache of being forced to marry someone you neither knew nor loved but she and her husband grew to love each other over time and she never regretted the day she married him. She had to leave another love behind for this marriage but now she knew that she was better off where she was. Her daughter would come to understand this in time as well. Whether it

Beautiful Pretender

was Kendrick or Eric, her daughter had a tender heart that would learn to love whomever it was she would end up with.

Once they were home, Arabella went straight up to her room. Ida helped her to quickly change from her clothing into a soft silken chemise and then she went to bed. The cloak that Edmond had leant her remained in her room, draped over one of the chairs. She looked over at it and felt a strange stirring in her soul. "Why did he have to act so... Uh!" She threw the covers over her head in frustration. "Stupid feelings!" She scolded herself. "I can't feel this way about him, its just wrong. He's my friend and that's all he can ever be to me." It wasn't the first time she had this speech with herself. Every now and then Edmond would do something that would stir this feeling deep within her and every time it made her angry with herself.

"Edmond could never love me that way, he's just my friend and to him we're both men. Something must be wrong with me." She pulled down the covers and looked at the cloak again. "I'm just being stupid, I don't love him. He just has a way of surprising me that's all." She sighed and then she thought, "Perhaps its better if I don't see him for a few days. That way I can keep myself from getting confused. I have to see him as he sees me and not confuse this day with how things really are between us. I just couldn't bear losing his friendship."

The door to her room opened and her father came in carrying a bowl of water with a cloth draped over the side. "How are you feeling princess? I heard you had quite a day today at the Wallace's." He placed the bowl down on a table near her bed and then sat down next to her. Apparently he just returned home and the frustrations he had towards her earlier in the day were no longer vexing his temperament.

"I was so embarrassed." She nearly cried as she spoke softly to him. "I'm sure the Baroness will never ask me to come visit her again after today." Honestly she didn't care but she was use to putting on these little performances to please her parents.

"I wouldn't worry about that. She has already sent a huge bouquet of flowers and sent the physician here as well. Mother is entertaining him downstairs."

"Uh…" She pulled the covers back up over her head. "Tell him to go home, I'm fine."

"He knows but he would still like to come and talk to you. After all he is supposed to be Aram's father. You have to be responsible for that part of your life too you know."

Arabella started laughing softly as she pulled down the covers. "He's still your best friend, isn't he?"

"Until our dying day, more likely then not." He laughed with her. "Shall I have him come up?"

"I guess it can't be helped since he is already here. Besides, I have something I'd like to ask him."

"You're mother will be pleased. She is still fretting over you." He stood up. "Would you like the cook to send up dinner for you?"

"Please do. I'm famished." She grinned.

"A sure sign that you're doing perfectly well." He laughed. "Alright then, you sleep well tonight my love. I have to leave early tomorrow for Eldardesh so I probably won't see you for a couple of weeks."

"Eldardesh?" She sat up quickly and asked, "Why?"

"Even though we are no longer citizens of the country I still have business and family there. It's been five years since I've been there and I'm long overdue for going back. Unfortunately part of the condition of citizenship was that we couldn't leave this kingdom during the five year period. Now that we are citizens, I must tend to my affairs in Eldardesh."

"I'll miss you father." She reached out her arms to him and he came back to her to embrace her. "I'm sorry for fighting with you earlier today." She whispered into his ear and then she kissed his cheek. "Promise not to stay away too long."

"Well I had considered bringing you with me because Eric has been inquiring about you so earnestly, but I'm glad I hadn't said anything to anyone about it before now. He would have been terribly disappointed if I had told him you were coming and you didn't. I don't want to endanger your health after what happened today. It is obvious you are in no condition to travel right now."

"Do you think he may end up coming here?" She asked as he released her.

"It's highly unlikely. There's bad blood between him and his brother. King Eric resents that Kendrick was left to take his father's throne and the greater of the two kingdoms. I am sure that within time, Eric plans to declare war and take back what he feels is rightfully his. He is a strong and determined leader, Arabella. I know he is young in body but he is an adult in spirit."

"I noticed that in Kendrick as well." She reflected. "Even though he looked young, he seemed old somehow."

"It's a terrible thing for those boys to have to assume such great responsibilities at such a young age. Eric has already taken his first wife and I am sure she will give him a child in the near future. Part of his strategy is to build both his kingdom and his family as quickly as possible."

"If he has a wife then why is he pursuing me?"

"You are the one who would sit beside him as a queen. You're a person from a family that is highly respected in Eldardesh and marrying you would bring him a lot of power and respect by the hierarchy of Eldardesh. Eric will most likely take on even more wives but his heart is devoted to you, Arabella. Don't ever forget that."

"I don't feel that way about him, father."

"Let's wait and see what the future brings, my dearest daughter. It may be that you will never again set foot in Eldardesh, so don't worry about it for now. Just enjoy this last year of freedom that I am giving you. Let your mother and I worry about the rest."

"Yes father." She kissed his cheek before releasing her embrace. "I'll try hard to do as you ask."

"That's my girl." He said proudly. "Now, I'll be off and I'll send the physician up to see you soon."

"Good night father."

"Good night Arabella. May you be blessed with dreams that bring you happiness." He left her room, closing the door gently behind him. "I really hate deceiving her like this." He whispered to himself before heading downstairs.

Arabella waited quietly in her room for the physician to come see her. Joseph Aldonmire had been a long time friend of her father's and now was a friend to her as well, not to mention that he was a valuable aid in keeping her secrets. He not only had he kept her secret about not being a boy but he also knew now that she had accidentally befriended a nobleman's son. Unfortunately he also had not known that Edmond was a noble because he didn't socialize in those circles. However, because of the deep bond she had with Edmond, he promised to never reveal her secret to her parents.

A soft knock sounded on her door. "Enter." She called out and watched as it slowly opened.

The dark brown hair of Joseph was the first thing to appear and soon she could see his dark eyes and handsome face as well. "May I come in?"

"Of course." She smiled.

He walked in and gently closed the door behind him. "Your mother was kind enough to fill me in on the details today."

"Yeah, some day it was too." She sighed.

"It sounds like you had yourself a near disaster. Did you really get sick?"

"I'm afraid I did. I panicked and ran from their home. I didn't know what to do… then he ran after me and it all just happened so fast… before I knew it, I was there being sick right in front of him." She sighed. "At least it should detour him from trying to have further contact with the Arabella side of me. Hopefully, I am safe from that now."

"Maybe…" He thought for a moment. "Edmond stopped by the house earlier. His first order of business was to let me know that you might need me and then second was him inquiring about Aram. He was worried because you had not shown up to meet him and the other boys today."

"I was afraid of that. What did you tell him?"

"I told him you were visiting your cousin."

"Did you say when I'd be back?"

"No, but he didn't ask. I had told him it was a last minute decision on my part, so you hadn't time to let him and the others know. He seemed to understand."

"Thank goodness." She said relieved. "Tell him I'll be back in a few days, should he come looking for me again. I just can't face him right now."

"I understand." He reached over and felt her forehead and then took up the cloth and dampened it in the water from the bowl her father brought in earlier. Gently he wiped her forehead and face with it. "Your mother informed me that Aram will only be with us for another year."

"Yes, father has decided that I will need to stop doing this soon."

"How do you feel about that?"

"Part of me is alright with it and part of me wouldn't mind doing it forever because it would mean that Edmond and I could keep being friends." She sighed, "I'm so afraid of what will happen should he learn who I really am. I don't want that to ever happen. I'd rather marry King Eric and move to Eldardesh then to have Edmond find out the truth and hate me for it."

"That may be but I believe that he deserves to know the truth about the person that is closest to him. You are the only person that boy has ever truly bonded with, Arabella. He needs you as much as you need him."

"I don't know." She got out of her bed and walked to where the cloak still remained hanging on the chair. "Would you take this back to him for me? I just can't risk him seeing me as a girl, at least not yet."

"I'm afraid I can't. This is something you must do yourself. Arabella…" He walked over to her and touched her elbow gently. "You must face him sooner or later and confess the truth to him. He deserves that much. What happens from there will be a testament to the man he truly is. You can't make these decisions for him."

"I don't know if I can." She groaned miserably.

"It's something you must do, especially if you truly care for him." He released his touch and walked to the door. "I look forward to your next visit, Arabella. Don't stay away too long."

She looked at him and smiled. "I won't. Please be sure to tell him that I'm at my cousin's still."

"I will. Make sure you rest well these next few days." His smile was warm and fatherly.

"Yes sir." She watched as he left her and then she looked down at the cloak and sighed. "Edmond you fool." Her voice whispered and she picked up his cloak and held it to her nose. It had his smell etched into the fibers. The fragrance of his horse, the gentle musk of his skin and the forest lay as a testament to the cloak's owner. She never grew tired of it either. She walked over to her bed and sat down.

Pulling the cloak away she noticed a small tear. Instinctively she reached for her basket of sewing supplies and pulled out a thread that was close in color to the black cloak and a needle. "It's the least I can do to repay his kindness, I guess." Carefully with small delicate stitches she began sewing it up. If she was careful, he may not even notice that it once had a hole.

She was so entranced by her needlework that she didn't hear her father come in with her meal. Quietly he sat the food down on the table near her and then he left the room again. It always amazed him how she could concentrate on one thing to the point that she could block out the rest of the world around her.

Chapter 3

"Is your daughter feeling any better, Baroness?" Edmond asked as he walked with Jocelyn to their visiting room.

"Much better, thank you for asking." She smiled. "Tea?"

"Yes, please." He smiled and sat down in the seat she offered him.

"Father caught her mending your cloak last night." She laughed softly. "I'd say you left an impression on her."

"That was very kind of her." He humbly took the tea she had poured for him and he carefully sipped down its hot fragrant liquid.

"My daughter has had a lot to deal with these past few years and I'm afraid it can get to her from time to time. I don't believe she meant to be rude to either you or your mother the other day…"

"You don't need to explain, we both understand perfectly well." He assured her. "Mother has been most anxious about her and so I thought I had better come to check on her condition."

"That is so kind of you." She smiled. "I'll send a servant up to fetch her now." Jocelyn nodded to one of the servants who immediately left to do a bidden. "I think my daughter might be a little shy about meeting you as well. She hasn't had the chance to meet any nobles her age yet and it seems to be unsettling for her to be back in the center of attention again."

"That is more then understandable, baroness. I tend to avoid spending too much time with people like that myself. In fact my best friend isn't even a noble but a commoner's child. Yet, I don't believe I could find a truer friend. It's nice to have someone like him, someone whom you can be completely honest with, you know, no secrets. I like that we can set aside our differences and talk to each other without worrying about what the other might think."

"Friends like that can be rare indeed." She said softly. In her social station you didn't have such freedoms because your weaknesses could be used against you without notice if someone thought it would benefit them.

"Miss, you have a guest downstairs." The servant told her after being allowed to enter.

"Really, who?" She asked. Arabella had been working on her lessons with a tutor her father had hired to teach her.

"The young master of the house of Baron and Baroness Wallace, milady."

Arabella nearly choked on her tongue, "What?" She coughed. "He's here... at my house?"

"Yes miss and he is inquiring about you. Your mother sent me to bring you down to see him."

"Impossible... Never..." She stood up from her seat. "Tell them I'm not feeling well and..." She picked up the cloak. "Give him this with my thanks."

"But miss I..."

"No, I won't go." She grew quiet as did the other servants for they could hear her mother's voice in the hallway.

"It's better this way. My daughter is a very stubborn girl and she might be too embarrassed to face you on her own after what happened the last time you saw her." Her mother's voiced said from the hallway.

"This can't be happening!" She whispered in fright and ran to her bed and flew under the covers just in time to hide her face.

"Are you sure she won't mind us dropping in like this?" Edmond asked her at the entry, the door was nearly shut completely.

"Goodness no." Jocelyn laughed and opened the door. "Oh." She said in a dumbstruck manner when seeing her daughter in bed. "What's going on?" She asked the others in the room, which consisted of the tutor, the servant she had sent up and Arabella's attendant Ida.

"She wasn't feeling well again." Ida informed her. "So she decided to lie down for a while."

"Isn't this a shame and after Edmond came all this way just to see you." Jocelyn said with disappointment in her voice.

Arabella peaked over the covers, only enough that they could see her eyes but not the rest of her face. She looked at her mother and Edmond, "I am terribly sorry for my poor health lately. Do forgive me?"

Edmond walked a few paces further into the room as he looked down on her. "Thank you for mending my cloak."

"Thank you for lending it to me." She would smile but there was no point since he could only see her eyes.

"Anytime." He couldn't get over how mysterious she was being but it only seemed to arouse his curiosity about her, making him want to know more about her. Again he managed to walk even further to try see to more of this mysterious maiden who continued to hide her face. "You don't have to hide your face from me, you know." His smile could melt any heart, it was different from his regular smile somehow and it was frustrating her.

Arabella could feel her heart skip a beat at his dashing smile. "Oh… no…it's just that… well, I might be contagious. I wouldn't want you to get sick as well." His smile seemed to brighten and her heart began to beat faster as his gentle eyes gazed caringly down on her. 'Stop it you stupid thing.' She silently scolder her heart, however it had no intention of obeying her and was beating even harder as her cheeks took on a betraying blush. 'You're absolutely useless.' She cried in defeat, 'I won't let you win. If you do, you could ruin the most precious relationship in my life.' She continued to silently scold it.

His handsome smile never ceased, "I think that if it you are contagious, just my being in here is enough for me to be exposed to it." He heard her mother laugh softly. "However, your mother has explained to me that you are a little uncomfortable around other nobles, so I won't force you to show me your face but I do hope you will someday. I would like to see the young woman that has captivated so many people."

"I'm afraid you'll be disappointed when you do. There really isn't anything that special about me I'm afraid." She replied from her quilted shelter.

"Perhaps it's because you are so mysterious." He laughed softly. "Will you be attending the masked ball?"

Arabella thought for a moment. Yes, that was the best thing to happen yet. She could go in disguise and stand next to Edmond as a girl without him finding anything out. "Of course, perhaps we can have a chance to speak with each other then." She suggested. "I'm sure I'll be feeling much better by that time."

"Then I will look forward to seeing you. Make sure you save a dance for me." He bowed.

"Yes, I would be delighted to." He took his cloak from the servant who had retrieved it for him.

"Then I will see you in a few days, milady." He bowed humbly and then waited for her mother to escort him out of the room.

"Ida." Arabella brought down her covers after the door was closed. "I feel so sick."

"Really?" Ida asked confused.

"Have the others leave."

"Yes milady." Ida waited for the servant and Tutor to leave and then she shut the door. "What's wrong?"

"Promise not to tell father and mother."

"I swear I won't breathe a word to them."

"Remember the noble boy whom I have been close friends with these last five years?"

"Yes."

"I know mother and father told me not to befriend a noble but I didn't know Edmond was a noble when I first knew him…"

"You mean, he's…?" Ida was speechless as she looked towards the bedchamber door as if she were trying to look at the man who had just left the room only moments earlier.

"Yes, it's him." She sighed. "When he comes near me when I'm Arabella, it literally makes me sick with fear of being found out."

"Everything makes sense now." Ida sighed. "You sure have yourself one very interesting problem on your hands."

"Tell me about it. What am I going to do, Ida?"

"I'm not sure." Ida walked over to the windows and looked out to where Edmond was currently mounting his horse. "He seems to genuinely care about you as both people. Maybe it won't be as bad as you might think should he learn the truth. Perhaps if you told him now it would go over better then if you waited. He might just understand why you've done what you've done."

"No, it would be the end of everything." She moaned. "He'll hate me for certain." She pulled the covers back over her head as if she were

Beautiful Pretender

trying to hide herself from the entire situation.

"Are you really going to the masked ball? It's possible he might recognize you there."

"Why shouldn't I? I can easily hide my face there. I'm sure it will be safe enough and that he won't recognize me if I'm careful enough to thoroughly disguise myself."

"I suppose you're right." Ida turned and looked back towards Arabella. "I have a feeling that Edmond might be hoping to spend some time with Aram today. Perhaps you should go to meet him at your usual place."

Arabella looked back out from under her protective covers at Ida. "Yes, I think I could use that as well." She got up out of bed and allowed Ida to help her transform into Aram.

Aram barely had enough time to get to the lake and lounge out under the tree before Edmond appeared. Thankfully he had taken his horse home before coming which allowed Aram to get there first. Edmond sat down next to his friend and then delivered a rather hard punch to his shoulder. "Hey!" Aram said and immediately grabbed his shoulder, "That hurt you moron."

"You have been gone long enough." Edmond scolded him and then laid down next to him, both of them looked up to the cloud scattered sky through the canopy of the oak tree's abundant leaves.

"It couldn't be helped." Aram looked over at his friend. "Something seems to be bothering you. What is it?"

"You always could read my emotions." Edmond sighed. "Mother has the list of possible marriage candidates down to two women. I'm supposed to meet them in the next couple of weeks following the ball. Neither one of them is able to attend it, thankfully."

"Then we're in the same boat."

"What do you mean?"

"My parents also have narrowed my choices down to two and neither of them are someone I care to spend the rest of my life with." Aram was referring to his choices as Arabella and the two kings.

"So they did decide to arrange your marriage after all." He reflected.

47

"Yes they did." Aram was silent a moment before continuing. "Tell me your opinion Edmond... shouldn't it be wrong for a man to marry a woman who is older then him? It just doesn't seem right."

"You're not serious are you?" Edmond sat up and looked down on Aram.

"Unfortunately I am. Not only that but I think I would rather marry Silas's sister then either one of those fools." Aram thought for a moment. "Well maybe I am not that desperate but I can't bare the thought of marrying someone I don't even like."

Edmond laid back down and picked a long piece of grass to chew on. They continued to lay there in silence for some time before either one spoke again. "Aram?"

"Hmm?"

"I've met someone... well sort of."

"A girl?" Aram looked over at Edmond who continued to look over at on him.

"Yes." Edmond looked back up to the blue sky through the canopy of leaves.

"Is she pretty?"

"I'm not really sure. Our meetings have been under odd circumstances. I suppose you could say that she is a complete mystery to me yet there is something about her that has me enchanted."

"You're not making much sense. Do you at least know who she is?"

"Yes and so do you. It's the Princess Arabella Mina Cordell." He heard Aram nearly choke in a gasp. "What?" He asked confused as he looked over at his friend who sat up quickly and looked down at Edmond, who was lying on his side.

"What could you possibly see in someone like her?" Aram wasn't sure what else to say.

"Well you've met her haven't you? You seem to know more about her then anyone else." Edmond sat up as well.

"Well I know about her family. Father does tend to them often." That was a twisted truth after all the Baron was her father, though she made it to sound like she was referring to the physician.

"That is true, I had forgotten about that connection. Have you seen her face to face?" Edmond asked with curiosity.

"I guess but she's nothing to get too excited about. What I mean to say is that she looks alright for a girl, I guess."

"She promised to meet me at the masked ball. Aram, do you think that maybe you could go there with me?"

"What?" Aram was shocked. "That ball is a place for nobles, there's no way they'd let me in there."

"They would if you were my guest. She knows you Aram and she might feel more comfortable if you were there with me. Please attend it with me." He begged.

"I can't. Besides you need to learn to stand on your own two feet when it comes to these things. What if she decides she likes me instead of you? How would that make you feel?" Aram grinned at him.

"I hadn't thought of that." He laughed at the jest.

"You know I'm much better looking then you are." Aram grinned proudly.

"Dream on. You're not even half the man I am." Edmond countered.

This made Aram laugh even harder, 'If he only knew.' Suddenly Edmond tackled him and pinned him to the ground by his shoulders while he straddled his body. "Hey!" Aram protested as he tried to struggle free.

"Seriously, Aram, are you sure you shouldn't come?"

He stopped struggling and talked with Edmond seriously. "Yeah, I'm sure. You'll just have to trust me that it would not be a good thing for me to be there. I have a feeling you will do fine on your own. Just trust your instincts and you will do well my friend." Aram smiled.

"Perhaps you're right. It wouldn't look good if I had you there to 'hold my hand' as it were." Edmond thought out loud and Aram laughed again as Edmond continued to look down on him.

"Why are you even bothering with her? I mean after all, you are about to meet the bride of your parents choice. It's not like they'll let you marry this girl if you fall in love with her. Perhaps you should just avoid her all together."

"I know I should but I can't. What's worse, she's the possible bride to one of the two kings…my uncles. I don't even know how she feels about that." He sighed.

"She hates the thought of marrying either of them, to be honest."

Edmond's gaze became intense and he asked, "You know this for certain?"

"Yes, this much I am sure of. Her parents raised her in the palace with Kendrick's and Eric's mother and she was favored by the queen. The queen's wish was that Arabella would marry one of her two sons. It seems King Eric is the one who has taken the greater interest in her though Kendrick's advisors are encouraging him to consider her as well. However, Arabella doesn't want to live the life of a queen, instead she…." Aram almost said too much. Obviously as a supposed outsider he wouldn't know more then this. "Well, I believe she probably wants to marry someone she's in love with. That's my guess anyways. That's what I would want."

"Yes." Edmond got off of Aram and sat down next to him again, "As do I but how do we go against our parents in these matters?" He pondered out loud. "The only conclusions are these, love while we can, deny our hearts or deny our parents' wishes and risk losing everything for the sake of love."

"In the end someone will be hurt no matter which path you choose to take." Aram reflected.

"I will meet with her this one last time." Edmond told him. "Perhaps I am just in awe of the mystery. Perhaps she isn't really what my heart thinks and I can leave the celebration knowing this. As things stand now, I can't find peace until I talk to her face to face."

"Perhaps that is best then." Aram agreed.

"Have you heard what her outfit and mask will look like?"

"No, I have no idea what so ever." Aram said honestly. Her mother hadn't told her anything about it yet. "Edmond?"

"Hmm?"

"If I had ever done something that grievously disappointed you… Would you hate me for it?"

"You're the best of friends, Aram. I'm sure we will eventually both end up disappointing each other at one time or another. Hopefully our friendship is strong enough that we can survive anything the other might do. Why do you ask?"

"Nothing really. I just…" Aram wanted to tell him but he just couldn't. He couldn't bear the thought of things changing from the way they were now. "I was just curious to see what your answer would be. I'm not sure I could bear losing your friendship, it means the world to me."

"As yours does to me. I wouldn't worry about it, Aram. I can't imagine anything that would make me dislike you anymore... well unless you shamed my future bride or something." This made both of them laugh.

"That's not likely to happen. No girl is worth dividing the two of us."

"That is for certain. Let's make a promise to each other." Edmond offered.

"What promise is that?"

"That no matter where life takes us in the future, let's always live near each other and stay friends as we are today."

Aram sighed. "If it's possible, I would like that. However there are no guarantees in life, Edmond."

"I hope we can try to do that. You're the only person I have ever been able to fully depend on and trust."

Aram's chest tightened. 'Trust'. There was no way Edmond could discover Aram's secret now. If that trust was broken then the relationship could very well end. "I know we are normally very open with each other about things Edmond, but even I have secrets that I haven't told anyone."

"I suppose we all have them." Edmond agreed with a sigh of realization.

'Some more then others.' Aram thought in silence.

"Arabella!" Her mother nearly ran into her daughter's room while waving a piece of parchment. She was smiling almost uncontrollably as she held her hand to her heart as if she were trying to slow the beating of it. It was obvious that she had run to her daughter's room with whatever news she just received. "This just arrived from the palace today and it has everyone in an uproar." She walked over to where her daughter was and sat down in a chair near the tub that her daughter was bathing in. Ida was assisting her.

"What is it mother?" Arabella asked with curiosity.

"The gracious and most adored, King Kendrick, has announced that he will also be attending the masked ball."

"So?" Arabella really didn't see what was so great about this news and she lost interest in the topic. Really, she couldn't see what the big deal was. Kendrick was just a relative who had occasional contact with the family on a somewhat regular basis. Sure she had only seen him once so far but she was sure she'd see him more often in the future. Now if he was to pay a visit to the commoners that would at least be slightly more interesting since he never paid any attention to them.

"He sent a notice to say he is coming especially to see you. Is this not the most wonderful news?" She was nearly in tears with the joy she felt from it.

"I suppose." Arabella replied with some uncertainty.

"Please dearest, try to show some enthusiasm. The king is going out of his way just for you. That's not something that happens everyday you know."

"I will be sure to greet him properly mother, I promise." Arabella looked deeply into her mother's eyes as she asked, "You don't think he will stay long do you?"

"Most likely he would not. He is still just a child after all and I'm sure that it would not be in his best interest to stay for too long. I'm sure as he grows older he will be more interested in these types of social functions." Jocelyn paused for a moment before continuing. "Arabella, if you do marry him, perhaps you could hold some of these social gatherings at the palace. They would be infinitely grander should you decide to do so."

"I guess they probably would be." Arabella couldn't have cared less. She was only going to this one to humor her mother and Edmond. They both seemed adamant that she attend. Personally she had other things she'd rather be doing. It wasn't that she didn't like dancing. To be perfectly honest she loved dancing but only with her father, who was the one who trained her in this particular subject. One of their servants was known for his skill in playing the lute and he would provide the music for them to dance by.

"This is truly wonderful." Her mother laughed softly as she stood up from the chair. "Oh, before I leave, I have one more thing to tell you. Our gowns and masks have arrived. They came just before this notice did. Our jewelry arrived yesterday morning. Apparently the jewelers, tailors and seamstresses have been working day and night to *have* everything prepared for this event. We can look at the gowns together when you're finished with your bath."

"Alright. I'll come right down as soon as I'm done." Arabella was ready to get out of her bath now but she decided to wait until after her mother left the room.

"Wonderful!" She grinned and stood up to leave. "I'll have the servants lay them out for us." Jocelyn left the room in high spirits.

"Princess…" Ida was concerned when she looked at the pale face of her charge.

"Ida?" Arabella began to stand up which indicated she was finished.

"Yes milady." Ida walked over to pick up the robe to wrap Arabella in once she stood up from the tub's water.

"Would you feel like going to Essica with me tonight?" (Essica was the name of the hot springs on the border of her father's estate. They were named after a maiden in Eldardesh lore who was the spirit of good fortune. She was often pictured having long white hair, wearing a somewhat transparent long white gown. She had wings and a laurel wreath halo. Other nobles would use the hot spring on occasion, with permission since it was only one of the few that the kingdom had and it belonged to her father.)

"You're feeling that poorly today?" Ida approached her mistress and held the robe up so Arabella could slide into it.

"I'm hoping it will help me to relax some. All this chaos is making me feel rather ill. Between this whole arranged marriage business with the kings and the situation that seems to be building with Edmond, I just can't seem to calm my nerves." She secured thick robe in front of her that Ida had put over her shoulders from behind. It was much like a man's cloak but it was a thick soft white fabric and it didn't have a hood.

"Of course, milady." Ida took Arabella's elbow and helped her step out of the bath. "If you don't mind it, I might like to enjoy the hot waters along with you." They had often done this in the past.

"You know I don't mind." She smiled kindly at her long time servant and companion. "We should probably humor mother and go down to look at the merchandise that came."

Ida knew this was her queue to move a little faster for the day was already in the latter part of the afternoon. "Yes mistress, I'm sure she would appreciate it if we did."

Edmond couldn't seem to think clearly. His eyes seemed to be filled with the sight of those beautiful hazel eyes and the long flowing light brown hair of Arabella. The memory of her sweet feminine voice still tickled his ears and every moment with her, though very limited, seemed to enchant his mind. He took from his pocket the broach that she had entrusted to his care. The sapphire rested snuggly in its golden filigreed bed. It would bring a fair amount of money if he were to sell it, but he wouldn't dare betray her trust in the man she referred to as 'Sir Robber'. He used the finger of his free hand and gently caressed the perfect jewel before placing it back into his pocket.

He longed for the night of the masked celebration, the night that he would have a chance to see her again. Edmond had scolded himself on more then one occasion for he had never been so entranced by the opposite sex before. Worse yet he had never even seen her face. All he knew about her looks was from the opinions of those who had seen her. However, it almost didn't matter. There was just something so familiar and charming about her that left him unable to concentrate on anything else.

"Damn it all." He breathed in frustration. There was just no way he could concentrate on his studies anymore.

"Is there something bothering you, milord?" His mentor asked as he looked up from the book he had been instructing Edmond from.

"Would it be alright if I cut the session short today? I am finding too difficult to concentrate."

"If we must, sir." The short stout mentor of forty seven shut the book he was holding in a gentle manner. "I suppose we have done enough for one day." There was no guarantee that Edmond would ever assume the throne but he had to be trained just the same for the possibility. Even if he didn't use these skills as a king, they would still be used in the service of His Majesty the King. "It is clear that you could use some time off from your studies. Why don't we take a few days off from doing your lessons so that you can clear your head?" The tutor suggested, not that it mattered much because Edmond had a tendency to disappear when his tutor came. The man was amazed that

Beautiful Pretender

Edmond could learn anything at all, yet he was a bright lad and even though the tutor only saw him once or twice a week, Edmond didn't seem to be struggling at all with his studies.

"Thank you for understanding, Sir Thomas." He smiled kindly to the man who had been his instructor since he was a child.

"I will go and speak with your father so he understands why we are taking a short break."

"I appreciate it. Will you also inform him that I will be out late tonight and to be sure to have the cook save my evening meal for me?"

"Of course. Make sure to take some time to rest, Edmond. I can't quite place it but you haven't seemed quite yourself lately."

Edmond sighed, "Yeah, I'm not feeling quite myself." Never had a woman come close to captivating his attention as Arabella had. He almost felt foolish when he thought of the affect he was allowing her to have over him. He stood up from his chair and walked over to his bed to lie down for a few moments. "Do not let on to my parents about your concerns, it will only make them worry needlessly about me. I'm sure I'll be feeling just fine by the time you return."

"As you wish, milord." Sir Thomas smiled and then left the room.

Edmond continued to lie down for a few moments longer in the silence of his room after his tutor left. "Arabella." He said in a soft voice, listening to the sound of her name made his heart quicken. "Who are you to cast such a spell over me, that I can't stop thinking about you?" A gentle laughed escaped his lips. "I must see you again or I'll go mad." Edmond sat up in his bed and looked around his room of wood and stone. He decided to get up and go for the walk he that he had been thinking about taking earlier. "I must try to clear my head." He nearly scolded himself. "I will see her soon enough at the celebration."

Arabella allowed Ida to assist her in removing her clothing. The waters of the heated pool sent billows of steam up in the cool summer night air. A lone lantern was all they needed to see by. The forest offered the screened in shelter needed in order to hide them from the public view, not that anyone was around to see them. No one ever came there without her family's knowledge. It was just a common courtesy. Once she was undressed, Arabella sat down on the stone

55

ledge of the water's bank and let her legs dangle in the heated liquid as a gentle breeze tasseled her hair that hung down her back and to her waist. "It's perfect." She grinned. "It is hot but not too hot."

Ida laughed softly. "It has been a while since we've been here. I'm glad you thought of it, milady." She carefully began hanging Arabella's clothes up over the branches of a nearby tree.

"Even the fragrances of the flora here are different. It seems to sooth every part of you." Arabella inhaled the sweet and spicy fragrances around her. In the distance she could hear the crickets and frogs singing their evening duets. Her gaze went up to the sky and she looked at the clear night filled with stars along with the hazy ribbon of the milky way's soft trail that gently lit up the night's sky. "I think I need to come here more often." She sighed with a smile.

"Yes princess." Ida agreed and then undressed herself. Arabella continued to sit on the stone bank as she drank in the scents and sounds of the night. Her feet gently moved back in forth in a slow kicking fashion to allow the heated water to caress her legs. She closed her eyes as if to shut out everything else around her that could disrupt this beautiful illusion of paradise she had found. Ida stepped into the hot waters and lowered herself down until they came up to her chin. She breathed a sigh of contentment as the hot waters worked into her tired muscles.

Edmond wasn't sure how long he had been walking and the fact that the day had grown dark was barely even noticed by him. He had fairly good night vision and could see well enough to get by. He hadn't even really paid attention to where he had been walking, for it didn't matter since he could use the stars to guide himself back home. No matter how much he tried to clear his head, it only seemed to make him think about her more. He was sure it was because of the mysterious feelings she had left upon him. "Why does she desire to hide her face from me?" He wondered out loud in a whisper as he unconsciously allowed himself to be lured towards a dim light in the distance.

Just for a moment his mind changed directions to his friend Aram, "I should have asked him to walk with me tonight. Perhaps he could have helped me to find other things to focus my mind on." His voice whispered. Within a short time his solitude journey led him into a dimly lit clearing and it snapped him out of his dazed state. His breath caught in his throat and he stood there in a dazed trance of freight and wonder. Before him, with her back to him, was a slender woman with hair that fell to her waist. She sat naked on a stone ledge with her legs dangling down into the steaming waters of a heated pool. He could swear that it had to be all in his mind, for he was sure he was seeing Arabella.

Ida gasped in fright and lowered herself down into the water as she saw the man who had appeared from the forest. Arabella looked down into her handmaiden's paled face. "What is it Ida?" She asked with curiosity.

"Come." Ida frantically waved for Arabella to come down off the stone ledge so that she might hide herself in the water.

"What?" Arabella asked confused.

"There's a young man behind you." She reached forward and took Arabella by the wrist to force her to come down.

Arabella half turned and her heart nearly stopped. "What!" She jumped down into the water and then quickly hid herself behind Ida who was down in the water far enough to cover herself. "Who goes there?" Arabella's shaky voice asked loud enough for the man to hear.

"I'm....I'm sorry, I didn't mean to..." He stumbled over his words.

Arabella instantly recognized the familiar voice. "Edmond, is that you?" She peeked over Ida's shoulder, but only enough that the lower half of her face didn't show.

"So I'm not dreaming then?" He started to step closer and then stopped himself when he realized what he was doing. Immediately he turned around to give the women their needed privacy. "I'm so sorry. I didn't realize you'd be here."

"Why on earth are you out here?" Arabella asked him and then quietly to Ida she said, "Go get my gown."

Ida replied just as quietly, "Yes, milady." She left the water and quickly put on her chemise before getting Arabella's belongings.

"I was just out walking trying to clear my head... I guess I wasn't really paying attention to where I was walking... well... what I'm trying to say is... I had no idea you would be here... nor that you would be in such a manner as you are…" He was having a difficult time talking to her. "Please forgive my intrusion." Now his voice was shaking but it was from the embarrassing situation he had gotten himself into.

Arabella looked at him for a moment and then decided that she'd take this opportunity to talk a while more with him. "Ida?"

Ida approached the water's edge with Arabella's belongings in her hands, "Yes princess."

"Leave my things there and give us a moment if you would."

"But princess…."

Arabella didn't allow her to continue, "Do not fear about me, I have no ill intentions. I just thought this might be an opportune time to speak with Edmond in private. However, I would appreciate it if you took the lantern with you. I'll call for you when I'm ready for you to come back."

Ida knelt down and Arabella came closer so her friend could speak to her without Edmond overhearing them. "Shouldn't you at least come out of the water and dress first?" There was a touch of fear in her voice.

"No one knows Edmond better then I do." Arabella whispered. "He won't do anything to shame me, I promise. If you leave me like this, he will be less likely to try to see my face, wouldn't you agree?"

Ida looked in Edmond's direction and took a moment to consider Arabella's words. Finally she looked back down to her charge, "I suppose what you say does hold some merit." She sighed, "Very well, do as you wish, but call out to me should there be even the slightest hint of trouble."

"You worry too much dearest." Arabella laughed softly. "Now go."

"Yes milady." Ida stood back up after carefully laying out her mistresses belongings. She then went to retrieve the lantern and walked down the path through the woods towards Arabella's home. She wouldn't go far but she wanted to be sure she stayed on a path she was familiar with.

Once the light had faded to nothing, Arabella spoke first. "Edmond?"

"Yes princess." He answered nervously.

"Don't be silly, come and talk with me." She carefully made her way to the edge of the pool that was closer to where he stood and leaned against it, folding her arms up on the surface of the ground above.

"I wouldn't dare come any closer."

"Don't be silly, you can't see anything, not really. All I can see are silhouettes. Please, come closer so we can speak with each other."

Cautiously Edmond turned his head just enough to see if she was right. The only light in this little clearing was that which was given by the stars. Not even the moon had the courage to defy her wishes of not being seen. The water she kneeled in twinkled but only on the surface. The water itself was as dark as pitch and made a suitable cover to hide her body from him. All he could make out was a dark silhouette of her head, hair, shoulders and arms. "Alright." He turned and walked towards her, stopping a couple feet from the water's edge. Then he sat down on the hard cool ground.

"You must have known that I was thinking about you." Her gentle voice reflected to him. "For why else would fate lead you here?"

"I was suffering the same ailment. I can't stop thinking about you either. Even now I wish to call to the heavens to afford me some light so that I might look upon your face, yet you are still clouded in mystery as they continue to hide your face from me."

She laughed softly. "As they should, for there is a reason why I keep myself hidden from you, milord."

"Why do you?"

"Perhaps we should speak of this matter some other time." Her suggestion informed him that she wasn't ready to talk to him about it yet so he decided to let the matter of the subject drop, for now at least. "I must apologize for the impression I must be leaving on you and your family, Lord Wallace. Even now you have managed to catch me in yet another unseemly and awkward situation." She was smiling and he could hear the smile in her voice even though he couldn't see it on her face.

"It is moments like these that make me even more curious about you and draw me to you, milady. You are unlike any woman I have ever met and to be honest, these situations tend to brighten my day. Only you and one other person have managed to reach into this dark and dreary world of mine, princess."

She started laughing, "I don't see how I could have such an effect on you, milord, for they tend to cause me to nearly die of embarrassment."

He reached forward carefully and touched her cheek which was damp from the water's steam. "Don't worry yourself about it. I see this as part of your charm." He brought his hand back.

"Oh." She smiled with embarrassment. "Still…" Her soft laughter kept her from continuing.

Edmond looked up to the sky, "Do you ever think that perhaps fate is the one responsible for these interesting encounters of ours?"

"Perhaps, but it is a cruel joke she's playing on us."

"Why's that?" He looked back down onto her darkened silhouette.

"Why do you think?" She laughed softly. "I have to ask a favor of you." Her voice was serious now.

"What is it?"

"Whatever you do… don't let yourself fall in love with me."

He thought carefully on her words for a moment before replying. "Yes, that could cause us both problems since we are to be promised to other people." He agreed. "But please tell me this if you can, how exactly do you forbid the heart to not fall in love with someone? I'm afraid mine has already been captivated by you."

Arabella sighed and then turned around so she faced away from him, not because she feared he would see her but because she was guilty of having the same weakness of the heart. "I'm not sure to be honest. I have to admit that you are a little too charming, sir. I find that I am in need of scolding myself, almost since the day we met, because my heart is so easily controlled by your affections towards me."

"Then we will have to fight this battle together I guess." He got onto his hands and knees and crawled over towards her and lowered his head down near hers. Then he whispered in her ear, "You will dance with me at the ball still, won't you?"

She turned slightly until her mouth came near his, "It would be awfully rude of me not to, wouldn't you say?" Her voice was in a near whisper. "After all I did promise you that I would."

"Then I'll look forward to it."

"Just remember my first dance is promised to the king."

"Then promise me the rest of them after he leaves."

Arabella laughed softly, "You're not making this easy for me, are you? I'm trying not to fall in love with you, remember?" She quickly kissed him and then moved further out into the pool of water, far enough that he couldn't reach her. "You had better leave or you will make my poor handmaiden be troubled over my well being. Already she is discomforted by the fact that we are alone like this."

Edmond was now on his knees and he touched his lips gently with the tips of his fingers where she had just kissed him. "I... I can't." He stumbled over his words because she had a way of disorienting him, especially with that kiss.

She turned to look in his direction, "Why not?"

"I'm not sure, I just can't go."

"You must try." She continued.

"I can't stop myself from feeling these feelings about you. All I can think about is how much I long to touch you and hold you. Arabella, I..." She didn't let him finish.

"Ida!" Arabella called out to her handmaiden. "You may come back now." She turned her back towards Edmond again so he couldn't see her face once the lantern was close enough for him to see her more clearly by.

Soon the lantern light lit up the area with its dim glow. Ida walked towards Edmond who was still kneeling and looking in Arabella's direction. "I believe it is a good time for you to go now, sir." Her voice was gentle and kind.

"Huh?" He looked up at her, "Oh, yes, I'm sorry." Edmond stood up and took the lantern from her, turning enough that Arabella could leave the hot spring without him seeing her. "I'll hold this while you help her out and then I'll leave."

Ida took a moment to study him to make sure he was on the level with her, before going to assist Arabella. "I can see now what it is that attracts her to you. You are indeed very handsome and charming young man, Lord Wallace." She laughed softly and then she left to assist Arabella from the hot spring. Arabella made sure to keep her back turned to Edmond, even after she was fully dressed.

"May I look upon your face before I go, milady?" Edmond asked Arabella when Ida came to fetch the lantern from him.

"Soon you will have a wife, Edmond and it would be best if it was her face that you see in your marriage bed and not mine." She told him in a sad but gentle voice.

"What about you? You have seen mine. Will you not suffer that yourself when you are with your king?"

"If I do, it may be my only comfort, for I do not desire to be with either of them. Besides," she sighed, "I didn't intentionally look. You were just suddenly there before me."

He walked up behind her and laid his hands on her shoulders. Her damp hair brushed against them as he leaned in close to her. "Very well, I will continue to wait." He moved her hair to one side and brushed a kiss on the back of her neck. Arabella gasped as unfamiliar sensations tickled her skin and body. "This is payback for earlier." His voice whispered and then he backed away from her and turned to leave. "Goodnight ladies, until we meet again."

Ida came over to Arabella after Edmond was far enough away to neither see nor hear them. "You two shouldn't be doing this." She warned her.

"I know but I can't stop myself." Arabella gently touched her neck that was still warm from Edmond's breath. "Oh God, help me." She whispered. "I can't let myself fall in love with him."

Chapter 4

"It has been a long time since I last saw you, Baron Cordell." King Eric said as he greeted his mother's favored nephew who had just arrived to Brie-Ancou, The capital of Eldardesh.

"Indeed it has been your majesty." The Baron said from his kneeling position before the twelve year old king.

"Rise and embrace me, beloved cousin." The baron did as his true king asked. "So you're finally a citizen of my brother's country."

"Yes milord, and as you predicted he gave me an esteemed position in his palace."

"Perfect. It seems everything is going as planned."

"Yes, your majesty."

"I was hoping you would change your mind and bring Arabella with you."

"I do apologize, milord, but she was very ill when I left Arminia. I couldn't risk her health to bring her with me."

"Was it serious?" Eric asked concerned. Eric was well aware of Arabella's fragile health. Though it improved as she got older, she still tended to fall ill if she wasn't careful. As a child she often had fever's that would lay her up for days at a time.

"No milord, but it could have been if she came with me."

"Then I will let the matter drop. Her health is too important to me." He looked to the corner of the room, "Come." He told a young woman who immediately did as he asked. "I don't believe you know my wife, Miriam." He smiled. "Be assured that Arabella will be my queen, but I wanted to begin creating heirs to my throne as soon as possible."

"She is very young, majesty."

"She is almost thirteen, Baron. She is plenty old enough to be producing heirs for my throne, should I need them."

"Yes your majesty. That she is."

"Should Arabella give me a son, he would be the one appointed as my successor, naturally."

"As you desire, milord."

"Has my brother taken any interest in her yet?" Eric grinned with anticipation.

"Possibly, though I must warn you that my wife, the baroness, is hoping that Arabella will become Kendrick's wife."

"Your wife is a fool if she thinks that she can overrule my desires." Eric grumbled.

"Yes milord. I am only loyal to you and will do whatever you ask of me." This brought a smile to Eric's face.

"I knew you wouldn't disappoint me, cousin." Eric laughed. "I can not wait for Arabella's return." He sighed. "These last five years seemed to have dragged by as I waited for you to fulfill that annoying law of citizenship. I am trusting you to be my eyes and ears in the palace in Celendra Desh, cousin." (Celendra Desh is the capital of Arminia where King Kendrick resides.)

"What do you want me to do about my daughter, my king?"

"Leave her in Arminia for now and let her beauty taunt my brother. She is the first key to bringing down his resolve. If we can get him to fall in love with her, then I can send word that a marriage agreement has already been made between the two of us." Eric motioned to a servant of his who disappeared from the room and within in moments, reappeared back through the doorway holding a rolled up parchment. Eric took it from him. "Take this back to Arminia with you and hide it. It is the marital agreement and it only requires your signature to make it final. When you receive word that leads you to believe that Kendrick will ask for her hand, sign this and present it to him on the day he makes his proposal." Eric handed the parchment to him.

"I will send word to you as soon as this takes place." Baron Cordell promised. "It should give you time to prepare for her arrival."

"I plan to meet you at the border of the two kingdoms. I will take her virginity as soon as she is in Eldardesh. This will dissuade my brother from trying to seek her further and assure her position as my queen."

Beautiful Pretender

Aldrich sighed and went to his knees to plead humbly with his king, "I understand your wishes and I will obey you without hesitation but please, your majesty, don't do anything that will hurt my little girl. I don't care what you do to take the throne from your brother but my daughter is the most precious thing in my life and my only child. I beg of you to treat her gently and with love." He lowered his head to the floor and waited for the king's reply.

"I have no other intention. She is the only woman I could ever hold dear in my heart. I have loved her for as long as I can remember. First it was more as if she were an older sister but now, it is much more. My mother also loved Arabella dearly, as one would her own daughter. How could I not have anything but love for Arabella. Baron..." Eric knelt down by the older man, "You were always like a father to me. I know I was only seven when you left, but you were the only one to show me fatherly affection. I never really even knew my real father but since he had no problem abandoning me, I have no loyalty to him nor do I to Kendrick. Arabella being from the only man to treat me like a son, only serves to secure my resolve to hold her in the highest esteem. Surely you must know this."

"I had hoped for this but I still had to hear the words from your majesty's lips to set my heart at ease. Thank you for indulging this selfish whim of mine."

"A father's love for his daughter is never selfish." Eric stood back up. "Come, let's dine together to celebrate the beginning of my brother's downfall and the beginning of my soon to be united empire."

"Yes milord." Aldrich rose up to his feet and followed the king from the room. 'I am truly sorry to deceive you my wife and child but I believe this all is truly in the best interest for, not only our family but also our kingdom, both of them.' He thought to himself.

Aram's one handed sword ricocheted off of Edmond's sword as they practiced in the sword ring near the palace grounds. At this time of day there was little activity on the tournament grounds, so Arabella felt safe going there as Aram because there was little chance of encountering other nobles who might recognize her. Edmond immediately turned to block the sword that Silas wielded. They were assisting Edmond in preparation for the tournament that would be held in Celendra Desh in the near future, though it was still months away. Edmond usually tried to attend at least four to five tournaments a year, but this particular year he choose to only attend the King's tournament. Most contestants would normally have to fight and win in four or more tournaments to compete in the prestigious King's tournament. However, those in line for the throne were given special privileges, especially those who were as close in succession as Edmond was. This was to keep them safe incase an ill fate befell the king.

Edmond was a champion fighter in his age range, and had yet to lose a match in the past four years. Currently he was battling three on one. Silas, Aram and Eustace were Edmond's chosen aids and Silas was his official Squire and Eustace his Herald during the tournaments. Currently they were all using swords made of hard wood to battle each other with. Edmond wanted to focus more on his technique since he hadn't been using his sword much in the last few months, other then when he used it for pirating purposes when robbing the selfish noble elite. He could work more on strength later since he really didn't need the others for that. Basically he would use one of his old swords to hack at a hanging log. The practice swords were tampered with to make them heavier then normal and the log provided the resistance of the blows. This made his current sword feel lighter in the tournament ring and also it made it much easier for him to wield and control it.

Edmond delivered blows and blocked as he fought with his friends. He only wore padded armor verses the metal armor he would wear when he fought them with metal swords. In fact they all wore padded armor for the blows not only hit other swords but they also would strike each other. "Ha!" Edmond yelled as he blocked Silas's blow, which he nearly missed. Quickly he turned and caught the strike that Aram delivered, "You're getting better." Edmond praised Aram. "Won't be long and you'll be as good as I am."

"I doubt that," Aram struck again only to have Edmond's sword block his blow again. "I will never be strong enough to handle the two handed sword properly." He struck again but failed to hit Edmond, which was his target. Edmond swung quickly and hit the side of Aram's leg.

"Four hits, one more and you're out." Edmond grinned as he spun to catch the blow that Eustace delivered.

Beautiful Pretender

"Damn." Aram complained and raised his sword to strike again. He watched as Edmond delivered the fifth blow to Eustace, who then lowered his sword and left the ring to sit on the side lines and watch the others. The fighting didn't continue much longer and Aram received his fifth strike. Now the battle was down to both Edmond and Silas. Aram knew Silas held back a little when it wasn't just him and Edmond. Once the two were alone in the ring, Silas got serious and presented his best performance. Edmond preferred it this way because by the time he got to this one on one battle, he was usually really tired and Silas was able to push him harder and present a worthy challenge.

"Not bad, you are a worthy squire." Edmond laughed as he received and delivered blows. Currently Edmond had only one strike against him and Silas had three. It wouldn't be easy for Edmond to get in the final two now that Silas was being serious. Truthfully, Silas was an excellent swordsman himself. He along with Eustace had come to Arminia from other kingdoms and in such a manner that when the king had called for recruitments a few years back, even though they were within the age limit, they were not yet citizens of Arminia. Therefore they were able to avoid joining the king's army as were their fathers.

Aram and Eustace never grew tired of watching Edmond and Silas battle. They were both amazing and they both had a flawless style and technique to their fighting. The serious concentrated look on both faces, the sweat that dripped from their brows, their battle ready stances and how they kept eye contact as they studied their opponent and waited for the other to make the next move was mind boggling. Finally Edmond got in a forth strike but nearly was struck himself, he moved his body and it missed by only a small fraction. "One more." Edmond smiled.

"We'll see." Silas swung his sword hard and Edmond barely caught it with his own in time. Silas grunted in frustration for he nearly had him. "I will beat you one of these days." He promised. The two had become friends shortly before they had met Aram. Immediately the two got along famously because they had so much in common. Silas's father had been teaching him the sword since he was just a child and it didn't take long for the two to realize they had a common love of sword play. Eustace didn't have that advantage but he was a quick learner and picked up the ways of the sword rather quickly. Aram was the last to join this group of swordsmen. At first he was reluctant but eventually the thrill of the sword and Edmond's method of teaching him, won Aram over. They were pretty good about not harassing Aram about not being able to wield the heavier swords. Aram was smaller then the rest of them and he wasn't built like the rest of them either.

Edmond was happy that Silas was a worthy opponent and presented him with a difficult challenge. Silas could easily compete in the tournaments, if only he had a title and came from an established noble family. On more then one occasion Edmond had been tempted to speak with Kendrick about finding a way to give Silas a title, even though he was still young, Edmond believed that Silas was a good candidate for a knighthood. A knighthood wasn't an easy thing to receive. It took more then just being able to wield a sword. However, he was sure that whatever condition Kendrick would set, that Silas would be up for the challenge, despite his young age.

Edmond found the gap that finally opened in Silas's defense and he took the final shot, delivering the last strike needed to put his opponent out of the ring. The strike hit on Silas's left side and he gasped as the wind was temporarily knocked from him. "Thank goodness." Edmond sighed and walked over to where Aram was and handed him his sword. "I wasn't sure how much longer I was going to last. We haven't really practiced in quite some time."

"Easy for you to say." Silas could barely talk as he hunched over to catch his breath. "Nice match though. We shouldn't have waited so long to start training again." Normally they would have started training months ago but since Edmond was only participating in the one event that year, due to the fact that his family was forcing him to pretty much retire from it because they wanted him to settle down to more serious matters, including marriage.

"Perhaps we did wait too long but I have confidence that I'll be more then ready to compete when the King's Tournament comes." Edmond boasted with pride. The others agreed in their own fashion as they waited for Edmond and Silas to exit the sword ring. The day was getting late and they were all expected to be home soon. Silas and Eustace had their chores to attend to and Edmond's father had matters he needed to discuss with his son when he came home from

Beautiful Pretender

his duties at the palace. Aram had already decided to stay the night at the physician's home because he wanted to spend time with the family that had adopted the boy part of him. He had grown rather close to the family and adored them almost as if they were his own. This was especially true because Arabella had no siblings of her own and she found that need for such a thing fulfilled in her second family.

Aram and Edmond sat down at the table that evening with the physician Joseph and his family for the evening meal. It wasn't the first time they had done this. Edmond wasn't in any hurry to go back home after his conversation with his father because his mother would only continue to go on and on about how the two maidens of noble birth, that she found for him to choose from, would suit him as a wife. Also, even though he had not originally intended to spend the evening with Aram, he had grown frustrated with his father's endless orders to him about being of the age of taking on duties that were expected from a young man of his station. Edmond had left home angry and sought the comfort of his closest friend. Aram, or should I say Arabella, was also trying to avoid hearing the similar thing from her own mother about the two kings, which was why she had originally intended to seek refuge at the home of her other family.

Joseph and his wife were more then pleased to have both of them there, as were the children. Both Edmond and Aram were rather fond of the little ones and they had often spent the evenings playing with them as a way to escape from the reality that awaited them outside the physician's home.

"I know this is getting a little late for me to be asking this but do you think it would be alright if I stayed over tonight?" Edmond asked Aram. "I really don't feel like going home tonight."

"I'll ask." Aram smiled. A room had been set up in the home for Aram's exclusive use, should he ever need or want to stay overnight. In fact, Baron Cordell even paid a generous rental fee for it so it wouldn't be an inconvenience the family. Aram left Edmond with the children to speak with the physician in private.

"You don't know what you're asking Aram." Joseph said quietly. "It's immoral."

"Only if he was staying with Arabella but you know that is not who

I am to him. Besides, we've slept next to each other before. The only difference was that is was outdoors. I really see no harm in it."

"Are you sure he won't discover anything?"

"Positive. I'm too careful when I'm around him for that to happen. Please, he really needs a friend right now and to be honest, so do I. We're both facing arranged marriages we don't want and we only have each other to lean on for support. It won't be long and we will be forced to live separate lives. Please, just give us this time to be friends and to support one another."

Joseph cupped his forehead in his hand and used his fingers and thumb to rub at his temples. "As long as you promise that this situation won't shame me or your family, I will allow it, but Aram…" He looked him square in the eye, "don't you dare disappoint me, do you understand?"

"Yes sir. I promise not to disappoint you." Aram smiled gratefully.

"I hope your father never learns about this or it will be my head." He sighed. "Very well, be off with you and enjoy what time is left of this precious friendship of yours."

Suddenly Aram leapt up from the bench they had been sitting on and embraced Joseph, "Thank you." She said in the voice of Arabella. "Thank you for being there when I needed you most." She kissed him before leaving to tell Edmond the good news.

"I would have felt much better about this if she hadn't sounded like Arabella just now. Please God don't let them do anything stupid." He said quietly and then left the house to walk outside for a while in order to clear his head. He really did want Arabella to be happy, as did her father. That was why they both agreed to this but he was worried about the fact that Edmond was a noble man from one of Arminia's highest ranking families, even to the point that he exceeded her own father's right as heir to the throne. "Arabella, you're playing a dangerous game my girl." He whispered to himself in the privacy of the night.

Aram had a hard time containing his excitement. One thing was confusing him though, as Arabella the feelings she felt towards Edmond were nearly uncontrollable, but as Aram, the feelings in her were different somehow. What she saw was her long time friend from when she masqueraded as Aram. True, she was still attracted to him but she was able to, by some unknown means, curve her feelings for him so they didn't control her, as they did when she allowed herself to be a woman. Aram grabbed Edmond's arm and whispered, "He said that it's fine."

"Great." Edmond grinned. "Well kids," he stood up after gently easing two of the physician's children off his lap, "Brother Aram and I are going upstairs now, so be good and don't disturb us." His request was met with moans of protest from the children. "We'll see you in the morning." He smiled and then he addressed Joseph's wife, "Good night mam."

"You're staying here tonight?" She asked confused.

Quickly Aram spoke up, "I already discussed it with father and he's fine with it."

"Well…" She hesitated for a moment, "I suppose if father said it was alright then I'll hold my tongue."

Edmond looked over to Aram and asked quietly, "What was that about?"

"Don't worry about it." Aram smiled, dismissing it without a thought.

"Alright." He shrugged his shoulders in confusion and then followed Aram up the stairs to the bedroom that had been set aside for his use.

It only just then that it dawned on Aram how small the bed in the room was. If Edmond was to stay over it meant they would have to share a bed and he now realized why Joseph and his wife were hesitant about the situation. "Umm…" Aram bit his lower lip nervously, "I forgot how small this bed was. Perhaps I should make up one for myself on the floor." He looked over to Edmond.

"Nonsense," Edmond grinned, "We can both squeeze into it just fine. It's only for one night, so it shouldn't be a problem, right?"

Aram thought a moment longer and decided that he probably would be better off just letting the matter drop. Too much protesting would only arouse Edmond's suspicions as to why they couldn't sleep next to each other. He would just have to be more careful than usual to hide the fact that he was actually a young woman. "I suppose you're right. I was just worried because I'm sure the bed you use at home is probably so big that you might feel uncomfortable sharing this one with me."

Edmond walked over and sat down on the bed. "Not bad, it's rather comfortable."

Aram sat down next to him, "I suppose so. I never really took time to think about it." Truth was, she had only slept on it maybe five times over the last five years during her ruse as Aram. She wasn't even sure if the clothes that she left in the closet would still fit her, since it had been so long since she had needed to use the room.

Edmond fell back on the bed and brought his arms up behind his head as a substitute for a pillow. "Aram?"

Aram looked back at his friend, "What?"

"Would you be mad at me if I fell in love with someone before you did?"

Aram's eyebrows drew in and his forehead wrinkled slightly at the subject of conversation, "What?" He asked confused. "Are you saying you fell in love with someone?"

"I think I might have." He sighed almost dreamily.

"No, I wouldn't be angry but I think you're being foolish if it isn't the girl your parents choose for you to marry."

"Perhaps I am being foolish." He closed his eyes and sighed.

"You know your parents are going to protest it should they learn of it."

"I know but is it really so wrong for me to fall in love with someone?" He looked up at Aram.

"It is, if you already know that you can't always stay by that person's side. Why torture yourself for a love that can never be?" Truly, Aram believed that if he could talk Edmond out of these feelings then maybe she could talk herself out of them as well. After all it would be easier to keep herself from getting too close to Edmond if he didn't fall in love with her.

"Perhaps I find some satisfaction in this torture." He suggested with a gentle laugh. "I don't really even want to try to keep myself from loving her, to be honest. She's just so adorable that I am unable to stop myself from thinking about her every moment of the day."

Aram started to laugh but then quickly stopped himself from doing it. "Adorable? Arabella is anything but adorable. Sure she's kind of nice in her own way but she's far from adorable."

Edmond reached over for a pillow, "That's because you don't know her like I do." He swung the pillow at Aram and hit him in the shoulder.

Aram then reached over Edmond for the other pillow and then

sat back up, "I know her more then you might think, my friend." He slammed the pillow down on Edmond, hitting him hard in the chest.

Edmond began laughing, "Oh you think so do you?" He sat up and began hitting Aram with his pillow and received many blows in return. Soon feathers were flying all over the room as both pillows were pounded to nothing but rags and flying fluff. They were both shouting at each other and laughing hysterically. Suddenly Edmond grabbed Aram by the shoulders and slammed his back against the wall to pin him. He was always amazed at what little strength Aram had for being a guy. "Are you ready to surrender? You know you have no hope of beating me." He asked laughing.

"No." Aram smiled in a challenge. Their smiles slowly disappeared as the both stood breathing hard from the exercise. Feathers were still floating about the room as they slowly made their way down to the floor. He noticed that Edmond seemed lost in thought as he looked into Aram's eyes. After some time had passed, Aram asked in a gentle but boyish voice, "What is it?"

"Huh?" Edmond seemed to slowly come out of his trance. "It's just that I never realized how nice your eyes looked before. It reminded me of someone."

Aram pushed Edmond away from him, "Well I hope it's someone nice." He sighed and looked about the room. 'Oh boy, I'm going to hear about this mess tomorrow.' He thought nervously as he looked at the room that was scattered with feathers. "I guess we won't have any pillows to use tonight."

Edmond looked around, "Uh… yeah, I guess we over did it a little." He laughed nervously. "Tell your mother that I'll have them replaced as soon as I get home tomorrow. I'm sure we have a score of pillows that have never even been used."

"I'll make sure to let her know." Normally Aram wouldn't care, that is *if* he were Arabella. However, if he told Edmond not to worry about it, it might raise a suspicion since the physician's family couldn't afford for one of their kids to be so reckless with their belongings. "Perhaps it will soften their frustrations concerning it."

They began sweeping the feathers off of the bed with their hands and they used their feet to push as many as possible off to one side on the floor so they wouldn't be dragging them around the house. This would be especially useful should they need to get up in the middle of the night to use the outhouse. "Wall or edge?" Edmond asked indicating the bed.

Aram looked over. "Edge I guess." He shrugged, and wondered if it really made any difference. "What do you want to wear to bed tonight?"

Edmond looked down at his clothing, "The usual I guess." He indicated his shirt, for it came down to his knees and it seemed handy enough to use as a night shirt.

"Guess I'll do the same then." Aram turned around and began removing his pants but then stopped and looked back at Edmond. "I think I'll run out really quick and use the outhouse. Go ahead and go to bed. I'll be back in a moment."

"Sure." Edmond finished removing his pants and crawled under the covers.

Aram walked over and took the candle into his hand that had been lighting the room, "You don't mind if I take this do you?"

"No, go ahead." Edmond yawned as he got under the covers.

"Thanks." Once Aram was out in the quiet of the outhouse, he took a deep breath and slowly breathed out. He regretted doing it immediately as the acrid scent stung his nose and burned his throat. Arabella was more accustomed to using a bedchamber pot that her servants would empty for her verses this small hut with the hole in the floor boards. She had used them before but the smell had often got to her.

When Aram spoke again it was in Arabella's soft voice. "I must be crazy to think he won't notice I'm a girl." She sighed miserably. "I forgot that I should have hair on my legs by now, that is 'if' I was a man. Not only that but I'll only have on a shirt." She brought her hand up to her chest. Their nights together before didn't require the removal of any clothing. "At least I know my bindings won't come off but if he lies too close to me, will he feel the bindings? I've always had a coat or cloak on to help conceal them before, not to mention that we never slept so close together like we will be doing tonight." Arabella moaned miserably and was beginning to regret this decision of allowing him to stay.

By the time she had gone back into the house, everyone but Joseph had gone to bed. "Are you alright?" He asked her.

"Yeah." She was still talking in her Eldardesh accented feminine voice as she came into the room where he sat. "I'm afraid we made a bit of a mess up there. I'll have one of our servants come and clean it up in the morning."

"It sounded like the two of you were enjoying yourselves." He smiled.

"Just rough housing." She smiled back, "Though you're out of two pillows now. Edmond wants to replace them, so I told him to go ahead."

Joseph laughed gently as he brought out his pipe and lit it. "I see." He said as he puffed gently on the hallowed out wood. "Mother has a few more pillows in the chest over there. Feel free to take those for tonight."

"Thank you, sir." She smiled and then went to gather the pillows. "We'll be quieting down now, so you needn't worry about us keeping you up."

"I'm afraid it will be difficult for me to sleep tonight. Mother asked that I stay up and watch over you two. It is bothering her that you two are sleeping together in the same bed."

"But we're guys... well sort of." She sighed.

"Like I said earlier, you only have a short time left to do be friends, so go ahead and enjoy yourselves." He gave his best reassuring smile. "I know that I can trust you not to do anything inappropriate."

"Thank you, sir." She bowed humbly. "Thank you so much!" She grinned and then left to head back up the stairs. When she got back into the room she found Edmond sitting on the side of the bed. "Oh, you're still up." She said in Aram's boyish voice with the Arminian accent that he had mastered.

"I was beginning to wonder if you fell into the hole, out in the outhouse." Edmond laughed softly.

Aram laughed as well, "Not this time. Here..." He threw the pillows at Edmond, "Father found some extra pillows for us to use tonight."

"Great!" Edmond smiled and laid them both on the head of the bed. Then he crawled back over to his side but stayed in a sitting position. "Was he too unhappy about what we did to the other ones?"

"No, he seemed alright with it once he knew that you were planning on replacing them." Aram placed the candle down on the table. "Need anything else before I blow this out?"

"No, I'm fine." He answered. "Are you going to undress in the dark?"

"Yeah, it's sort of a habit of mine." He bent down and blew out the candle so he could undress in the security that the dark had to offer. As quietly as possible he took a slow deep breath and then let it out. 'We're both guys, there's nothing to be concerned about, as far as he knows, I'm just another guy.' He reassured himself and then got into the bed. Quickly he pulled the covers up to his chin.

"Whoa, give me a chance to lay down first." Edmond laughed and then scooted down under the covers as well.

"It's a little cramped but not too bad." Aram did his best to make a light conversation.

"Just pretend I'm Silas's sister and snuggled close to me." Edmond laughed and grabbed Aram about the waist, pulling him closer.

"Stop that!" Aram scolded.

"Oh come on dearest. Now don't be shy." He pouted.

Aram back elbowed Edmond in the ribs causing him to gasp. "As if you'd even come close to looking like a girl. Take your hands off."

"Alright, I'll just pretend you are Arabella then." He clung on tighter.

"Don't you even dare, you pervert." Aram warned him with a nervous laugh and then he thought to himself, 'why Arabella of all people?' A slight groan of frustration escaped his lips.

Edmond was laughing harder now but he ended up releasing Aram. "Well you do have to admit that you do look like a girl. I can't help it if I get confused sometimes." He knew it drove Aram crazy when people told him he looked like a girl but every now and again, Edmond had to play that card. It just couldn't be helped when Aram responded so dramatically to it every time.

"Go ahead and laugh it up you moron." Aram sighed and turned his back to Edmond.

"Aw, come on now… don't be mad." He laid his hand on Aram's shoulder. "I'm just jesting."

"I realize that. Go to sleep."

"Aram?" Edmond's voice was more serious now.

Beautiful Pretender

"Yeah."

"What does she look like? You have seen her face to face, right?"

"Her who?"

Edmond sighed, "Who else would I be talking about but Arabella of course."

"Oh her." Aram yawned. "She looks like a girl."

"So do you but that's not the point."

Aram elbowed him again. "Go to sleep already."

"Come on." He begged. "Anything will do."

"She has nice sized breasts and a pretty smile. Is that enough?"

"Hey!" He pulled on Aram's shoulder, "You were looking at her chest? How could you?"

"Like you didn't?" He countered. "I'm sure you noticed them too."

"Well yeah but...well...just don't look at them again, got it."

Aram laughed softly, "You devilish pervert. You really were checking them out, weren't you?"

"Oh, just go to sleep." Edmond complained. "At least I got to do something you didn't."

"Oh, and what's that?"

"I saw her swimming. She had absolutely nothing on and her soft pale skin glistened in the star light."

"Liar."

"It's the truth. Just last night I accidentally ran across her on one of my walks and she was swimming in her family's hot spring. And you know what else?"

"Let me guess, she kissed you." Aram yawned again.

Edmond leaned in closer to Aram, "How did you know?"

"Wild guess... goodnight." Aram could feel his temper beginning to grow short. He really had no desire to talk about this because it was stirring the feminine feelings that she was trying to hide when she was Aram.

"You're upset with me, aren't you?"

"I just don't want to see you get hurt, that's all." Aram said honestly.

"She just might be worth it." He sighed and rolled onto his back.

Arabella couldn't help smiling when she heard his honest words.

Truth was she was thinking that it just might be worth it too, as long as Edmond never discovered the truth about her and Aram being the same person. Still she was going to continue to try and use Aram to convince him to stop the relationship. After all, it seemed like it was the right thing to do for both their sakes.

The next morning Edmond awoke to the sun's rays shining on his face. He looked down and noticed that Aram was still fast asleep with his head near Edmond's chest. Aram was lying on his side facing Edmond and had one fist under the temple of his head and his other hand was lying palm down on the bed near his face. 'Why does he have to look so adorable when he's sleeping?' Edmond complained silently. Then he gasped as Aram moved closer into him and took a fist full of Edmond's shirt as he snuggled closer. "Whoa." Edmond laughed softly. "A whole other side of you I never noticed before." Aram groaned in a feminine tone.

Edmond reached up and brushed a few stray hairs that had managed to come out of the leather bound ponytail Aram was known to wear on the back of his head. "I almost forgot how found of sleeping you were. I don't think an earth quake could rouse you from your slumber." He laid his head back down but he continued to watch Aram as he slept. Edmond then reached over to pluck a feather off of the sleeve of Aram's shirt when suddenly a knock sounded at the door. "You boys should get up now, breakfast is ready." The physician's wife called to them.

"Yes mam." Edmond called back. His voice seemed to reach Aram who yawned. "Come on beautiful, wake up."

"Huh?" Aram's voice was barely audible.

"You're mother just called us down to breakfast."

Aram slowly opened his eyes, "Mother?" His quiet voice was more like Arabella's then Aram's. Then he realized his situation and let go of Edmond's shirt and returned his voice back to that of Aram's. "Oh." He sat up feeling rather embarrassed. "You go first." He told Edmond nervously.

"Huh?" Edmond replied in confusion.

"You go ahead and go down first. Let mother know I'll be down shortly."

Edmond looked at Aram in confusion, "Alright." He said with some hesitation and then got out of bed. Aram quickly turned his head to avoid looking at Edmond as he used no caution when getting out of bed and his shirt revealed just a bit too much of his body. After he was out of bed he straightened his clothing and then picked up his pants and put them on. "Are you feeling alright?" He asked his friend.

"Um... Yeah, I'm fine." Aram looked at him and yawned. "I just need a moment."

"Alright, I guess I'll see you down stairs then." He looked at Aram a moment longer before turning to leave.

After he left, Aram breathed deeply and then fell face first down on the bed. "How embarrassing..." He said quietly into his pillow in Arabella's voice. "I can't believe I was snuggling into him like that. I could just die." She slammed her fist into the pillow several times. Finally she got up out of bed and put her pants on and straightened out her hair the as best as she could. It would only be a few more hours before Ida would transform her back into Arabella again. At least that was only *if* Edmond went home after their morning meal. She was pretty sure that was his plan. In her opinion it would be best if he did because she was looking forward to going home and taking a nice long hot bath. She was still feeling rather disgusting after all the practice in the sword ring the day before. "You really have gotten yourself into a rather fine situation." She scolded her reflection in the mirror. "Even if I manage to keep my real identity hidden, how on earth am I to continue hiding it from him should I become Arminia's queen?" It was something that only just dawned on her as she watched her reflection. "I really doubt I could hide this that long anyway." Her fingers on one hand came up to touch her cheek, "I have to end this somehow before I hurt him. I just don't know what to do." She lowered her hand and turned to look at the door. "What should I do?" Her soft voice whispered as she sighed in remorse.

Chapter 5

Jocelyn was ecstatic with the excitement that flowed through her veins. The day of the masked celebration was at hand. She had the entire household of servants in a flurry of activities as she prepared for that evening. Her list felt endless yet she wanted to do even more. The smell of pastries, meats and vegetables were rising up from her kitchen and more then once her stomach growled in anticipation for the feast and activities that awaited them at the masked celebration. The very much anticipated event would transform this into the most enchanting day, even more so because the king himself was coming to see her daughter.

She was one of the few noble women who delighted in helping prepare for these kinds of festive activities, though her servants really were the ones who did the majority of the work. "If only Aldrich were here." She sighed. "His absence is the only thing that is keeping this day from being absolute perfection." A smile crept across her face, "Still, with the king coming to see my daughter, it is as close to perfection as a celebration could possibly be." She squealed happily and danced around her bed chamber with an invisible partner, humming one of her favorite tunes. Her heart was racing and her cheeks were flushed with excitement for she had never felt as wonderful as she did now. With all of her heart she hoped that Kendrick would set his sights on her little Arabella and make her his bride. It was the moment she had anticipated for a long time now, the moment her daughter would be chosen as a queen.

Arabella looked out her window into the grey morning. "It looks like it might rain today." She yawned.

Beautiful Pretender

"Will you need Aram's clothing today miss?" Ida asked her.

"No, we tend to not gather on days like this." Arabella was referring to Aram's group of male companions. "There is no sense in doing so if it means getting soaked to the bone. Besides, I can't hide my womanly features that well when my shirt is wet."

"Yes, I had forgotten about that." Ida came and stood next to her mistress. "Milady, may I ask you a personal question?"

"Of course you may." Arabella looked at her and smiled.

"Eventually you will have to marry someone, but what I was hoping to know is whether or not I will go with you to continue serving you."

"I suppose I really hadn't thought about it before." She confessed. "I am so use to you being by my side that it wouldn't seem right if you didn't continue to do so. I will talk to father and mother about it and see if it can be arranged… that is, if it is what you desire…" Arabella didn't want to force Ida to stay in her service if Ida was hinting about leaving instead of asking to stay.

"It is, milady. You may be a bit odd for someone in your station but it is one of the many things I love about you. It would be dreadfully boring to tend to someone else after being by your side for this long." Arabella laughed softly for Ida had been her handmaiden for nearly nine years and they were more like sisters at times then like mistress and servant.

"I'm glad to hear it." Arabella smiled. "However, I'm afraid that Aram can only be with us for a short while longer and then I will have to behave like a lady of my station. Are you sure you can handle that?"

"Yes, milady." Ida smiled.

Arabella looked over to the gown she would be wearing soon for the festive occasion to come. It was a crimson red gown with gold and black trim. It had a narrow skirt which meant she wouldn't have to fight the farthingale (a hoop skirt) or the several skirts that were usually worn under the dresses. It would also accentuate her slim figure without a doubt and she was sure her mother may have had it made this way on purpose in the hope that the king would come to see her and enjoy seeing her in it. Her mask was crimson red and just like her dress it was trimmed with gold decorative gilding around the edges and a delicate pattern down the nose and it boasted large black plume feather with smaller black feathers in front of it on the right hand side of the upper corner of the mask. The mask was the kind that would strap on nicely to her head so she wouldn't have to spend the night trying to hold one up on a stick.

"It's beautiful isn't it?" Ida smiled as she too looked at the rather becoming gown.

"Yes, I would be lying if I said it wasn't." She walked over and felt the fabric. "It certainly won't leave much to the imagination though. The low bust line, the lack of sleeves…"

"It is daring. I haven't seen this fashion on very many women but the workmanship suggests your position as a future queen."

"Is my cape ready?"

"Yes, it awaits you downstairs."

"Very well then. I think I would like to rest a while longer so that I may enjoy the celebration tonight to its fullest. Please inform mother."

"I will." Ida smiled. "I'll make sure that a bath is ready for you when you wake up."

"Thank you." Arabella yawned sleepily. She laid down and fell asleep and ended up resting for quite a bit longer then she had intended, however it did what she had hoped it would do for it left her feeling refreshed and in a good frame of mind.

Arabella looked into her mirror and frowned. "It's still not going to be enough."

"I don't understand." Ida responded in confusion and looked closer at Arabella's reflection.

"Even with the mask, I'm sure he'll recognize me." She continued to look into the mirror. Her hair being up looked too much like Aram's in her opinion. "What if we allow some hair to hang down on the sides of my face and then pile the rest on top as it is now? Also if I put a touch of color on my lips…" She continued to think for a moment. "He knows that Aram's ears are pierced but he never has seen him wear any jewelry in them, so it should be alright…" She was mostly thinking out loud to herself more than she was talking to Ida.

"Yes milady." Immediately Ida set about doing as Arabella suggested.

Beautiful Pretender

When she was finished they both looked at her reflection in the mirror again.

"Hand me my mask, Ida."

"Do you think this will work, milady?"

Arabella allowed Ida to put her mask on. The inside of it was lined with a soft cushioned fabric to provide comfort to her face. "I think it will." She smiled as she saw her face transform into one of a strangers. "Perfect." She grinned happily and then her hand went up to her mouth. "My smile..." She whispered. "He'll recognize my smile for certain."

"What do you mean?"

"Edmond has told me before that I had a nice smile, as Aram that is. I can't let him see it or he's sure to figure it out." A sigh escaped her lips. "I'll just have to do my best to hide it." She looked around and then asked Ida, "Don't I have a fan that would coordinate with this outfit?"

"I believe so." Ida set about looking for it. When she found it she brought it to Arabella.

Arabella opened it and practiced smiling behind it in the mirror. "Now it's perfect or at least it will have to do. After all it isn't uncommon for a woman to hide behind her fan." She reasoned with herself and then closed it, placing the strap on its handle around her wrist. "Yes, this should do nicely."

The door to her room opened and her mother came in wearing a dark blue gown that belled out from her waist to the floor. The top rode low and the sleeves flared out at her wrists. There was a golden V that went from the top of her bodice to her waist and a thin rope of gold crisscrossed on the outer sleeves of the gown's arm. On her head sat a simple gold tiara, much like the one on Arabella's head and they both had similar gold jewelry on their ears, necks and wrists. Only Jocelyn wore rings on her fingers.

"My child how lovely you look tonight." Her mother beamed. "I do believe that we will be the two most beautiful women there tonight. She walked over and stood next to her daughter and they took a moment to look at themselves in the mirror. "You certainly are not a little girl anymore."

"Nor should I be considered a woman yet." Arabella reminded her. "I'm still growing."

"In more ways then one." Her mother teased for she was referring to her daughter's womanly features that were finally coming to a point that would attract men. "It took you a little longer then most young women, but you seem to be making up for lost time."

"Yes. I'm not sure if I can hide the fact that I'm female for much longer when I dress as Aram. I'm afraid I won't get my full year at this rate."

"Well, I know you have your reasons for not being happy about that but I'm glad that it will soon end."

"I know." Arabella sighed in annoyance.

"I hardly even recognize you, Arabella." Jocelyn reflected softly as she reached over and fingered the hair that hung near her daughter's cheek. "Why not put it all up, dear?"

"I like it this way." She smiled. "Mother, if we don't leave soon we won't arrive before the other guests do. Our hostess made it clear that she didn't want the other guests to see me before my presentation."

"Yes, I had almost forgotten about that." She glanced in the mirror one last time. "Are you ready to leave?"

"I am."

"Very well then, I'll inform the staff." Jocelyn left Arabella's room. "We'll be taking separate carriages tonight. I'm going with a few friends of mine and since this is your debut, I thought you might enjoy having some time alone before you are forced to mingle with all those people."

"You are very perceptive mother." Arabella reached for her mother's hand. "I really appreciate the forethought."

"Try not to take too much longer. You don't want to be late for such an important event." She leaned down and kissed her daughter's cheek.

Once Arabella was ready to leave she allowed Ida to assist her with putting on the black cape that coordinated with her gown. It had a nice soft feel to it and would provide moderate warmth that was suitable to the late summer evening on her journey home. "I hope you have a wonderful evening, milady." Ida offered to her mistress.

"I'm sure I will." Arabella smiled and then left for her carriage. It wasn't anything too fancy, just a simple black carriage with a touch of gold trim and some carvings of geese in flight on the door. It wasn't

Beautiful Pretender

used very much anymore but the stablemen seemed to keep it in good shape. She could tell that the seats had been recently reupholstered and it also had new curtains on the windows, which were tied back so she could look out of them as they drove.

The early evening drive was pleasant. The sun had already began its decent and the rain from earlier in the day left the air feeling cool and refreshing as it made its way into her open windows. It was only a gentle and mild breeze so she didn't have to worry about it messing up her hair or clothing. Her eyes glanced down at her mask which sat beside her on the seat. She still wasn't sure if it would hide who she was from Edmond. All she could do was to pray for a miracle and hope that he wouldn't notice anything.

Her carriage slowed down to a stop and it brought her attention back to her window, "Surely we can't be there already…" It looked like they were still on the road. "Huh…" She reached for the cane to signal the driver but her attention was brought to the door on the other side of the carriage.

"We meet again, princess." The familiar voice said.

Quickly Arabella pulled her hood up over her head to hide herself. 'Thank God he didn't come to this side of the carriage or he would have seen me for sure.' She thought nervously. "Well, isn't this a surprise, Sir Robber." She kept her face hidden under the hood of her cape as she turned to face him. 'He was trying to catch me off guard. I bet he thought he could see my face if he did.' Now she was frustrated but she didn't let on. "Have you come to relieve me of my jewelry again?"

"No… not this time." He laughed softly.

"Oh?" She asked curiously. "Then how might I help you?"

"May I come in?"

"In the carriage?" Her voice betrayed her surprise.

"Yes. I thought perhaps we could ride together for a short while."

"You are awfully bold, sir." She hesitated for a moment as she thought of how to answer his request. Finally she decided to give in. "Very well." She heard him open the door and could feel the bounce and jostling of the carriage as he climbed inside and sat down beside her. He was so close to her that his arm rested snuggly against hers. After the door closed, Arabella picked up the cane she needed to use to tap on the roof to signal the driver to move on.

When he heard the tap, he opened the small door in the roof so he could speak with her. He was surprised to see the bandit sitting next to his mistress. "Are you alright, milady?" The concern was evident in his voice.

"I am well, thank you. This man means me no harm, please carry on."

The driver looked at the bandit who smiled good naturedly at him. "I promise I won't do anything, sir." Edmond told him.

"Very well." The driver obviously seemed unsure about this man being in there with Arabella, but he also didn't sense any fear from her. He closed the hatch and soon the carriage took off with a jolt and was again moving towards its destination.

"Were you alone?" Arabella asked.

"Yes. I must confess that when I saw that your mother wasn't traveling with you, I went out of my way to come find you." He heard her laugh softly. "Are you not at all afraid of me? I am a bandit after all."

"I'm terribly sorry." She said through her laughter, "It's just that…" She couldn't continue.

"What?" He asked curiously.

"You must promise to not talk to the other nobles as you do with me or they will know who you are." She brought the back of her hand up to her lips to try and still her laughter.

"Then you know who I am?"

"Please don't hate me for knowing, but your voice is too familiar to me now, Lord Wallace."

"Ah." He couldn't believe that she figured it out so soon. "So I have been discovered."

"I'm afraid so."

He sighed and then reached for her hand. "I assume you'll keep my secret, right?"

"Of course I will. I did tell you that I supported your cause didn't I."

"That you did." He squeezed her hand gently. "So you're not mad at me then?"

"No, why would I be?"

"I did rob your family…"

"Don't hesitate to do so again. My darling father is just as guilty as the other nobles."

"True." He had a hint of laughter in his voice for indeed her father was rather stingy when it came to helping those in need. "However," He added more seriously, "your mother is rather charitable and I felt bad for taking her things. I haven't even had the nerve to try and sell them yet. Also…I couldn't bear to sell the things you gave me either. You also seem to be very charitable and I don't think its fair of us to take those things from you."

"You didn't take those things from me, silly. I gave them to you."

"I suppose." He said with some hesitation. "I keep that broach you gave me with me at all times." He pulled it from his pocket. "Whenever I feel life bringing me down, all I need to do is to look at it for a few moments and then I start feeling better. I promise I will keep it until you ask for it back."

"It is a rather priceless family heirloom. Mother was terribly unhappy about me giving it away, however I just knew it should go to you."

Edmond put the broach back into his pocket. "I know it will only be a short time before we see each other tonight, but I couldn't help taking this opportunity to see you again. I hope you don't mind."

"You may stop my carriage anytime you wish, milord." She freed her hand from his and used it to removed the bracelets from her other wrist. Then she handed them to him. "Take these so your efforts at thievery this evening aren't a total loss."

"No, you've already given more then enough." He protested.

"Just take them." She let them fall onto his lap. "You may have the rest after the party tonight if you'd like. I doubt that I'll be wearing these things again."

"No, I will take what you gave me and the things from before but I will not let you give anymore for now." He placed the gold bracelets into his pocket with her broach. "Perhaps you can come and help my friends and I distribute food, clothing and medicine to those we rob for." He suggested.

"Perhaps someday." She couldn't promise anything. "Close your eyes for a moment."

"Why?"

She laughed softly, "Just do it."

"Alright." He did as she asked. Arabella lifted her hood just enough to expose her mouth and nose and then she kissed his cheek gently. Immediately she let the hood lower again. "What was that for?"

"I just felt like kissing you." She smiled. "Take it as a token of my great esteem for you and what you do for others."

"Oh?" He looked at her even though he couldn't see her face. What he could see however were her slender arms and her delicate hands that were toying with the black fan that hung off one of her wrists. "Thank you." Finding words wasn't easy for him at the moment as her actions had left him slightly flustered.

"You may want to get out of the carriage before we get too close to your house. It would be simply dreadful should someone see you in my carriage and learn that Arminia's beloved son was the same boy who robs them blind."

Her statement made him laugh, "True. I do have a rather polished reputation among the nobles. They seem to have high hopes for my future even if I never become a king. Apparently Kendrick has a rather esteemed position waiting for me in his court when I'm ready to take on the responsibilities."

"Really?" She sounded surprised but it actually made her nervous. If this was true and she did end up as Kendrick's wife then seeing Edmond on a regular basis would be unavoidable. Still, it was better then becoming Eric's wife and being miserable with him. Her future seemed to have a dark cloud that hung over it and it only seemed to grow bigger and bigger with time. She used her cane to signal the driver to stop so Edmond could get out before they came to a point where they'd be more likely to get caught by someone. "I will see you later, milord."

"Until then, milady, I bid you ado." He gently closed the door and hit the carriages side twice to signal the driver to leave and he didn't hesitate to do so either. Edmond watched as the carriage left to finish the short distance to his home where the evening's festivities would take place. His hand slid into his pocket and he wrapped his fingers around the broach that rested in it. "How can I not fall in love with you?" His voice whispered into the stillness of the setting sun. "You always leave me enchanted and breathless."

Beautiful Pretender

Not long after Arabella arrived to the anticipated event, the young king did as well. He desired to speak with her and her mother before the celebration began. He knew all too well that once he was around the noblemen in his kingdom they would monopolize his time and he would no longer have time to spend with this prospective bride. While Kendrick, Arabella and her mother, who had joined her daughter once the king arrived, waited they didn't bother wearing their masks for it would be more then enough of a burden to wear them during the remainder of the night.

"I'm pleased to see that you and your mother are doing well, Arabella." He smiled. He was aware that her father had returned to Eldardesh to attend to family matters, or at least that was what he had been told.

"Yes we are your majesty. Have you been well also?" She wasn't sure what to say to this boy king or how to address him. Normally she would talk down to a boy of his age, since he was two years younger then she was, but because he was the king and acted like a grown up, it made her unsure of how to behave, so she treated him like an adult.

"My advisors have suggested that I consider not waiting to ask for your hand in marriage because my brother seeks it as well, but I'm not sure if I'm ready to be a husband yet."

"I see no reason for you to hurry, your majesty. Eric is still only twelve and he is on good terms with my father. I'm sure that he doesn't feel rushed to ask for my hand because of this. I know he has already taken a wife but if he was worried about anything he wouldn't have waited so long to make me his wife as well."

"Perhaps." He was silent for a moment before speaking again. "Arabella?"

"Yes."

"Would you be happy living here in Arminia for the rest of your life?"

"Yes sire, I would." She smiled.

"Don't you miss your home in Eldardesh?"

"Sometimes I do but not enough to go back. To be honest, Eric frightens me a little. He doesn't mean to but there is something about him that doesn't sit well with me. My parents have the final say as to whom I marry but to be honest, I really hope they don't choose Eric." She quickly held up her hands, "I'm not saying that you have to decide on me or anything like that, though. I'm just saying that I would prefer not marrying him."

"I understand." He smiled. "I am very fond of you, Arabella. So never worry about my feelings towards you. It is possible that I will ask for your hand in the near future. I just need a little more time to think about this."

"I am honored that you are willing to consider me as your potential wife, milord." She smiled in return. If worse came to worse she felt that if she had to choose between the two brothers, that Kendrick was by far the better choice. Though he had his moments where he seemed a bit arrogant and domineering, he also had a gentle and tender side to him. He also never seemed to hide his true feelings or thoughts when he talked with her.

The door to the room opened and one of the king's guards stepped in. "They're ready for you, sire." He announced.

"Has it been that long already?" Kendrick asked and that was when he noticed that Arabella's mother was no longer in the room. "I didn't realize we had been talking that long." A grin stretched across his face and then he stood up and offered his hand to Arabella. "Come my dear, it's time for your début into society."

Arabella took his hand and then she looked over to Ida, "My mask." She reminded her.

"Mine too." The king addressed one of his servants. The servant fetched the king's white masked that was trimmed in decorate gold on the edges and on the nose with red trimming the eyes with gold swirl trimming around that. Both of them stood still while their masks where strapped onto their heads. "I had almost forgotten about them." He laughed gently.

"Then I suppose I have been of some service to you tonight, milord." She smiled sweetly.

"You're company is far better then the service of a subject, princess. Shall we?" He began to escort her from the room. Once they were out they walked to the stairway where they would descend. It led down to the main room where the remaining guests were waiting for them patiently. "Are you nervous?"

"Just a little." She looked down into his eyes. "Does it not bother you at all that I'm taller then you are?"

This made him laugh, "That is only a temporary matter. In time, I'll be taller then you and it will all work out fine."

She couldn't help smiling at the thought of how awkward they must look together. She was nearly half a head taller then he was. "I suppose that is true. At least that is what mother keeps trying to tell me."

"We will be expected to have the first dance together. You do know how to dance, right?"

"My father and I have often danced together. He taught me every dance he knows." She assured him. The fleeting memories of the evenings her father spent with her as they danced in the family's banquet room made her heart feel warm. She missed her father when he left on trips like this. She knew she had grown spoiled over the last five years while he was forced to stay within Arminia's borders because of the residence law. However, now that they were official citizens, it was obvious that he would be spending a great deal of time away from home like he used to when they lived in Eldardesh. She wondered if it would be like that for Edmond also when he took up his position in Kendrick's service.

"Then I will truly enjoy these festivities after all since you are the only one I plan to dance with tonight."

"I am very honored, your majesty." They came to the top of the staircase which barely concealed them from the others below and there they stood and waited for their cue to descend. One of the king's guards went down before them, to let their host and hostess know that they were ready to come down. Two of the king's personal guards would follow them down from a short distance away. Though the security was tight, the king still required at least two guards near him at all times.

Finally the sounds of the crowd died down and they could hear the voice of their hostess, Kendrick's older sister, rise above the audience to make her announcement. "My most esteemed and honored guests, as you may know tonight we have the rare honor of not only entertaining our most beloved king but also his prospective bride. On top of this, Princess Arabella Mina Cordell will be making her first appearance in society as one of our most cherished nobles in our beautiful kingdom and also as our newly established princess. Please bow in honor of our king, long may he live."

A loud rustling sound came from below and the trumpets blasted their familiar tune that meant that the king was about to appear before his people. "Are you ready?" He smiled up at her warmly.

"I am." Together with her arm resting lightly on his they walked with slow coordinated steps down the stairway. Arabella was amazed at the number of guests that were bowing before her king.

About two thirds of the way down he stopped and said loudly for all to hear. "Please rise and see our honored guest." Everyone then stood upright and looked up at them. The sea of masks of gold, silver, red, blue, green, and every other color, many with and without feathers, accompanied by coordinating and beautiful clothing of the men and women, was nearly breathtaking as the crowd gazed up adoringly at them.

"How lovely." Arabella whispered.

"I thought you might like seeing it from this view." He led her to begin their final descent.

When they reached the last stair, the Baroness announced. "Please stand aside as his majesty and Princess Cordell dance the first dance." Immediately the center of the room cleared as he led her out onto the dance floor. Then a soft yet somewhat lively tune struck up from the musicians and the two began to dance. Thankfully it was one that Arabella was more then familiar with. She assumed the time her father spent dancing with her was one of the many ways he used to prepare her for the life that he and her mother had wanted for her.

Arabella couldn't help but to smile as she and the king danced. They didn't touch in this dance. It was called 'The Dance of the Lover and the Spirit'. It is a dance about a young man who had lost his lover to death. In his dream she was there calling to him but try as he might to reach out for her, she was always just out of his reach.

Arabella would dance near Kendrick, portraying the spirit of the deceased lover. Gently she clapped her hands off and on as twirled about him. It was to symbolize the spirits efforts to call to her lover since he couldn't hear her voice. They would put their hands up and come near each other as if to touch but at the last moment she would gracefully turn away, as would he. They would then dance in a somewhat large circle, gently twirling and looking for one another at the occasional moments when their eyes could meet. As the song grew to a close they were in a breathes reach of each other. It ended with her bowing with her face lowered to the floor before him and him reaching down to her.

The audience erupted in praise at the flawless execution of the dance. Arabella looked up and smiled at the king. "You are very good at this your majesty."

He reached down and took her hand to assist her up. "As are you, princess. That was the most fun I have ever had dancing with someone."

"Your majesty, the Duke…" One of the king's men started to say. They were both slightly startled because they hadn't even noticed him approach.

"Yes, yes, I know. Tell him I'll be there momentarily."

"Yes sire." The man immediately left.

"So it begins." Kendrick moaned miserably. "I am glad we were allowed this one dance, Arabella."

"As am I, sire." She smiled and he lifted her hand to his lips to kiss it.

"Until we meet again."

"Yes your majesty. I'll look forward to it." She curtsied before him.

She watched him walk away and then the voice of her mother said in a gentle tone next to her, "It seems you two are getting along rather well."

"He is a nice boy." Arabella agreed.

"You'd do best to refer to him as a man because of his station." Her mother gently warned.

"Perhaps you're right." She sighed with a hint of frustration. Arabella knew her mother was hoping that the two of them would end up together.

"Come dear, there are many people who want to spend time with you." Jocelyn escorted her to a rather large group of masked women who had gathered together. "I'm sure you'll get a chance to dance with some more gentlemen shortly." She winked at her daughter through her white and gold mask.

"I'm in no hurry." Arabella smiled. She allowed her mother to lead her but Arabella couldn't help but to look around to see if she could find Edmond. Too many of the men in the room looked like they could possibly be him, mostly because she only got a glimpse of each one. She tried to hide the fact that she was looking for someone by keeping her observation of the crowd as casual as possible. "Everyone looks so wonderful tonight."

"They do, don't they." Her mother agreed. Soon she was introducing and reintroducing her daughter to the many noble women that were waiting patiently to meet her. Arabella did her best to be polite and play the part she was born into but her mind was unsettled with knowing that somewhere in the room, Edmond was waiting to see her. Even with her mask and gown, she was still frightened that he would discover her secret.

Suddenly a gentle hand touched her elbow and a soft male voice broke the prattling tongues of the women around her. "May I be so bold as to steal this beautiful young woman away from you lovely ladies for awhile?" This caused many of the women to laugh softly. Arabella swallowed hard to hide her fear.

"Well, it's about time you came." Edmond's mother, The Baroness Wallace, said with delight. Her mask of white with sliver trim and light blue feathers in the upper right hand corner completed the look of her gown with similar coloring and trim. The style suited this lovely petite woman with light brown hair and brown eyes. "This young lady has better things to do then cackle with all of us old hens."

This caused more laughter and then one woman said, "Speak for yourself, Baroness." Again the laughter erupted.

"Very well then, shall we?" He smiled down at her.

"Yes." Arabella answered barely above a whisper. Her heart was pounding so hard she could barely breathe. He led her by the arm to the front porch. "Why are we out here?"

"You're looking rather flushed. I thought you could use some air." He reached down and took her hand into his own.

"Yes, thank you." She was finding it a little difficult to speak with him.

"Are you feeling well tonight?"

"I am." She spread her fan, with her free hand, to prepare it, incase she needed to hide her face.

"I'm glad we can finally have a chance to be alone again."

"As am I, though I really didn't have a chance to properly thank you for all you did for me when I was feeling poorly that day when I last visited here. Your gesture really meant a lot to me, as did your visit to our home. I…" She was beginning to feel nervous and unconsciously began prattling to him.

"Would you like to walk the gardens with me?" He asked. This unexpected nervousness in her was striking him as being rather cute when only just earlier she had boldly kissed his cheek.

"I'd love to." She was still having a hard time being Arabella around him. Even now her heart was fluttering almost out of control. His demeanor was so much different now then it had been with Aram. His voice wasn't the boyish voice that teased her and talked carefree with her as it did when she dressed as Aram. His voice now was gentle and tender and it had an almost erotic sensuality to it. It had a man's compassion that seemed to search her very soul. It almost felt as if he were two different people, much like she was, but without the gender confusion.

"You don't have to keep wearing that mask if you don't want to. Not that it matters because it is much too dark for me to see you that well where we are." He removed his simple mask of black with silver trim, and she could tell that the night would hide her face from his eyes. "May I?" He was asking if he could assist her with taking hers off.

"Yes please." She smiled. For now, she wouldn't need her fan to hide her face so she closed it again. Once her mask was off, he held onto to it for her.

"There's barely a cloud in the sky tonight." Edmond observed.

She looked up. "No, there doesn't seem to be very many clouds at all. It does allow one the most spectacular view of the stars, doesn't it?"

They continued walking. "Arabella, may I ask a question of you?"

"Yes."

"Are you still against me falling in love with you?"

"Of course I am." She laughed softly. "Didn't I already tell you that I would only end up breaking your heart if you did?"

"Yes…" He was silent for a moment, "But I'm afraid your warning came too late, for you are the only woman who has managed to capture my affections. I must admit that I have found you to be my one weakness. No matter how hard I tried, I couldn't keep myself from falling in love with you."

She sighed. "Why did you have to go and like me in that fashion?" She backed away from him a few paces. "I'm really not worthy to receive such affections from you."

He came over and stood before her, "Why ever not? Is it because of those boy kings?"

"No, it's not that." She was having a difficult time speaking to him about this.

"Then why?" He smiled.

She looked up into his shadowed downward gaze, "It's just..." He didn't let her finish. He gently cupped her face in his hands and kissed her tenderly. "Lord Wallace..." His kiss silenced her protests.

"I want you to address me by my name, please, do me the honor of calling me by my first name. I really want you to address me as Edmond." He smiled and then kissed her again.

"We must not do this. If you are caught kissing me it will anger his majesty." Arabella was nearly breathless from receiving such passion from him.

"Is that all that is bothering you?" His lips caressed the tip of her nose in a soft kiss.

"Well..." She was at a loss for words.

"Arabella!" They heard the distant childish voice of Kendrick. "Where are you?"

"I'm here sire." She called back and then to Edmond she said. "You see he's looking for me even as we speak. What if he saw you kissing me?"

Edmond gently kissed her again. "And your point is." He smiled.

Arabella raised her hand to his cheek, "Why? Why do you feel this way about me?"

"It is as if my heart says that I was born to love you. Even when these unavoidable circumstances tear you away from me, and I from you, I know that you are the only one that my heart will ever chose to truly love."

Arabella couldn't control her feelings and she took the initiative to kiss him this time, "Then I will allow you love me for this moment but after this moment passes, you must forget about me or I will surely break your heart." She whispered.

"Then let it break." He whispered back. "I don't really mind at all." His kissed her once more with more passion but quickly broke away as the light from the king's men's lanterns began to come into view.

"Arabella!" Kendrick's youthful voice was closer then it had been before and a soft glow from lanterns could be easily seen in the distance.

"Just a moment, milord." She called back. "Edmond, this must end here. Neither one of us is free to fall in love with someone other then the person of our parents choosing." She backed away from him and then looked out over the lake. It was the same lake that connected to the property of the king's palace and also the same one that they would spend time at, however the oak tree they loved to meet at was not on either property.

"So you could not care for me in this way?" His voice seemed a little sad.

"I can't let myself give way to my heart."

"Do you feel anything for me? Your kiss suggested that you did."

"I beg of you not to pursue this. I can't let myself fall in love with you. If I did, I would only cause you misery." Her voice had lowered as she pleaded her case.

"If it meant you returning my affections then I don't mind." He didn't say anymore for it was obvious the king would be able to hear their words at anytime now.

"My mask." She whispered almost urgently as she realized that soon there would sufficient light for him to see her by.

"What?" He asked in a daze.

"Hurry, I need to put it back on before the king gets here."

He lifted up her mask and looked at it, "Yes, we should probably get them back on." He came around behind her and helped her to put hers on and then he put back on his own just as the king's party came into view.

"There you are." Kendrick smiled. "I had wondered where you went off to."

Arabella reached towards Kendrick and laid her hand gently on his shoulder. "Have your men extinguish the lanterns." She grinned.

"Why?" Kendrick asked.

"You'll see." Her smile brightened though she made sure she was turned away from Edmond enough that he wouldn't have a good view of it. She had to make sure he didn't recognize her. They stood there and waited as the king's guard snuffed out the lanterns lights. "Look." She pointed to the sky, after their eyes had a moment to adjust to the darkness. "Aren't they beautiful?"

Kendrick's breath caught in his throat, "I never really stopped to look at the stars before." He said and she let her hand fall from his shoulder, but immediately he took it into his own hand. He had been asked to study astronomy by his tutors but he thought it was something he would do later on. He never realized how magnificent the night sky could be. "What was that?" He asked as a streak of light crossed the sky.

"Some call those shooting stars. I think you're supposed to make a wish when you see one."

"Really?" He looked up at her.

"Uh-hmm." She affirmed.

"Do you think it's too late for me to do it?"

"I think exceptions are made for kings who are as great as you are, sire." She laughed softly. Right at this moment, Kendrick was more like a little boy then a king. "Just close your eyes really tight and make your secret wish."

"Alright." He did as she instructed. "Now what happens?"

"I guess you'll just have to wait and see if heaven chooses to grant it." She smiled down at him again, though it was too dark for him to see her smile.

"Your majesty…" One of his guards whispered.

"Oh yes, I almost forgot. Arabella, I came looking for you because I have an urgent matter that needs my immediate attention back at the palace. I'm afraid I must be leaving now."

"Already?" Her voice was laced with disappointment. One of the king's men relit a lantern and Kendrick watched as her masked face slowly came back into full view as the light from the lantern's fire danced its shadows on it.

"I'm afraid so." He adjusted his position so he could look up to her face to face. "May I kiss you goodnight?"

"Oh…" She looked over at Edmond who just smiled in response.

"Yes, I suppose you can if you wish to, sire." She bent down so that their faces were more level with each other.

"Good night Arabella." He kissed her cheek. "Come and visit me at the palace sometime soon."

"Yes milord. May I kiss you in return?" She asked.

Even in the semidarkness she could see him blushing, "Alright." He turned his cheek to her so she could kiss it.

"Goodnight my king." She stood up straight but her smile never left him. "Until we meet again."

"Yes…" He had a difficult time answering her. "Let's go men." He said in his most grown up voice. "I will send for you soon, milady."

"I will count the days, your majesty." She was having almost too much fun. It wasn't everyday one had the chance to fluster a king.

She continued to watch as the king's party disappeared into the distance. Suddenly Edmond started laughing softly behind her. "That must have been the funniest thing I have ever seen. I have never been witness to Kendrick being so unsure of himself before."

"Be nice." She scolded while gently laughing herself. "I must admit it was rather amusing."

"Arabella." He put his hand on her shoulder. "I meant what I said." He brought her into his embrace and started to kiss her neck gently several times.

"Edmond, if you don't stop this… I'll…. I'll…." Her voice was failing her.

"Cry out for help?" He asked laughing softly and then continued to nip and kiss the soft pale skin of her delicately shaped neck.

"I might do the one thing we'd regret the most."

"And what is that?" He teased as he inhaled the perfumes that she had used when she washed her hair.

"I'll fall hopelessly in love with you."

He laughed again and kissed her cheek with a gentle peck. "Is that all? Well, that isn't much incentive for me to stop."

"Please, don't make me fall in love with you." She begged breathlessly. Try as she might to deny it, she knew that it was possible that she had already fallen in love with him a long time ago. This feeling was one she had always attributed to a deep admiration but now, with him gently kissing her and the way he gently held her close to himself to restrain her from trying to move away from him, she knew that these feelings she had were more than just friendship. Now she knew why the doctor had hesitated about letting Edmond stay over that night and why Ida had warned her not to let things continue as they were with Edmond. They were all worried that something like this might happen. Arabella tried to gently struggle to free herself from his embrace.

He pulled her deeply into his chest and wrapped his arms even tighter around her as Arabella closed her eyes to absorb this moment with him. "You said I could love you for this moment. Don't be in such a hurry to leave me behind just yet." His voice whispered, his lips were almost close enough to touch Arabella's. He could feel her warm quick breaths betraying the pleasure she found in his attention.

"This isn't like you..." She had never once heard him reveal to Aram any desire to be with a woman the way he was being with her at this moment. Like Aram, when women were present, he was very nonchalant and cool. He would join in with some mild teasing but he never had shown any real interest, even when he allowed a girl to pay attention to him.

"No, but how would you know?" He laughed softly and then kissed her lips tenderly.

"I must go." She whispered. "Mother will be looking for me."

"Not just yet, she can wait a little longer." He whispered and kissed her more passionately. "Stay with me just a little longer."

"Please Edmond... she'll be worried if I'm gone too long." Her soft feminine voice pleaded with him though she didn't hesitate to return the passion he was raining on her.

"Then let me come and see you again."

"No, you mustn't see me anymore." She tried to push herself away but he wouldn't let her.

"Please." He begged in his hushed voice.

"Our love is forbidden. We are promised to others." She reminded him.

"Not completely. Not yet." He reminded her. "No contracts have been made by our parents on our behalf yet. We are still free to pursue this as long as we are not promised to someone else."

"We just can't do this." She tried to protest but he silenced her with yet another kiss. Arabella's body nearly went limp in his snug embrace.

Beautiful Pretender

She simply couldn't fight off his affections for her any longer, especially when she craved each touch and sensation that his attentiveness brought upon her. "Alright," she sighed with the pleasure his lips brought to her as his lips worked their way down to her throat and then back up to her ear before searching for her lips again, "but it can only be during the night, under the cover of darkness, when no one will be able to see us." Her resolve was broken and she finally gave in to his pleading.

"Agreed. I will refrain from meeting with you during the day but at night, you belong to me and me alone." His kissing continued.

Finally she forced him to stop. "I must go now."

"It's still my time. You promised me the night, remember." He tried to go back to kissing her again but she wouldn't let him.

"Not right now, my mother is waiting for me. She will be worried if I don't come back soon." Arabella reminded him. "I really must go."

He sighed heavily. "I guess it can't be helped if you made a previous promise." He released her. "I will come to you tomorrow. Where shall I wait for you?"

"You are hopeless." She laughed softly.

"I don't mind." He reached up and touched her cheek gently with his fingertips.

Arabella brought her hand up and touched his hand with it, "You will find me near the tallest tree on my family's land after the night has fallen." She said quickly and then she turned to run back to the house. 'Oh you idiot!' She scolded herself in her thoughts. 'How could you let it go this far?' She felt like crying in frustration and dancing in joy at the same time. She had no intention on falling in love with him but what was done was done. 'How will I ever be able to face him as Aram again, knowing what I know and feeling what I feel?' She ran all the way to the house, only just stopping outside of it to adjust her clothing, mask and hair. 'How could he make me love him like this?' She looked back over at where she had come from but there was no sign of him.

Slowly she ascended the stairs that led back into the house. Once inside she was immediately greeted by her mother, "My dear, are you alright? You look positively out of breath and flushed."

"I was running?"

"Why?"

"The king kissed me mother, but only on the cheek." She added the last part quickly.

Jocelyn beamed as they continued to talk quietly to each other so as not to be over heard, "He did?" She hugged her daughter, "You returned the kiss, right?"

"I did." Arabella said with some embarrassment.

"You did beautifully. The king has definitely found favor in you." Her mother congratulated her.

"There you are." Baroness Wallace smiled at her guests. "I have been looking all over for you, your highness."

"How may I help you?" Arabella asked sweetly.

"Your mother had mentioned once that you have trained on the harp and I was hoping that perhaps you would honor us tonight with your talents."

"I couldn't possibly...." Arabella felt extremely nervous because she had never preformed in front of anyone outside of her parents, her tutor and a few servants who happened to be in the room while she practiced.

"Of course you can, dearest." Her mother encouraged. "You play so beautifully, you really must share your talents with our friends and family."

"I don't have my harp."

"Not to worry, your highness, we have one you can borrow." The Baroness smiled.

Arabella sighed but kept her 'noble' composure and smiled. "Then I will oblige our gracious hostess by honoring her request."

"Wonderful!" The Baroness smiled also. "Wait here for a moment and I'll make the arrangements." Immediately she left.

"Mother!" Arabella scolded. "You know how I feel about these things. I don't like performing in front of people. I'm really not that good."

"Nonsense, you play beautifully." Her mother encouraged. "Seeing as how this is your début into society, the other nobles are curious as to what kind of young woman you are. This includes displaying your many talents. In fact, I think that you should also sing as you play. You do have the most enchanting voice...."

"Please, don't make me do this..." Arabella begged.

"It's just too bad Kendrick isn't here to enjoy it as well. I was hoping you could perform before him." This was said more in thought then to her daughter.

It was only moments before Baroness Wallace returned. "Everything is set." She beamed to her two guests.

"My daughter will be performing with a song as well." Jocelyn said joyously. "You must hear the angelic voice she was blessed with."

"Then this will be an enchanting evening." The Baroness took Arabella's hand and led her to where the other musicians were playing. She waited for the music to stop and then made her announcement to all of the curious faces that looked their way. Arabella just happened to notice Edmond sneaking back in while everyone was distracted. He seemed curious as to what his mother had in mind with Arabella standing at her side. "My most esteemed and honored guests; we have been blessed with such a wonderful night of music, food and entertainment." She paused as her guests agreed with her with nods, smiles and mumbles. "Tonight, our guest of honor has graciously agreed to perform for us with voice and harp. Also, this will be her very first public performance." This announcement was met with great approval. She led Arabella to a stool that had been set up for her to use and then a servant brought the lap harp to her.

Arabella reached out and took it from him, almost as if it were a baby. She really did love the harp and she gently brought it down to her lap and wrapped her arms about it so that her fingers gently lay over the strings. Almost as if she were caressing a lover, her fingers began to pluck at the strings. Edmond noticed how her entire being transformed as her eyes closed and her face took on a sensual glow. He could tell that she liked playing her harp but he could also tell that she seemed to block out everything around her so that she could give her best performance.

Edmond was mesmerized as he listened to her angelic voice and the softness of the instrument she played. The song she did was a love song called 'The Prince of the Night' and he wondered if she picked out this song especially for him. This was because it was about a prince who had been under a curse where during the day he was a wolf but at night he was allowed to change back into a man. During this time he would come to visit his lover when he would confess his undying love for her. The song was beautiful but also sad because in the end the two chose death over separation. The music ended slowly and when she finished her head hung gracefully and she brought her hands up to the top of the harp's frame and she held it close to her. Her expression was unmistakably sad and he wondered if she was taking a moment to compose herself. Around him the audience applauded. Truly she was very gifted in both the harp and voice.

The Baroness came to Arabella. "That was truly lovely, milady." She praised. "Your mother understates just how talented you truly are."

Arabella waited until the instrument was taken from her, by a servant and then she stood up before replying. "Thank you." Her voice was soft as she spoke and her cheeks took on a gentle glow that betrayed how the situation was slightly uncomfortable for her.

"Edmond my love..." His mother smiled at him while reaching out her hand towards him, indicating that she wanted for him to join into their conversation as the musicians began the next song. "What did you think of our little song bird?"

"It makes me wish that I was a cat." He smiled mischievously.

"A cat?" His mother was surprised by his answer.

"Yes." He leaned over to whisper to Arabella. "It makes me want to devour you." Arabella gasped softly and it made him smile.

"Edmond?" His mother was still confused.

"It was truly the most beautiful thing I ever heard." He smiled.

"You should dance with her." His mother suggested.

"It would be an honor." He smiled handsomely and offered his hand to Arabella. "May I?"

Arabella blushed slightly, "Of course." Her soft voice replied and she took his hand. He led her out to the floor and they joined in with the others that were dancing. Finally Edmond had what he had been looking for. The dance didn't last long and when it had finished he took her off to one side so they could talk in private.

"Is your mother finished with you?"

Arabella laughed softly. "I can't leave again, if that's what you're asking."

"Would you like something to drink?"

"Yes, please."

"Then wait here and I will return shortly." He reached forward and touched her arm gently just above her elbow. "You really did play

Beautiful Pretender

wonderfully. Perhaps you could play for just me sometime."

"Perhaps." She smiled and then he left to find something for her to drink. Arabella looked around to see if she could locate her mother and found that she was talking privately with Edmond's mother. The two seemed to be pretty close friends, or at least that was the impression that Arabella was getting. Her attention was diverted with Edmond's return. She took the goblet of wine that he offered her and she drank from it. The beverage had a slightly sweet fermented taste and it gently burned down her throat as she drank from it.

Jocelyn and Edmond's mother watched as their children conversed with one another. They seemed to genuinely enjoy each other's company. "Edmond seems to have taken quite an interest in your daughter." The Baroness smiled at her friend.

"Indeed, it does appear that way." Jocelyn answered. "She seems rather comfortable around him as well."

"Perhaps if one of my brothers doesn't take an interest in pursuing marriage with her, maybe we should consider the two of them." She suggested.

"Yes, it would be something to consider." Jocelyn hoped that Kendrick would take interest, for she really wanted her daughter to be a queen. However, she did have to admit that Edmond was the next best choice. He came from an ideal family and his mother was the king's sister. Age wise he was much more suitable and Arabella did seem to like him. However, she hoped just the same that she wouldn't be forced to consider something less then what they had been preening their little girl for. Her husband had to do a lot to capture the late queen's favor and he would be terribly disappointed if Arabella was unable to be what the late queen had wished for her to be, they wife of one of her sons.

"I know I'm probably setting my hopes to high, for my brothers would be fools to not be interested in her. However, a mother can always hope for the best when it comes to her son."

"Just as a mother hopes for the best when it comes to her daughter." Jocelyn agreed. "However, should neither king decide to marry her, I do agree that this would be a suitable match." She watched as Edmond leaned in closer to Arabella to whisper something into her ear. Arabella laughed softly in response to his words and she could tell that her daughter did indeed seem to be found of the young man.

"Your highness," The older feminine voice of a woman disrupted Edmond and Arabella's private conversation.

Arabella looked towards the elaborate red and black feathered masked face of the middle aged woman who stood next to a young man with the half red and half gold mask who was a head taller then his graying mother. "Good evening." Arabella smiled.

"I don't know if you remember me from the other day at Baroness Wallace's…" she hesitated and looked at Edmond, "Good Evening, Lord Wallace."

"Good evening Lady Ellington." He bowed slightly.

She turned her attention back to Arabella, "I wanted to introduce you to my son, Rupert Ellington."

Rupert, a young man of twenty five bowed humbly. His black hair glistened in the glow of the lights around them. "It is an honor, princess." He stood back up. "Lord Wallace." He was sure to pay his respects where it was due. Edmond nodded in return.

"The honor is mine sir." She allowed him to take her right hand and kiss it.

"I was hoping that perhaps you would honor me with the next dance." He asked humbly.

"I'm afraid that dance is promised to me." Edmond spoke up.

"Then perhaps later…" Rupert wasn't allowed to finish.

"They all belong to me." Edmond challenged without threat.

Arabella, sensing the tension spoke up, "Please pardon us." She smiled, "I'm afraid I have been left in Lord Wallace's care by our king. Seeing as how Lord Wallace is his nephew, he was made responsible for my care in the king's stead. It was decided that it would be best if I respected my king during this time of indecision…"

"What she means to say is that only I'm allowed to be by her side in the king's absence." Edmond finished for her, Arabella just smiled apologetically.

"I see. Then I will take my leave." His voice remained formal. "Good evening."

"Good evening." Edmond and Arabella answered in unison.

Beautiful Pretender

"I'll be sure to let the other's know." Lady Ellington smiled. "We didn't realize how the king felt."

"Thank you." Arabella felt bad that they had lied but she truly didn't want to dance with anyone else.

Edmond waited until they were alone again before he spoke, "Come."

"What?" She asked in confusion. Edmond reached over and took her wine from her, placing it down on a nearby table. Then he took her by the elbow and led her out of the main area of the house where all of the guests were to a more private area. "Where are we going?"

"I want to show you something."

"Really? What?"

He looked down at her and winked, "You'll see."

Arabella made sure she took the time to look about his home as they traveled through it, soon they came to a stairway and they both went up. She felt his hand slide down her arm so he could take her hand. Finally they came to a doorway. "Where are we?"

Edmond reached down and took the handle of the door so he could open it. "My room."

"Your room?" She asked nervously.

"Come on." He grinned and led her inside. The room had a very masculine feel to it. The furniture was wood, leather and hide. The colors were dark but the number of windows and the current supply of light from the candles, made the darkness tolerable. "I thought you might like to see my room, since I saw yours."

"You're not going to do something weird are you?" She asked with suspicion.

Edmond laughed, "Not unless you want me to."

"Pervert."

"Who's the pervert? I wasn't thinking along those lines at all until you said something." He was still laughing.

"So what did you want to show me?" She asked.

He led her over to the wall to where the table he worked at sat. He picked up the broach she had given to him when he had first met her and he also picked up a simple gold ring. "Here" he told her and took her left hand. He slid the ring onto her pinky finger on her left hand.

"What's this for?" She asked as she brought her hand up to look at it.

"You left this broach in my care, so I leave this ring in yours." He took her hand and kissed it near the ring. "You mustn't let any man but me, kiss this hand. Promise me, that this hand will only belong to me."

"Alright." True, it was normal for a lady to offer her right hand, seldom was the left one offered for it was the marriage hand. Arabella didn't mind bending the rules for him and she was sure no one would really notice it. "Is that all?"

"No." He took her hand and led her towards his bed, "Now Edmond, you promised…"

"Just sit next to me." He sat down and tugged gently on her hand and she did as he wanted. "I just wanted some time alone with you before you had to leave. I know your mother will worry if I keep you too long."

"Thank you for the ring."

"It belonged to the late king's mother. She had given it to my mother when she was a child."

"That would explain why it's so small." She smiled as she admired the ring."

"I want you to keep it as a sign of our promise."

"Promise?"

"The promise we made tonight, that until we are promised to the person of our parents choosing, the nights belong to me. I want to see you whenever I can." He turned to face her and turned her to face him so he could look into her eyes.

"Alright, then I will accept this token and my broach will be my token in return. Keep it with you as a symbol of my affection and loyalty to you until my future husband has been decided." She leaned forward and gently kissed his lips to seal the promise.

"We should probably return to where the others are before we are missed."

"Not yet." She whispered and then wrapped her arms about his shoulders. "I want to stay here just a moment longer, before our night is over."

Edmond smiled, "Yes, I will obey." He took her into his embrace so he could hold her to him. How he longed to see the beautiful face

Beautiful Pretender

that hid so secretively behind the mask. He adored the fact that her dress was form fitting and revealed the natural curves of her body. He couldn't help but to let his hand take in the feel of her back, shoulders and sides as he held her. As a man he wanted to take in more of her, but he didn't want to risk losing her.

After some time had passed they finally went back down to the festivities. They had a chance to dance with each other a few more times and no more young men were either introduced to Arabella or asked to dance with her. It was apparent that word did get around about her not being available for such things. The celebration ended with a very large bonfire on the estate as people toasted one another and their kingdom, wishing it prosperity and wishing the king a long and prosperous life.

Chapter 6

When Arabella awoke the next morning it was as if the previous night had been just a sweet and distant dream. Every time she thought about Edmond's unbridled affection towards her from the night before, it made her smile and blush. In fact, she couldn't stop smiling no matter how hard she tried. He brought out feelings in her that she never knew existed, both emotionally and physically. She brought up her hand to feel the places where he had kissed her to see if she could still feel the warmth of his lips, but it had all cooled down during the night as she slept.

Edmond told her he was in love with her, the Arabella part of her. It made her want to give up being Aram forever. As much as she treasured the friendship, it was nothing compared to the feelings she was having at that moment. However, she also knew that if she gave up Aram, she'd lose something very precious that she and Edmond shared. A friendship like theirs wasn't something that came along everyday.

"Good morning, milady, did you sleep well?" Ida asked as she opened the curtains to the room.

"I had the most wonderful dream last night." She grinned. "I dreamed that a handsome prince came and declared his undying love for me. He held me in his arms and kissed me over and over again." She hugged her arms about her body.

"You seem a little too happy for it just to have been a dream." Ida smiled. "You're mother confided in me that the king kissed you last night."

"That was just the kiss of a child, Ida." Arabella laughed softly.

"Then there is more?" Ida pried.

"If you breathe a word of what I'm about to confide in you to either of my parents, I swear I will never forgive you nor will I take you with me when I leave." She told her seriously.

"I swear to never breathe a word. I haven't yet, have I?" She was referring to Aram befriending Edmond who was a noble man.

Arabella grinned, "Then come sit by me and I will tell you everything." Immediately Ida was sitting on the bed near her mistress. "I think I'm in love." She said excitedly.

"With whom?"

"Whom else, but the one man I can't reveal myself to." Her voice had a hint of sadness to it.

"Edmond!" Ida said knowing full well who it was.

"Isn't it terrible?" Arabella pouted. "I honestly tried not to let my feeling get the best of me but it was useless. I couldn't say no as he gently kissed me over and over again under the soft glow of the midnight stars." Her eyes closed and she smiled. "His familiar scent and the gentleness of his touch still remain with me even now."

"This can't be." Ida grabbed firmly onto Arabella's arm. "You can't let yourself get carried away like this. Any day now you will get a proposal from one of the monarchs and you will have to do as your parents say and marry him. Even Edmond isn't free to give away his love like this, you must know that."

"I do and so does he. Yet here we are breaking all the rules for our selfish desires." She smiled.

"You know you are the most important person in the world to me, don't you Arabella?"

"I know."

"I realize that I'm not much older then you but I do know for certain that you can't do this. Eventually he is going to discover who you are as well. You're only setting yourself up for a horrible heart break and him too. You must stop this now before it goes too far."

"I'm to meet him again tonight." Arabella changed the topic. "It will be under the canopy of the largest tree on our land."

"Then take my advice and end this. I will keep my vow to never breathe a word of it to either of your parents, no matter what you decide to do, but you should do right by you and Edmond and end this immediately. Not only should you end the relationship with Arabella, but also his friendship with Aram. Your bond with him as Aram was fine as long as love wasn't involved, but now that it is, you may be even more tempted to act on your feelings."

"Then what am I to say to him?" She asked with disappointment and even some resentment.

"As Arabella, tell him the truth. Tell him that you need to break this off in honor of your future husband. As Aram, if you can't tell him the honest truth about who you are, then tell him that your father is having you move out to live with your cousin's family and you will marry her and live there with her."

"I can't do that." She gasped as tears began to fill her eyes.

"You must. Arabella, if you want a future with no regrets then take this action now." She warned her.

Arabella looked at Ida with sadness, "A future with no regrets." She whispered. "I should have considered Edmond's future more then my own. I know he would be miserable if I allowed this to continue and then he'd be forced to marry someone he doesn't love while loving another." She sighed in misery. "Why do you always have to be right Ida, it just isn't fair?" Her hands came up to hide her face as she flopped back down in her bed. "I just can't face him."

"You must. You're just as guilty as he is that it was allowed to get this far." Ida warned her.

"I suppose you're right." She had to admit that if she really had wanted things to end the other night, she could have easily made it stop. Her protests to his attention were a poor half hearted attempt at trying to do what was right. In reality she earnestly wanted him to do it and to love her.

"First things first then." Ida stood up and straightened out her dress and apron. "He'll most likely be looking for Aram today, so Aram will be the first one to end things."

"No…not Aram…not yet." She begged. "This is going to be hard on Edmond. He's never been in love before. He'll need Aram more then ever, at least for a while. I promise I will behave myself. You know how scared I am of him discovering that I am Aram."

"I suppose you have a point there. Very well, Aram can wait for the time being." Ida agreed, "I guess we should be a little considerate of his feelings after all and it would be suspicious if both Arabella and Aram cut their ties with him on the same day."

Beautiful Pretender

"That was my thought too." Arabella was happy that she could at least continue this connection with him, even if just for a short while.

"Just the same, he will want to see Aram, of that much I'm sure. Therefore, I will not urge you to discontinue that relationship yet. However in the near future you must do it."

"Hurry then and help me get ready Ida, so I can go to him straight away." She got out of bed but her mood was no longer cheerful. She knew Ida was right but she dreaded having to hurt Edmond in this way. However the sooner she did this, the easier it would be for him… the easier it will be for them both. Arabella's heart ached knowing that no matter how little or how long they waited, it would still hurt to say goodbye. Even their friendship was going to have to come to an end and it grieved her.

"I beat you here today." Edmond looked up at Aram from the lounging position that Aram was famous for.

Aram laughed softly, "So you did." He sat down next to Edmond. "It's looking rather nice out today." He laid down and then he picked up a twig nearby to play with. "The others should be along soon."

"Aram?"

"What?"

"Have you noticed anything different about me?" He looked over at Aram who looked back at him in return.

"You're getting facial hair."

"Stupid, I've been getting that for some time now." They both laughed. "No really, do I look any different today?"

"Hmm?" Aram seemed to be studying him intensely. "I'd say you have more nasal hair and some growing from your ears now too." Aram couldn't stop laughing. Edmond rolled over on his side and then delivered a hard blow to Aram's shoulder. "Ouch!" Aram grabbed his shoulder which stung from the blow. It had to be the hardest one Edmond ever gave him.

"Stop teasing me, I'm being serious." Edmond warned him. He could tell his punch may have been a bit too hard the way Aram was holding his arm.

"Alright." Aram sighed. "I'd say you look like a man in love, happy?"

Edmond grinned, "You're right." He rolled over onto his stomach and propped himself up on his elbows, his gaze remained on Aram. "She's the most enchanting creature I've ever met." He sighed.

"More enchanting then me?" Aram pouted teasingly.

"I'm afraid so." Edmond laughed softly. "It was beautiful. We kissed under the starlit night and confessed our love for one another. The whole night was magical in its own right." He smiled as he closed his eyes.

"Magical, huh?" Aram sounded doubtful.

"I never knew what it meant to be in love before now."

"I'm going to go home if you can't find anything better to talk about." Aram warned him. "You've never talked about girls like this before."

"I never knew a girl like this before."

"So who's the lucky girl that won your heart?" As if he didn't know. Even if Aram wasn't really Arabella, the way Edmond carried on about her made it obvious who it was.

"Princess Arabella Mina Cordell." He nearly sighed her name as he spoke it. The fact that Aram should have easily known who it was didn't seem to register with him.

"You're hopeless. You know she can't have a relationship with you. She's promised to marry one of the two kings. It will only break your heart if you keep this relationship going and you'll break hers too. Can you live with that hanging over your head for the rest of your life?"

"You sure know how to spoil the mood." Edmond returned to lying on his back and put his arms under his head. "I suppose you have a point though. She did try to tell me that it would be a mistake for us to fall in love but I wouldn't listen to her." He looked over at Aram. "Perhaps she was only humoring me last night."

"No, I'm sure she probably does feel something for you. Arabella isn't one to give her heart or her affections away that easily. I'm sure this isn't going to be easy for either one of you but you should stop this before it goes too far. Just my advice as your friend."

"You have the same hair color that she has." Edmond reflected.

Aram sighed and sat up. "That's it, I'm out of here."

"Why?"

"When you're thinking about a girl to the point that you see her

Beautiful Pretender

in your best friend, then it isn't safe to be around you anymore. Next thing I know you'll be trying to kiss me thinking that I'm her." He stood up.

"Do you think it's that bad?" Edmond asked as he stood up.

"Worse. It might do you good to go and swim for awhile. Just try not to see her in the fish. That would be disappointing." He laughed.

"Maybe you're right." He began to remove his shirt since the lake was only a few feet away. "Why don't you join me before the others come? You don't have to worry what I'll think of your swimming skills or whatever it is that keeps you from swimming with us." He threw his shirt on the ground.

The girl in Aram suddenly found herself blushing and she turned away from the sight of his bared chest. It hadn't bothered her before if she saw him without a shirt but this time it did for some reason. "Not today, I have some things to attend to on my father's behalf so I had better get going."

"You only just got here, Aram. What's bothering you? I can tell something is wrong." He walked up and placed his hand on Aram's shoulder.

"My parents are talking about the possibility of sending me to live at my cousin's house for a while." He said softly. It was the only thing he could think of saying. Silently Arabella thanked Ida for this idea. It couldn't have been better timing.

"Why?"

"So that I might learn to love her I guess." He hated telling blatant lies to Edmond. Skirting around the truth was one thing but telling an all out lie was another.

"Oh. No wonder you're being unusually agitated today." He put his arm about Aram's shoulders as he stood behind him. "Would you like to come over tonight and stay at my place? I know it won't change anything but maybe it would help to take your mind off of it for a while."

"What about Arabella? Didn't you say you were meeting her again tonight?"

"Did I say that?" He tried to remember. "I guess I must have or you wouldn't know about it, huh?" He sighed, "I could send word that I can't make it tonight."

"It's better if you don't. You should take this time to break the bond that is developing with her. I'm sure she'll understand."

"Maybe." He let his arm drop. "So, do you really need to go home or do you think you could convince your father to let you spend the day with me?"

"I'm afraid he really needs me to come home today. Perhaps we can get together again in a couple of days. Father has asked for me to stick around for a while to help him out with things."

"I see. Well, then I'll let you know how it goes with Arabella when we meet next."

Aram began walking away and waved his hand, "I know you can do it. Just remember you're doing it for not just you but for her as well."

"I know." Edmond called back as he finished removing his clothing. Soon the sound of him going into the water could be heard but Aram didn't dare turn around to look.

Arabella looked at her image in the mirror. Tonight she would leave her hair down for extra shielding should she need it. She wondered how Edmond would like seeing all of her hair down during the day, for it was uncommon for a young woman of her age and station to not tie it back in one fashion or another. "You're going to do it tonight, right?" Ida asked her. "You will stop this from going any further."

"Yes, tonight it will end." Arabella reluctantly told her, even though she wasn't convinced that she could do it. That was why she had tried to talk Edmond into doing it earlier in the day when she presented herself to him as Aram. 'I'm depending on your strength, Edmond. Don't let me down.' She said silently in her thoughts. "Make my excuses to mother." She asked Ida.

"I will." Ida promised. She looked out the window. "Are you sure you can get around out there alright. The moon is only in the first quarter and it isn't providing much light."

"It's better if it doesn't."

"I suppose you're right. He's less likely to recognize you if it is like that. Just promise to be careful."

"I will. Watch for my return."

"Yes milady."

Arabella went to the door and opened it slowly. She held the cape she wore together at the neck, though she really didn't need to since it was held by a clasp. The hallway was clear so she began her journey to the servants' side of the house so she could escape out the backdoor. Most of the servants had retired for the night so she was less likely to be discovered. Quietly she walked through the corridors until she came to the kitchen. She would use that door to come back in the house when she returned.

Carefully she walked through the gardens that led to the forest on her father's land and made her way towards the tallest tree. "It is already so late... I wonder if he is waiting for me or he gave up and went home." She whispered to herself. The air was filled with the sounds of the night. Owls, bugs and frogs talked to each other in a sort of rhythmic melody. The forest was dark to the point that she had troubles navigating the debris on the ground and her dress snagged on fallen branches and bushes.

When she finally reached the predetermined tree, she placed her had on the trunk and took a moment to catch her breath as she looked around. There was no sign of Edmond anywhere to be seen. "Edmond!" She whispered loudly and then fell silent in order to hear his reply as she continued to try to find his silhouette in the darkness. "Edmond, are you here?" Still there was no answer. "Ed..." She was cut off by a hand touching her shoulder and she gasped in fright. Her hand fled to her heart as she struggled for air.

"I was beginning to wonder if you were going to come." He whispered to her.

"Don't scare me like that." She was barely able to whisper to him. "I nearly died of fright."

He laughed softly. "I truly am sorry for frightening you."

"I didn't mean to take so long to come but I was detained. I had to wait until mother went to bed before I could leave." He came around to face her. "Have you waited long?"

"Time is of no importance. I would have sat here by this tree all night if I needed to." He reached forward and took a handful of her hair and worked it between his fingers. "You wore your hair down."

"I usually do at night. I suppose I should have left it up until after our meeting..."

"No, I think it is lovely this way." He brought her hair to his lips and kissed it. "I met with Aram today."

"Really? How is he doing?"

"He's struggling with a dilemma much like our own. He too is suffering from an arranged marriage and will probably have to leave to live with his cousin soon."

"How awful, the poor fellow." She said sympathetically.

"He suggested that we stop meeting each other."

"Oh." Her soft voice replied. "Perhaps we should take his advice then."

"What do you mean?"

"My handmaiden also suggested that we should not meet anymore. She said it would only lead to our suffering and heartache."

"Are you sure it is safe to confide in her about us?" He asked concerned.

"I trust her."

"As I trust Aram." He released the hair he had been holding and then leaned against the tree. "What are we to do?"

"I don't know. I know that this is foolish but part of me is curious too."

"Hmm." He laughed softly. "Perhaps it is foolish but I also would like to see how it feels to love and be loved by someone. Arabella?"

"Yes."

"Do you want me to end this?"

Without thinking she answered, "No…" then she remembered why she was here, "but perhaps we should to stay faithful to those whom our parents have chosen for us to spend the rest of our lives with."

"If you had to choose this moment between Eric and Kendrick, who would you choose?" He asked her with curiosity and to change the subject. "My mother said that Kendrick plans to ask for your hand as soon as your father returns from Eldardesh but she also said that Eric is planning for you to marry him as well. So, if you were given the choice, which one of them would you choose?"

"Is neither an option?" She teased.

"No, its not." He laughed softly.

"Then most probably it would be Kendrick. Eric is much too frightening of a person. I know he's young and was fairly well behaved when I was with him, but I can't seem to erase the memory of the malice

I saw in his eyes. He hates his brother with an unbelievable passion. To be honest I would rather die then to be forced into marrying him."

"I've heard many things about him as well." He reflected.

"What about you?"

"I believe my parents have settled on Countess Alicia D'Winter. Her family has a great deal of influence and power."

"Do you like her?"

"I've never met her, only her father."

"I see." She sat down on the ground and leaned against the tree. He sat down beside her. "So then it won't be long before we will have to part ways."

"Most likely."

"Father should be home soon. I was looking forward to it but now I am beginning to dread it, especially if what you say is true."

"As am I." He reached over and took her small hand into his. "I had fully intended on following Aram's advice about ending this but I honestly don't want this to end, not yet."

"Perhaps it wouldn't hurt to let it go on a little longer." She agreed and then yawned. "Oh, I am terribly sorry."

"No, don't be." He also yawned. "Why don't you lay your head down on my shoulder and rest for awhile?"

"What if I fall asleep?" She asked as she nuzzled her head on his shoulder.

"Then I will make sure that I don't." He promised. "I'll make sure that you make it home long before the sun rises." He placed his arm behind her and held her closely to him. Her hand gently went onto his chest and she could feel his heart beating, even though he wore more then one layer of clothing. "I love you, Arabella." He whispered.

"I love you too, Edmond." Her voice was barely audible. It wasn't long before they both had fallen asleep.

The morning lark sung his sweet song and the sound aroused Arabella from her sweet slumber. A gentle breeze caressed her face and a strong arm tightened about her as she snuggled in closer to the warm body next to her. Suddenly her eyes snapped opened as she realized that the morning had come and she hadn't gone home. "Oh no." She breathed in fright and then she quickly leapt to her feet. She hadn't brought her mask with her because she hadn't planned on being out for so long.

She started running away when she heard Edmond call out to her. "Wait! Arabella!" He began to run after her. "Please!"

"I can't. I have to get home before my mother notices I'm gone. If I don't there will be hell to pay." Her frantic voice called back.

He continued to run after her. 'Why?' He thought to himself, 'Why won't she let me look upon her?' His heart ached with the desire to see the face of the woman he loved.

"I'm sorry." She yelled back at him.

"When can I see you again?"

"I don't know. Goodbye!" She waved her hand in the air, which pushed her cape off of her arm and onto her back. He was surprised to see a large bruise on her shoulder.

'Did someone hurt her?' He wondered silently. He had no idea it was from when he punched Aram in the shoulder the day before. Finally he stopped pursuing her as her parents' home came into view. "Arabella, what are you hiding from me?" He asked quietly in defeat. "What can be troubling you so much that you can't face me?" His breathes revealed that his body hadn't been ready to exert itself so soon after waking from a deep sleep. Each breath was more labored then it should have been. He turned around and walked back to where he and Arabella had spent the night so he could gather his belongings and go home.

Arabella ran through her house and to her room without a second of hesitation. When she was safe in her room she threw herself down on her bed. "That was too close." She panted. "He promised he would wake me before sunup." She placed her hand on her stomach as waves of nausea came upon her. She was use to this side affect coming upon her when her fear of being discovered reignited.

"You're finally home." Ida said from a chair in the far corner of Arabella's room. "I waited here all night for you to return."

Arabella propped herself up on her elbows, "I'm terribly sorry, Ida. I didn't mean to fall asleep out there."

"Well I hope you at least ended this relationship with him." She stood up from her chair and began rummaging through her mistress's clothing to find something clean for her to wear, since the clothes she

Beautiful Pretender

wore now were soiled from sleeping on the ground.

"I had every intention…" Arabella began to answer.

Ida stopped what she was doing and looked Arabella in the eye, "You mean to tell me you didn't end it?"

"What's the point?" She flopped back down onto the bed and sighed. "Edmond told me that Kendrick intends to propose to me when father returns."

"Seriously?" Ida came over and sat down next to her.

"He also heard that King Eric is planning on proposing as well."

"So it's a matter of who asks first then." She pondered. "Your father should be returning within a few more days."

"This is why we saw no point in rushing to end this relationship. For it will end itself within the week." Arabella wiped at the few tears that managed to escape.

"When will you be meeting him again?"

"I don't know." She sighed. "I think I might have hurt his feelings when I ran away from him this morning."

"Oh."

A notion then came to Arabella, "Ida, maybe you could go and talk with him on my behalf."

"Milady, I really don't want to get involved in this."

"No, please Ida. Please talk to him for me and send my apologies. You know I can't face him right now."

"Why don't you have Aram do it?" Ida suggested.

"I can't face him as Aram right now either, Ida. I'm afraid I won't be able to keep my composure. Please, you have to do this for me."

"Alright, but only just this once." Ida sighed. "Really Arabella, you must stop this. I won't be your face during the day."

"I know." She sat up and embraced Ida, "Thank you."

"Alright, that's enough already. There's a basin of water for you to wash up with and I'll finish getting your clothing ready for the day. You're mother will be expecting you to come down for the morning meal soon, of this much I'm sure." Outwardly Ida was frustrated but secretly she found this adventure of forbidden love between her mistress and Edmond to be thrilling and almost addictive as she waited silently to discover what would happen next. It was the kind of romance that young women like her could only dream of and hope for. The suspense of wondering what would happen next was nearly killing her with anticipation. Secretly she was glad it hadn't ended just yet, but she'd die before she ever let Arabella know how she truly felt about the situation.

Ida had only seen Edmond once (this didn't include the night in the forest because it was rather dark and it didn't allow her the ability to see him all that well.) She wasn't sure if she could really remember exactly what he looked like because of this. She had already tried to find him at the location that Arabella had mentioned, where they usually met near the lake and where Aram would lay under the tree, but no one was there. Arabella had said that Aram had told Edmond he wouldn't be able to see him for a few days, so Edmond may not be at any of their usual places.

Finally she saw her first glimmer of possibility as she came upon a group of boys walking in her direction on the road. "Gentlemen?" She called out to them as they approached her.

One boy about her age with blond hair and blue eyes answered, "Young maiden, is it wise to walk these roads alone that lie hidden in the forest?" He and the others laughed.

"Perhaps not but I am looking for someone and I had hoped you might help me." She smiled graciously.

"Maybe." He walked up to her, while the others hung back a few paces. "You are a very lovely maiden." A wink finalized the statement. "Don't you think so *gentlemen?*" He emphasized the last word.

"Don't you have any manners boy?" She scolded.

"Oh I do, fair maiden." He grinned. "But we are bored and we need to amuse ourselves." It wasn't uncommon for them to gently harass the young woman they came across and Ida was no exception to this rule.

"Amuse yourself with someone else, sir. I've been sent by my mistress to find the man that has captured her heart so that I may speak to him in her stead."

"That someone wouldn't happen to go by the name of Lord Edmond Wallace, would it?" Another boy who had been behind the others asked as he came closer to her.

"It is that very name sir. Do you know him?" Ida was hopeful that her search was nearing its end.

Beautiful Pretender

The blond boy put his hand in front of the other to stop his approach. "You're mistress, is she the Princess Arabella Cordell by any chance?"

"Yes, 'tis the same." This sent the boys in an uproar of laughter and teasing, for it was Aram's group of friends and Edmond was indeed among them.

Edmond approached Ida and then glared at his friends. "Quiet down and let me speak with her." He scolded them because they were having a little too much fun teasing her. "Come." He told her and they walked away from the noise so they could talk in private. "You are her handmaiden, are you not?"

"Aye, that I am, milord."

"Tell me what message she sends to me."

"First of all she apologizes for running off on you the way she did."

"Did her mother find out that she was with me?"

"No, but if she had waited any longer to return, she surely would have been noticed coming back home."

"I'm glad. We hadn't meant to stay out all night like that."

"I am disappointed that she didn't break off this foolish relationship of yours but she explained to me what you had told her about the kings and so I will hold my peace for now. I also have to admit that I can't scold her too soundly about this relationship because it is making her very happy right now and I believe it will make the times ahead a little more bearable for her. But you had better not hurt her in anyway or I will personally come after you to avenge her honor."

"I know that I am forbidden to touch her, milady." He saw the others were listening in so he led her further away. "Is she alright?"

"What do you mean?"

"Her arm bears a rather large bruise. Is someone hurting her?"

"Oh? I hadn't noticed it. However as far as I know, there is no one."

"What else does she want said to me?" He asked.

"She doesn't know when to meet you again. There wasn't time for her to arrange it so she sent me to do it in her stead."

"Could I come to her room? I could sneak in and…"

"You aren't being serious are you?" She was shocked that he would even suggest such an outlandish idea to her.

"Well, yes, I am. I thought perhaps it would be easier on her if she could stay in her room and I could come to her. This way I could hide if someone comes to check on her and it would make her parents less suspicious of her activities."

"My master would have my head if I were to allow such a thing to take place." She scolded him.

"I swear that I won't touch her. I just need to be with her while I can, since the time we will have to share this love is coming to an end."

Ida sighed and stopped walking. "Arabella was right, you are hopeless." This made him laugh softly. "Alright, I will agree to let you come see her but you may only meet with her on her balcony. It's right off of her room and on the eastern end of the manor. No one should be around there to see you during the night. I'll stay in her room to keep watch should someone approach but also to make sure her innocence stays intact. I know she trusts you but I'm not as trusting as she is, for love isn't blinding me."

Edmond grinned. "Thank you." He leaned over and kissed her cheek. "Thank you with all of my heart."

"Go on now, they're waiting for you." She indicated the other boys. "Don't breathe a word of this conversation to any of them, is that clear?"

"Yes milady." He turned and went back to the others. Immediately they began to badger him for information.

'Thank goodness the house will be able to shadow the moon's light enough to conceal her face.' She thought to herself with some relief. Arabella's balcony, at least at this time of the year, sat on the side of the house that wouldn't see the moonlight for some time. Not only that but there was a huge walnut tree that practically towered over it, so even if the moon could shine her light down on the two lovers, it would be muted.

However, unknown to Ida and Edmond both was that fate had planned to play yet another trick on the two secret lovers, for Edmond's mother, the Baroness Wallace had planned to make a social call on Baroness Cordell, Arabella's mother, that afternoon.

She had two reasons for this social call, one was because she knew that Baron Cordell had gone to Eldardesh and had been gone for over two weeks now. The second reason was that she was determined to formally introduce her son to Arabella. Arabella's family was a very

Beautiful Pretender

prestigious one and she wanted to make a close relationship with them. Not only that but Arabella was most likely going to be the next queen in Arminia and currently held the title of Princess. She also kept it in mind that if for some unheard of reason neither king should choose her, then she could quite possibly be her son's future wife. (This was why they had yet to announce their choice for his future bride. Baroness Wallace was waiting to see whether or not one of the kings did indeed decide on marrying Arabella. She was sure one would most likely do so but part of her had hoped that they might decline, so she could negotiate with Arabella's parents.) In any case, she felt it necessary to bring the two kids together, for no matter how she looked at it, it would be very beneficial to her family's position in society.

The Baroness had planned on detaining her son from leaving the house that morning but by the time she had gotten out of bed, he had already left. So instead she sent a few of her servants to go out and look for him. The only draw back was that no one had a clue what he did and where he went on these little outdoor excursions of his. He would simply disappear for a day or two and then return home. Never did he disclose any information concerning his activities and she had no idea who his friends were. She knew it could take awhile before one of the servants found him and brought him home.

Arabella sat quietly as she did her daily studies. It was something she did *almost* daily. She had a tendency to sneak off before the tutor arrived sometimes. It infuriated her parents to no end but they did little to reprimand her for her actions. Arabella listened to the male tutor of about thirty as he carefully went over the daily duties that would be expected of a queen. She had to practice sitting tall with a straight back, keeping her hands in her lap and her legs and feet in an appropriate position. Even when she ate her mid-day meals he reprimanded her if she did something incorrectly. He controlled the way she walked, talked, sat and even thought when he was able to. He forced her to learn the harp and how to sing, as a way for her to entertain which ever king she ended up marrying, should she indeed marry one. On and on the list of expectations and lessons grew.

A light knock sounded on her door and Ida, who had returned several hours ago from her meeting with Edmond, went to answer it.

125

When she came back, she informed Arabella of the news but first she dismissed the tutor so she could talk to her friend in private. Once they were alone Ida sat down in the chair the tutor vacated and spoke softly with her. "You have a visitor, well actually two to be exact."

"Who?" She asked curiously.

"That's the problem. You're mother has asked for you to join her downstairs."

"Yes, I figured that much, but who is it?"

"Baroness Wallace and Lord Wallace, your forbidden love."

"Oh." She said softly. "That is a problem."

"I'd say it is. So what are you going to do now? You can't very well go down there in your mask, for it would raise too many questions." Ida warned her.

"No, that won't due at all, will it?" She sighed and then stood up and began pacing back and forth as she pondered this unexpected situation she was now facing. "What should I do?" She thought out loud.

"You probably shouldn't play sick again, you've done that too many times already."

"But what other excuse could I possibly use?" She looked at Ida with pleading eyes that begged for her help.

"Give me a moment to think about this."

With an urgent tone to her voice, Arabella said, "Well make it quick before she comes up here like she did last time."

"Be patient with me and let me have time to think about it, child." She scolded. The room was quiet until she finally answered with, "Perhaps I can say that you twisted your ankle and you must lie down because it is too painful for you to walk on it."

Arabella look down at her feet as she pulled her skirts up. "Which ankle?" She asked and then looked up at her hand maiden.

"Does it matter which one?" Ida had a bit of an annoyed voice.

"Of course it does. If some asks which one, I don't want to hesitate in telling them."

Ida sighed in frustration, "Then have it be that one." She pointed to Arabella's left ankle. "I'll go and let them know about it and you had better go to bed incase your mother comes up to check on you."

"Alright." Arabella answered in her 'fine whatever' like attitude. She dropped her skirts and then she went to sit down on the side edge

Beautiful Pretender

of her bed. Suddenly a thought popped into her head, "Where's my mask?"

"Your mask?"

"Yes, incase Edmond wishes to come up to check on me. If he does, I should have it nearby."

"Very well." Ida walked over to the box that she kept it in on some shelves that lined a portion of one wall in Arabella's room. She opened the box and carefully took out a red and gold mask. It was a simple design with a red silk background that was adorned with gold trim around the edges and eyes. "Will this do, milady?"

Arabella grinned, "It will do just fine." She reached out her hand towards Ida and took the mask from her, once Ida walked to where Arabella had been waiting for her. "Now hurry and go before they get suspicious."

"Yes princess." Ida's voice gave away the fact that she wasn't too happy about having to cover for Arabella like this but she knew this problem wasn't entirely Arabella's fault. It was also her parents' faults for allowing their daughter to go out disguised as a young man. Therefore she felt like she had no choice but do this for her mistress.

A few moments after Ida had left Arabella got up off her bed and quietly snuck out of her room. She was much too curious to stay put. Carefully she snaked her way down the hallway to the top of the staircase. She positioned herself just right, so she could see into the 'visitor's room' downstairs without anyone seeing her, or at least they wouldn't if they were not looking for her. She brought her mask with her, just incase she accidentally bumped into Edmond during this little adventure.

Once she came to where the wall ended at the top of the stairwell, she carefully peeked around it, only exposing the minimal of one side of her face. Her hair hung down over her shoulders and nearly to her waist in soft brown waves. She could just see Edmond's face as he talked with her mother, his own mother and Ida. So far he didn't seem to notice her but she could unmistakably see the look of concern on his face. Then he suddenly looked up and saw her. The look of concern melted away and he smiled at her. "Excuse me ladies, it seems you have a little mouse in your midst." After the terrified gasps were heard from the women below, he assured them that he could take care of it before he left the room to pursue his 'prey'.

He casually left the guest room, but his eyes never left her. He made his way to the bottom of the stairwell and began his accent. Immediately Arabella turned so her back was towards him. It wasn't long before she felt his hand gently touch her waist. "Hello, my beautiful little mousy." He whispered into her ear.

Arabella laughed softly. "You are the devil to come here without me knowing."

"Ah, but every devil needs his angel." He wrapped his arms around her and pulled her close as he kissed the back of her head. "Do you have your mask or should I wait here until you retrieve it?" He kept his voice quiet so the women below wouldn't hear him. Arabella lifted up her mask and he took it from her. Then he helped her put it on. "Is there somewhere we can go?"

"I have a sitting room off of my bedchamber, we can go there." She answered. "Are you still coming tonight?"

"I was planning on it." He turned her around to face him once he finished putting on her mask. "Did you really injure your ankle?"

"Maybe." She grinned and received his smile in return.

"I thought not, but let's pretend you did."

"Why is that?" She laughed softly.

"So I can do this…" He scooped her up into his arms, "I now have a good excuse to carry you." He brought his head down so he could kiss her. "Show me where to go." He had no clue where her sitting room was, only her bedchamber, since he had been there once before. Once they were in the room, he carefully laid her out on the chaise lounge. Then he went down to where her feet lay exposed and asked, "Which ankle?" His grin gave away the fact that he saw this as some sort of love game and knew she wasn't actually injured.

Her soft laughter only made the game more interesting, "The left one."

"I see." He lifted her skirt up just enough to expose her ankle and then he tenderly took it into his hand. "This one?"

"Uh huh." She watched as he brought it to his lips and kissed her ankle and the top of her foot tenderly several times. His hand took the liberty of gently cradling the calf of her lower leg, under her skirt while the other one tenderly held her foot. She giggled nervously, "That tickles."

"Does it feel better now?" He grinned.

"Yes, but the other is feeling rather poorly." She watched him as he gently put her leg down and then he moved her skirt up slightly to pick up the other one in the same style before repeating the 'healing technique' to it.

"Is there anything else that is not feeling well?" He laid her foot down gently and brought her skirt back down.

"Um..." She couldn't stop smiling and she showed him her wrist and he walked over on his knees to where he could reach it. Then he gently brought it to his lips. His kisses tenderly worked their way up her arm and to her shoulder. His lips gently and hesitantly came to her collar bone and he lingered there as he caressed that part of her before moving up to her neck. "Edmond." Arabella whispered in delight. Her breaths were betraying her as he awoke her senses with each tender kiss. "My lips." She whispered. He didn't hesitate to work his way up her throat and bring the healing there as well. He brought her tightly into his embrace as he continued to 'play doctor' with his lips. His hand gently caressed her back, arms and neck. His fingers found her hair and he gently ran them through their soft wavy folds.

The door to her sitting room opened and immediately Edmond stopped kissing her and they both looked to see who had caught them. "You two just don't know when to stop, do you?" Ida sighed in frustration. "You should feel lucky that it was only me coming in here and not the others." She closed the door behind her before coming further into the room. "The servants will be up shortly with refreshments for both of you. I came up to see how you two were doing. Obviously you are not having a difficult time finding your way around, Lord Wallace." Her voice was sarcastic.

Edmond gently eased Arabella back down onto the chaise lounge before standing up and then he approached the handmaiden, "Saint Ida, our beloved angel who watches over us and keeps our deepest secrets." He grinned and then kissed her cheek. "You are my savior."

"Oh hush up." She laughed softly in embarrassment before scolding him. "How dare you take liberties with milady and in her own home too?"

"She needed my healing touch." He teased and then looked over to

129

Arabella who was slightly flushed from the excitement. "You feel better now, don't you?" She smiled and shook her head to affirm that she was indeed feeling pretty good at the moment.

"I can't believe I have to endure all this nonsense." Ida huffed in frustration.

"Name one thing you want, anything, and I'll do all I can to get it for you to thank you for keeping our secret." Edmond promised Ida.

"Anything?" She asked.

"Anything."

Ida thought for a moment, "How about if you two don't see each other anymore."

"Anything but that." He laughed.

"I thought you would say that. I suppose this won't be lasting much longer, so I'll get my wish eventually." She thought for a moment. "Well, there are some blue roses in the king's garden... If you get me a bouquet of them, I promise I will not say another word about my reservations to you."

"Seriously?" Edmond asked surprised. "I'll just ask Kendrick...."

"No, you have to take them without him knowing." She smiled wickedly.

"Ah, now that might be hard." He thought for a moment. "I guess that means I will have to sneak onto the palace grounds without being caught."

"I guess you will, but I'm not finished yet." She grinned. "That is what I want you to get, but I also want each of your friends to take something as well."

"Ida!" Arabella gasped in disbelief.

Ida laughed, "If you can do this then I will allow you to meet with milady without complaint."

"But why?" Arabella asked.

"Well, if he really loves you, then he should be willing to do the impossible for you. The palace is heavily guarded, so accomplishing this task won't be easy."

"What will you do with the things they take?"

"They'll just be practical things that the king won't miss. I don't even really need them or want them, but that's not the point."

"What is the point?" Edmond asked her.

Beautiful Pretender

"I want to see to what extent you are willing to go to for her sake." She said in a matter of fact tone. "I want to see for myself how much you are willing to risk on her behalf or if you are just taking advantage of her."

"Ah, now it all makes sense. Alright, I have eight other guys I hang out with on a regular basis. So, what are the items you want us to gather?"

"I'll give you a list before you leave." She smiled and then a knock sounded on the door. "I believe your refreshments have arrived. Please take a seat over there, Lord Wallace." She pointed to a seat that was across the way from the chaise lounge that Arabella was still lying on.

Chapter 7

Arabella had the foresight the day before to assume that Edmond would want to try and fetch Aram from the physician's home to accompany him on his 'quest'. Technically she had planned on not being Aram for another day or two but this suggested adventure of Ida's was much too exciting for her to not join in on. As expected, Edmond did indeed show up and only moments after Arabella herself arrived, as Aram of course.

"So will he let you out of working today?" Edmond asked excitedly.

"I'm sure he will, why, what's up?"

"We're going to raid and plunder the Celendra Desh palace." He grinned.

"Are you trying to get me killed?" Aram acted offended.

"Hurry up and get his permission so we can leave. It won't be easy to get past the palace guards and we still need time to go and round up the others."

"You're serious aren't you?" He had to play up the part in order for his role as Aram to be believable.

"Dead serious. I'll explain everything to you on the way. Hurry up we have no time to waste."

"Alright, alright." Aram sighed, "I'll run and ask. I'm sure it will be fine since we got everything done quicker then expected."

"Great. I'll wait here for you."

Aram took almost no time at all before returning, "Alright, let's go." He smiled. "Father said he wouldn't need me today." Naturally Arabella ditched her tutor again without notice. She knew he would be arriving at her house any moment to instruct her. It tended to give

Beautiful Pretender

her great pleasure knowing that he'd come to her room and not find her there again. 'Serves him right.' She laughed silently, 'He should be made to suffer too from time to time. It's only fair after all he puts me through.' She wasn't the only one guilty of this, for unknown to her Edmond was doing the exact same thing to his tutor as well.

Once all their friends had been gathered, they went to their usual place under the oak tree near the lake. Edmond addressed them, "Alright, you all have a pretty good idea what we are doing today."

"Yeah, but why are we doing it?" Silas asked. "I'd at least like to know what I'm putting my neck on the line for." The others agreed with him.

"It's a game and if we win, then Arabella's handmaiden has agreed to let me see Arabella in secret with no objections." He smiled proudly. "She gave me a list with eight items, one for each of you."

"What about you?" Aram asked. "Obviously the eight items are for the rest of us."

"Right, they are. I have a special item to collect, exactly sixteen blue roses from the king's prized rose garden."

Silas gasped, "You have to be joking."

"Nope, I'm dead serious. So are you in or not?"

"I'm in." Aram stated without hesitation. "It sounds like fun."

"It sounds dangerous." Silas countered and the others agreed.

"Well Edmond, I guess we can't count on them after all." Aram sighed dramatically. "So much for friendship."

"Hey!" Silas complained. "Just because it sounds dangerous doesn't mean we aren't going."

"So you are going then?" Edmond grinned.

"Of course, we can't let you two have all the fun." He laughed. "So what are the eight items and does it matter who gets what."

"No it doesn't matter that much who gets what, we just have to get everything on the list." He pulled the parchment from his pocket and unfolded it and then he read off the items. "We are to get one of each of the following items, size, color and other details are not important unless otherwise noted, all that matters is that you get what is listed. Alright, here we go… a candle, a shoe, a pillow, a mug, a loaf of bread, a wine skin with wine in it, a sword or dagger, and a piece of jewelry."

"That's it?" Aram asked confused. "They seem kind of odd for things to steal and why only one shoe…"

"Take a pair if it bothers you that much." Edmond folded the parchment back up and placed it back into his pocket. "Alright, who wants to do what?" They took some time to determine who would fetch each thing, but only after Edmond said, "I want Aram to get the sword or dagger and Silas the piece of jewelry. Don't ask why, but they are the ones who have to do it." His real reason was because he wanted them to stay by him while they were there. Those two particular things would be more hazardous to collect then the others and his close relation to the king might prove useful should they get caught, or at least he hoped it would. Also, Aram and Silas were his best friends and he knew they wouldn't do anything stupid to get them caught.

"The roses will be the last item to collect because they will take some time. I have to gather them alone but I will need you two to stand guard for me." He informed Aram and Silas.

"What will you do with everything once it's collected?" Silas asked.

"I'm to bring it to Arabella's home and give everything to her handmaiden. However if I get caught by the Baroness then all our efforts will have been wasted. The three main points of this game is to collect everything, bring it to Arabella's handmaiden Ida and most importantly, we are not to get caught." Everyone seemed to understand. "Now, once we're there we will split up into three teams. Mine has been decided and you can decide among yourselves who should make up the other two remaining teams of three. Try to team up with someone who has similar items to yours, this might make your search a little easier and quicker." He suggested.

Once they had separated near the palace each group had to find a way to get on the grounds. Edmond had a card up his sleeve for this one. "We'll be using one of the secret passages into the castle located near the north entrance." He informed his two companions.

"You know where a secret passage is?" Aram asked surprised. "If you knew that, why didn't you tell the others?"

Edmond sighed, "There's a reason it's called a 'secret passage'. I trust you two not to abuse the knowledge of its location but I'm not as sure about the others."

"Aren't you abusing the knowledge by showing us?" Silas asked.

"Would you like to find a different way in on your own?" Edmond threatened.

"Point taken." Silas smiled charmingly. "Lead the way, master."

Edmond looked over and saw one of the teams. The boys in that team were horsing around with each other. "Better yet, you should probably go and join them."

"Aw, come on I was just..."

"That's not what I meant. Take a good look at them. They're going to get caught for sure at the rate they're going. I'll get your item for you. Just keep a close eye on those three guys and make them settle down before they get caught. I'm counting on you to keep those three out of trouble and to make sure they get the items I need them to get in the most efficient and timely manner."

Silas watched as their friends goofed around, "I think your right. Thanks for getting my item it will help me out a lot." He took off to calm their three friends down before they drew attention to themselves.

"Come on." Edmond told Aram and they both took off for the North entrance to the palace grounds.

"Have you ever been through the passage before?" Aram asked him.

"Twice. It was part of my training should I ever need to occupy the throne on short notice. The passageways are the king's life line should the palace ever be attacked."

"It's a little scary when you think about it."

"I try not to. Besides, I'm sure I'll never have to serve on the throne. It won't be long before Kendrick takes a wife and begins producing heirs."

"Right." Aram said slowly in a soft voice. She wondered if that person would be her. Aram shook his head to clear his mind.

It took a short while before they came to the hidden doorway for the underground passage. "Since we will have the most risky job, we will have a decent chance of escaping because of this passage way." Before approaching the door he looked around quickly to make sure no one saw them and then he grabbed Aram by the hand and quickly pulled him into the alcove that was hidden by hanging vines in the side of the palace's outer wall. Once inside he searched the stones on one of the walls near the door. Finally he found the loose stone and removed it so he could borrow the key. Once the key was removed he placed the stone back into the wall. Then he carefully unlocked and opened the door so no one would hear. Once inside and with the door shut he pocketed the key and then said, "I know this might be uncomfortable but you'll have to trust me."

"What do you mean?" Aram asked nervously in the pitch black tunnel. His voice echoed off the invisible walls.

"We have to navigate the tunnel in the dark and unfortunately there are several false paths...."

Aram didn't let him finished and quickly grabbed Edmond's hand. "Say no more, but are you sure you know your way around in here?"

"Pretty sure." Edmond replied. It hadn't been that long since he last went through the tunnels and he did it both in the light and darkness. There was no guarantee that if you had to use them, light would be available. "I was taught to count the step and when to turn before I even stepped foot in here for the first time."

"I trust you." Aram told him and moved closer to Edmond.

"First of all there are five footsteps from the door to the top of the first stair. Then we'll have to descend eight steps until we reach the tunnel's floor." Edmond backed up to the door and then began counting steps. Once he reached the top of the stairs he said, "Now down eight steps. Carefully feel the depth of the first step before you continue."

"Alright." Aram let go of Edmond's hand and felt for the wall to balance himself.

"Don't let go of me, you could easily get lost. You'll just have to trust me."

"Alright." Aram looped his arm through Edmond's and relied on his guidance to navigate the stairway.

"Tell you what, if I ever become king, I will have you come and live at the palace as my aid." Edmond was trying to ease the tension.

"Can I be second in line until you have kids?" Aram laughed.

"That decision is up to the advisors, but I'll try." He laughed as well. "We now have to go ten steps forward and then turn right."

"You know I'll never remember this, don't you?" Aram sighed.

"Don't worry about it. I took me forever before I could remember everything myself."

"Is it a long ways?"

"If we were walking a straight line, it would be about three hundred steps to the palace. However because of the maze down here we'll end up walking quite a bit further."

"So in other words, it would be really unwise for me to get lost." Aram clung tighter to Edmond.

"I think you understand this situation perfectly. Now…" They turned down the next path, "Now fifty steps forward and then left." Aram brushed up against the wall when they started down the next corridor and gasped. "Sorry, I should have felt for the walls first. You didn't get hurt did you?"

"No, it just frightened me a little, that's all. I didn't expect the wall to be so close to me."

"I'll make sure to take an extra step so I end up closer to the wall on my side next time."

"Alright." They continued to navigate the pitch black labyrinth for what seemed like half the day. Finally a dim light could be seen at the far end of the next corridor. "Thank goodness." Aram sighed in relief.

"Don't get too anxious, it's a false lead. There's a pit down there. I guess you could say it's the last attempt at fooling people who don't belong here."

"Do you know if anyone has ever fell victim to it?" Aram asked.

"I really don't know, to be honest. I also don't know if anyone fell in it and no one knew about it."

"UH, that would be awful if that were true." Aram replied in disgust. "I would never want to die alone in a dark place like this." A cold shiver ran down his spine as he thought more on it. Suddenly Aram gasped and jumped in fear.

"What?" Edmond asked.

"Something just ran over my foot." He said nervously.

Edmond thought for a moment, "It was probably just a rat." He suggested.

"A rat?" Aram could handle many things in his role as a boy but rats were not one of them. Instinctively he clung to Edmond, "I can't do this, let's go back." His voice was shaking with fear.

JM Howard

"We're almost there." A distinctive squeak from a rat could be heard and Aram buried his head in Edmond's arm. "Very well." He sighed and squatted down, "Get on." He told Aram.

"What?"

"Get on my back and I'll carry you. That would help you not to be as worried about them, right?"

"I couldn't possibly…" Aram tried to protest.

"Just get on already and stop acting like such a baby." He scolded.

"Alright." He replied in a near whisper and got up on Edmond's back.

"The ceilings are all high enough that you most likely won't bump your head on anything." More squeaks could be heard and Aram clung on tighter to Edmond. "Now don't suffocate me or we'll both end up as rat food." He teased.

"That's not funny." Aram said in a frightened voice. "I really hate rats."

"I couldn't tell." Edmond said in a sarcastic voice and then laughed. He then took a moment to remember what sequence of steps and turns were left to take. When he remembered he began walking again. "Hopefully I haven't mixed up the last few turns." He commented, it couldn't be helped he had to take advantage of Aram's moment of weakness.

"What do you mean?" Aram asked nervously.

"Well when we stopped and started talking with each other, I sort of lost count."

"You did what?" Now his voice sounded frightened.

Edmond had to fight his laughter, "Well the most dangerous part of the tunnel is here near the palace. Like I said before it is their last chance to stop intruders." Just then he buckled his knees so they'd drop about a foot and he yelled out, causing Aram to scream. Unfortunately, Aram was too scared to remember her boy voice. Edmond stood back up laughing almost uncontrollably, "You sounded just like a girl with that scream."

Aram let go with one of his arms long enough to smack Edmond on the back of his head, "Don't do that you moron." He remembered his boy voice.

"I can't believe you scream like a girl." He laughed even harder.

Beautiful Pretender

"Let me down." Aram began kicking. "I'd rather face the rats then your mean comments." He kicked harder.

"Now stop it or I really will drop you." He had to hoist Aram back up again because he really was about to drop him.

"I said, let me go." Aram began pounding his fists on Edmond's shoulders.

"Fine." Edmond let go and Aram went crashing to the floor.

"UH!" He gasped as he hit the ground. "I didn't say drop me!" He scolded hotly.

"Come on, we're almost there." Edmond reached down to search for Aram's hand in the darkness. "Where are you?" He asked but no reply came. "Come on, this isn't funny. You don't want me to leave you down here do you?" He got down on his hands and knees so he could search better. "Look, I'm sorry I dropped you, alright?"

"Whatever." Aram sighed. "Can we maybe just rest for a few moments before we go in?"

"Sure." He crawled to where Aram's voice had come from and reached forward to find him.

Aram gasped when he felt Edmond's hand touch her chest. Despite the fact that she was bound tight, she was still very aware of where his hand was on her. "What are you doing?" She asked in her male voice.

"I don't want you to be too far from me. It really isn't safe for you to be down here without knowing your way around." He lowered his hand and took a seat beside his friend, sitting against the wall.

Aram's heart was racing and the familiar pangs of nausea swept over, 'I wonder if he might have felt something?' She thought nervously to herself. 'Surely he would have said something if he did.' She reached up and felt her chest to discover for herself what he might have felt. It felt like she had on a vest or something of that nature underneath her shirt. 'Perhaps he didn't notice anything.'

"Are you alright? I didn't hurt you did I?"

"No, I'm fine. It surprised me more then anything." Actually Aram's backside was hurting pretty bad from the fall, but he'd never admit it.

"Are you about ready or do you need more time?"

"Let's do this." Aram began to stand up and the pain from the fall intensified, however he fought any trace of verbal acknowledgement of it so that Edmond wouldn't know that he was hurting. "Give me your hand." Aram said as calmly as possible. Soon he felt Edmond's hand on his shoulder and he could tell that Edmond was already standing up. Aram took his and allowed Edmond to help him stand the rest of the way up.

"We only have two turns left before we come to the stairs." He informed him as he led him by the hand. Sooner then not Edmond stopped. "Nine steps up and then seven more to the door."

"Alright." Aram carefully walked towards the stairs until his toes bumped into the first step. He reached over and felt the wall and used it as a guide up while still clinging to Edmond. Finally they were at the door that led into the palace. "Where does it lead?" Aram asked in a whisper.

"It leads to a closet in the servant's hall. They keep it locked but the key I have and also one that is hidden outside the door, will open both the tunnel door and the closet door." Edmond took the key from his pocket and then he carefully used his fingers to find the key hole. "By the way, I was just kind of curious about what you are wearing under your shirt."

'Oh God, he did notice it after all.' Aram winced silently.

"I've noticed it before when touching your back and I always meant to ask you about it."

"Um, I guess you can say that it helps to keep my body aligned properly." Aram had no clue what else to say about it.

"Do you have back problems or something?" He asked concerned.

"I have problems but I'd rather not talk about them, if that's alright."

"I suppose, but don't worry, I won't tell anyone." He reached over and gently patted the back of Aram's head before inserting the key into the hole that he had finally located. Soon they were standing in the servant's closet. "Now we just need to listen carefully and make sure the corridor is clear before we go into the palace." He placed his ear against the door and stood there silently for several moments.

"Are you not going to close and lock the door to the tunnel?" Aram asked.

"Only on the way out. I want to leave it ready for a quick escape if we need it."

"Oh." Aram also laid his ear against the door. "What do you think?

Beautiful Pretender

Are we safe?"

"I believe so." They both stood back some from the door and soon Edmond had it unlocked and then he opened it, but only just a crack. Again he placed his head near the door and listened carefully. Finally he gave the all clear, "Come on." He grabbed Aram's hand and led him from the closet. Edmond shut the door but he didn't lock it. "They won't know that we left it unlocked." He assured Aram.

"So where are we going?"

"Straight to the king's chambers. He's sure to have both a dagger and jewelry in there."

"Do you even know where it is?"

Edmond thought for a moment, "I'm pretty sure I do. I saw it once but this place is so big that a person can easily get confused."

"That's not very reassuring." Aram sighed.

"Come on, we need to hurry before someone discovers we're here."

"Yeah, yeah." Aram groaned. He found himself amazed at the beauty of the palace. The walls and floor were of white stone and marble. The walls and corridors were littered with all sorts of old décor from the ages past. It amazed her that this overly accented place could soon become her new home. 'No, you have to stop thinking about that for now.' She scolded herself. There were no guarantees who she'd end up with yet. The last thing she needed was to be imagining herself in a life she couldn't have.

They had walked a long time, though there was a need for them to hide from time to time so they wouldn't be found by the palace staff. Finally they made it to the corridor that the king resided in. "It should be just a few doors down this way." He told Aram in a whisper.

Aram also spoke in a whisper, "How long has it been since you came here? All these corridors look the same, are you sure this is the correct one?"

"I was given this tour about five years ago, just before I met you actually." He smiled over at Aram.

"So what if you're wrong?"

Edmond shrugged his shoulders, "Then I'm wrong."

Aram sighed in frustration, "Let's just get this over with."

"I wonder how the others are doing."

"Who knows."

"I think I'd like to find something pretty to give to Arabella while we're here." There was a hint of a dream like sigh to Edmond's voice.

"That is not a good idea, especially if she marries Kendrick."

"I don't care. I want her to have a memento of my love for her."

"I think this little adventure of yours is enough of one, wouldn't you agree?" Secretly for Arabella it was. Even though she was showing Aram's cranky side, she was actually enjoying this time with Edmond. Even the fact that he was constantly thinking about her, was enough of a gift. A small smile traced her lips. Soon they stopped in front of a door. "Is this it?" Aram asked.

"It's either this door or the next. You try this one and I'll go down to the next one. If this is the room, don't bother coming back out to look for me, just grab the two things we need and get out quickly."

"Alright." Aram waited for Edmond to get a short ways down the hall before he snuck into the room. To his surprise it was quiet dark, but he could manage to find his way around well enough. Quietly he shut the door behind him and went to the window to open the curtains so he could see around the chamber better. He could tell this room was someone's bedchamber but he wouldn't know if it was the king's until he could see the room better. As quietly as possible he opened the curtains about halfway. Then he turned to look around the room.

A smile stretched across his lips when he realized that this was indeed the king's bedchamber, or at least it appeared to be. Then he walked over to a table and began rummaging here and there looking for a piece of jewelry and for a dagger or sword. A slight rustling noise came from the bed behind him and he froze solid in fear. 'Oh please God, don't tell me there's rats in here too.' Aram scrunched his eyes closed tightly.

"Whose there?" A familiar boyish voice asked.

Aram felt himself relaxing, but only just a little. Apparently Kendrick had been sleeping in the room. Slowly Aram turned and looked over at Kendrick. "Hi." Arabella said in her normal voice with a smile as she waved her hand nervously at him.

"Arabella, is that you?" He asked in disbelief.

"Yeah, sort of."

"You look like a boy." Kendrick got out of bed to come and have a closer look. He reached out his hand and touched her chest. "What the..."

"I bound them up." She told him, slightly embarrassed. That was twice now that a member of the opposite sex had touched her bound chest. Only difference was one did it unintentionally while thinking she was a boy and the other did it on purpose, knowing that she was a girl.

He removed his hand, "Why?"

She laughed nervously, "Well you see, there is this whole other side of me you know nothing about and if my parents find out you know, I'll be in big trouble, so promise you won't let them know you caught me. Please?"

"Perhaps you should fill me in."

"Well you see, about the time we came here from Eldardesh, I discovered a group of boys playing and I really wanted to play with them because I didn't have any friends yet. However they wouldn't play with a girl so father bought boy clothes for me so that they would believe that I was a boy. I guess it just became a habit but unfortunately they still think I am a boy. But don't worry... this won't be lasting much longer, I understand once I am betrothed I can't do this anymore." She fell to her knees, "Please don't be angry with me about this." She begged.

"I don't understand." He said quietly.

"What, sire?"

"Why people want to pretend to be something they're not. I had always thought it was something that the peasants did to entertain themselves because they wanted to be like the nobles, but to discover that a noble does this too..." He was beside himself with confusion.

"Actually sire, if you'll pardon my forthrightness, you too pretend on a daily basis to be someone that you're not." She looked sincerely at him and smiled.

"What do you mean?"

"Well you've been forced to grow up and act like a mature man even though you are still so young."

"Oh." He said sadly. "I guess I never really thought of it being that way." He walked back over to his bed and sat down. "Come sit by me."

"Yes sire." She stood up and did as he asked.

"Is that why you treat me like you do?"

"How's that?" She asked still smiling.

"Like a child."

"Well I wouldn't say I treat you like a child, but more like someone your own age..." she had to think for a moment, "I really just like playing with you (she was referring to the somewhat childish game they played when gazing at the stars). You do like it when I do that, right? I mean, seeing you as both a grown up but also as someone more my age. My friends and I play with each other all of the time, yet they are on the verge of being adults too."

"So what you do with me is normal for people our age." This seemed to spark his interest.

"More or less, though I don't go around kissing people." She laughed softly when she saw a gentle blush on his cheeks. "You're so cute." She leaned over and kissed the temple of his head.

"Arabella..." he complained from embarrassment.

Suddenly the door opened, "Did you find them?" Edmond asked with an elevated whisper into the room and then he quickly stopped when he saw Aram sitting next to Kendrick.

"Why are you here too?" Kendrick asked confused, "In fact, how did you both make it this far without being seen and detained?" Now he seemed worried.

"It really wasn't that hard." Edmond shrugged and walked into the room, closing the door behind him.

"So much for having personal guards." He sighed in disappointment. "If you two could get in here with no trouble, then so could one of my brother's assassins."

"Oh, don't worry too much." Aram said in his boy voice and then winked at Kendrick who gave him an odd look. He wasn't use to hearing Arabella talk like that. She not only sounded like a boy but also like a native Arminian. Quickly she leaned towards him and whispered into his ear, "Edmond doesn't know I'm a girl either, so please don't tell him my secret."

"Oh." Kendrick replied quietly. "We'll talk more about what we were discussing at a later time."

"Sure." Aram stood up and then looked around the room. "Sire, would it be all right if we borrowed a few items from you?"

Beautiful Pretender

"Is that why you're here?" He stood up and walked towards her.

"Yes. We were given a list of things to get from the palace, us and a few of our friends."

"There are more of you?" He asked in disbelief.

"Yep, though I'm not sure where they are at the moment." She admitted honestly. "We each had something different that we were supposed to find."

"What are you looking for?" He asked.

"Well, I'm supposed to find a piece of jewelry and a dagger or sword. Edmond is supposed to get a bouquet of your unique blue roses, sixteen to be exact."

"My blue roses?" Kendrick couldn't believe what he was hearing.

"Yes. You see it's a test."

"What kind of test?"

Quickly Edmond came over and answered the king, after he made his way to Aram. He gently placed his hand on his friends shoulder to indicate that it was best if he answered the king. "It's really not important sire."

Aram laughed, "It's a test of love."

Edmond grabbed Aram to him and covered his mouth and then whispered, "Shut up." in a serious voice. Then to the king he smiled and said, "It's just a silly game."

"You're in love?" Kendrick asked surprised. "With who?"

Aram tried hard to break free so he could tattle tale but Edmond held on too tightly for him to escape. "Just a girl, sire. It's only temporary until my parents name the one I am to marry."

"I see." He looked at Arabella in confusion and wondered if he should order Edmond to release her. Then he saw her find the opportunity to elbow Edmond in the stomach and he finally let her go. "Are you hurt?" Kendrick asked Aram with concern.

"Nah, I can take it, your majesty. Just look at what he did to me the other day." Aram said proudly and pulled up his sleeve to boast the large bruise on his arm that Edmond had given him with the punch from the other day.

"Doesn't that hurt?" Kendrick reached forward and touched it gently.

"Only when someone touches it." He teased and then laughed when

145

Kendrick quickly pulled his hand away.

Edmond looked at it, "Sorry, I didn't mean to hit you so hard."

"Why are you apologizing?" Aram laughed, "This is a trophy."

Edmond laughed also, "I guess so." He stood up and then pulled up his shirt. There were several red marks and even a couple of bruises on his stomach and ribs. "These are mine." He grinned.

"Are those all from today?" Aram asked laughing.

"Every one." He said proudly.

"Oh yeah…" Aram placed his hands on his hips in an almost defiant gesture, "well I bet you that there's a huge bruise on my backside from when you dropped me in the tunnel."

"Drop them and let's see it." Edmond was referring to Aram pulling down his pants so they could see his rear end.

"No don't!" Kendrick said frantically as reached to grab onto Aram's hand to prevent 'him' from doing what Edmond suggested. "Have you forgotten that sh…." He almost let it slip by saying 'she's a girl' but he corrected himself. "Have you forgotten where you are and in who's company you're in?"

Edmond looked confused for a moment, "Oh, I had nearly forgotten. Please grant us your pardon, sire."

"Kendrick, why don't you get dressed and finish helping us search for everything?" Aram suggested. Currently the king was only in his night shirt, much like the one Edmond had worn when he stayed the night with Aram at Joseph's house.

"I really ought to do something about this security problem first. Go ahead and find what you need." He smiled. "Also find something for Arabella and take it to her for me."

Edmond seemed surprised by the remark. "Could we both take something to her, sire?" He knew it was selfish but he really wanted to bring her something as a memento.

"That's fine. You'll find a box with ladies jewelry in the cabinet over there. I'm not sure why its there, but feel free to help yourselves to it. You'll find a dagger in there as well."

"Thank you very much, your majesty." Aram grinned.

"I'll let the staff know you are here and that I gave you those things so you will not face any problems concerning them."

This time Edmond spoke up, "Thank you cousin, we really appreciate

Beautiful Pretender

you letting us do this."

"Kendrick?" Aram called out before the king could leave the room.

"Yes?"

"Could we maybe stop by tomorrow and get you?"

"What do you mean?"

"Come out and play with us tomorrow." Aram smiled. "Please? I know you'll love it."

He thought for a moment. "I'll have to take my personal guards with me."

"That's not a problem. Alright then, we'll come by after the morning meal. Make sure you wear a disguise."

"Huh?"

"You and your guards should dress like commoners, so you're not easily recognized."

"Couldn't we just play here on the palace grounds?"

Aram thought for a moment, "We could but I really would like to show you our favorite place by a lake near here."

"The only lake near here is on the palace grounds." He said after thinking about it.

"Is it really?" She asked in confusion. "Still, you should dress down because you could bump into people on the way there."

"I'll send some servants to get us some commoners clothing then." He wasn't sure why he had to dress down but he was too curious to fight with her about this. More then anything he wanted to see this other life that the princess lived.

Just then the door opened and one of the guards walked in, he seemed shocked to see two strangers in the room. "Sire…" He asked with hesitation.

"I need to talk with you." Kendrick's voice almost sounded angry. "Just be glad that I know these two and trust them."

"We found more intruders in the palace and on the grounds."

"Let these two get what they came for and bring them down to where you're holding the other intruders. Anyone they tell you to set free is one of their friends. Let them go and get whatever they came here for. When they are finished, escort them back off of the palace grounds. When these two boys come back tomorrow, let them in."

The guard looked worried but answered, "Yes sire, as you wish." He left the room and closed the door quietly behind him.

"I'll see you both tomorrow then." Kendrick smiled. "I think this adventure of yours should be rather entertaining."

"Yes sire." They both said in unison and bowed from the waist to their king and both were grinning from ear to ear.

Chapter 8

That evening, Arabella had barely enough time to get home, bathe and put on her fresh, feminine clothing before Edmond came to see her. He climbed up the walnut tree to access her balcony and came into view right as she was tying on her mask. "It took you long enough." She grinned teasingly. "What is that rope you're holding for?"

"It's tied to a basket that contains all the items you're handmaiden requested." He smiled proudly.

"Really!" She said with excitement and peaked over the railing's edge. "You were able to get everything?"

"Yep, everything." He began pulling the basket up. "I was even able to get a few things for you too, with permission from the king of course."

"Oh, you mustn't breathe a word about getting caught to Ida or she'll say you failed the mission." She saw him making a buttoning motion on his lips with his fingers and thumb.

"I wanted to give you what I brought for you without her around anyhow." Once he brought it up, he opened it and rummaged around for the items. "Here." He handed her a couple of jeweled bracelets and a dagger designed for a woman.

"How pretty." She nearly squealed in delight. "Anything else?" She grinned.

"Only these." He produced a bouquet of red roses.

Arabella was speechless, 'He must have taken these after I left.' She hadn't remembered him cutting them when they were in the king's garden.

"These are from my mother's garden." He told her proudly, almost as if he had read her thoughts.

She brought them up to her nose and inhaled their strong sweet scent. "They're perfect." She sighed in delight. "Thank you."

"I won't be able to come tomorrow night." He informed her. "I made plans with some friends."

"Really?" She smiled. "I'll miss you but I do hope you'll enjoy yourself."

"I think we will. Aram and I have talked the king into...oh..." He suddenly stopped.

"What?"

"I forgot we weren't supposed to tell anyone."

"You can tell me though, right?" She reached over and touched his hand. "Please?"

He looked to the door to make sure Ida was still away and when he was sure she wouldn't overhear he said, "We're kidnapping him, but only for a day."

"What on earth..."

"He's agreed to spend the day with us."

"Really?" She acted surprised. "I really have hoped to see him find some opportunities to just have some fun and act more like a kid his age." She said almost as if to herself. "This would be a wonderful opportunity for him to do that."

"So you don't mind then?"

"Just take care of him." She gently placed her hand on his arm. "Don't let anyone hurt him. After all..." she sighed and looked almost a little sad, "He may very well be my husband soon."

"Try not to think about it." Edmond did his best to comfort her. He knew all too well that she wasn't looking forward to her arranged marriage, whether it was to Kendrick or his brother Eric. After setting the basket aside he walked over and took her into his embrace. "Right now belongs to us, so don't think about those things which lie ahead." He kissed her tenderly.

"Alright." Her sweet voice whispered back. "I'll do my best to just focus on what I have right now." She snuggled into his chest. "I wanted to ask Ida if she'd give us some time alone tonight."

"We're alone now." He reminded her.

"But she may come at any moment. Actually, she should be here already. I wonder what's detaining her."

Beautiful Pretender

"Arabella?"

"Yes."

"I want to do everything I can to make our short time together to be as wonderful as possible. Is there anything you want me to do for you while I can still do it?"

"Do for me?" She asked confused.

"If I could do, even just one thing for you, what would you like me to do?"

"I'm not sure really. Can I think about it?"

"Of course." His hand gently rubbed her back with gentle strokes as held her close.

"While I'm thinking about it, I want you to do the same. Think of something I can do for you too. I'll do anything you ask of me."

He laughed softly, "Anything?" There was a hint of teasing in his voice.

"I know what you're implying, but my word is my truth. I'll do anything you ask."

"Alright, I'll take time to think about it as well." He kissed her again, "And don't worry, I won't ask anything from you that would hurt either of us in any way."

"I know, silly." She looked over as her bedchamber door opened. "There you are." Arabella smiled.

"Sorry I'm late, milady." Ida looked like she had been working hard. "Did the young master bring everything I asked for?" She looked over at him.

"Yes miss, there in the basket." He pointed to it.

"Everything came from the palace itself?" She asked in suspicion.

"Ida!" Arabella scolded

"Sorry milady, I didn't mean to offend him." Ida apologized because she understood that Arabella had also gone on the 'mission' and that she had already told Ida that they were successful in gathering the items from the palace. "So you'll keep your promise not to bother us about seeing each other, right?" Arabella asked.

"Yes princess. I will hold my tongue." She walked over and opened the basket. "Everything seems to be in order." She closed the basket again and the headed for the door.

"Aren't you going to take it?" Edmond asked confused.

"No. There is no need to. Return as much of it as you can, when you get a chance to." She turned and smiled at them. "I'll come back later with some refreshments."

"You're leaving?" Arabella asked in a bewildered voice.

"I see no need to stay." Ida then left the room and gently closed the door behind her.

"Weird." Edmond looked over to the untouched basket. "She didn't even look through it to see if everything was there. The blue roses were covering almost all of the items."

"She trusts you." Arabella smiled. "If she didn't, she would have looked through it and she also wouldn't have left the room."

"I see." He was still a bit surprised at the turn of events. "So now what?"

"It sounds like you have a rather big day before you tomorrow. Perhaps you should go home and rest." She suggested.

"But I only just got here and you're sending me away already?" He pouted.

Arabella laughed softly, "Then stay if you wish." She stood up and walked over to her bed, "If it's alright, I think I'll lie down. I've had a pretty busy day today and I'm rather tired." A lazy yawn escaped her lips. "You can stay with me if you want."

"Don't you need to change first before you go to bed?"

"I'll change later." She sat down on the bed's edge. "Come and sit by me."

He walked over towards her, "If you're that tired, maybe I should go."

"You're so mean." Arabella yawned again and then she laid down.

Edmond laughed, "How's that?"

"At least stay until I fall asleep." She patted the bedside near where she was lying. "Tell me about everything you did today."

He looked over towards the door and wondered what Ida would say if she caught him sitting on Arabella's bed while she was laying on it. Finally he resolved that Arabella was trying to make a point by telling him that Ida trusted him and so he sat down and began to tell the story of what happened that day. She seemed very interested in his story and even more interested in his retelling of what happened in the king's bedchamber.

"So would Aram really have shown his back side to you if Kendrick hadn't spoken up?" She asked laughing.

"Who knows?" He laughed as well. "To be honest, I doubt it. Aram's never undressed in front of any of us before."

She grinned, "Maybe he has something to hide."

"Maybe." He leaned down and kissed her forehead. "Or maybe he is just insecure about his manhood after seeing mine." They both laughed.

"You're so bad." She hit his arm, just like Aram would have done when he heard a good joke.

For a moment Edmond was stunned. There was something about the way that Arabella behaved that seemed so familiar to him, almost comforting. It was if they had known each other for years and not days. He reached over and picked up her small hand into his own. Even this small hand seemed like it had always held his. It was certain that they only just met, for he was sure he'd never forget knowing her. Yet when he was with her, he knew this was where he belonged. "May I lie down next to you?" Immediately he wished he hadn't asked. He didn't mean to do anything to embarrass her.

"I don't mind." She smiled up at him.

"Really?" He seemed surprised.

"We've slept next to each other before. I really see no difference now." Arabella moved over to give him room.

"I suppose we did that night in the forest. I have meant to apologize to you about that. I really didn't mean to fall asleep that night." He reached up to move some hair off of her face (actually it was more on her mask then on her face) after lying down.

Arabella snuggled into him, clinging tightly onto his shirt. 'This feels so nice.' She thought happily. 'I can hold onto him all I want as Arabella, at least until…No, I can't think about what lies ahead', she scolded herself. 'I can only think about what I have right now.' The words of advice that Edmond gave her would be locked in her heart during this precious time. "I love you." She whispered. "Can we stay like this forever?"

"Let our today be our forever." He gently stroked her soft hair. "Now go to sleep." It was amusing how tightly she clung on to him. It reminded him of the other night when he woke up to Aram doing the same thing. It made him want to laugh, because it made Aram appear to be even more girlish since Arabella was now doing the same thing he did.

He felt a little guilty about the way he felt towards Aram. It was really hard not to be attracted to a guy like him. He was way too much like the opposite sex and Edmond had a hard time with his feelings and thoughts at times. Now that he met Arabella, it did help some because he found someone who could capture his thoughts and attention. She and Aram were a lot a like and he wondered if that was why he was so attracted to her. He fell in love with her almost instantly, even though he tried to meet other girls, he could never feel anything for them and he had started to worry that something might be wrong with him. However, now he knew everything would be alright because of this beautiful young woman by his side.

Already Arabella was breathing the soft rhythm of sleep. She still clung tightly to him but he could tell that she was indeed sleeping. He brought his hand to her mask and ran his finger along the outer gold trimmed edge of it. The temptation to take it off was nearly overwhelming. He was aching to see the face of the woman he loved, however he loved her enough to fight the temptation to defy her wishes. Instead, he brought his hand to her small waist and laid it down there. Both she and Ida had to be blissfully unaware of the amount of other temptations that he had to fight. As a man he had to fight the urges that were streaming through him. He wanted to do more then just lie by her side. How easy it would be for him to touch her in desired places as she slept soundly. Would she even know if he did? Would she care if he touched her in an intimate way? He wasn't sure. All he knew was that he had made a promise not to violate her and he meant to keep it.

When he felt himself starting to drift off, he knew it was time to go. Carefully he tried to release her hands from his shirt. Arabella moaned in complaint. "Hush now." He whispered tenderly but she only tried to snuggle in closer to him. "I need to leave, Arabella."

"No." Her soft voice whispered.

Edmond sighed, "I can't fall asleep here."

"Stay with me." She told him in a sleeping voice. "I only have you for a little while."

"Alright, I'll stay, but it may cause problems with Ida." He leaned down and kissed her.

"Ida?" Arabella looked up at him. "You're right." She yawned as she released her hold on him. "She said she would be up with refreshments, didn't she?" She looked into Edmond's eyes, "If I violate her trust, she won't let you come anymore. This is so unfair." She moaned miserably as Edmond sat up. "Perhaps you should go after all."

He took a deep breath and let it out, "Alright then." He stood up. "I'll come back to see you the night after next." He brought her back into his embrace.

"I'll be waiting." She smiled as she nestled her head into his chest.

"Would you like me to bring you anything when I come?"

"Umm.... How about giving me a new mask to wear when you come to visit me?" She suggested with a charming smile.

"A new mask?"

"Yes, I want to wear one that is from you."

"Only on one condition." He teased.

"What's that?"

"That you promise that someday you will let me see your real face. I know you won't do it now, or even before you marry, and I've accepted that. However I do hope that one day you will let me see the face of the only woman I have ever loved."

"You'll let me do it in a time of my own choosing?"

"Yes. I'll try to wait until then."

"Then I'll agree to your terms."

"You will?" He seemed surprised for some reason. "You will show me someday?"

"Of course I will. To be honest you have already seen my real face." She couldn't help but to tease him a little.

"Yes, I have been told that but I must have not known who it was that I was looking at, for I can't recall ever meeting you before. I wish I could remember."

"I'll make you something."

"Huh?"

"If you're going to give me something when you come again, then I want to give you something as well."

Edmond blushed slightly, "Oh." He reached up and touched

her cheek tenderly. "Make sure it is something I can keep with me always."

"Alright." Immediately her brain began thinking of what she could make to give him that he would like.

"Good night, my princess."

"Good night, milord." She initiated the kiss and it lasted longer then any previous one they shared as of yet. Arabella hated it when he took his arms from her and turned to leave the way he came. It was well into the night, so he would have to navigate the balcony and the tree in the darkness. "Be safe." She called to him.

"I will my love." He winked at her. "Rest well."

Arabella watched him disappear into the darkness of the night. Then after a few more moments she went to her bedchamber door to look out into the corridor. Ida was sitting on the floor with her back against the wall and she looked up to her mistress when the door opened. "How long have you been sitting out here?" Arabella asked.

"I've been sitting here for a while now. I had planned on bringing refreshments in for you but then I thought that you might like to have some time alone without my disruption. Has he gone home?"

"Only just. Why don't you go ahead and come in for a while." She noticed that Ida had the tray of refreshments sitting beside her. "We can share what you brought before retiring for the night."

"Yes milady." Ida stood up and then gathered up the basket. "Will he come again tomorrow?"

"No and I won't be home either. We're spending the day with Kendrick tomorrow."

"The king?" Ida seemed surprised. "Are you going as Aram?"

"I am. Kendrick promised to keep my secret, so his knowing about it shouldn't cause any problems for us."

"Perhaps not but I don't feel well about this, milady. Please be careful."

Arabella reached over and touched her handmaiden's arm. "I actually feel better knowing that he is aware of my other side. It will make this situation easier on both of us if we marry and it comes out that I've done this."

"I suppose that is one way of looking at it." Ida decided not to worry about it for now. She would instead wait to see what else might come

Beautiful Pretender

of this situation.

As promised, Edmond and Aram waited by the gate of the palace for the young king. When they saw him, they had to try hard not laughing because his commoner clothing looked like the clothing of a nobleman. His guards looked a bit more like commoners though, except that they had their swords on their sides. "I think that is about as common as he'll get." Edmond whispered to Aram.

"I think you're right." Aram whispered back. They both put on their best faces for greeting the king. "Good morning, your majesty!" Aram called and waved.

Kendrick looked a bit surprised by Aram's casual behavior for a moment but then he decided to join in on the excitement. "Good morning." He smiled brightly.

Once they were together and ready to leave, Edmond spoke next. "I have to admit that I wasn't completely convinced you'd come today, your majesty."

"We have to do something about that." Aram commented.

"What's that?" Kendrick asked slightly confused, confusion was also evident on Edmond's face.

"Your name. What's the point of you coming out here in disguise? If we keep referring to you as the king, everyone will know who you are."

"I hadn't thought of that." Edmond reflected. "How should we address you today, your majesty?"

"I suppose Kendrick is out of the question." The king spoke up in thought.

"Perhaps we could refer to you by a different name." Aram suggested.

"But what?" Edmond asked as he pondered an alternative. "Perhaps if we shortened his name to Ken..."

"Ken?" Kendrick didn't seem to care for the name.

"Well it's better than us calling you Drick." Aram added and they all laughed.

"Ken will be fine." Kendrick told them. "After all, it's only for a day." He reached over and took Aram's hand. "Please, whatever you do, don't call me Drick, it sounds terrible."

157

Aram smiled, "Yes Sire but it will be awfully hard not to."

"Yeah, you just gave Aram something to torture you with but I'll let you in on a secret."

"Yeah, what?" Kendrick seemed excited to learn a secret.

"Don't you dare Edmond, I'm warning you." Aram scowled.

"If he calls you Drick, just tell him he looks like a girl."

"You moron!" Aram yelled and released Kendrick's hand. Then he slammed his fist into Edmond's shoulder.

"Ara…" Kendrick almost said Arabella. 'I'll never get use to this.' He sighed in his thoughts. "Aram." He scolded.

"Ouch." Edmond laughed. "I forgot to mention that there is a drawback to knowing Aram's weakness." He rubbed his sore shoulder. "This kid may look like a girl but he has a lethal punch."

"I told you to stop calling me a girl." Aram glared at him for a moment and then he looked back over to Kendrick. "Come on Ken." Aram reached down and took the king's hand again. "The others should be at the lake by now."

Edmond came over and put his arm around Aram's shoulders. "We're planning on swimming today, right?"

"Maybe." Aram smiled up at him and then looked over to Kendrick, "Do you like to swim?"

"I'm not really sure. I've never done it before." He confessed.

"Well you'll have to try it at least this once." Edmond suggested. "I'm sure you'll love it."

"Alright." They had a ways to walk before they were able to get to the designated area where the others were. When they arrived the other boys were playing a game of tackle tag. "That's a game right?" Kendrick asked as he watched the other boys play.

"Yes." Edmond answered. "One person is selected to be the one to chase the others. If he tackles you then you're out of the game. In other words he can't just touch you but he must also bring you down to the ground. The first person to be tackled is the one who must chase the others in the next round."

"That sounds interesting, can I play too?"

"Sure. We'll just make sure that they are not quite so rough with you."

"Majesty?" One of his guards asked in a concerned voice.

"Leave him alone." Aram interrupted. "He'll be fine. It won't kill him if he gets a few scrapes or bruises. Just let him have fun for once."

The guard looked to the king for advice on what he should do. "Just do as Aram says. I want you to stand over here and watch over me from a distance."

"Yes sire." The guard answered but it was easy to see that he was uncomfortable with this assignment. The three joined in the game and Kendrick caught on quickly. Soon he was laughing and talking with the other boys as if he had always been one of them. Once the game was over they headed for the lake's shore.

"Everyone is going swimming now." Aram informed Kendrick.

Kendrick looked over to where the other boys were. "What are they doing?"

Aram looked over to the others, "Oh, they're just taking their clothes off. Don't mind them."

Kendrick turned Aram to face him, "Taking their clothes off?" He asked in a 'You can't be series!' voice.

"Well they can't swim in their clothing. It would be much too cumbersome."

"They swim naked?" He looked around her and a slight blush came to his cheeks.

"You are coming, aren't you?" Edmond asked.

"But they don't have anything on." Kendrick looked up at Aram.

"Oh, I see." Aram laughed softly and then looked up at Edmond, "Give us a moment."

"Sure, I'll go ahead and go in."

"Alright." Aram smiled and then he looked down at Kendrick. "Just so you know, I don't go swimming with the others. Instead I usually nap under this tree here."

"But their naked." He whispered to her. Since Edmond and the others were too far off to hear him whisper he spoke openly with her.

"Don't worry your majesty, I don't look at them, or at least not when they are out of the water. Sometimes I'll watch them play for awhile but they always go deep enough to hide the lower halves of their bodies."

"A woman shouldn't see these things." He warned her. "How do you

JM Howard

think they'd feel if they knew the truth?"

Aram laughed softly, "Most of them would probably get a kick out of it, if I know them as well as I think I do."

"This isn't funny." He scolded. "Have you ever accidentally seen... well, you know?"

"I'll be honest and say yes. A couple of times I accidentally saw things I shouldn't have, but it really isn't a big deal. It's not like I looked on purpose or anything."

"That's not the point."

"Go on and join them. I promise I won't watch until after you're in the water."

"I can't."

"Sure you can."

"Arabella." He scolded her.

"Don't call me that." She reminded him and she glanced around to make sure no one had overheard him. When she was satisfied that no one had, she told him, "Go on and have your one day of fun and spend time with guys who are your own age." She leaned down and kissed his forehead. "It really is alright."

"Why did you kiss me?" He asked as he touched his forehead.

"You looked like you needed one." Aram grinned. She watched as his jaw dropped and he seemed to be staring behind her. "What?"

"Just don't turn around." He warned her.

"Come on you two." Edmond's voice said from behind Aram. "I doubt Aram's coming in, but how about you Ken?"

"I think we should make Aram swim with us today." Silas added. "He never swims with us."

"Make me and you'll regret it." Aram warned them without turning around.

"Oh really." Silas grabbed Aram's arm. "I'll drag you in if I have to." He laughed.

Aram tried to yank his arm from Silas's grip, "Don't you dare."

"That's enough!" Kendrick stood with his fists on his hips. "If he doesn't want to do it, then he shouldn't have to."

"How about you?" Edmond asked him. "You'll come, right?"

Kendrick looked up at Aram, "I will because Aram wants me to."

Edmond wrapped an arm about Aram's shoulders from behind him

Beautiful Pretender

and put his face close enough so their cheeks touched. "Nice job. I didn't think he'd do it."

"Just go already." Aram huffed and could feel her cheeks blushing knowing that Edmond wasn't wearing anything as he held onto her, "And stop hugging me when you don't have anything on, it feels weird."

Edmond laughed, "Ah darling." He whined in jest. "You know I just can't go even a little while without a little skin-ship." He reached down and pinched Aram's bottom.

"You moron!" Aram whipped around and tried to hit Edmond but he caught his arm before Aram could make contact.

"You're just too cute when you're mad." He laughed.

"Why you…" Aram warned in anger.

"Aram!" Kendrick scolded. Aram looked back at him. "Enough."

"Huh?" He looked back at Edmond and then realized the awkward situation. "Oh." Quickly he turned his back to Edmond. "I suppose I'll let it go this time." He walked to his place under the oak tree and sat down. He avoided looking at any of the others.

Kendrick walked with Silas and Edmond to where they had left their clothing. "He'll be fine in a few." Edmond assured the king. "He can be a little hot tempered at times, but he never holds a grudge."

Kendrick looked back to where Aram lounged on his side in the grass with his back towards them. "I guess I'll just have to take your word for it."

"Edmond told us that you're one of his cousins." Silas said suddenly.

"Yes, actually I am. I came to visit him." Kendrick smiled, though technically he was Edmond's uncle and not his cousin, but that was a secret.

"How long do you plan to stay with him?"

"I plan on going home tonight."

Edmond looked down at his 'cousin', "You should stay the night." He suggested.

"I couldn't possibly…" Kendrick began to protest.

"Really you should stay. Both Aram and I were hoping you would."

"Oh." He looked back at Aram again. "I suppose I could if you really want me to."

"Then it's settled." Edmond grinned. "That should cheer Aram up."

"Do you think so?" Kendrick asked.

"Aram and I are the closest of friends. No one knows him better then I do." Edmond boasted.

Kendrick nearly laughed and thought to himself, 'You don't know him as well as you think you do.'

Aram played with a piece of grass as she fumed in her normal voice, "Stupid boys." She whispered and then rolled from her side onto her back, placing an arm behind her head. "You can be such an ass sometimes, Edmond." She stuck the piece of grass in her mouth to chew on as she looked up at the clouds. "Still, I can't help loving him." A small smile forced its way through her clouded feelings as she thought about the night before. "Even as a boy he thinks I'm adorable, even though it's cute it's also a little disturbing. Oh well." She sighed. "I can't blame him any, I am adorable after all." She laughed softly and then turned her head so she could watch the guys playing in the water.

Kendrick seemed to be fitting in well despite his years of being sheltered from such things. She had thought that he might enjoy being with boys his own age for once and she was glad that she was right. "Miss." Someone said near her and she turned her gaze towards the voice. It was one of Kendrick's guards. "May I sit by you for a while?"

"Sure." She smiled up to him and took the blade of grass from her mouth. "I guess our beloved king filled you in on my little secret."

"It was for your protection that he did, milady. We're to watch over you today as well."

"Thanks but I'm sure I'll do fine without it."

"This is rather a compromising situation for you to be in, isn't it?" There was concern in his voice.

"I'm use to it. I've been hanging around with these guys for five years now and I think I've seen them all naked at one time or another. I just figured it was one of those life lessons." She put the blade of grass back into her mouth.

The guard couldn't help laughing. "I suppose that is one way of looking at it."

Beautiful Pretender

"I can't let it bother me or they'll know something is wrong."

"True." He continued to watch the king carefully as he spoke to her. "Lord Wallace seems to be rather fond of you. Are you sure he doesn't know that you're a woman?"

"I'm sure. I know he tends to associate Aram with one though."

"Doesn't it hurt you to bind your chest like that? I know I may be out of line but when I've seen you as Arabella and you're not all that flat."

"I have to admit that it's not very comfortable but I'm use to the discomfort. Besides, I honestly think that it's worth it. These boys are my only friends and we are really close to one another. It isn't something that a person can give up that easily."

"Your friends mean that much to you?"

"They do. Sure, we fight a lot and badger each other all the time but I don't think I could have found a more trustworthy and loyal group of friends as I have found in them."

"You and Edmond are the only nobles in this group, correct?"

"Yes, though they believe that the physician, Joseph Aldonmire, is Aram's father. He even has a room for me to sleep in should I need it."

"Is he being compensated for this?"

"Yes, father is paying him."

"Amazing." He seemed fascinated. Then a new thought dawned on him. "This group of friends...they wouldn't happen to be the Black Bandits would they?" He was slightly hesitant in asking.

Aram laughed softly, "What brought that up?"

"Well, I couldn't help noticing that they're about the right age and the number of boys here matches the number of bandits, if I include you."

"Well now, that is something isn't it." She sighed as she looked again to the young men horsing around in the water. "I suppose your right now that I think about it. I could see how one would come to that conclusion."

"Then they're not the ones? That's a relief."

"Are you married yet?" She asked from out of the blue as she turned to look back over at him.

"No princess. I really don't have time to look for someone to court."

He looked down at her and smiled fondly before returning his gaze back to watching over the king.

"How old are you?"

"I just turned twenty."

"Perfect." She grinned.

"Why is that?" He looked back down at her.

"I know someone you should try courting."

"I beg your pardon?" He laughed.

"No, really. You two would make a cute couple."

"And who might this woman be?"

"Her name is Ida, she's my handmaiden. I know you'll love her. She's beautiful, responsible, courteous and kind. When could you come to my home and meet her?"

"Oh I...."

"Just come as my guest and see her. If you're interested just tell me and I'll help you work things out. If you're not, she'll never even know the difference."

He grinned and laughed softly, "You are something. Now I have a much better understanding of why the king is so taken with you. You're not shy, that's for sure."

"Why, should I be? Nothing would ever get done if I was shy." She spit out the blade of grass and yawned. "I wouldn't have the friends or life I do today if I was shy. I really love my life right now."

"I'm truly happy for you, milady." He cleared his throat. "It looks like they're done swimming."

"Already?" She glanced over and saw that several of the guys were already coming out of the lake. Quickly she glanced away again to avoid seeing any more of them then she already had. "It was nice talking with you."

"The king doesn't seem to be too happy with me for doing it." He watched as the king scowled at him.

"I'll have a talk with him." She looked up at the guard, "By the way, what's your name?"

"Simon, milady."

"Just Simon?" She teased.

Smiling he added, "No, it's Sir Simon Griswold II."

"So you've been knighted." She seemed impressed.

Beautiful Pretender

"Yes Princess." He scooted back and prepared to stand up, "The king and your friends are just about to come. I should return to my post."

"Come by and visit me soon, Sir Griswold. I really do think you'd like my handmaiden and she could use a nice man like you."

"I'll be sure to do so." He stood up and walked back to where the other guard was waiting.

Aram waited patiently as the boys dressed. Finally Edmond, Kendrick, Silas and Eustace made they're way back to where he patiently waited. "It's about time." Aram yawned lazily.

"You wouldn't be saying that if you came with us." Silas scolded him. "One of these days we will dump you in the lake with the rest of us."

"Whatever." Aram dismissed his comment.

"We were thinking about snagging the swords off of Kendrick's guards." Edmond informed him.

This seemed to catch Aram's attention and he stood up so he could talk with them better. As he was doing so, he asked, "Do you really think they'll let us?"

Kendrick answered the question. "If I order them to, they'll have to."

"What will you do with them once you have them?" Aram asked.

"Silas and I thought we'd entertain Ken with a duel." Edmond answered.

"My cousin tells me that Silas is quite skilled with the sword and I thought it would be fun to watch them." Kendrick smiled.

"It is rather entertaining but I'm not sure how wise it is to do this without armor. They usually dual only with wooden swords and they also wear padding. Your guards' swords are the real thing. Even in a tournament the blades are dulled to help prevent injury, your guards are sharpened with the intent to kill if need be." Aram reminded them.

"True." Edmond agreed, "However, we'll make sure that we're careful. We won't be competing for points. We just want to swing the blades a little. I'd like Ken to see your skills as well." He told Aram.

"Aram's skilled with the sword?" Kendrick seemed surprised.

"Very skilled, though a two handed sword can be a little more then he can handle. However, your guards' swords look like they'll be fine for dueling with." Edmond smiled.

"This does sound rather interesting." Kendrick looked at Aram.

165

"You never cease to surprise me."

"Glad to be of service." Aram bowed with a smile. "Shall we?" He placed his hand on Kendrick's back and they walked over to where his guards stood. It took some convincing but they finally talked them out of their swords and soon the rest of their friends gathered around to watch Edmond and Silas compete. Kendrick's guards hovered closely near him, should they need to protect him. They weren't too concerned about one of the boys intentionally hurting him but if one should lose his sword or get too near the king, they wanted to be sure they could protect him in time.

Kendrick was delighted to see that Edmond wasn't exaggerating his praise when it came to his friend's ability's with the sword. He quite enjoyed this heated match between two very skilled swordsmen. He glanced up at his guards, even though they were guarding him, he could tell that they were impressed with the skills to the two young men who were battling each other had. It was obvious that Edmond and Silas were having fun but they were also giving it their all to make this a great show of their exceptional talents.

After a rather long duel, Silas finally held up his sword in defeat. "I'm done." He smiled as he panted hard from the physical exhaustion that was claiming him.

"Nice match." Edmond congratulated his friend and then he looked over to Aram. "Ready?"

"Yep." Aram grinned and then he stood up and walked over to Silas so he could take his sword.

"I have him all prepped for you." Silas grinned. "Give him hell for me."

"You bet." Aram gently hit his friend's shoulder before gripped the sword's handle with both of his hands. Then he got into his stance that indicated he was ready to fight anytime Edmond was.

Edmond was panting hard from his battle with Silas but he still had a lot of fire left in him. At least the competition would be more evenly matched for Aram since he wasn't as strong or as skilled as Edmond. By fighting Silas first, Edmond lost much of his strength and vigor which made Aram's skill level a little more challenging. However, it didn't mean that Aram couldn't give him a good fight, for the kid was pretty skilled himself and also had a lot of stamina. "Ready?" Edmond asked Aram.

"Anytime you are." Aram watched as Edmond raised his sword. Aram was the first to charge and soon they were in a heated battle. Their swords clashed noisily off of one another as they dueled. Aram fought with everything he had, proving to be a worthy opponent. Kendrick was amazed at how skilled Arabella was. He never dreamed that a pretty girl like her was living such a life. As Arabella, she was very feminine and defined but as Aram she was a skilled 'warrior' and very boyish, as far as Kendrick was concerned. It was obvious that she wasn't afraid of much and that she really did love to have fun playing with these boys she hung around with. He couldn't help smiling as he watched her battle seriously with his nephew.

"Are you about ready to surrender yet?" Edmond asked laughing when he noticed that Aram was beginning to slow down.

"Dream on. I still have a lot of fight left in me." Aram grinned as he delivered another blow. "You must be tired, how about if you surrender instead?"

"Sorry but it won't happen. I have a reputation to uphold." They both laughed as they struck at each others swords again and again. Finally Aram had to admit defeat. As much as he had hoped to win, he just couldn't keep up with Edmond. The guards didn't hesitate to reclaim their swords from the two boys. "We should fish for our dinner." Edmond announced.

"Eh?" Kendrick asked in confusion.

"On days like today we usually fish from the lake for our food and dig up edible roots to eat with them. You'll really enjoy it." Aram assured him.

"Um…" He looked up at his guard Simon who only shrugged his shoulders in confusion. Finally Kendrick decided that he should give in and just do whatever they wanted to do. "Very well."

The rest of the day they played, went to the market to buy their dinners (the afternoon meal of fish and roots seemed to bother Kendrick so they decided to do something different for their evening meal. The meal was Edmond's treat and later on they just goofed around in town, the poorer side where Kendrick's identity was more likely to stay safe.) Most of the boys went home as night fell but Edmond, Aram and

Kendrick returned to that place by the lake, along with the two guards. This was after they stopped by Aram's 'home' (the physician's place) to gather the few things they would need for the night.

"You can't be serious." Kendrick said in shock as they walked to the lake. "We're sleeping outside?"

"Yep." Aram grinned. "There's nothing like sleeping out under the stars." He sighed.

"I'd have to agree." Edmond joined in. "The night can get a little cold but there's nothing like laying in the cool grass and looking up into the heaven's while the frogs and crickets sing you to sleep."

"I love listening to the wind rustle the leaves." Aram told Kendrick. "You must experience this, even if it's just this once."

"You make it sound like paradise." Kendrick told them.

"It practically is." Edmond agreed.

"Unless it rains on you." Aram's comment made them all laugh.

"I can see how that would spoil the mood." Kendrick reflected. "Do you think it will rain tonight?"

Edmond looked up and then answered, "I don't think so but you never know for sure."

"It'll be fine." Aram assured him. "That is unless the wolves come around." He couldn't help himself.

Edmond began laughing as Kendrick said nervously, "Would they really?"

"Maybe." Aram shrugged. "You never know anything for sure until it happens."

"Well, I'm not going to be afraid." Kendrick said with determination. "Besides, I have my guards to watch over me should anything happen."

Once they came to the tree, Edmond and Aram laid out the few pieces of bedding they brought with them and tied the food sack up in the tree so the animals of the wild would stay out of it. Then they all laid down and looked up to the stars through the tree's shelter of leaves. "This really is nice." Kendrick agreed after he took some time to take in the sights, sounds and fragrances around him. "It's almost as if I have stepped into an entirely different world."

"I'm glad you like it." Aram looked over at Kendrick. "I really wanted you to have a day like this, even if it was just this one time."

Beautiful Pretender

She could see Kendrick's smile, even though it was getting fairly dark.

"Thank you. I'll never forget this day for as long as I live. I just hope that maybe I can have more days like this with you."

"You're embarrassing me, sire." Aram laughed softly.

"What about me?" Edmond teased.

"Of course you too." Aram was still laughing.

"Of course." Kendrick agreed. "If I had known earlier that spending time with my nephew could be this much fun, I would have done it long ago. "Perhaps you would consider visiting me in the palace more often."

"I would like that uncle." Edmond said proudly. They continued to chat for a while longer but soon the exhaustion of the day caught up with them and they all fell asleep.

The next morning, Kendrick was the first one to wake up. He smiled when he realized that Arabella was holding him to her. Her breathing was even and soft as she slept. He snuggled his head closer into her bound chest and instinctively her arms wrapped tighter around him. 'I could easily get use to this.' He thought silently and at that moment he realized that he didn't want Eric to have her. He wanted her to stay by his side for the rest of his life. Not only was Arabella beautiful, but she also helped him learn how to enjoy his life. He knew if he had her by his side that she would bring joy to all of his days. It seemed nothing ever soured her mood and though she might have a bit of a temper, she easily snapped out of it with a smile.

He could tell that she was honest with her feelings too. She was the first woman he met that didn't try to cater to his every whim just to gain his favor. Arabella took the initiative and she seemed to understand what it would take to make him happy, without even asking. Even now she didn't hold back on showing him attention and she seemed to understand his feelings even better then he did himself.

Right there and then he decided that it was time to make his decision concerning her future. He planned to make arrangements to visit her parents, upon her father's return, to inform them that he truly did want Arabella for his wife. His love for her was certain and so was his decision. Before now he had been wavering because of his age, for the most part but even that didn't seem to matter anymore. All that mattered was that he had to have her.

When Arabella woke up she was slightly surprised to find Kendrick snuggled up into her, in fact his head was lying quite contently on her bound chest. She could feel her cheeks growing warm with embarrassment but she had yet to release him from her embrace. She looked over to where his guards were, however only Simon was awake and the scene seemed to amuse him. Then she turned her head just enough so she could see if Edmond had woke up, he was currently lying on the other side of her with his back to her. 'I can't believe how pathetic I am.' She scolded herself. Unfortunately if someone was sleeping close to her, she had a bad habit of latching onto them. Apparently Kendrick was the victim of her latest 'assault'. However he seemed to be enjoying himself so she decided not to worry about it. Arabella brought her lips down to kiss the top of his head as he slept and her hand that had been lying on his back holding him to her, she moved up to his shoulder.

Arabella wasn't sure if Kendrick was even aware of the fact that she was holding him like this but the way he moaned when she tried to move away, indicated that he wasn't willing to give up her warmth and comfort to the cold harsh morning. Breathing in a sigh of defeat, she looked up to the heavens. The first of the morning birds were out flying and singing. Every now and then one would land looking for its morning meal before taking off again to the freedom of the morning sky. There were very few clouds that littered it and as far as she could tell it was going to be a rather nice day.

She heard Edmond begin to stir and then he rolled over towards her. "Are you up?" Aram whispered in his boyish voice.

"Not yet." Edmond yawned and scooted closer to him. "It's colder then I thought it would be this morning."

"Ah…" Aram said in surprise as Edmond grabbed onto him so they could share body heat. "What are you doing?"

"Getting warm." His sleepy voice said. His hand reached over and he felt that Kendrick was on the other side. "It seems he beat me to it." He laughed softly.

"You two are hopeless." Aram moaned miserably.

"That's what you get for sleeping in the middle." He brought his hand

Beautiful Pretender

up and laid it on Aram's chest. "Does it feel awkward to be sandwiched between two guys like this?" He laughed.

Arabella was nearly dying with embarrassment because, yet again, Edmond was laying his hand on the unknown forbidden area. Not only that, but Kendrick's face was near the other one. "Even if I was a girl this would be too weird." He scolded. "Get off."

"No, it's too cold." He complained and brought his body up against her back.

"Damn it!" She nearly yelled. Her voice aroused Kendrick from his sleep and he rolled partly away from her.

"Did you say something?" He asked in a sleepy voice.

"It's time to get up." Aram was quick to change the topic and he could feel Edmond roll away from him as well. Finally, Aram was able to sit up. He choose to ignore the cold air and quickly got out of the make shift bed. 'Never again.' He promised himself. Being sandwiched between to guys like that was anything but fun. He was so embarrassed that he thought he would die.

Kendrick yawned lazily as his guard approached. "We should consider returning to the palace, your majesty." Simon suggested.

"Yes, perhaps you're right." Kendrick sat up and rubbed his eyes before looking over to Aram and Edmond. "Thanks for inviting me to spend this time with you."

"Anytime, your majesty." Edmond smiled and Aram agreed with a nod of his head and a smile. "I'm glad we could have this chance to get to know each other better."

"Indeed, milord." Aram told Kendrick. "Perhaps we can find some more time to go out together in the near future."

"I'll look forward to it." Kendrick allowed Simon to help him to his feet. "Farewell."

"Farewell, sire." They said in unison.

Chapter 9

"Ida, where have you been?" Jocelyn said in a near frenzy when Ida finally got back home from the market.

"I was running an errand on behalf of your daughter, milady." She replied with a question as to the urgency that Jocelyn was displaying. "Is something wrong?"

"Yes! Kendrick will be here any moment to visit Arabella and she needs your help to prepare for him."

'Figures'. Ida complained to herself. The one day she has to go and run errands is the one day the king decides to visit. The number of tasks before her now seemed overwhelming. Had she known sooner, not only would she have put off the errand to the market, but she also would have woke up hours earlier then she did to start preparing things. She knew he wouldn't see most of her efforts, but they still mattered to her none the less. "Yes milady, I will do it now." She answered and then immediately ran upstairs to help Arabella.

"Did you see him?" Arabella asked excitedly.

"I did but now it is not time for your foolishness. The king will be here anytime and we have to make sure you're presentable." Ida's assigned task was to go to the market to meet with Edmond. His mother had been ill and he had to stay home and help take care of her the last two nights, so he and Arabella communicated with each other through Ida. The two hadn't 'seen' each other since the night before the outing with Kendrick. "Here." She handed Arabella the gift that Edmond had promised along with a note. "He said he really wanted to give it you himself but he couldn't wait any longer. He said you should wear it tonight when he comes."

172

Arabella opened the velvet drawstring bag. Inside was a white mask that was trimmed in silver and decorated with white feathers. It had a lace overlay and the inside was covered in silk. "How lovely." She grinned and ran to the mirror so she could hold it up to her face to see how it looked. "Oh Ida, this is my most beautiful mask yet."

"Come on child, we don't have time for this. The king will be here any moment."

"Just hold on for a moment, I want to read Edmond's message first." She ignored Ida's unspoken protest and opened the note to read it.

"My Dearest Little Mousy… (He was referring to that day he visited and used the excuse of seeing a little mouse, when she was peeking down at him from the top of the stairway. This was when she had supposedly twisted her ankle. He used this as an excuse so he could go up and visit her.)

"I long for the day when you hide from me no more. However, until that time comes I will adore you from **afar**. Here is the mask that I had promised you and I look forward to seeing you wear it for me. I grieve that I was unable to bring it to you in person but I promise that I will come back to you soon, my dearest love. Your gift was the most beautiful that I have ever received. The embroidery on the handkerchief was exquisite and I will treasure it always, next to my heart. Until we meet again, ado my beautiful Little Mousy and be well. With all of my undying love, I will be your faithful *Prince of the Night*, Lord Edmond Wallace."

"Oh." Arabella squealed joyfully and spun in a circle. "Isn't he so romantic?" She asked Ida. She knew that he understood the song she had sung at his mother's home the night of the masked ball, the song called *The Prince of the Night*. It was her silent proclamation of love to him, a name which seemed fitting to him.

"Indeed milady." Ida said somewhat short tempered. "Now please, put those things away and let me help you prepare for the king's arrival."

"Oh, alright. I do hope that Simon will be assigned to come with him. I really want him to meet you." She carefully placed the mask down on the table below the mirror. After taking another second to look at it, she then did as Ida asked and allowed her handmaiden to help get her ready.

JM Howard

"What was that milady?" Ida asked as she began rummaging through Arabella's wardrobe, looking for a suitable outfit. So far Ida had only managed to comb out her mistress's hair.

"Nothing, I was just thinking out loud." She told her and then said, "Why do I have to fret over my looks so much? Do you really think he cares all that much about what I look like? What I have on should be suitable enough, do you not agree? After seeing me dressed like a boy, I'm sure he'd be satisfied with what I have on right now."

"You're mother cares. She would whip me raw if I allowed you to go before the king in your everyday clothing. You must dress like a queen or she won't be happy."

"Well I don't care. I have no need to impress him and my attire is suitable enough." She walked past Ida and quickly left the room.

Ida was about ready to lose her temper, "Please mistress..." She went after her but Arabella was too quick and was soon no where to be found. Finally she gave up looking for Arabella and instead she went in search of her mother. When she located her she bowed humbly and said, "I'm sorry Baroness but milady has chosen not to allow me to assist her in changing into something suitable for the king's visit."

"Where is she?" The Baroness asked with some anger.

"I honestly don't know, milady. I'm truly sorry for my incompetence." Ida was hoping for understanding for she didn't want to experience the Baroness's wrath. The Baroness was a good woman, but if you defied her, she could be rather scary to be around.

"What has gotten into that girl lately?" Jocelyn sighed.

"Mam..." One of the servants came into the 'visitor's room'.

"Yes."

"His Majesty the king has just arrived."

"Thank you." Then to Ida, "Let us go and greet him Ida. Obviously Arabella has left some positive impression on him or he wouldn't be coming today."

"Yes mam." They walked together to the entryway and then outside. What met their eyes was unexpected.

There, near the carriage, Arabella was talking animatedly with Kendrick and they were both laughing. "Oh!" Arabella said as she looked their way, "Hello mother!"

Both Jocelyn and Ida bowed when the king turned to look at them.

174

Beautiful Pretender

"Majesty." Jocelyn said in a formal manner.

"Come Kendrick, let's go." Arabella smiled and nearly dragged him away with her.

"Where are you taking me?" He asked confused as he laughed nervously.

"It's a secret but it will be fun." She turned and looked at the men who were following them. "Can't you call the dogs off so we can be alone for a change?"

"I suppose so." He looked back at his guards, "Stay here."

"But your majesty…" One tried to protest.

"Just do as I say. That's an order."

"Yes sire." They stopped their pursuit.

"Now what?" Kendrick asked her.

"I'm going to take you to a secret place but you have to promise not to tell anyone about it."

"Alright but what are we doing?"

"We're going to play." She grinned.

"Play?"

"Yep. You look like you need to have some fun today. So I have decided that this is my self appointed duty. I will spare you from another one of my mother's dreadfully boring visits and we'll just go and have fun."

"Oh, I see?" He held on tighter to her hand. "You really do like to play a lot, don't you?" He laughed.

"When we're together, I want our time to be enjoyable." She grinned and continued to hold onto his hand as she quickened her pace. Soon they came to an area that had a pool of water and on one tree nearby was a swing that was hanging from it. It was located in a small opening in the forest where wild flowers of different colors and varieties grew in the tall grasses.

Kendrick stood for a moment to take the sight in. "It's really pretty here."

"Isn't it?" She agreed. "Father put up that swing for me. Come on, try it out." She pulled him over to it. "Get on."

"I couldn't possibly…"

"Please cousin, would you stop being a king and just act like a boy your age?"

175

"Alright you win." He held up his hands laughing and then walked over and sat down on the swing. Arabella sometimes reminded him of another girl he knew years ago named Jasmine. She too had encouraged him to act his age and play with her. He wondered what possessed these girls to bring him down off his throne and play with them like a commoner. Worse yet, he hated to admit it, but he loved the attention from them, even more then he loved the actual playing part. Sure he was having fun but girl's like Arabella and Jasmine seemed to make his rather dull life enjoyable. He wondered whatever happened to the little girl he knew when he was twelve. Jasmine seemed like a distant memory now.

"Hold on tight." Arabella told him and she grabbed the wooden seat of the swing and pushed him as hard as she could.

"Ah!" Kendrick said in fright as it took off fairly high up into the air. He hadn't truly realized just how strong she was.

"Just hold on silly." She laughed.

"Alright." He felt her push his lower back to help keep up the swing's momentum. "Is there suppose to be something else to this, cousin?"

"Just have fun, Kendrick." She laughed.

"Shouldn't I be the one pushing you though?" He looked back at her and saw her sweet smile.

"You can if you want to."

"How do I stop this thing?"

"Just put your feet down and use them to stop yourself." He did as she said and then they switched so he could push her. However he didn't push her very high because he wanted to talk to her.

"Arabella?"

"Yes." Her voice always sounded so sweet when she talked and he had to admit that he was attracted to her Eldardeshian accent. The only thing Kendrick could compare it to, was his favorite treat of honey on sweet bread, especially when it had rose petals on it.

"Do you know why I'm here today?"

"I have a pretty good idea." She looked back at him and smiled. "You're beginning your courtship, right?"

"Yes. I have decided that you are my choice for a wife and I would be honored if you will be the one that will sit beside me on the throne

Beautiful Pretender

as my queen. I just need to discuss the terms with your father before making it official."

"I'm glad."

"Why? That is, if you don't mind my asking."

"Partially it is because I was dreading the thought of havening to marry Eric. We pretty much grew up together and I didn't like the anger and resentment that was in his eyes and personality. He frightened me. Also, I really enjoy spending time with you. I know you're a king and we will have to be serious most of the time, but I hope that we will have more days like today, days that are spent simply enjoying one another's company with no royal duties weighing us down."

"Eric behaves the way he does because he resents that father didn't make him the heir to the Arminian throne, not that he had a birth right to it since I am the oldest. I was hoping he would be happy with just Eldardesh, but apparently he wants both kingdoms for himself. He feels that they both should belong to him."

"Do you think he will try to take you're country by force?"

"Maybe, but I don't want to think about that right now. You said it yourself that right now I'm not a king but a boy."

She started laughing, "Oh yeah, sorry." She pumped her legs to make the swing go higher. Once she was finished she got off and started picking a small bouquet of wild flowers for her mother. "Do you really want to get married this soon, Kendrick?"

"What do you mean?"

"You're still fairly young. I mean, I understand why you are doing it but is it really what you want?"

"What I want?" He pondered the idea for a moment. "Actually I'm not sure what I want. I'm always told what to do and where to go. People ask for my decisions concerning the affairs of the kingdom and the people who live in it… honestly that is all I know."

"Haven't you ever just wanted something just because you wanted it or wanted to do it?"

"Only a few times as a child. Once my father died, I haven't had time to know if there was anything for my heart to desire."

"What about me?"

"What do you mean?"

"Do you desire me or are you just marrying me because your

advisors told you to?"

"Oh." He thought for a moment. "What do you mean by desire you? I mean I do know that I like being with you and that I would like us to always be together but I'm not sure what you mean by desire."

She stopped picking flowers to look up at him and then she smiled. "Do you want me to show you?"

"Um... alright." He watched as she walked closer to him.

"Have your advisors told you what husbands and wives do?"

"Well they get married and then in our case you would provide heirs to the throne."

"No, I mean what they do together." She placed her hands on his shoulders. "They desire one another and love one another." She leaned forward and kissed him gently on the lips. "Do you understand?"

Kendrick was blushing from ear to ear. "Um, I'm not sure."

Arabella laughed softly, "If you marry me, I want you to love me and desire me. If you can do this then I will do the same for you." She dropped her bouquet of flowers and then wrapped her arms around him, lowering her face to his. She kissed him again but with a little more passion.

Kendrick could only stand there with his hands at his sides. Finally between her kisses he spoke, "Arabella?"

"Yes." She backed off and smiled down at him.

"Do you love me?"

"I admire you with all my heart but I still don't really know you that well. Love is something that can happen suddenly with one person and with other people it comes with time." It was the best she could do to answer.

"Have you ever loved someone?"

A smile crept across her face, "I'll be honest with you, Kendrick. I want there to be no secrets between us if we are to spend the rest of our lives together as husband and wife. Yes, I have loved another and I still love him very much. However, even though there is a mutual love, he knows that I can never be his because I will soon belong to you."

"Will you be able to love me and only me even though you love another right now?"

"I will do all I can to do so, milord." She allowed her hands to drop from his shoulders. "Kendrick, you'll have to have faith in me. Once

Beautiful Pretender

my father makes our engagement official, I will willingly disregard my former love and focus my eyes only on you." She knew this would be nearly impossible to do but she knew it was what she would have to do when she chose to allow herself to love Edmond. He too knew this day would come and that she would have to leave his side for the sake of the king she was destined to spend her life with. "The man I love right now is also going to have to marry someone of his parents choosing soon, so we are on mutual ground. We understood the consequences of our actions and we are willing to part when the time comes."

Kendrick reached forward for her hand. "Thank you for bringing me here and doing everything you have done with me. It was nice to be able to spend time with you and get to know you. I would have never understood how wonderful you were if you hadn't come into my life the way you did." The coloring of his cheeks brightened again as he asked, "May I kiss you again?"

"Do you like kissing me?"

"Yeah. I've never done something like this before and I like the way it makes me feel."

She laughed softly and bent down to kiss him. Even though she acted carefree about it, deep inside she was doing this to try and dissolve the love that her heart felt for Edmond. By doing this she hoped that it would help her to transfer her love to Kendrick who would soon be her betrothed. He brought his arms about her and held her to him.

Jocelyn watched her daughter and Kendrick from the safety of the forest where she hid behind a tree. She couldn't help smiling at the affection her daughter was raining down on Kendrick. "I'm so glad she is trying. It seems this affectionate way of hers is pleasing to the king." She had been worried that her daughter's manners would turn him off but it had the opposite effect. Apparently her daughter's insistence on making him behave more like a child and also her carefree affection towards him were the very things that the young king needed and desired.

Kendrick looked up at Arabella after they had finished kissing. "I'm not completely sure what love is Arabella, but if it means you want to live the rest of your life with someone, then it is the closest thing to love that I can think of. Not only that but I really like being with you like this, like grownups."

"Is that how you think of me, Kendrick, as a grown woman that you feel this way for?"

"Yes Arabella. I really like you a lot and I want to spend the rest of my life with you by my side. I know together we can make a great family and build a great kingdom as well. Besides…I really like kissing you too."

She laughed merrily. "Alright, time to cool off soldier."

"Huh?" He asked and suddenly she picked him up in her arms and carried him towards the pond that was near by. "What are you doing, Arabella?" He asked in a frightened voice.

"You'll see." She laughed and began walking into the small pond.

"Arabella!" He yelled, "Don't you dare drop me in this."

"I don't plan on dropping you, kiddo, only soaking you through."

"Hey!" His feet were in now, "Arabella!" He grabbed tightly to her neck as they both went in further. His feet began to kick madly. "Stop, that's an order from your king."

"I thought you were just a boy right now." She laughed disregarding his order.

"No fair, put me down." He demanded. Again he was surprised at her strength.

"Alright." She released him and he dropped into the water but it wasn't long before he was back on his feet. "I'll get you for that." He laughed and began splashing water at her and she returned it.

Two of the king's guards came running from the forest, "Majesty!" They yelled terrified as they made their way to him. "We're coming just hold on…"

Kendrick stopped for a moment and looked at the two guards and then he whispered to Arabella, "Should we soak them too?"

"Yes, let's." She laughed. Once the two guards were in the water near them, Arabella and Kendrick simultaneously attacked, by jumping on them and trying to sink them. Finally they ended up splashing water on them until the two bewildered guards were thoroughly soaked.

Kendrick was laughing hysterically, "That's what you get when you try to stop me from having fun with the woman I love."

"Yes sire." They said humbly and walked out of the water though they continued to stay close by. Arabella was slightly disappointed when Kendrick first came because Simon wasn't with him, but now she was glad that he didn't come. If he had she wouldn't have brought Kendrick there to play but instead she would have been trying to play 'matchmaker' with Simon and Ida.

"This was fun, Arabella, thank you." Kendrick smiled warmly at her.

"Anytime, your majesty. I just thought you looked like you needed to have some fun verses sitting through one of my mother's boring retelling of how wonderful our family is and how much she admires you...." She sighed. "I really do get tired of that stuff."

Kendrick changed the subject. "Did you and Eric use to play like this?" They walked out of the water together.

"Yes, but without the kissing part." She giggled. "I would never want to kiss him."

"I would hope not." He smiled up at her. "I will come again when your father returns to ask for your hand in marriage."

"I'm honored sire." She bowed humbly.

"Thank you for seeing me and not just my throne. You don't know how much it means to me."

"I will look forward to your next visit." She leaned down and kissed him one more time. "Farewell until then, dear cousin."

"As I wish for you as well, cousin." He allowed his guards to escort him back to the carriage and she followed behind.

Arabella and her mother waited to go indoors until they saw him off as properly as possible and then her mother spoke. "You could lose your head for such behavior, child."

"If Kendrick is going to marry me then he must accept me on my terms."

"That is not how it is done. You must accept him on his terms."

"I plan to. Mostly today I just wanted to see how he would react to a few things and I got my answers."

"You must like playing dangerous games. First this Aram nonsense and now treating the king like a child and making love to him in public."

"We were only kissing and I'd hardly call where we were 'public'. I just wanted him to understand what being married meant."

"Are you trying to turn him away?"

"No, just wake him up to reality. I wanted to make sure he knew what to expect."

"That's hardly a job for a young maiden to be performing."

"Who better to teach him then his future wife?" She countered. "I would prefer it was I who taught him then some other woman."

"I suppose you have a point." She sighed. "Come on and change before you catch your death."

"Yes mother."

Chapter 10

"Father!" Arabella smiled when she came down to her morning meal and discovered that her father was sitting there next to her mother. "When did you get home?" She laughed as she ran to sit on his lap.

"Goodness child, such behavior." Her mother scolded.

"Don't scold her mother." He laughed. "I don't mind coming home to a reception as grand as this." He kissed his daughter and held her tightly to him. "You're unusually energetic this morning."

"I missed you so much." She grinned as she clung to him as she inhaled his familiar scent of earth, pine and tobacco. "Never go so far from me again for so long. It was nearly unbearable."

"I'm not sure I can make such a promise but I will always be with you right here." He pointed to her heart. "So tell me of everything that happened while I was away."

"Nothing much really."

"Arabella, that's not true." Her mother corrected her and decided to talk on her daughter's behalf. "It seems our dear King Kendrick has given Arabella his favor and plans to ask for her hand in marriage. I believe Arabella is the best thing that could have happened to him. You should just see the two of them together, a match made in heaven." She grinned.

"I see." He said more seriously. "King Eric wanted me to inform you that he has missed you very much over these last several years and he also sends you his best."

"Will you have to go back there any time soon?" Jocelyn asked.

"It depends. If he summons me, I will go."

"I see." She finished the last of her melon and then excused herself from the table.

Aldrich could see the confusion in his daughter's eyes and he decided to change the subject. "I brought gifts back for you."

"Really?" That seemed to snap her out of her daze. "Where are they?"

"Come with me and I'll show you." He smiled and helped her off his lap. He then took her hand and led her outside. "There." A grin consumed his face as he pointed to an elaborately decorated carriage.

"The carriage?" She asked in surprise.

"That and what's in it."

"But that is much too fancy for an everyday carriage."

"It's a carriage made for a queen." He put his hand on her shoulder and squeezed lightly.

"Oh. I guess that makes sense since I am to marry a king." She slowly walked towards it and then ran her hand over some of the gold trimming that lay on the painted white carriage. "It's so beautiful." The wood was as smooth as silk and there lay upon it golden daisies and vines that surrounded the outer trim of the carriage. Each of the two windows on the side and the window of the door boasted a golden daisy as well. Under each window there was a framed golden feather and framed on the door a raised golden scroll with the king's crown craved into it. Center in the crown was a large jewel of red in a diamond shape. The queen's crown adorned the roof, engulfed by a fully opened golden rose.

"Open it up and look inside."

"Alright." She took the handle of the door and slowly opened it. There inside, were dozens of packages piled up. "What is all of this?"

"Clothing, jewelry and every other finery a queen would need to start off her new life." He walked up and stood beside her. "This carriage will take you to your future husband someday soon."

"It's just too much." She said softly.

"I hear that Kendrick is coming to speak with me today."

"He said he would come as soon as you came home." She reached in and touched the ribbon of one of the packages.

"Then perhaps we should go and prepare for his visit." He reached in and picked up a couple of the packages. "Wear these. I especially picked them out for this occasion."

Arabella took the packages from him. "How did you know he

would be coming?"

"Just call it a father's intuition." A gentle reassuring smile was his way of setting her mind at ease. He watched as she began to walk back to the house. "Arabella?" He suddenly called out. "You know that I love you more then anything in this world, right?"

"Yes father." She smiled.

"Will you trust my decisions concerning your future?"

"Yes father." She thought he was referring to accepting Kendrick's offer. Little did she know the control that King Eric had over him, nor the plans that Eric had set into motion in order to destroy his brother.

Ida helped Arabella to put on the delicate dress that her father had given to her to wear. It was a white slender dress that was sleeveless with a low bodice that tied in the front. The outer fabrics were light and airy, much like clouds. The outer fabrics on the skirt were layered to give it a slightly puffy look. "I feel like I'm getting married." She said softly as she looked at her reflection in the mirror. Her hair was partially piled on her head, though the sides were allowed to hang. Little golden spirals with diamond accents were carefully placed on the hair that was pinned up. Gold and diamonds hung from her ears and circled her neck and wrists. She lifted her skirt to see the soft white shoes that adorned her feet over her white stockings.

"You look like an angel." Ida smiled. "All you need now is a set of wings." She lifted up the last accessory to Arabella's collection, a tiara that coordinated with the other jewelry she wore. Carefully she placed it on her mistress's head. "At least you have your halo."

Arabella couldn't believe the expense her father went to in order to give her this. "It is just too much, Ida. Why is he doing this?"

"Just be happy he did." Ida smiled and then she turned when she heard a noise from outside the house. She walked over and looked out the window. "The king is here."

"Already?"

"I would assume so. It looks like his carriage."

"Then I had better go down to greet him." Arabella said and lifted her skirts slightly so she could walk without dragging them on the ground.

Ida quickly made her way to the door to open it for Arabella. "I'll stay here and wait for you, if that is alright."

"Yes, of course." Arabella smiled. "Oh… Ida?"

"Yes."

"Let me have this one last night with Edmond alone so I can say goodbye to him."

"Yes miss. Just make sure it doesn't last all night." As true to her word, the last few nights she had not said anything more about the time the two spent together and she also wasn't disappointed in their behavior. They stayed true to their word and kept their love innocent. It was actually a very romantic love affair, the things they would say to each other and the way they were with each other made Ida wish that she too had a love of her own. There was no doubt in Ida's mind that the two of them were in deeply in love with one another and it almost made her sad to think that they went into this knowing that they could never stay be each others side.

One thing that stuck in her mind was something that Arabella had told Edmond. She knew it was just an excuse Arabella used to keep her face hidden from him but there was also some sound logic to it. He had asked her why she would never allow him to see her face. The answer was one that Ida hadn't expected.

Arabella's answer was basically, "It is best that I don't, Edmond for I don't want you to be seeing my face when you are with your wife. It could do no good for you or for her." To Ida the answer was probably the most mature thing that ever came out of her mistress's mouth. Arabella was still very immature when it came to most things but every now and then she would surprise Ida with such sound logic and foresight.

"Welcome to our home, your majesty." Baron Aldrich said as he and his family bowed before Kendrick.

"You may rise, cousin." Kendrick smiled and then he walked over to Arabella and took her hand and brought it up to his lips so he could kiss it. "You look lovely today, princess."

"Thank you, sire." She smiled in return. The Baron led the way to the family's 'visiting room' and offered Kendrick their best seat.

"How was your journey, Baron?" The king asked.

"Too long for my liking, your majesty. However the weather

cooperated in our favor for the most part, so it went well enough." He took the goblet of wine that the servant had poured for him, after pouring and serving one to the king first.

"Is my brother doing well?"

"Quite well, sire. His wife is expecting their first child within the next couple of months. Naturally this child won't be his first choice as an heir because his wife is not his queen."

"Naturally." Kendrick sipped from his cup. "I assume you know why I am here today."

"I am."

"I am proposing an agreement for marriage to your daughter. She will sit by my side as queen of Arminia and her first born son will be the heir to my throne." He looked Aldrich straight in the eye. "Cousin, I want you to know that I am not just proposing out of duty. I love Arabella very much and I promise I will be a good husband to her in everyway possible."

Aldrich cleared his throat before speaking. "I am truly honored that you found such favor in my daughter your majesty." He looked to a servant and nodded. The man immediately came over with a rolled up parchment that sat on a silver tray. "Thank you." He told the man when he came. "Please hand this to his majesty."

"Yes milord." The servant answered and did as bidden.

Kendrick took the parchment and carefully opened it. For a few moments he read what had been written inside and then he carefully rolled it back up again and placed it back onto the tray. His expression remained emotionless. "I see." He took a slow deep breath and then looked at Arabella. "Do you know what that parchment contains, Arabella?"

"I'm afraid I do not know at all, your majesty." He knew she was being honest by the look in her eyes.

"It appears that your father has already made an understanding with my brother, the King of Eldardesh, concerning your future."

"What!" She said in utter shock and looked over to her father. "No, this can't be true! Why didn't you say something sooner?"

"I'm sorry Arabella but I have decided that King Eric should be your rightful husband. He needs you and he has loved you for a very long time. I believe he will make the most suitable husband for you."

"No father. I don't want to marry him." She pleaded.

"I'm sorry daughter, but it is a contract and I must abide by it."

"He's right Arabella." Kendrick said as evenly as he could. "Since this matter is closed, I will take my leave now." He stood up and started to leave the room.

"I'll walk out with you." Arabella got up quickly and stood by his side.

"Alright." Kendrick agreed and together they walked out without giving her parents the chance to properly see him off.

Once the two were out of the room Jocelyn looked over at her husband. "Why did you have to do that in such an underhanded manner? It was nothing short of cruel to not only Kendrick, but to your daughter and me as well."

"I'm just following orders. You had best stay out of this wife if you know what is good for you. I feel bad that you and Arabella had to be hurt in this but I am first loyal to my king and I will do anything he asks of me." He warned her.

"And what about what is good for Arabella? You never even gave Kendrick a chance and you knew I wanted her to marry him over Eric." She was nearly in tears.

"King Eric is the only king I will acknowledge. He is the true king of not only Eldardesh but also of Arminia. This arrangement was not only for our daughter's hand but also to break down Kendrick's countenance. If you even dare to breathe a word of this to anyone, I will personally take you before Eric to answer for it, is that clear?"

"So you have always planned on fully betraying Kendrick?"

"I'm sending you and Arabella to Eldardesh this evening. I'll send your things at a later time when I'm finished here."

"You wouldn't dare." She stood up and placed her hands on her hips. "Not only are you betraying the Arminian king but you also are betraying your family. Arabella wanted to marry Kendrick and he loves her. Eric already has a wife and I'm sure many concubines. Most likely he will take on more wives as well. Why give him our only daughter? At least Kendrick respects her enough to decide to only marry her. Everyone knows he only plans on taking one wife."

Aldrich slammed his hands on the arms of his chair and then stood up. "I told you to stay out of this, wife! My decision has been made

Beautiful Pretender

and I'm not going to back down. Now go and prepare to leave."

Jocelyn wanted to say more but she held her tongue. "Fine!" She turned and left the room crying.

Aldrich sat back down in his chair and sighed as he placed his hand to his forehead. "I'm so sorry." He whispered. This wasn't how he wanted it to happen but orders were orders and he had to follow them to the letter.

"Kendrick, I am so sorry." Arabella said through her tears. "I honestly didn't know."

"I know." He said quietly. "I'm sorry that he is forcing you to marry Eric."

"Isn't there anything that you can do to stop this? Please don't let this happen. I wanted to be your wife not Eric's."

"I'm afraid not. If I did, Eric would declare war without hesitation. I do love you Arabella but we simply can't afford to go to war right now. We've only just declared peace with one of our neighbors and we are still recovering from that war. We're also not on good terms with another neighboring country. If we went to war with Eldardesh our country couldn't possibly win and Eric knows that. He's just looking for a reason to attack."

"So I have no choice then." She said through her tears.

"I'm afraid not." He climbed up into his carriage after the attendant had opened the door. "I really had hoped to marry you. I just wanted you to know that."

"Thank you." She watched as the door was shut. Suddenly she ran up and stepped up on the step so she could see inside the open window.

"Milady you must step down." One of the king's guards told her.

"No!" She yelled back at him and then looked in at Kendrick. "I really do like you Kendrick. I'm so sorry about all of this. If I had known…"

"Don't be sorry." He did his best to smile at her. "I really enjoyed spending time with you. If anything, you gave me a chance to be a kid, even if it was for a short time. That is something I will never regret. Also…" He touched his lips with his fingertips, "you showed me what love is. You never hesitated to show it to me. I will remember this until the day I die."

"Kendrick...." She couldn't finish, one of his personal guards took hold of her and brought her down. When she looked to see who it was she saw that it was Simon.

"I'm sorry princess." He held her firmly until the carriage was well on its way. When it was a fair distance away, he released her and mounted his horse so he could follow. "Congratulations on your upcoming marriage." He told her before leaving.

Arabella dropped to her knees. "No." She cried softly. "How can this be happening to me?"

"Daughter..." Her father said gently as he made his way to her. "You told me you would trust my decisions concerning your future."

"Why are you making me marry someone I hate?" She cried. "You knew I wasn't fond of Eric."

"He loves you Arabella. When you're with him, he is a good person. You have a way of quieting the wild spirit that resides in him. Your child will be the one to inherit his throne so you needn't worry about his other wives and children. He will make you and your children first among them all." He tried his best to reason with her.

"I thought I was the most important person in your life? You said I was." She cried.

"I meant it."

"Then why are you making me do this?"

"It is the best thing for everyone involved. I'm sending you and your mother to Eldardesh tonight. I believe it would be best for you both to put Arminia behind you as soon as possible."

She turned and looked at him in surprise, "No! I won't go."

"Yes you will. Now go and prepare what you will need. I'll send your remaining belongings at a later time."

"Why are you being so hateful to me?" She cried.

"Go up to your room now and do as I say, child." He tried to keep his voice gentle and even.

Slowly she rose to her feet and she looked over at him. "You should have stayed in Eldardesh with your beloved king and left mother and me alone." Her voice was close to seething. "I will never forgive you for doing this, especially to Kendrick. He's a good king with a tender heart. Even though I don't love him right at the moment, I do admire

Beautiful Pretender

him very much and I was willing to give everything up to be his queen, even the man I that I dearly love."

"Man you love?" This was new to him. "Who is this man you love?"

"It doesn't really matter now does it? He and I both knew that we couldn't be together because we both faced arranged marriages. I knew that I might be able to let go of him when the time came if I had someone like Kendrick to help me forget about him... but now..." She broke out in uncontrollable tears and ran into the house.

Aldrich sighed and looked in the direction in which Kendrick's carriage had gone in. "I hope these sacrifices are worth it." He said softly to himself. "I just hope it really will make Eric a better king. It's all I know to do now. Everything we as his advisors have tried has failed thus far and this is the only other course of action left for us to take." Then in the direction Arabella once stood, he said softly, "I'm sorry my precious daughter but you're our last hope at giving Eldardesh a good king."

Arabella threw herself face down on her bed and wept. Ida was beside herself to know what to do. This was supposed to be a happy occasion yet her mistress was in the utmost distress. "Milady, what grieves you?"

"My life is over." She cried bitterly. "I have been betrayed and deceived by my own father."

"I don't understand."

"It's Eric! He's forcing me to marry King Eric."

"No." Ida gasped and put her hand to her mouth. "He never even indicated..." Her own tears began to fall. "My poor girl." She went over and laid down near Arabella and took her into her embrace. "What can I do to help sooth your tears my dearest princess?"

"Nothing. He's forcing us to leave tonight."

"Tonight?" She looked over at the door. "This can't be." She released Arabella and sat up. "Then there is no time. I can think of only one thing to do." She got up off the bed and went to the door. "I'll send someone up here to assist you, milady. There is something I must do before you leave." Arabella continued crying without answering. "Just don't leave until I get back milady. Promise me." Arabella only continued to cry in her uncontrolled grief and Ida knew she wouldn't get another word out of her for a while. So she quickly left the room for she couldn't afford to lose anymore time.

"Is Lord Wallace at home?" Ida asked frantically.

"One moment miss." The servant said in a low even tone.

"Please hurry, sir, this is an emergency."

"Yes miss." His tone never changed.

"Move!" She didn't have time to wait for this man to do as she asked so she shoved past him and ran into the house uninvited. "Lord Wallace!" She screamed. "Lord Edmond Wallace, please hurry and answer me." She looked frantically about her and soon she saw him at the top of the stairwell.

When he recognized Ida he ran down, "What? What's happening? Is she hurt?"

"No… yes… actually, what I'm trying to say is that her father turned down the marriage proposal made by our beloved King Kendrick and he is forcing her to leave this very night to meet King Eric to be his new bride. She is beside herself with grief and fear. You must come to her."

"What can I do? I can't force her to stay against her father's will?"

Ida grabbed the front of his shirt in both of her fists. "She needs you, you fool, are you unable to comprehend what it is that I'm trying to say to you? At least come and tell her farewell. Please… She had so hoped to see you one last time."

"Alright. I will go." He walked quickly with her out of the house and grabbed his cloak from the servant. "Tell my father I will be gone for a time."

"Yes sir." The man bowed and then handed him a fully loaded coin purse. This was a normal thing that was done when any of the family left to go somewhere.

"Come with me to the stables, Ida and I will fetch my horse. We'll get there quicker that way."

"Yes sir." She ran with him out of the house.

"Is she ready?" Baron Aldrich asked his wife.

"Nearly." She answered in a voice void of emotion. "I know she has

Beautiful Pretender

changed into suitable traveling clothes and her servants are preparing what she'll need during the journey.

"She will ride in the carriage that Eric sent for her. You will ride in ours behind hers." He tried to reach for her hand but she pulled it away.

"Don't you dare touch me." She warned him.

He sighed. "I have no choice but to obey my king, wife. You must understand that this is for the greater good."

"No. This is no good at all. You have been blinded by that selfish little spoiled brat of a king. He will be cruel to Arabella and break her heart but you don't seem to care about that, do you?"

"I do care about her very much…"

"Silence. I don't want to hear anymore of this foolishness. Once I am back in Eldardesh, I am going to go back to my father. Don't bother trying to see me for I won't give you an audience. If you don't reconsider this decision, you can consider our marriage finished. I will not live with someone as heartless as you."

"Jocelyn…" He couldn't believe what she was saying. "I can't disobey my king…"

"Then this is goodbye." She turned and went out the front entry door and headed straight for her carriage.

"Oh Jocelyn," He sighed miserably, "I just hope you will change your mind in time." His gaze took his line of view to the stairway that his daughter had yet to descend. "I wonder what is taking her so long." He looked over to one of the female servants. "Go see if Arabella is ready to leave yet and then report back to me."

"Yes sir." She answered and obeyed him immediately. Only moments later she reappeared at the top of the stairs. "Sir, she's gone and so is her handmaiden."

"What do you mean she's gone?" He asked in surprise.

"She's not in her quarters."

"Well look around and find her. She hasn't come down so she must be up there somewhere."

"Yes sir, unless she took the stairway that the servants use."

"What are you talking about…" He heard a loud commotion outside the house and he ran to the front entry. When he looked out he could see the carriage that Eric had sent for Arabella's use, driving away at its fastest speed. "What the…" He looked over to the carriage that was meant for his wife and saw her standing there with a grin on her face. "What on earth is going on here, wife?"

"Don't ask me, ask your daughter." She countered with a smirk.

"Well where is she?" He watched as she pointed towards the carriage disappearing in the distance. Then with one last smirk of enjoyment she got into her own carriage. He looked over to where the bewildered driver stood, the one who was suppose to be driving his daughter's carriage. "What is going on?" He asked him.

"She stole it." The man answered with a shrug.

"Who?"

"Your daughter, sir. I'm sorry sir, it happened so quickly I didn't have time to stop it."

"Damn it all!" Aldrich ran down the stairs, "Someone fetch me my horse." He yelled angrily. "NOW!" Several men ran to do as he asked. He turned to look at a new commotion that was approaching them. "Now what?" He watched as a man and a woman came up to him on a horse. "Ida?" He asked in confusion when he recognized the female passenger as she dismounted.

"Where's Arabella?" She asked nearly out of breath. "Sir, where is milady?"

"She stole a carriage and took off in that direction." He pointed the way.

"Alone?" Edmond asked.

"Yes, but who are you to her sir?" He asked.

"I am the man she loves and who has also fallen madly in love her." He replied and then yelled, "Haw!" to his horse and it immediately began running in the direction of the carriage.

"Ida." Baron Aldrich said in a low voice. "Do you care to explain what is going on here?"

"Well, uhm…" She didn't like being put on the spot like this.

"Who is that man?"

"He is the Lord Edmond Vaughan Wallace, son of Baron and Baroness Wallace."

Beautiful Pretender

"I see. I thought I recognized him." He looked in the direction that both Edmond and Arabella were now in. "Is that really the man that Arabella said she loved?"

"Yes sir."

He huffed in annoyance and then yelled, "Would somebody bring me my horse already!"

Part Two

Chapter 11

Arabella wasn't able to think clearly. All she knew was that she had to get away. She meant it when she said that she would rather die then marry Eric. She couldn't stop the memories of the things he did. For the most part his cruelty hadn't been directed towards her but she saw the way he treated others and it frightened her as she wondered how long it would be before he would treat her in such an ill mannered way as well. She had not only her memories of him but also the rumors that circulated about him bothering her. His cruelty towards others was no secret. She knew that many people were hoping that her presence would help to calm him down but she honestly couldn't allow herself to find out.

As far as which direction she was currently traveling in, she had no clue. All she knew was that she had to get away from her home as quickly as possible. Had Ida stayed by her side she might have been convinced not to do something so impulsive but without Ida there to restrain her, she took the opportunity to run. Not even her mother had tried to stop her. In fact the look on her mother's face almost seemed to encourage her to break free from this situation and run away.

"I'm sorry I couldn't say goodbye, Edmond." She cried. "You are my only regret. I really wanted to see you one last time but I have to get away from this as soon as I can. I just can't marry Eric, I won't marry him!" She slapped the reins again because the horses were starting to slow down. Immediately they picked up their speed again. She continued pushing them as hard as she could until she heard someone call her name.

"Arabella!" Edmond screamed over the sound of the horses and the wagon. He pushed his horse as hard as he could in order to catch up with her but it was tiring for the poor thing, for he had rode it hard not only to her house carrying two people on it, but also to catch up with her. He knew the beast couldn't take much more of this. "Arabella, please slow down." He yelled again.

Arabella peaked around the side of the carriage and recognized Edmond right away. "Oh no." She gasped. It would be hours before nightfall and she hadn't thought of bringing a mask with her. "I can't let him see me." She said frantically and hit the reigns on the horses again, yelling at them to go faster.

"Arabella!" He yelled and forced his horse to go even faster. 'I must stop her before she gets into an accident.' The carriage was having a hard time already because of her inexperience at driving one. It was weaving in the road and rocking rather hard. All it would take was one good sized mound or pit in the road and it would most likely topple over, taking her with it. Finally he was able to pull up along side the carriage, paying mind to not let it hit him or his horse. Soon he would be close enough to grab the reigns from her. "Hand me the reigns!" He yelled to her loud enough to be heard over the commotion of the horses and carriage.

"No! I won't submit." She yelled back taking great care to keep her face hidden from him.

"Please. You're going to kill yourself if you keep this up." He tried to reach for the reigns but missed grabbing them. "Damn." He grumbled and then thought to himself, 'There is no way I'm going to stop this carriage unless I get on there with her.' He stood up in the saddle, though it took an intense amount of skill and balance.

"No, don't!" She screamed at him when she realized what he was about to do. "You'll kill yourself if you miss."

"Then stop the carriage."

"No. Just let me go." She cried.

"I can't do that." Suddenly he jumped and landed hard on the carriages foot board below the front seat. He nearly fell but was able to grab hold of a handle that had been placed on the side, for the driver's mounting and dismounting of the vehicle. He immediately grabbed the reigns from her hands and then eased the carriage to a stop after sitting down next to her.

Arabella hung her head in her hands while she cried. "Why? Why

Beautiful Pretender

is my father doing this to me?"

"I do not know." He told her gently and then he took her into his arms as best he could since she wouldn't lift her head. "Hush now." He soothed as he gently rubbed her arm that was furthest from him. "I am not sure why this is happening to you but running away isn't the answer."

"I can't marry Eric. I would rather die then marry him."

"I know. Why couldn't you marry Kendrick? You were fine with that weren't you?"

"I was willing to except it, yes. However when Kendrick asked for my hand, father announced that he had already made a contract with Eric. He waited to announce this to purposefully hurt Kendrick. Why would he be so cruel? I even thought that he was going to allow my marriage to Kendrick until the very last moment." She couldn't talk for a moment because she couldn't control her tears. "Kendrick loves me and he's a good king. Why is father purposefully hurting him?"

"I believe your father may be a traitor to Arminia. Sending both you and your mother away to Eldardesh is a good sign that he may be working for Eric. Especially with his place secured in the Arminian government, it is likely he is one of Eric's spies. However, nothing can be done unless there is proof against him. This problem with the marriage contract isn't sufficient proof that he may be a traitor to the crown, though no one doubts his love for his former king."

"Father does love Eric as if he were his own child." She confessed. "He believes that my marriage to him will make Eric a better king, but I don't want to marry him."

"My Little Mousy... I know you had a reason to keep your face hidden from me." He paused for a moment. "I know you're worried that it will be your face I see in my marriage bed when I am with my wife and that I will have regrets because of it." He held her closer. "But I think I will regret it even more if I never know the face of the woman I hold dearest in my heart. Not knowing what you look like will haunt me until the end of my days. Please, let me look at you."

"I beg of you not to ask this of me." She whispered through her tears. "I will confess that there is another reason why I can't let you look upon me. You must trust me when I say that you will regret doing so."

"No, I won't, I promise. I know it can't be the way you look because all of those who have seen you say you are the most beautiful woman they have ever laid eyes on."

"Though I do not agree with their appraisal, it is not that which keeps me concealed. Please Edmond…"

"Your majesty." The captain of Kendrick's personal guard approached his king with caution. "I know this is a difficult time for you…"

"You know nothing!" Kendrick yelled at him. "I am a king and I can't even lift a finger to help her. If I do, many people will die in a needless war. I love her! I wanted to marry her and now she is being given to my enemy. He will only bring her pain and misery yet I can't do anything about it." He started to cry. "How could you possibly understand anything?"

"I'm sorry sire, but there are matters requiring your attention and…"

"I don't care!" He screamed. "If you all don't leave me alone until I summon you again, I will have your heads removed. Is that clear?"

"Yes sire, it is impeccably clear. I'm sorry to have bothered you." The captain bowed and then left.

Kendrick picked up the cup he had been drinking from and threw it across his bedchamber. Then he found more and more things to throw until he couldn't throw anything more. He wept bitterly for the first time in his life. To him Arabella was the closest thing to love that he had ever known. She accepted him for who he was and showed him tenderness. She allowed him to be a boy instead of a king and she enjoyed just being at his side. Her ways made him leave the world of adults behind, his kingdom behind and his responsibilities behind so that he could enjoy a freedom he had never known before. Now it was gone and he could never get it back again. No matter how much he wanted to use his authority to bring her back, he knew that all it would do would be to destroy the kingdom that he loved and it was his responsibility to put it first above all else. He learned that day that there were some things that even a king couldn't have, no matter how much he wanted them.

Beautiful Pretender

\-

"Arabella…" Edmond said gently and placed two of his fingers under her chin. "Please let me see the face of the only woman who could capture my heart and affections." Gently he encouraged her to straighten her posture though she continued to hang her head.

"Please, don't do this." Her hoarse voice whispered. "I know you will hate me if you do. I couldn't bear it if you hated me."

"I could never hate you, Arabella. That much I know for certain."

Arabella sighed in misery. "You will." She whispered. "Is there nothing I can do to change your mind about this?" She pleaded with him in a quiet voice.

"If you really do love me, you will let me look upon you." He kissed the top of her head.

"Very well then." She wiped her eyes. "But remember that I tried to dissuade you from doing this, just as I had tried to dissuade you from loving me in the first place."

"I will keep this in mind."

'Lord, please give me the strength I need to do what he asks of me.' She thought to herself, and then she slowly lifted her head up so she could look into his eyes. However midway up he stopped her.

"Wait, I want to kiss you first." His gentle voice said. "Only then will I look upon your face." He heard her sigh miserably. Edmond closed his eyes and lifted her face to his so he could kiss her soft lips tenderly. It was meant to reassure her. Inside Arabella was dying from her fright and she felt nauseous. She felt him pull away from her and it took everything she had to find the courage to open her eyes and look at him. The look in his eyes was one she knew she'd never forget as he gazed at the all too familiar face before him. "Oh God." He gasped and then his mouthed moved but now words came out, though she knew he said the name 'Aram'.

"I told you not to look upon me, didn't I?" She wiped away the tears that continued to fall.

"Aram…? Are you telling me…?" He couldn't finish.

"I never meant to deceive you, nor did I ever intend to fall in love with you." She told him softly through her tears. "I tried to stop you from loving me but I failed miserably."

"Everything seems to make sense now." His weary voice uttered. He looked down at where her dress partially exposed her chest and he could tell that she was indeed a woman and that what he had felt under her shirt were the bindings that hid this fact. He looked back up into her eyes. "Why did you pretend to be a boy?"

"It was supposed to be something I did only a few times because I wanted to play with the group of boys I saw five years ago. I knew that if I tried to do so as a girl you guys wouldn't have let me, so father let me dress as a boy. He felt sorry for me because things had been so hard on me at the time, that is, when we moved to Arminia. You boys so easily accepted me and I had so much fun spending time with you that being Aram became second nature to me. You and I had become close friends as we grew up together and I treasured the friendship you shared with me. When I began to take on the features of a woman, I bound my chest because I couldn't bear the thought of not having you for my friend anymore." She sighed as she tried to control her emotions. "I'm not asking you to understand why I did what I did because it was wrong of me to let you believe that I was a boy. However, I thought you should know why I did it."

"I'm honestly not sure what to say." He brought his hand up over his eyes as if to hide his own face from the truth. "I told you things I would have never dared tell to a girl. I undressed in front of you too, we all did."

"If it makes any difference, I never looked at you intentionally or any of the others for that matter. There were a couple of times I accidentally saw things I probably shouldn't have seen but I tried really hard not to."

"I trusted you Aram... I mean... Arabella. How can I look at you and not see the friend who betrayed my trust?" He started crying softly as he continued to hide his face from her. "How can I see you as the woman I have grown to love and not the friend that hurt me?"

Arabella drew in a breath as her body shook in grief. She hung her head in shame and said as gently as possible to him, "Go home, Edmond and marry the Countess D'Winter. Live a life that will make you happy and forget about me." She whispered. "I know that I will always be your one regret and I am really sorry for deceiving you."

A horse could be heard coming from the direction of Arabella's

Beautiful Pretender

home. "How can I possibly forget about you?"

"I am not worthy of you remembering me." She was silent for a moment as her tears kept her from speaking. "My life is over now that I am being forced to marry Eric. I am not asking you to rescue me from my misery because your future doesn't have me in it." She choked on her tears as her heart continued to break. "All you can do is to forget about me if you're to have any hope of a life that is happy with the countess."

The horse drew up to the carriage and stopped. "Thank you, son." Baron Aldrich said. "I will compensate you for your troubles."

"There is no need sir." Edmond did his best to keep what little composure he had left, though he knew he couldn't hide the obvious grief his face had betrayed. "I have to go. Have a good life, Arabella." With that he jumped off of the carriage and walked back to where his horse waited for him.

"Arabella?" Her father asked.

Suddenly she stood up and looked back to where Edmond was walking away from her and she called out to him, "Edmond!" She sniffed back her tears and continued, "I truly do love you. If you remember anything about me at all, remember that my love for you was never a lie and I promise I will love you until the day I die." At that she broke down in uncontrolled tears again and sank back into the driver's seat of the carriage. Edmond wanted to turn and look back at her as she talked to him. He did stop walking momentarily but after she had finished he continued on his course. Quietly Arabella whispered to the ears that could no longer hear her voice, "I really do love you with all of my heart."

"That's enough of this foolishness daughter." Her father said in a stern voice. "The driver and the rest of our party will be here shortly so we can be on our way. I have decided it would be better if I escorted you to your husband before dealing with matters here. It wouldn't do at all if another incident like this should arise."

"I hate you." She said through her tears and clenched teeth.

"What?" He asked in disbelief.

She looked up at him, "You are no longer my father. I disown you."

"You can't do that." He tried to reach out to her but she pulled away.

"Arabella, you know you're the most important person to me."

"No, I'm not. What you say is nothing but a lie to deceive me and make me do what you want. That poor excuse for a king you hold even more dearly then I. For if you truly loved me, in the manner in which you told me, then you wouldn't be forcing me to do the one thing that would hurt me the most. If you make me marry that horrible little boy, then I will never again acknowledge you as anything but a stranger and my enemy."

"That is not fair, Arabella. Do you think that this arranged marriage is an isolated incident? Do you believe you're the only one who has ever been forced to endure something like this? Even your mother and I had to leave behind people we cared about to fulfill the contract that our parents made on our behalf. We learned to love each other…"

"Mother believes as I do on this matter." She reminded him.

His voice became angry, "Your mother is just bitter because I chose Eric over Kendrick. In time she will see that Eric is the better choice when compared to that weak and useless king that can never be a proper ruler." He lowered his voice again and regained his composure. "Arabella… you must stop acting like a child and fulfill your responsibilities to this family and accept what has been decided on your behalf. You will marry Eric and you will love him. You will bear him a son who will sit on Eldardesh's throne and he will govern her people with dignity and pride. You will become the queen and companion that Eric needs without regret or complaint."

"Then from this day forward, I have no father." She whispered and then she got down from the carriage because she heard the rest of their traveling companions coming.

"You will change your mind in time, my precious child. I know you will. You're just angry because the man you love left you to marry another woman. He knows his place and his duty. Lord Edmond Wallace will marry the Countess D'Winter as he should. You will learn from his example and do as you should."

"Go to hell and take that snot nosed kid of a king with you for all I care." She seethed and then opened the carriage door and climbed in. "I always knew I couldn't marry Edmond and I was willing to except that, but I had hoped that you would show fairness and allow me to wed the king of my choosing. The only king who truly cared about me

Beautiful Pretender

and loved me."

"In time, Kendrick will lose his throne. He is a weak king. The kingdom that I am giving you will stand for all time because even though Eric is young, he is strong and powerful. Other kingdoms fear him and that says a lot for a boy of twelve."

"I don't care." She told him evenly and then slammed the carriage door closed.

Edmond rode for a ways and then turned his horse into the forest until he knew that he was in a place where no one would disturb him. There he let his emotions flow from his body. Anger, grief, sorrow, confusion and pain were only some of the feelings that seemed to consume him. Most of all he felt betrayed by the one person he trusted the most. He picked up a fallen tree branch that was thick, long and sturdy and used it to hit the nearby trees as hard as he could until it broke. Then he found another and continued to slam out his frustration. He cried out to the air and his allowed his tears to flow freely.

Although he was angry and bitter, he couldn't stop the love he still had for her. Even now knowing that she had been Aram, all it did was make it harder for him to let her go, for she now represented the two most dearest people he had ever loved. She was his best friend and his lover combined. He wanted desperately to tear his breaking heart out so he couldn't feel the pain that it held, yet it was her hurting look that was nagging for him to run back to her so that he could comfort her and protect her. He was beyond angry with her yet he wanted to hold her to him for all eternity more then anything else. With kisses he wanted to dry away her tears and sooth away the sorrow that was burdening her from her heart. He wanted to wrap himself around her like a living shield to guard her against the adversities of the world around them.

Finally his strength gave out and he fell to the earthen floor. "Why God?" He asked brokenly. "Why did it have to be this way? Why couldn't they have been different people? I loved them both. Aram was the friend who shared my pain and understood my thoughts and feelings. Arabella was the gentle creature who made me feel like I could be a real man. I loved her without reservation. I loved them both without hesitation. She was like an angel that enchanted me with her charm and beauty. The personalities of the two were so different that I never even dreamed that they could possibly even be the same person, yet in some ways they were also very much alike."

He sighed as he brought his knees up to his chest and he hugged them to himself tightly. "What am I suppose to do?" He cried. "I know she truly did try to discourage my love but how could I not love her? We were both willing to set our love aside to do as our parents asked, but how can I let her go to that boy who is only going to destroy her? Please God," His sobs made it nearly impossible for him to continue, "Please God, tell me what to do." He allowed himself to cry without restraint.

Arabella looked out the window of the carriage as it moved southward towards her future. She would never forget the pain she had seen in Edmond's eyes, the pain she had hoped never to cause him. That look would haunt her until her dying day but she was sure that it was a punishment that she deserved for betraying his trust and loyalty to her.

Baron Cordell, whom she chose to never call father again, rode his horse not too far from the carriage. Occasionally he would look over towards his daughter with both hope and regret. He hoped that one day she would come to forgive him for hurting her and that she would see that he was trying to do what was best for both her and Eldardesh. He regretted the painful way in which he had to do this to her. If at all possible he would have done things differently for her sake, but he didn't want to risk losing King Eric's confidence in him. It wouldn't be much longer before they reached the border of the two kingdoms, for they had been traveling nearly two days already.

Edmond still couldn't decide what to do next. At the moment he rode towards Eldardesh but at a slow pace. Several times he had turned around and began a journey back to Arminia but then he would change his mind again and head back towards Eldardesh. Part of him wanted to run away from the situation and hide from the truth and part of him wanted to run to Arabella and save her from her cruel fate. Part of him knew he should go home and fulfill his duties to his parents by marrying the countess and part of him wanted to leave everything

Beautiful Pretender

behind to be with the one he loved. Anger and hurt were in a constant battle with love and devotion.

Many times he had screamed out to the sky his frustration about the situation and his indecision. After all they knew that the love they had shared could only be for a short period of time. He had resolved that he couldn't keep her forever and he had convinced himself that he could let her go when the time came. If it had been Kendrick, he might have been able to do it, though he wasn't completely sure if he could really have done it. Unfortunately he had to admit that she was right when she told him that he would regret it if she showed him her face, for he did indeed regret it, but not so much in the way that she meant. Now he wanted her more than ever, despite all that happened. He couldn't bear to lose both Aram and Arabella, the two most important people in his life. Now that he knew they were in fact the same person made her only that much more precious to him.

"Why?" He asked in a hoarse voice. "Why do we have to suffer like this? Why must love be so painful?" He thought about the Countess D'Winter. He was supposed to meet her for the first time fairly soon. His father had yet to announce when that would be. Already Edmond had been away longer then he had expected and he wondered if his parents were worried about his absence.

Baron Cordell came of to the side of the carriage so he could speak with his daughter. "The king's camp is just ahead. We should be arriving well before sundown." He didn't even get so much as a sigh from her in response. "Eric has been waiting for you patiently and it would be nice if you would greet him properly. After all he is a king and he is going to be your husband. I believe his wife will be there as well. I do hope you can show her kindness and treat her like a sister. She'll be having a baby soon and Eric hasn't exactly been kind to her."

Arabella continued to ignore him as if he wasn't there. She had no intention on ever speaking to him again. As far as she was concerned he was dead. Instead of listening to him further she closed the curtain to the window on the side he rode on and she looked for the blanket that she had found the day before. The carriage was still filled with the gifts that it had come with. She only looked through enough of them to secure fresh clothing to change into and a blanket to cover herself up with when she needed one. Once she had these things she ignored the rest.

Her mind had gone into survival mode and all she did now was what she needed to do in order to survive, even though part of her wished this could all end. Her one saving grace was that she loved Edmond too much to add yet another pain to his heart. Should she die, no matter how angry he was with her, she knew it would hurt him deeply. So for his sake, she chose to live on so he wouldn't feel any guilt on her behalf.

Eric had left the day after the Baron did because his spies had informed him that Kendrick was indeed going to seek the hand of Baron's daughter upon his return. He wasn't sure how long he would have to wait for the Baron to arrive with his daughter to the designated place by the border but he knew he wouldn't have to wait too long. He trusted the Baron to keep his word and bring his daughter as soon as he had told Kendrick of her betrothal to Eric. How he wished he could have been there to see the pain this caused his brother.

"Husband?" The thirteen year old Miriam addressed Eric. "Do you think she will be kind to me?"

Eric looked over at his wife of thirteen, with her raven black hair and blue eyes, "If my memory of her is accurate, I see no reason why she wouldn't. I'll place you in her care if that would make you feel any better." Eric didn't love his wife but he also didn't hate her. She was simply just there. What he cared about was the child within her. For the present, that was his only heir to the throne and he wanted to make sure the child was well cared for. "She has no need to be hostile towards you since she will be above you and her children will be above your own. If anything concerns me it would be your attitude towards her. I have loved Arabella for as long as I can remember and you will treat her as the head wife."

"Yes sire." His young bride did her best to bow to him over her pregnant belly. "I only desire to please you."

"Make sure her tent is prepared and keep a fire going so that she can have a hot bath when she arrives."

"As you wish." Miriam left to do as he instructed. Eric followed her towards the tent that was to be Arabella's temporary shelter when she

Beautiful Pretender

arrived. When he arrived, he went inside to make sure everything was perfect and fit for the future queen of his kingdom. Its colors were a mix of deep blues and whites. Everything was made from the finest fabrics, woods and any other material that was needed to make the dwelling perfect for his new bride. Miriam peeked in and asked, "Is it to your satisfaction, milord?"

"Yes, I am pleased with it." He walked over and sat on the bed. It was to be their marital bed, where he would take her as his wife for the first time. The thought of what was to come made him smile. "Perhaps I should move my things in here as well." He said to himself and then he laid down and stretched out his body. "This should most definitely please her." A sigh escaped his lips.

"Sire." A male voice came from just outside the tent. "The princess's carriage will be arriving soon."

"Already?" Eric smiled as he sat up. "This is good news." He got up off the bed and left the tent. While he walked he addressed the captain of the guard, "Make sure everyone is lined up properly to greet her. I want everything to be perfect for when she arrives, do you understand?"

"Yes sire."

Arabella felt the carriage slowing down and she had the feeling that they had arrived to Eric's camp. It had only stopped for a short time and then her door was opened up for her. "We've arrived daughter." The Baron told her in his most tender voice. "Please come with me." He put his hand into the carriage with the palm up to assist her. "I think you will be pleasantly surprised when you see your cousin. He is quite a handsome man and he looks more like he is closer to your age then twelve. This should help make it easier for you."

Even though she resented this man, she had little choice about taking his hand in assistance. He simply wouldn't let her not do it. She gracefully stepped out of the stuffy vehicle and down to the hard earth below. The Baron placed her arm through his and he was pleased that she didn't fight with him about it. 'I really hate you.' Arabella screamed silently. 'I hate you for doing this to me!' Though her soul screamed out in protest to what she was being forced into, her breeding made her act as if this was just another one of her everyday motions. She held her head high, kept her back straight and walked with graceful, even steps. Her eyes faced front and she showed no emotion.

"You look so beautiful, Arabella. Everything about you shows that you have what it takes to be a suitable queen." The Baron praised her.

Edmond stopped his horse far enough away so as not to be detected. Then he dismounted and walked through the shelter of the trees to where he could watch the camp's activities. He had hoped that maybe things would go well for Arabella. If they did, then perhaps he could leave knowing that things were not as bad as they had both feared. Currently, Arabella was walking with her father to where some men stood. Edmond's best guess was that they were currently inside Eldardesh, near the border. It seemed odd that Eric would arrange to meet them there but he must have had his reasons for doing it.

"Welcome home, cousin." Eric smiled when Arabella and her father stopped before him. He couldn't help grinning at her perplexed expression. "I look older then twelve don't I?" He stepped up near her, "You see we're nearly the same height." He boasted proudly.

"Eric? Is that really you?" She asked as she looked into his greenish blue eyes. He certainly looked different from the last time she had seen him. Of course he was only seven then. However he still had the same reddish brown hair like his brother and she could even see a little of Kendrick in him, but only physically.

"Kiss me." He beamed.

"Huh?" She replied in confusion.

"I want you to kiss me. After all we are going to be married soon."

"Oh… alright." Her words came out slowly. She stepped closer to him and then she leaned forward and kissed his cheek.

"Why did you do that?" He asked and placed his hand on his cheek.

"You told me to." She replied softly.

"Your daughter is an idiot." He scolded the Baron.

"I do apologize, sire." The Baron bowed humbly. "Please forgive her." Then he leaned over and whispered to her, "Kiss him properly dear, as a wife should."

"But I'm not his wife yet." She stated the obvious. Suddenly she

212

Beautiful Pretender

gasped as Eric's hand struck her face.

"You foolish woman." He then pulled her to him and kissed her the way he wanted her to kiss him on the lips with some passion. "That is how I want you to kiss me."

"Yes sire." She backed away and lowered her eyes. She wanted to hold her hand to her cheek because it stung but her breeding wouldn't let her. Instead she took a position of humiliation and waited for Eric to tell her what he wanted.

"Come with me and I will show you the tent I had prepared for you. I made sure that everything was of the best quality…" He continued to talk on and on about all he had done for her to prepare for this day but her attention was else where.

Arabella interrupted him, "Eric, who is that over there?" She asked pointing to a pregnant woman.

Eric was irritated at her but he looked to see whom she was referring to. "Oh her? That's just my wife Princess Miriam."

"She's very beautiful, sire."

"Yeah, she was at one time." He sighed. "Don't worry about her. She won't do anything to offend you." Eric reached over to grab her hand but she started walking away towards Miriam and he missed it.

"Hello." Arabella smiled at the king's young wife. "I'm Arabella. It's a pleasure to meet you."

Miriam dropped to her hands and knees bowing her head to the ground as best as she could. Arabella wondered if doing that was such a good idea for the young woman to do in her delicate condition. "I am honored to be in your presence, your highness." Miriam's voice almost had a hint of fear in it. "I beg of you to look kindly upon both me and my child."

"I wouldn't do anything to hurt you." Arabella told her in a tender and sincere voice. "I am hoping that perhaps we can be friends."

"Really?" Miriam looked up at her and smiled.

"You needn't worry about Miriam." Eric told her. "You will be considered as my head wife and you will be the queen. Your children will be the first heirs to my throne. Should you give me a prince he will be the eldest and have first rights to my throne upon my passing. I know that having more then one wife and concubines isn't practiced much anymore but I want to make sure that my offspring are abundant in the future I have planned. It will require children of superior breed and the children you and I have will be superior to all."

"What if you have other sons before we do? Shouldn't they have first right to your throne?" She asked.

"There will be no princes older then yours, only princesses."

"I don't understand."

"I will dispose of those who would stand in your son's way." His words were almost too clear.

"You would kill them?" She asked with a frightened voice.

"I would have to." He didn't seem to be bothered in the least at his cruel words.

"You wouldn't kill a child, would you?"

"I will kill anyone who stands in the way of what I desire. Man, woman or child, it doesn't matter in the least. I am king and my word is the law and it is my right to decide who lives or dies."

Arabella began to back away from him in fear. "Do you really believe this?" She could feel her throat tightening in fear.

Eric advanced towards her as she continued to back away. "Where do you think your going?" His temper was rising.

"I… uh…" Suddenly she turned and began running away.

"Guards!" Eric shouted and immediately several men chased after her. It didn't take them long to catch her.

"Let me go!" She shouted, "I can't do this, I can't marry someone like him." Try as she might, she couldn't struggle free from the two men who held her. "Please." She cried in desperation. "Please let me go."

"You do disappoint me, Arabella. Here I have been, waiting these last five years for you to come back home to me," He stopped just before her and his face was growing red with his anger. "Is this how you show your gratitude for all I have done for you? I give you the finest dwellings, I set you and your children above my wife, and I bestow upon you the honor of being my queen. How do you repay me? You repay me by humiliating me in front of my men."

"Eric, please forgive her, she's had a lot of hardships lately. I'm sure that she is simply overwhelmed…" The Baron tried to reason with him.

"You will not speak so informally with me sir." Eric warned him. "Go back to your post in Arminia. You're no longer needed here unless

Beautiful Pretender

you can provide me with information that will help lead to my brother's downfall."

Arabella looked over to her father, "This would be a good time to redeem yourself, father." She was letting him know that if he helped her, she would give him a second chance.

"I love you daughter. You will always be the most important person to me. Listen to Eric and allow him to lead you in all things." He bowed before the king and then left to find his horse.

"Don't leave me here!" She cried out to him. "Please father, don't leave me."

"I've had just about enough of this." Eric seethed. "You have humiliated me twice now." Arabella turned to look at Eric as he continued talking. "For that you will have to be punished. I will continue to punish you until you learn your place and obey without complaint."

"Punish me?" She could barely speak the words.

To his men that stood nearby he ordered, "Strip her down to her smock and tie her to the flogging post. Open the back of it so I can make sure the strap hits her skin."

"Yes sire." One of the men answered and then to his men he said, "Do as the king commands."

"No!" Arabella screamed as some of the men, who weren't holding her, came towards her. She looked towards Eric who was walking away. "Please forgive me." She cried.

"I will when your punishment is over." His voice held no emotion. "I can not allow you or anyone else to behave in such a way that displeases me, no matter who they might be."

"Please don't do this to me." She fought as hard as she could but she was no match for the men who held her in place. They already had her gown off and were making quick work of the other items. "Please stop!" She cried.

"Take your hands off of my wife." A strong deep voice called from a short distance away. All the soldiers looked up at the man who was approaching on horse back.

"What?" Eric said as he turned around. "Who are you and what do you mean by your wife?" He demanded.

Arabella knew the voice and turned to look at the man in which it belonged to, "No Edmond." She warned him.

"Who is he to you?" Eric asked as he walked back over to where she was.

"I'm her husband and I demand that you release her at once." Edmond announced firmly. "I will not tolerate you laying even one hand on her."

"Where's your proof that she belongs to you?" Eric sneered. "I have a contract signed by her father saying that she belongs to me." He pulled the contract out of his vest, her father had given it to him when they arrived.

"Her father doesn't know we are married yet. We did it in secret." Edmond told him.

"Edmond." Arabella protested as she continued to try and struggle free from the two men holding her.

"Unhand her this instant." Edmond demanded again.

"Kill him." Eric said without hesitation. "Kill him and bring me his head on a pole."

"No, please don't." Arabella begged. "He's not my husband but a friend. He doesn't understand what's going on here. Please Eric, show him mercy and allow me to explain things to him."

"Silence wife." Edmond told her firmly.

"You're just going to get yourself killed doing this." She pleaded through her tears.

Edmond dismounted and placed his hand at the ready to the butt of his sword. "If I have to I will fight for her."

"Please Edmond, don't do this, I'm not worth it." Arabella begged as she cried.

"You are the dearest person in this world to me, Arabella. Even though things are not at their best between us, I will not stand by and watch this little snot nosed brat hurt you in such an abominable way." He pulled his sword from its sheath. "I said, release her at once."

Eric looked at his men, "Why are you all still standing there? I told you to kill him. Obey me at once." Immediately the men drew their swords. One of the soldiers released Arabella, but the other wrapped his arms tightly around her from behind to hold her so she couldn't escape.

"Edmond." She whispered as she watched him attack with all his might. One thing did set her a little bit at ease and that was in knowing

Beautiful Pretender

that Edmond was a very skilled swordsman. He never had to fight in a life and death situation as he needed to do now, but she took comfort in knowing that in the past when he fought in tournaments, he had never lost to anyone, never. Arminia was one of many kingdoms that hosted yearly tournaments that included jousting, swords and many other forms of combat and skill. Nobles of all varieties and from many of the surrounding kingdoms participated in them. It wasn't uncommon for many nobles to travel from kingdom to kingdom to participate in these events during the season, unless they were needed for military purposes in their own kingdoms. As Aram, she would occasionally assist Edmond during these events and she loved every moment of it. Now he was putting his skills to use and she prayed that he would be victorious yet again.

Edmond wasn't use to fighting so many opponents at one time. He had to keep his wits about him and not let his concentration and focus waver, even in the slightest or it could mean his death. He was currently fighting five men at one time. Never before had he ever fought more then three and even then it wasn't life or death. He had to keep track as to where each man was around him at all times. Right now Eric's men were playing more then fighting because they believed that they had the upper hand. He didn't want to kill anyone but he wasn't sure if he would have a choice.

Thankfully Edmond did have a few tricks up his sleeve for disabling the enemy but it would require great skill and a whole lot of luck. If he could hit key points on their bodies and limbs, he could disable them without killing them. The problem was that he had to cut them in strategic places in order for it to work. Mostly if he cut the tendons in one of their legs, on the back side, he could probably make it so they couldn't stand again. If they were determined to continue fighting relying on the other leg, he would be forced to cut that one too. It would leave them crippled for life but they would most likely not die by his hand.

He could also cut their fighting hand off at the wrist so they could no longer hold a sword and fight. Though cruel, this method was also an option. His preferred choice was cutting their thumb on the sword fighting hand. If he cut deep enough they couldn't use it, though they might use their other hand to assist the injured one. He preferred this one because it was the least devastating in the long run. However, it was also nearly impossible to do and if he didn't do it just right, they could still hold a sword. Death, however, was not an option. These men didn't chose their king and he could tell that they were not happy about the orders Eric had given them concerning Arabella.

Arabella watched as Edmond skillfully fought his opponents. One by one he took them out. They were too injured to continue the fight. She could see that he tried to only injure the hand but it wasn't enough to stop them. He had to move on to more drastic measures of disabling his enemy. She had never felt so proud of him. Soon, one by one he eliminated each opponent until all that was left was the one that held her. "Release my wife at once." He seethed through his teeth as he breathed hard for each breath. Edmond didn't escape totally uninjured, but the injuries he did have were minor and didn't seem to set him back much. His worst enemy at the moment was exhaustion.

"Release her and take care of him." Eric ordered.

"Yes sire." The solider replied and he did as ordered.

"You may have beaten those men but this one has had time to study your moves and learn your weaknesses. He's a very skilled fighter and has never lost to anyone yet." Eric grinned. "The others were weak compared to him." He walked over to where Arabella stood. "Watch my dear, for this will be the last day that your beloved friend will ever see. My man will show him no mercy, I promise you that."

"It is because of that Eric, that I detest you." She replied without looking at him. "I would have gladly accepted you if you were a good man like your brother."

"My brother is a coward and he is weak." He countered. "Once I build up my armies, I will take his throne."

"You are pure evil."

He turned to look at her, "Don't you dare mock me, princess." He turned her to face him. "I may be a child in your eyes but have am a very powerful king. My throne has forced me to become a man at a young age and I will prove to you who is in control around here." He grabbed her wrist and began pulling her towards the tent he had set up for her.

"Where are you taking me?" She asked in a frightened voice as she struggled to break free from his grip. She was amazed at how strong he was.

"To your marriage bed." He laughed in an evil manner. "I doubt that man is your husband, but I suppose I will know soon enough, whether or not he has spoiled you."

"Arabella!" Edmond yelled out to her when he saw Eric hauling her away.

"Don't worry about me." She looked back at him and gave her best smile. "Just concentrate on the matters at hand." She was afraid he would be struck if he didn't pay complete attention to his opponent who was indeed proving to be very skilled. Arabella heard Edmond whistle and knew it was the whistle he used to summon his horse. She could tell by the clanging swords that he was still fighting. Eric nearly had her to the tent. "Let me go, please." She begged.

Eric stopped pulling her, "Tell me the truth, is he really your husband?"

Arabella sighed, "In law and in body, no, but in my heart he is the only man that I desire to spend my forever with. In my heart he is my husband."

"Then I have the unhindered right to claim you as my own." He laughed victoriously.

"I will never love you Eric." She wanted to make that clear to him.

"I just need to break you. You're like a wild horse, Arabella. You're defiant and head strong, but when I'm through with you, your attitude about me will change. I will become the only man you in your eyes, in your mind and in your heart."

Suddenly Arabella felt herself being lifted into the air by a strong arm. She looked to see who had her. "Edmond." She gasped in a surprised voice. Edmond yelled at his horse and it took off in a run.

"Stop him!" Eric yelled. "He has your queen!" Immediately the few remaining men but two who stayed to guard Eric, were running for their horses to pursue.

"Hold on to me as best as you can." Edmond told her. She was sitting sidesaddle in front of him. Arabella wrapped her arms about him and held on with all her strength as she buried her head into his chest. "I will try to out run them and head into the forest. I'm hoping we will be able to lose them in there." He yelled at his horse again. "If we can make it into Arminia, we will be safer then if we stay here in Eldardesh. However, we won't be completely safe no matter where we go."

Edmond's shirt was soaked in perspiration but she didn't mind the smell. It was that familiar earth smell that was so memorable to her. She could see that there was at least one gash on his upper right arm and his side was also bleeding. She couldn't see whether or not if there were any other injuries. "Will you be alright?" She asked concerned.

"We must get you somewhere where they can't easily find you. I can worry about everything else later." He brought his head down just long enough to kiss the top of hers. This small gesture was Arabella's breaking point and she began weeping as she clung to him. Everything that had happened had built up inside of her and his gentle kiss gave her permission to relieve her frustrations and pain in the privacy of this moment in his embrace. Only he would have any knowledge of the tears that she was shedding. The noise of the horse and wind would drown out the sound of her grief.

Chapter 12

Edmond had driven the horse nearly to death before he eventually allowed it to slow down as he looked for a suitable place for them to rest for the night. Even now the sky boasted its array of brilliant red on the horizon. He could hear the sound of water in the distance and instinctively his horse made its way to it for a long over due drink. Arabella had fallen asleep from crying. She clung to him in the fashion in which he was now growing accustomed to and he wondered if she did this because of the fear of losing him. He wasn't sure but it seemed to make sense.

All Arabella had on was the smock that Eric was kind enough to let her continue wearing, when he order his men to undress her. Edmond knew it wasn't going to give her the sufficient warmth she would need when the night's cool air settled in on them.

He sighed as he silently scolded himself for allowing things to go as far as they did. He should have not run off when he discovered who she was and he was sure his words just prior to leaving her with her father, wounded her deeply. 'Have a nice life?' How much more insensitive and stupid could he have been. Here she was, hurting and scared and he turned his back on her, just when she needed him the most.

Finally he brought his horse to a stand still and then he began to gently work at waking her up from her sleep. "Arabella." He said in a gentle voice. "We should probably give my horse some time to rest now." She moaned and snuggled in closer to him, which brought a smile to his face. He wrapped his arms about her and held her for a few moments before he tried to wake her up again. "Come on Arabella, I need you to wake up so we can get off."

She slowly opened her eyes and felt the comforting warmth of

Edmond's embrace. "Are we safe?" Her tired voice asked. "Will they find us here?"

Edmond looked around for a moment and listened to the sounds of the forest around them. All that he could hear was the temperate sound of the breeze rustling the leaves of the trees and the melody of the birds as they serenaded him and Arabella in the gentle warmth of the day that would soon draw to a close. "I think we might have lost them, or at least I hope we did. I neither see nor hear any sign of them near here."

She carefully pulled herself away from him, keeping in mind that he was injured and then she too took time to survey the forest around her. When she was satisfied that no one else was there, she told him in a soft voice, "Thank you for helping me. I was so frightened."

"You weren't the only one. I was worried that I mightn't be able to win that battle. I only just barely escaped, for my opponent was still able to fight when I got away from him. I didn't win, I just found the opportune time to make my retreat." He brought his hand up to wipe away the sweat that was running down his brow into his eyes. "Let me help you down." He took her hands into his own so she could slide off the horse without falling. Once she was down he dismounted and immediately took his horse to the creek to drink.

"She looks really tired." Arabella told him with some concern as she looked at his horse. "Will she be alright?"

Edmond patted the neck of his horse and replied, "I have to admit that I pushed her too hard but she is healthy and strong. I'm sure she'll be doing fine in the morning if I let her rest." Then to his horse, "You did well. Thank you." He patted her neck and she stomped in reply.

"Where are we?"

"In Arminia, or at least I think we are. It is rather hard to tell exactly where the border is and we have traveled pretty far into the forest, so I'm not exactly sure of our location since there are no road references out here to rely on for navigation and boundaries."

"Are we lost?" She asked nervously.

"Not really. I have a general idea of where we are. I just am not sure where we should go from here."

"Oh, I see." She felt a little uneasy, not only because he wasn't exactly sure of their location but also because she too, didn't know where to

Beautiful Pretender

go or what to do next. She couldn't go home because her father would take her back to Eric. Kendrick would be no help because he didn't want a war. Eldardesh's borders had Eric's men looking for her and Edmond had a future fiancé to go back to. She sighed miserably as she leaned against a nearby tree. All she had now was a smock to cover her body. The future queen of one of the two greatest kingdoms was now reduced to rags and had nothing to her name.

"Are you alright?" Edmond asked as he watched her.

Arabella looked up at him. "We should tend to your wounds." She watched as he looked at them. "If we don't they could become infected."

"You're probably right." Now that his horse had satisfied her thirst, he took her to a tree and tethered her reigns to one of its low and sturdy branches. Then he took off his shirt as he went back towards the cold running water, so he could wash his wounds.

"Let me help you." She offered and walked towards him, "It's the least I can do since it's my fault that you got these to begin with."

"It's not your fault, Arabella." He told her in a soft but firm tone. "It's mine for not stopping this from happening in the first place."

"We can argue about this later." She grabbed the sleeve of her smock and before he could stop her, she tore it off. Then she placed it in the creek's clear water. Once it was thoroughly soaked, she brought it up and squeezed the icy water over the cut on his arm and then she carefully wiped the skin around it. His face showed the pain that the cleansing brought. "I'm sorry. I am trying not to hurt you." She apologized.

"I know you're not." He placed his hand on the one she used to hold the cloth. "You don't need to do this. I'm sure I can do it just fine on my own. You really should go and try to get some rest while we are here."

"No." She placed the cloth back into the water, "I need to do this." She cleansed the cloth and then let it absorb more of the fresh clear water. Then she squeezed the cool liquid carefully over his wound again. "This one is not very deep and the bleeding has pretty much stopped." Her gaze then went to the wound on his side. "It would be easier to clean that if you were lying down." Without protest he did as she suggested and she did her best to clean the gash on his side as

223

gently as possible after she carefully pulled up his shirt to expose his side. "These really should be bound…" She thought out loud and then looked around for something she could use. Then she looked down at her smock and sighed. "This will have to do for now, I guess."

"Arabella, you can't afford to tear that up anymore then it already is. You're going to freeze to death as it is." He protested but she didn't listen. Instead she reached for the dagger that peeked out from the top of his boot and she used it to cut her smock enough so that she could tear some strips from the bottom of it. Thankfully, despite the day's activities, her smock had remained rather clean. "You just won't listen to me, will you?" He told her with some frustration for now her smock only came to just above her knees and it only had one sleeve left.

"You're more important than this piece of cloth that I am wearing. If I will freeze to death with it being whole anyways, then it won't hurt for me to have a little less of it on. As long it will do you some good, it will be worth the small sacrifice." She knelt down by him and bound the cut on his arm first. Then she had him sit up so she could bind the one on his side.

"You sure are a stubborn woman aren't you?" He gasped as she tied the knot near the wound on his side.

"Perhaps." That was all she would say to him in return. When she finished, she stood up and started walking away.

"Where are you going?"

"I thought I'd gather some wood and look to see if there might be some edible vegetation around here. You really should eat something."

"Wait, I'll go with you." He began to stand up.

"No, you should take a bath while I'm gone." She had yet to look back at him as she walked away. "You should also rest since you're the one who is injured."

"Stop it." He ordered her. "Why are you acting so cold towards me?"

She stopped walking but she still didn't turn around. "I really do appreciate what you did for me. You'll never know how much that meant to me." He heard her sigh. "Now that I am out of Eric's hands, you need not worry about me anymore."

"What are you talking about? How could I not worry about you?" He was deeply confused by this foreign behavior.

"It's alright if you hate me for betraying you. I knew that it would probably happen once you learned the truth about me." Then she turned and looked at him. "You needn't feel responsible for me, Edmond. Once you've rested and have had something to eat, you should go home. Your parents are probably very worried about you."

"My parents are the least of my concerns at the moment." He told her with frustration and then stood up and walked towards her. "I told you before that I could never hate you and I meant it. True, I was angry about your deception but once I had time to think about everything and why you did it, it wasn't all that hard for me to forgive you."

"You have obligations in Arminia." She reminded him. "You should go home."

"Am I supposed to just leave you here? I think not." His temper was starting to rise. "How could you even suggest that my only reason for saving you is out of obligation?" He advanced towards her. "I still love you, no matter who you are or what you did, nothing will change that. The truth is, I loved Aram nearly as much as I loved Arabella. The love was different for each person but never the less, I refuse to lose you both. The reason I saved you was because I want to keep you for myself and I don't want to share you with anyone else. To be completely honest with you, I'm not even sure that I could have stood by and not have taken you away from Kendrick as well." His words to her were honest and from his heart. He then reached out to take hold of her. However she back away just out of his reach. "Why are you doing this to me?" He begged to understand.

"We made a promise." She reached up to wipe away a tear. "When the time came, we would let go so we could marry the person of our parents choosing. I won't marry Eric, so I am guilty of lying to you. However, you still can do as you're supposed to..."

"Stop it!" This time he successfully took her into his arms. "Just stop it." He buried his face in the hair on the top of her head and began weeping. "Stop saying such stupid and meaningless things to me. Haven't you hurt me enough?" He couldn't stop his tears.

Arabella wasn't sure what to do, so she just stood there as he held her and cried. She wished that she could go back and stop the promise she made to let him go. The desire to give into her greed and to keep him for herself was nearly overpowering. Finally she spoke again, "You really should take a bath. You're sweating all over me."

Edmond backed up and looked down into her feminine face. "Are you suggesting that I smell bad?" They stood there for a moment just looking at each other.

Suddenly she started laughing softly and couldn't look him in the eye anymore, "Yes, you smell awful." She covered her mouth and nose with the back of her hand and turned away so he couldn't see her face as she laughed. "I'm sorry. I don't mean to be laughing about it."

"Now you sound like Aram." He wrapped his arms about her shoulders. "I'm really glad you're a woman." He kissed the back of her head. "Alright, I'll go bathe while you look for something for us to eat."

"Thank you." She didn't turn around because if she did, he would see the tears in her eyes. The laughter was forced to hide her grief. "It shouldn't take long. I'll just make sure to stay away long enough for you to have some privacy."

"It's not like you haven't seen me without clothes on before. To be honest, I'm a little jealous."

"Don't forget my parents' hot springs. You got to see me there, so we're even."

"Hardly. I barely got to see anything." He pretended to pout.

Arabella had to get away from him before her silent tears were silent no more. "Maybe I'll give you another chance sometime." She did her best at a realistic giggle.

"Don't tempt me." He leaned forward and whispered in her ear, "We'll have to sleep close tonight to keep warm since neither of us has any extra clothing to put on." He reached down and slightly flipped up the back of her shortened smock.

She swung back her elbow but stopped just short of hitting him since he was injured. She heard him gasp in anticipation of the familiar pain her elbow would bring. "That's a warning. Do it again and I'll really hit you." She laughed and then began walking away again. "Hurry up and bathe so you'll be done before I return."

"As you wish, my most beautiful princess."

'You stupid fool.' She scolded Edmond in her thoughts. 'Things can't go back to how they were before.' Unfortunately she would have to wait to cry until she was further away. 'I don't even really know how

Beautiful Pretender

I should act around you anymore. Should I only be Arabella? With Aram being so much a part of me, how can I not be him as well?' To be honest she loved 'playing' with Edmond. The rough housing and bantering were just as much a part of her as the sweet and innocent demeanor that she set aside, for the side of her that was Arabella. However that wasn't her only dilemma. Edmond really didn't belong to her. Sure he sort of did for a short period of time but now his parents had arranged for him to marry the countess. Technically he belonged to her now.

Edmond was worried about Arabella. Something was very different about her and he was sure it was his fault, even though she wouldn't admit it. He quickly washed up and dressed the bottom half of his body. As nice as it would have been to have clean pants to wear, it would have to wait. Instead, he washed his shirt. It was something he knew that as long as it was clean, he could stand to continue wearing what he had on a little longer. Right now he wasn't sure what to do about Arabella. She most definitely couldn't go around in the clothing she had on. Not only was it thin and offered no real protection to her, but it also barely covered her up now.

He was hanging up his shirt and the sleeve from her smock, both of which were now washed, though her sleeve now bore blood stains from his wounds as did his shirt. Arabella carried several branches of wood and had a few roots. He was sure she couldn't possibly hold one more thing, she carried so much. Immediately he went over to help lighten her load. "This should be fine for now." He smiled. Though she tried to hide it, he could tell she had been crying. However he chose not to say anything about it.

"These turnips were all I could find for food." She apologized because she knew how much he hated them.

"I'm sure they'll be fine." He laid the wood down once they reached a clearing large enough that he felt it would be safe for a fire. "We should gather some stones for the fire pit." He suggested and then reached to take the turnips from her. That was when he noticed that her hands were scraped up and even bleeding in a few places. 'It only makes sense.' He sighed knowing that she had never had to do any manual labor and so her hands were delicate and the skin would be easily injured. She did have some calluses from using the sword but only on a few areas of her hands. He saw that her bare feet also were scraped up.

"You go ahead and work here and I'll collect them for you." She offered.

"Sure." He decided it was best to let her do as she wanted. The area needed to be cleared of the bits of debris before he could lay out the wood. Arabella was able to gather the rocks, each were about the size of a small loaf of bread. Thankfully Edmond had his flint stone on him and so starting a fire was a breeze. Soon the smell of roasting turnips filled the air and even though he hated them, he was starving since he barely ate anything in the last three days.

"You sure are hungry." She smiled and handed him the last turnip, there had been three in all.

"I really don't mean to be so selfish." He took it greedily from her and wolfed it down.

"I could go and get some more…" She offered as she looked around as the last rays of light were disappearing from the sky and then she finished with, "tomorrow." It was obvious that trying to find anything above or below ground would be nearly impossible now. "I'm sorry, had I known how hungry you were, I could have dug up a couple more."

"Don't worry about it." He popped the last piece in his mouth. "I can only handle eating so much of these. The only reason why I can stomach them now is because I am so hungry. I doubt I'll be able to do so tomorrow."

"I can't say that I would want to either." She looked towards the creek, "I think I'll go wash up now."

"In the dark?" His voice reflected his concern.

"I feel awful being so dirty." She lifted her hands up and looked at them. "I feel like I'm caked in filth."

"Would you like me to make you a torch?"

"I'd have no way to hold it." She started getting up.

"Then I'll hold it for you." He offered and grabbed a tree branch.

She started laughing, "You're just trying to get a peak at me with nothing on, aren't you?"

He couldn't help smiling, "No, I swear that isn't my intention, or at least it wasn't." He stood up. "However, now that you suggested it, it would only fair that you return the favor."

"You pervert." She laughed. "Sit down and rest. I'll be alright and the creek isn't all that far away. I'm sure I'll easily be able to see the fire from there, so I don't think I'll get lost."

"Alright then, have it your way." He sat back down. "Don't hesitate to call if you need anything."

"Thanks." She turned and started walking away. As she walked, she tried to remember what was lying on the ground on the path she took. Her feet were burning from the cuts and bruises they already had and she didn't want to do anymore damage then necessary to them as she walked. She made it a point not to flinch or cry out in pain when she stepped on something. All it would do would be to make Edmond worry about her again and she had resolved to stop making him be troubled so much over her. She really didn't want him to feel obligated to stay by her side because he felt sorry for her.

"Are you doing alright?" He yelled to her.

"Yes." She answered in a 'please just let it the subject drop already' like manner.

"Alright, I was just checking. Let me know if you want me to wash your back." He started laughing.

She sighed in frustration. "Try it and you'll regret it." She threatened back.

"You're just no fun are you?" He was still laughing. It did amuse her to a degree that he was acting in the same manner as he did with Aram. It was one of the personalities that she admired about him, his carefree spirit and his quick wit remarks. She could easily tell that he was adjusting to the fact that Aram was a part of who Arabella really was. It was the part of her that she wasn't allowed to be at home or in society. As a lady of breeding she was expected to be the perfect young woman. However, that wasn't really who she was. True, the way she was with Edmond as Arabella, was also her personality but the sweetness and innocence that she conveyed could get a little tiresome at times. She preferred playing with him and saving the romance for more serious times.

'You have to stop thinking about having a relationship with him.' She scolded herself and then began removing her smock because she had come to the creek. She laid it off to one side before carefully stepping into the cold water. Her breath caught in her throat as the icy water touched her skin. Quickly she used her hands to splash it up where it wouldn't reach on its own. Unfortunately it wouldn't be the best bath she ever had but it was better then nothing. Once she was done she quickly got out and snatched up her gown. Her entire body was covered in goose bumps and she was shivering, almost uncontrollably. Her teeth chattered and her breathing was more labored as her body fought to regain some degree of its lost warmth.

On the way back to the fire she used her hands to rub at her arms in an attempt to warm up. Edmond heard her returning and looked up. He could tell she was nearly frozen to death. He quickly grabbed the blanket that was used under his horse's saddle and got up to go meet her. "Here." He wrapped the blanket about her shoulders as soon as he reached her. Even in the dim light offered by the fire he could see her lips were looking more blue then pink. "Come on, we need to get you warmed up."

"Th...th...thank...you..." She chattered through her teeth and allowed him to put his arm around her shoulders as he escorted her to the fire. They sat down together. "I didn't know it would be so cold." She struggled to say.

"Come here." He told her gently and nearly forced her to get up on his lap as he sat. He took the blanket from around her shoulders and placed it over her. He used his body to warm up the side of her that the blanket wouldn't cover. "You'll warm up quicker this way." Her smock was damp and cold against him, but he didn't really mind that much. He knew within a short amount of time that both she and it would begin warming up. He used one arm to hold her close to him and allowed the other to rest on her lap. "We should probably think about going to sleep soon. If we sleep near the fire, it will help to keep us warm, at least while it's lit."

"What will happen tomorrow? What are we..." She wasn't allowed to finish.

"We'll worry about tomorrow, tomorrow." Carefully he laid down, making sure as they went down, he kept her closer to the fire.

"Edmond..." She began to protest.

"Go to sleep, Arabella. I don't want to hear another word of complaint from you." He said firmly. "I'm tired and I'd like to sleep for a while."

"Goodnight." She whispered as she snuggled into his warm body. "I am feeling a little bit warmer then I had been."

"Good." He leaned forward and kissed the top of her head, since her face was snuggled into his chest. His uninjured arm served as a pillow for her head. Unfortunately it was slightly uncomfortable for him, but he knew he'd survive it. He didn't get much sleep that night and he had to get up more then once to rekindle the fire, however it really wasn't a chore for him. He rather enjoyed this moment alone with her. It always amazed him how much she trusted him. The fact that she was incredibly vulnerable in times like this, it didn't even seem to cross her mind, even when he teased her with suggestions of intimacy.

"You fools!" Eric bellowed when his men returned to camp that night empty handed. "Where is she?"

"I'm truly sorry sire, but once he went into the forest we lost sight of him. We searched for a long time but..." One of his men replied in defense.

"Uhhh!" Eric grunted in anger not allowing him to finish. "How dare he steal her from me?" He took his cup and threw it at the man who had just spoken. It spilled wine everywhere, yet the man never flinched, none of them did. They all remained on one knee, bowing before their king. "That useless ingrate! I'll kill him if we should ever cross paths again." He kicked a chair and sent it flying. "Go back out there and look for them." The king ordered. "If you find them, bring her back to me. Kill him immediately and bring back his head."

"Yes sire."

"Show them no mercy. Make her watch his execution."

"As you wish sire." The men rose and left to do as their king instructed.

"Is their anything I can do to help?" Miriam asked as gently as she could.

Eric turned and looked at her. "I want her back." He seethed. "Unless you can bring her back to me, you're useless." He raised his hand and slapped her as hard as he could on one of her cheeks. Miriam bowed her head and backed away into the darkness. "Stupid girl." He grumbled. Eric wanted to do worse to her but he didn't want to injure his only child that still slept within her. "I'll make Arabella pay for this. She'll still be my queen but she will pay for this unforgivable insult." He used both of his hands and flipped over the table that was near him, sending the items it held crashing onto the floor along with the table itself. His breathing was labored as he finally resolved to go to bed. There really wasn't anything he could do at the moment, so there was no use staying up any longer.

When Edmond awoke the next morning, he was lying alone on the hard cold earth. The blanket was still lying over him. He sat up and looked around. The fire was still burning. It was obvious that Arabella had added more wood to it to keep it fueled. "Arabella!" He called, but she didn't answer. Again he called for her but still he received no reply. "Where is she?" He sighed and stood up. His muscles cried for a good stretching and he obliged them before he began his search for her.

First he would retrace their steps to the places they had been the day before. He wasn't going to allow himself to panic, until he knew for sure she was gone. "Arabella." He called again, "Where are you?" Still she didn't reply. "Damn that woman sure knows how to ruffle a guy's feathers." He grumbled. "She could have at least told me where she was going before she left."

Arabella was trying her best to find something that would better suit Edmond's refined pallet. She really wasn't much of a cook and she was afraid to gather most of the things she found because she wasn't sure if they were poisonous or not. "There must be something around here." She sighed in frustration. Unfortunately she hadn't paid attention to how far she had wandered from camp and didn't realize that she was lost. "This is hopeless." It seemed that the season for anything edible being available was pretty much over. Really all that was still good this time of the year was still underground. "I might as well head back to where I found those turnips. So much for my intentions of making him a nice meal this morning." She hung her head in defeat. "I wasted all that effort for nothing."

She turned around to head back but she couldn't remember from which way she came. "Well this just figures." Her voice nearly growled.

Beautiful Pretender

"Edmond!" She called but then she shook her head and scolded herself. "Stupid, there is no way he'd be able to hear you." She tried to listen for the creek but it was too far away to hear. "Well Arabella, you really did it this time. I guess I'll just try to find my way back on my own and see what happens from there."

Edmond was starting to worry. He had been searching for her for some time now and still there was not a single trace of her. "Perhaps I should go see if she's back at camp." He turned and headed back. Really there was nothing else he could do for the moment. He continued to call out to her, hoping that maybe she would hear him.

Suddenly he had thought he heard something in the near distance and he changed course. He figured it couldn't hurt to check it out and see if it might be her. However, common sense demanded he use caution because there was no guarantee what you might run across. For instance it could be a bear wandering around looking for another meal to pack away before retiring for the winter, or even a wolf. He shook his head to clear it. All he was doing now was thinking about Arabella running into danger. His line of thinking would have to be more optimistic if he wanted to keep control over his emotions.

He stopped near a tree as the noises grew louder. There was an eerie rustling noise coming his way and he felt that it would be best to use some caution. "Edmond!" A female's voice called out and he sighed in relief. She was safe and best yet, she hadn't run off as he feared she would.

"I'm over here." He called back. "Where have you been, you silly girl?" He walked in the direction her voice had come from.

Arabella couldn't help smiling when she saw him. "I'm sorry. I didn't mean to worry you." She continued to come closer to him as he walked towards her. "I got turned around when I went to look for something for our morning meal."

When he reached her, he quickly snapped her up into his embrace, "Don't ever wander off like that again. I might not be able to find you next time and it isn't exactly safe to be alone out here."

"I'm sorry." She repeated, though his embrace was so firm it made it difficult for her to breathe. "I promise not to take off again without letting you know where I am going first."

He released her and looked down at her bared feet. They were raw with injuries because she wasn't wearing anything on them. "You must be in a lot of pain."

Arabella looked down, "Some, but its nothing I can't handle."

"Get on my back and I'll carry you back to camp."

"Don't be silly, I'm perfectly fine to..."

"Stop disobeying me and get on." He scolded.

"You're sounding way too much like a husband then like a friend." She laughed. "Very well." She waited for him to crouch down and then she climbed on, taking care not to touch the wound on his side or arm. Once he was up and walking she told him, "Thanks."

"We need to find you something more suitable to wear, but I'm not sure where we can go to get it."

"Even if we find a place to go, I have no money."

"That's not a problem, I have plenty enough for us to get by on for awhile if we're careful how we spend it."

"It would be nice to have something to wear other then this smock, but perhaps we should part ways once I do get something."

"Why?" He seemed a little offended.

"Eric and his men are probably still searching for me and they'd be looking for both of us. Honestly, Edmond, you're not safe around me. If they should find us, they will kill you for sure. It was obvious yesterday that Eric desires your death."

He needed time to think about her words. They were very logical and he knew she was right, as much as he wished to deny it. "So what should we do?"

"I was thinking that perhaps if we do find a place, you could buy me what I need to disguise myself as Aram."

"Aram? Why?"

"Eric and his men are looking for Arabella. If I'm disguised as Aram, they're less likely to find me."

"So after we do that we'll go back to Arminia..."

She didn't let him finish, "No. You'll go back to Arminia. I'll go to Eldardesh to live with my mother and her parents."

"Eldardesh?" He asked surprised.

"I know it sounds crazy but I am sure that Eldardesh would be the last place Eric would look for me. If I live as Aram, no one will be the

Beautiful Pretender

wiser as to who I really am. Until I can figure out what to do, it could be the best place for me."

"Why can't you be Aram in Arminia?"

"Aram wouldn't work in Arminia because father would know it was me since he still resides there. No, it must be in Eldardesh."

"Wouldn't your former friends recognize you? It doesn't sound like you would really be safe there either."

"Where my grandparents live is far from my former home near the palace. I should be safe enough, especially if I don't go out too much."

"May I come with you?"

Arabella smiled and hugged him gently, "You're a true friend." She kissed his cheek. "I think you should go home. I'm too worried that Eric will find you. I can bear us being apart if I know you're safe. Besides…" She sighed and then tried her best to sound happy, "You have someone waiting for your return."

"Who?"

"The Countess D'Winter, of course." She laughed softly. "Have you forgotten about her already?"

"Not exactly but I'm not really happy about havening to marry her. I'd much rather stay by your side." He brought his lips down to kiss her arm that rested on his collar bone.

"Thank you." She whispered. "Wouldn't it be wonderful if we could do that?"

"You still want me to go back to Arminia?" He asked in defeat, even though he already knew the answer.

"It would be for the best. Besides, you have a family who adores you and their waiting for your return." She kissed his cheek after he hoisted her up so she wouldn't slide off his back. "I'll be alright, you'll see. You know me."

"You're too optimistic for your own good. It certainly would take a lot to get you down and keep you down, wouldn't it? Your like a ball, when you fall, you come right back up again."

"Yeah, I guess you're right." They both laughed even though neither of them really felt like laughing. "I'll find a way to come and see you again someday." She promised. "You'd do best to stay clear of Eldardesh while Eric's alive, however."

"I really don't want to leave you and go back to Arminia, Arabella."

"I know. Let's not talk anymore about this right now so we can enjoy this time together until we have to part."

"Alright." They finally arrived back at the camp site and he gently let her down off of his back. All that was left was to make the preparations to leave so they could search for a town nearby where he could purchase some clothing for her to wear as well as a horse and anything else she might need for her journey.

Chapter 13

As Arabella, disguised as Aram, rode the horse that Edmond bought for her back to Eldardesh, she had many things that occupied her mind. First of all she was sad because the best part of her was being left behind in Arminia. Edmond, the first man and quite possible the only man, she could ever love was now on his way home to Celendra Desh. There he agreed, though reluctantly, to follow through with his parents wishes and marry the Countess D'Winter. It would be awhile before the actual marriage would take place, he would first have to meet her and then follow through with the traditional courtship before they would exchange vows. This process took about a year.

She felt bad for him, only because he honestly tried to leave everything having to do with his life in Arminia behind so that he could stay with her. However, she was afraid if he did, he might come to resent her for losing everything that he was to inherit from his family and through this marriage. Arabella assured him over and over that this was for the best and that she would be fine in Eldardesh. Eventually, he stopped asking her if he could stay with her and she left when it came time for them to part ways. Arabella was sure that her grandfather would take her in without hesitation, so there was no fear of having no where to go. Her grandfather wasn't at all fond of Eric but he lived in Eldardesh for so long that he couldn't bear the thought of leaving his beloved country. She also found comfort in knowing that her mother was there as well and that she was probably worried about Arabella.

The past two weeks with Edmond were ones she'd never forget. They decided to spend the two weeks together in a village called Kinshek. She relived the past two weeks moment by moment as a way to pass time while she took the long journey to her grandfather's home.

JM Howard

Edmond was generous enough to provide her with funds to see her through in comfort until she got there. At first, she had protested his generosity. After all he had already purchased for her clothing, a horse and other provisions. It felt like she was beginning to become a burden on him financially and it was bothering her greatly. Eventually he told her that she could send it back to him when she was able to and then she was able to accept it from him. Of course she'd have to get it from her grandfather first.

Two Weeks Earlier
Just Outside Kinshek's Village Border

"Here." Edmond handed her the clothing that he had purchased for her to wear. "Are you sure that you want to wear men's clothing? It's possible that Eric and his men won't look for you here."

"You're probably right but I can't risk taking any chances." She almost greedily took the items of clothing from him, which consisted of a long sleeved shirt, a pair of trousers, stockings, boots, a cloak, leather stripping to bind her hair and a long rolled up strip of cloth to bind her chest. "This is perfect." She grinned and then began looking around. The trees were rather thin where they were and she'd have to walk a long ways to find somewhere that she could change where Edmond couldn't see her.

He seemed to sense her concerns, "Don't worry, I won't look. The village is far enough away from here that it is doubtful that anyone from there will see you. Besides, I can easily look around and see if anyone is coming for quite a ways."

"I suppose you're right." She waited for him to turn around before she removed the only piece of clothing she had to wear for the last four days, a torn up smock. It felt good to finally be rid of the humiliating piece of clothing and have real clothes to wear again. First she put on the trousers and then she took the time needed to carefully bind her chest. It was never an easy or comfortable process. When she looked down, she was slightly disappointed, even with the bindings she couldn't completely hide the fact that she was a woman anymore. However, it made her flat enough to get by on. "Edmond."

Beautiful Pretender

"Hmm."

"Would you like to help me with my hair when I'm done dressing? It's not something I've ever done on my own. I've never bound my chest on my own either but I think I'll be able to manage it."

"I don't mind." He told her.

"Thanks. I know I'll have to learn how to do these things on my own but I'll make time to learn it all later." She tucked the end of the binding cloth under the wrappings near her navel. Then she reached down to pick up the shirt. Normally this would go on first but she didn't fancy the idea of standing around half naked while she took the time to bind her chest. Once the shirt was on, she carefully tucked it in. "I'm dressed enough that you don't need to conceal your eyes any longer." She informed him.

He turned around and looked at her. "It still blows my mind." He walked towards her. "It's amazing to watch you transform." He reached down and picked up the leather strapping that would be used to tie up her hair into the bound tail that Aram wore. "How do you shorten your hair? Aram's tail wasn't this long."

"It has to be folded up. Basically bring my hair back into a tail, twist it gently and then fold it so that the bottom of my hair comes almost to where the strapping would begin, closest to the top. This helps to disguise its true length."

"So that's how you did it." He handed her the roll of leather stripping to hold before taking her soft hair up into his hands. Then he pulled it all back to form a 'tail' at the bottom back of her head. He then loosely twisted it and folded it up to reduce its length to half. "How do I bind it?"

"Just hold my hair for me and I'll do the binding." She reached back and began wrapping the leather (at its center) around the tail in a crisscross fashion, slowly working her way down. Once she reached the bottom, she tied it off. Only just the tiniest amount of hair showed through the bottom. She turned and smiled at him, "See, it really is me." She grinned, still speaking in Arabella's voice.

He laughed softly, "So it is." He reached down and picked up her boots and stockings. "You should probably get these on so your feet can start having a chance to heal." He looked around for a place off of the ground for her to sit. Finally he saw a fallen tree that would make a rather nice bench for her. "Come." He reached down and took her hand to lead her there.

"Wait." She quickly picked up her cloak. "I don't want to leave this on the ground." They walked together hand in hand the short distance that it took to her make shift bench, which was really just a fallen tree. Then Edmond knelt down to help put on her footwear. "I can do that myself you know." She told him smiling.

"I know." He replied but didn't look up. "Just let me do this for you."

"Alright." She took a deep breath of the cool afternoon air as she leaned back on her hands, that steadied her on the log and she looked up to the sky. "Winter is in the air. It won't be long before the snows begin to fall."

"They may very well come early this year." He agreed as he continued to work. Before he could put anything on her feet, he had to brush off the debris and dirt that they had picked up since her last bath. It didn't take long for her feet to get dirty from walking around with nothing on them.

"Do you think she's pretty?" Arabella's voice was almost dream like.

"Who?"

"The Countess. I've never met her before." She was just making idle chit chat.

"Father said that she is nice to look at. Unfortunately he says that about a lot of women, no matter what they look like." He laughed. "However, how a person looks isn't much of a way to judge them. An angel can be a demon in disguise and an ogre can be the truest of companions."

"I see your point." She looked down at him. "But then again, an angel can be the greatest blessing to someone's heart. You're my angel and guardian, Edmond." He looked up at her for a moment and smiled, before going back to the task at hand. "Part of me wishes that our lives were different. That things like arranged marriages and duty to family and country, didn't exist for us."

"They no longer exist for you." He reminded her.

"Not for the moment, no they don't. However, once I go home to grandfather, he may decide to arrange new possibilities for me. If

Beautiful Pretender

he does, I will honor his decision." She sighed, "I wish I could choose though." He finished and stood up before sitting down next to her. Arabella held out her legs so she could see her new footwear. "I like them."

"They should hold up for awhile anyways."

"What would happen if you decided not to marry the countess? What would your parents do about it?"

"I'm not completely sure to be honest. I have never tried to cross them in such decisions. However, it is possible that I will be disinherited if I defied their wishes. If that happened, father would probably bestow his estate on his late brother's son."

"I wondered if that would be the consequence." She sighed. "That is why I want you to go back home. I would feel horrible should I be the cause of such misfortunes." Arabella laid her head down on his shoulder. "What should we do now?"

"I thought perhaps we could spend some time in Kinshek and rest before starting our journey. I talked with a few people there and they found a place for us to rent on the edge of the village. The widow who lived there died not long ago and the place has been vacant since. Her family could really use the money, even if it's just for a few days."

"That worked out well."

"It will also give me time to secure everything we each will need before leaving and..." He placed his arm about her waist, "I was hoping that maybe we could..." He seemed a bit uncomfortable with his words.

"We could what?"

"Remember we made a promise to each other where each would do one thing for the other, no matter what it was?"

"Yes, I remember."

"I know my request."

She sat back up and looked at him, "What is it?"

"I want you to be my wife for two weeks." He had a slight blush to his face.

"How's that possible?"

"Obviously it wouldn't be a real marriage, so to say, but I want you to be completely mine, just for this little bit of time."

Arabella looked away and stared out into the forest as she thought about his request. "A wife for two weeks..." She whispered. "That's a

JM Howard

lot to ask."

"I know." He admitted.

She got up off the log and started walking away. Then she turned and looked at him, "What do you mean by wife, exactly?"

"First of all, all matters of our futures can't be discussed in any fashion. Only that which will take place during our time together, can be discussed. I want you to allow me to give you the affection that I wish to show you. In these two weeks, we are to only exist for each other and for no one else." He wasn't sure how else to explain himself. "I know you will have to dress as Aram to keep you identity secret, and I know it will cause rumors of a questionable nature to spread about us but I don't care. I know who you really are and that is all that matters to me."

"This could be a problem should you ever inherit the throne." She reminded him.

"These people are unaware of who we really are, other then the fact that we are wealthy nobles. You are safe keeping your name, because Aram doesn't truly exist and should your name leave the village, by the time anyone we know hears of it, you will be long gone. Therefore, you need not worry about your father learning of your presence here."

"What about you?"

"I told them that I am the son of Count Eldritch of Compton. He is a deceased great uncle of mine, but very few people ever knew about him. I should be safe. However I did use my first name, so call me by that name." He stood up and came to her. "Let's have fun and raise a few eyebrows in the process. Let's create memories to take with us into the future that we are being forced to face without each other."

"Very well." She smiled and walked back over to sit beside him again.

"Have you thought of your one request yet?"

"I still have two weeks to think of one." Her arms then wrapped tightly about him as she snuggled closely to him. "I want to make sure it's a really good one."

"Anything at all that you ask, I will give you, even if it means leaving behind my family and fortune."

Her soft laughter was followed by, "I doubt it will be that extreme. I do have to live with my conscience you know. I couldn't be the cause

242

Beautiful Pretender

of your disinheritance. I would never be able to forgive myself if I caused your family grief."

Truthfully, Edmond felt that he was willing to give it up for her, though he could also understand her feelings about it as well. He also would never want to be the cause of such grief in her life either. So he decided not to bring up the subject again. It was obvious that she was not going to change her mind about this and he was going to have to learn to let her go, but not until after these two weeks were over. He didn't care that it could be considered being unfaithful to the woman he never even met yet. Right now she didn't exist, his family didn't exist and the entire world outside of this forest and Kinshek, none of them would exist for the next two weeks. Already this temporary new life seemed to be bestowing a sense of nostalgia on him. His concerns and tension seemed to be melting away like the spring snow. "Shall we?" He offered her his arm in escort. "My horse is already at the dwelling and I had some provisions sent over, so we can eat a real meal for a change."

"I think I could live my life without eating another turnip, ever again." She laughed. "At least we didn't starve."

"True enough."

Baron Cordell was working with Kendrick on some documents of minor importance concerning the matters of a nearby village when one of the king's guards came in. "Sire, please pardon my intrusion, a messenger from Eldardesh is here to see you. He has a message from your brother, King Eric and it is of urgent importance. Should I allow him an audience?"

"Yes, send him in. Baron, your excused."

"Actually sire," the guard spoke again and in somewhat of an apologetic manner, "this matter concerns the Baron as well."

"Very well, send the messenger in." Kendrick did his best to keep a civil attitude with the Baron and only allowed him to assist on matters that didn't involve the kingdom's welfare or security because his loyalty was in question, though it was never discussed.

The messenger came into the room that the king used to address his kingdom's affairs. He bowed humbly, even though King Eric had told him not to, and he cautiously approached. "I have a message for you

JM Howard

from the king of Eldardesh." He unrolled the scroll and began reading. "Princess Arabella has been kidnapped and I believe that she has been taken back to Arminia. If you wish to avoid war, then you will return her at once, should you have any information to her whereabouts. I wish to speak about this further with Baron Cordell, so please send him to me immediately. If he informs me that you are innocent of this matter then I will reconsider initiating further actions against you. However, I do request that you allow my men access to your kingdom to look for her. Approximately one hundred men will be assigned to this task and you will be informed of their location at all times." The messenger looked up. "How do you wish to reply sire?"

Kendrick sighed and looked to the Baron, "You saw that she arrived safely to my brother?"

"Yes sire." He seemed worried. "Who would do this? Do you think there might be someone who is trying to start a war between the two of you?"

"I'm not sure." Kendrick looked at the messenger. "I'll agree to the conditions. Tell Eric that I haven't lifted a finger to stop him from marrying Arabella and that I too will deploy one hundred men to search for her as a sign of good will and of my innocence in this matter."

"Yes sire." The servant bowed again and left the room.

"Baron, you will take charge of the hundred men. Take them to Eldardesh's border with you and have them begin their search on our soil from there. If you find her, send someone to let me know. Despite our differences, I am hoping that you will change your opinion of me in the years to come."

The Baron's face paled, "What do you mean, sire?"

"It is no secret that you harbor resentment and ill will towards me. It is well known that you are of the opinion that I am not the one who should be Arminia's rightful king, despite the fact that I am the first born and my father the king, may he rest in peace, specifically called me to this position. However, I am resolved to prove myself to you, which is why I left peacefully the day you told me of your daughter's engagement to Eric and why I now, not only employ you but also why I choose to assist him in finding her. As much as I hate the thought of her being his wife because I still hold her dearly in my heart, I am a man who will not go against the preexisting laws for my own selfish

244

Beautiful Pretender

desires. Arminia must come first, her and her people."

"Yes sire." The Baron answered slightly embarrassed. "I understand you perfectly now. I will prepare to leave at once."

"Safe journey, Baron. I look forward to any news you may bring to me." Kendrick's voice remained formal and devoid of emotion.

Without another word, the baron left the room. Once he was alone he spoke quietly to himself. "It seems that I may have misjudged you. Perhaps you're not as weak of a king as I was once led to believe. Still, only time will tell if this is true."

"As you can see the place has some furnishings and it's been kept fairly clean by my wife." The man with short dark hair of about forty addressed Edmond and Aram. "You gentlemen are free to use what you need to make yourselves comfortable. I know it's out of town a bit, but it should give you your privacy. You are free to use the buggy out in the barn as well, if you would like too."

"Thank you." Edmond smiled gratefully at him. "I'm sure all of this will work out just fine, thank you for letting us use it."

"Yes, well then I'll be off." The man smiled and then left to walk back to the village that was nearly to the point of becoming a real town. The growth had brought in a good amount of new people to the area and its location was right on one of the main roads used by not only Arminians but also by Eldardesh to the south and those from the northern kingdoms who traveled south.

"So," Edmond said with a hint of nervousness to his voice. "Shall we?" He looked to the front door that would lead them inside.

Arabella blushed, and replied in her normal voice, which she would use when they were alone, "Yeah, I guess we should. It would be kind of awkward if we stood out here all day." She too was feeling a little nervous and she began wondering if this was such a good idea after all. For the next two weeks they would be living together in the same home with no one around to keep an eye on them. Somehow it was different then the last few days in the forest. Then they were alone too but it seemed that it was more of a circumstance of survival, this time it was different. He wanted her to be his wife. She still wasn't sure of exactly what that meant either.

Suddenly he picked her up in his arms, "Might as well do this right."

He grinned.

"You're going to carry me in?" She said in a somewhat shocked voice.

"Of course." He leaned down and kissed her. "After all, we are married."

"Not really." She countered.

"For two weeks we are. The first thing I want you to do when we get in is…"

"Make you a descent meal." Arabella finished hoping he wouldn't ask for more.

Edmond laughed, "That's the second thing."

"Oh." She said embarrassed, "What's the first?"

"Take off your bindings. I don't like them and you shouldn't wear them when we're alone. It can't be good for you to be doing that all the time."

Arabella looked down at her flattened chest. "No, perhaps it isn't." Once they were inside she had a better view of the small home. It was basically one large room. In one corner there sat a fire pit that would serve two functions, keeping the house warm and it also would be for cooking their meals. A table sat against the wall with two chairs pushed under it. Three shelves sat over the table and held two cooking pots, two plates, two mugs and a few other needed items. In the center of the table was a wash basin that would serve for cleaning dishes, bodies and clothing. Another corner held a bed, it was larger then the one Arabella had used at the physician's home, but not by much. The third corner of the room held a cabinet, which Arabella assumed was where their clothing would be stored and the fourth corner stood bare. One tattered rug was laid out on the floor in the center and that was all there was to their little temporary home.

"It's not much…" He began to tell her.

"No, it's perfect." She smiled up at him as he continued to hold her. "Really, I couldn't be happier." '…or more nervous.' She silently finished in her thoughts.

He carried her over to the bed and gently sat her down. "I'm going to tend to our horses," he had already purchased one for her use, "why don't you take this time to take those bindings off."

"Alright."

Beautiful Pretender

"When you're done, go ahead and fix us something to eat." He walked over towards the table. Then he reached down and stuck his finger in the floor, soon a door opened up and he looked down into the pit. "This is where the food is kept."

"A food cellar?" She asked with curiosity and came over to look into it. "Joseph has one of these as well. His wife showed it to me once. But..." she looked up at him, "It's awful dark down there."

"I'll leave a candle lit for you." He offered and then closed the door. "I'll bring some water in when I'm done out there."

"Thanks." She watched as he left their little home, closing the door behind him. Arabella walked to the window and watched him for a few moments before taking off the shirt she was wearing, so she could start the process of removing her bindings. Once the binding was off, she rolled the heavy cloth strip up and then opened the cabinet to find a place to put it. The cabinet held a few extra outfits for her and Edmond to use, only men's clothing plus a chemise gown. She didn't want to know what he had to do to get that gown without arousing suspicion. "I suppose the rest of the clothing would have been suspicious if he bought outfits for a girl." She said to herself and then closed the cabinet. Her shirt was laying a few feet away, so she walked over to pick it up and then she began to put it on.

She gasped as she heard the handle on the entry door unlatch and she did her best to cover herself. "Is it safe to come in yet?" Edmond asked.

"Honestly, do you really think I had enough time to change?"

"No." He laughed. "I'm just trying to get a rise out of you."

Arabella smiled and decided she'd play his game to see if she could fluster him instead, "Oh?" She said nonchalantly. "Well, I don't have my shirt or bindings on, but if you really need to come in, please don't hesitate."

"Seriously?" He seemed confused.

"You did say there was payback coming for me seeing you naked. So here's your chance, milord." She walked over to the door that was only opened a crack. She positioned herself behind the door, so he wouldn't see her, and then she grabbed the handle and quickly opened it, sending him stumbling inside. She held the shirt over her chest to hide what was necessary. "Please, don't be shy." She laughed. "We are married after all."

Edmond refused to look her way, "Arabella?" He nearly choked, "I was only playing around."

"You're always hinting at it, so why don't you make up your mind already." She sighed.

"Very well then." He finally realized what she was doing. In this little game she had turned the tables and was trying to fluster him instead. He wasn't about to let her win. "Since you're offering, how could I possibly refuse?" Edmond looked her way as she peaked at him from behind the door. "First things first." He walked over and placed his hand on the door. "It's a bit drafty out there, so let's close the door."

"What?" She was beginning to wonder if her little game had backfired.

Edmond grabbed the door and pulled hard, forcing it from her hand. Once it was shut he grinned. "So…"

"What?" She asked nervously.

"Let me see." He folded his arms in front of him as he congratulated himself in victory. He knew she wouldn't do it. There was no way she would. Still he did get to see her shoulders and arms bared, for him that was enough.

"You're crazy." Arabella huffed and walked towards him. "I know you won't do it."

"Really?" He smirked and reached down to finger the knotted string that held her pants up. He gave the bowed string a little flip with his finger. "You should take these off as well."

"Get out you pervert." She brought up the one hand that wasn't being used to hold the shirt against the front of her and she punched his shoulder.

He began laughing. "Then you give up? You know you won't win this one."

"Oh really?" She stepped back. "Then I'll do it."

"Do what?"

"I'll let you look."

"Fine." He was sure she was bluffing. He watched as she took the shirt into the two of her hands and she began pulling it away from her body. Instinctively he turned around.

Beautiful Pretender

"Hah!" She laughed. "I won." She brought the shirt back around her front and walked over to him. "I won, I won." She sang in a teasing voice.

"I had better get back out there to finish with the horses before it gets too dark." He said nervously.

Arabella came up behind him and laid her head against his back. "I won." She sang again.

"Yes, you won." He sighed and then he reached behind him and snagged the shirt from her. Arabella cried out in surprised, "It was only a temporary victory though." He laughed.

She did her best to reach around him, "Give it back!"

He held it just out of her reach, "Now what should I do?" He seemed like he really had to think about what to do next.

"You cheated!" She continued to reach for her shirt. "Edmond Vaughan Wallace, you give me my shirt back right now."

"Only if you say that I'm the winner." He boasted.

"No." Her reply was defiant. "Give it back."

"Just declare me the winner and you can have it back. It's really very simple."

"Forget it." She huffed and then wrapped her arms around him. "If you won't give me mine, I'll just have to take yours." She began pulling his shirt out of his pants.

"I'm glad to see that the personality I admired in Aram wasn't reserved just for him." He placed his free hand on one of hers and she temporarily stopped what she was doing. "You do love me, don't you?"

"Of course I do." She tried to reach for her shirt again. "Why?"

"Promise you will tell me that you love me as much as you can while we're here. Give me a life's time of those words these next two weeks. Maybe then, when the time comes, I can allow myself to say goodbye." He felt her embrace him tenderly.

"I love you, I love you, I love you." She whispered. "I'll always love you, no matter where we end up in life, you can be certain, that I will always love you." With deep affection she kissed his back through his shirt. "If this world hadn't been so cruel we might have been able to share our love for the remainder of our lives. I would have been happy being your wife for real."

JM Howard

Edmond hung his head and used his arms to cradle the ones she held onto him with. She didn't even try to take her shirt back at the moment. "I will always love you as well. There could never be another woman who could capture my heart the way you have. You're like a wild fire at times, you're fun to be with and you like to play around. You hardly fear anything and you go for whatever it is that you want. At other times you are like a gentle breeze, soothing and refreshing. You're gentle and adorable when you show your love towards me. I also wish that we could take this temporary marriage and make it a life long reality."

She grabbed hold of her shirt but she didn't take it from him yet. "Perhaps, you will be the only one." Her voice whispered.

"What do you mean?"

"You'll be the only one I will allow myself to truly love. I don't want to truly love anyone else but you. I don't want to marry anyone if he isn't you. I won't marry anyone else, at least as long as I have any say about it."

"You shouldn't isolate yourself like that." He said with concern. The thought of her having to spend the rest of her life alone, made his heart grieve.

"I want to." She let go of her shirt and it fell to the ground. Then she began working at his again. "Make me your real wife these two weeks. Love me enough to last me a life time."

"Arabella, I couldn't possibly..." He could feel himself losing confidence in his strength to deny himself what she was now asking for. It was easier to deny himself when she brushed off his advances then it was when she gave into them.

"You don't have to do this if you don't want to."

"Wanting to do it isn't the problem." He cleared his throat, "Whether we should or not is." After she loosened his shirt, she brought her hands up into it and caressed his stomach. "You don't know what you're asking." He was about to lose control.

"I'm pretty sure I know what I'm asking." She pulled up his shirt so she could kiss his back without it being a barrier.

He could feel the heat rise to his cheeks as he felt her unclothed chest resting on his bared back. That was when he realized that this was no longer a game of seeing who could get a rise from the other first. She

Beautiful Pretender

was being very serious. A sigh of content escaped his lips. "If that is what you want then I'll give in. You win."

She stopped for a moment, "Huh?"

"You win. I can't fight you at this level. If you want me to love you then I'll love you." He was about to turn around to embrace her but there was a sudden knock on their door.

"Oh God!" She gasped and dropped to her knees to retrieve her shirt.

Edmond pulled his back down and tucked it in as quickly as possible. He couldn't help but to glance down on her and he saw the back of her torso unhindered by clothing. "You're so beautiful." He whispered.

The knock sounded again. "Are you going to get that?" She whispered back as she sat up with the shirt being held tightly to the front of her. Her breathing was still slightly labored for the earlier excitement.

"Stand behind the door and do your best not to be seen."

"Alright." She quickly turned around to face away from him and then put the shirt on over her head, despite the knowledge that he continued to watch her. "You better answer it."

Edmond tore his eyes from her and took hold of the latch to open the door. "Can I help you?" He asked the visitor that Arabella couldn't see.

"I brought the saddle and other equipment that you ordered for the horse." The male voice said. "I'm sure you'll be satisfied with the condition and…" He wasn't allowed to finish.

"Let's go and try them out, shall we. I was just about to head out to work with the horses anyways." Edmond told him and then he peaked around the door at Arabella, "I'll be back later. Make us something to eat, alright."

Arabella used her male voice to answer, "I was just about to do it."

Edmond winked at her. "We can finish that project we started later." Arabella coughed in embarrassment. "I win." He whispered and blew her a silent kiss before leaving.

"That moron!" She huffed. "Like I'd give him a second chance." Arabella made her way to the food cellar and opened it. "He didn't even leave me a candle." Carefully she navigated the ladder down and did her best to look around. To her delight she found some dried meat, onions and potatoes. All she needed now was some water to cook it all in. She brought it up and then placed it on the table. The pot was on the shelf and she used a chair from under the table to get the needed elevation to reach it. Everything needed to be cut up so it would cook quicker but she couldn't find a knife to do it. "Figures." She groaned.

Arabella sat down on the chair she had just used to stand on. "He's in for a pretty big disappointment. I really don't even know how to cook. That wasn't part of my training to become a queen. Even a nobleman's wife wouldn't do such a lowly job." She knew a few things for cooking out doors, mostly because the peasant boys that she and Edmond befriended knew how. For instance, placing fish, rabbits and roots on sticks to roast over a fire, was really all she knew, thanks to them. She looked at the fire hearth, "Even if I had sticks to put through these things, I still haven't a fire. How exactly does he expect me to cook this stuff?" Edmond was always the one to start the fires when they were alone. He had the flint stone and other materials that were needed to make one.

"I give up." She sighed and then went to go lay down on the bed. "I'm just too tired to care." Before getting in bed she first pulled down the covers. "That's great, there's only one pillow for us to use. What else will we be lacking in this place?" True she had told Edmond that it was perfect, but anywhere looked perfect after the last four days of sleeping in the woods and only having a torn up smock to wear. Now reality was sinking in. She also was feeling a little embarrassed about her behavior with Edmond earlier, before they were interrupted. She wasn't quite sure what had possessed her to act so carelessly. Sure, she loved Edmond very much and it really would have been nice to truly have been his wife, but she wasn't really his wife and she had to keep that in mind.

Arabella slid down into the old bedding. The musty smell left much to be desired but she wouldn't complain. "It's so nice to have a real bed to sleep in again." She smiled with delight. It nearly swallowed her in its soft feather stuffed mattress and the blankets that were piled on, provided her with an almost instant warmth.

Edmond was just finishing putting the saddle and other supplies away so they would stay safe from the horses and the weather's elements

Beautiful Pretender

should it decide to rain. He was looking forward to a nice hot meal, devoid of turnips. Edmond couldn't help wondering what 'his wife' was going to make for their first dinner together. He grinned at the thought as he closed the barn up tight. "My wife..." It had such a nice sound to it as he whispered it into the night air. As he headed towards the house, he couldn't help but to let himself wonder what it would be like if all of this were for real. He really wanted it to be. The sacrifices for this to happen would be high and he understood why Arabella was not in favor of making this real but he was pretty sure that it would be worth it to keep her by his side. When he reached the front of their little home he was a little surprised that no fragrances of food were coming from it to greet him. "Huh." He shrugged his shoulders.

Then he saw the wooden bucket sitting by the door and figured he should fill it from the property's well before going in. It was already getting rather dark and he didn't want to have to try and find his way around in a strange place when it was too dark to see by. Besides, getting the water would be the last thing he would need to do for the night, so he figured he might as well get it over with.

When he came back he felt a tinge of disappointment as he went inside, there still was no aroma of food, the house was cold because there was no fire and he couldn't see Arabella anywhere. He set the bucket of water down on the table and then lit the fire in the hearth. It sent a soft warm glow throughout the little abode. That was when he saw Arabella, sleeping soundly on the bed. He could see now why he hadn't noticed her there before. She was partially sunk in the mattress and the number of blankets also helped to hide her tiny form.

Edmond smiled at her pretty sleeping face, he couldn't really be too unhappy with her, after all the last several days were really hard on her. Even so, as much as he would have liked for her to sleep, he knew she hadn't had any food all day and barely anything to drink. He went over and knelt down beside the bed. "Arabella?" He called to her gently. "Dearest, you should wake up for awhile." She groaned sleepily. "Come on, get up." He pulled her blankets off and then sat down beside her. Then he lounged down next to her on his side, facing her, and using his elbow to prop himself up so he could look down on her. "Hey beautiful..." He moved some stray hairs from her face and wondered why she left her hair bound in the leather strapping. He

253

JM Howard

never did think that it looked all that comfortable to sleep on.

Arabella felt suddenly cold as the blankets were removed but she found it difficult to wake up from her deep slumber. Edmond's gentle voice was speaking to her but she was unable to comprehend the words he said. She found the sound of his voice and his words to be comforting and familiar as she slowly awoke. She moaned softly and then turned into him to seek the lost warmth from him.

Edmond laughed softly as she grabbed two handfuls of his shirt and then snuggled her face into his chest. "You should get up and eat something, dearest."

"It's too cold." She mumbled.

"Come on." He sat up with some difficulty and brought her up with him.

"What are we going to eat? I had neither fire nor water to cook with. Besides," she wrapped her arms around him to keep him from getting up out of bed. "I really don't know how to cook."

"Ah, so the truth comes out." He laughed again.

Arabella hit him gently in the back with her fist. "You moron, I was never taught how to. It isn't something that a person of my station should need to know."

"True enough. I'm sorry. I just assumed since you were a woman that you would know how to cook."

Arabella looked up at him, though she continued to lay her head on his chest, "You've known me for five years now. Did you think Aram had any ability to cook?"

"I guess I forgot about that. Aram could hardly do anything domestic."

"Next time you think about assigning me such tasks, keep him in mind." She then sat up the rest of the way, for she had been lounging against him and then she moved to the edge of the bed so she could get out. "So what should we do?"

"Well…" he had to think for a moment. "There's a tavern not far from here. I'm pretty sure we could get something to eat from there. We'll figure out what to do about our future meals tomorrow."

"Alright." She got out of bed and began trying to fix her hair without needing to take out the binding to rebind it. Then she looked down at her chest. "Damn."

Beautiful Pretender

"What?"

"I'll have to flatten my chest again before we can go. It'll be too noticeable even with the cloak on."

Edmond looked at it and smiled. "Yeah, I suppose it is."

Arabella blushed and crossed her arms over her chest, "Hey, stop looking at them you pervert." She scolded him but he just laughed and stood up.

"Where did you put the binding?"

With her arms still crossed to hide herself, even though her shirt concealed them from his eyes, she said, "In the cabinet over there." She nodded her head in the direction it was in.

"You don't have to hide your chest, its not like I can see them through your shirt or anything."

"Yeah but you were looking at them just the same." She complained.

"And your point is? You're a woman. Of course I'm going to look." He grinned at her before going to open the cabinet and located the rolled up binding. Then he brought it to her. "Isn't this hard to put on?" He held it up and looked at it.

"It is rather difficult but I manage." She snatched it from him and then looked into his eyes. "Well?"

"Well what?"

"I can't do anything with you standing around here. Go." She pointed the way to the door.

Edmond sighed, "I want to help you."

"Edmond!" She couldn't believe the nerve he had.

"I'm starving woman. Just turn around and let me help you." He demanded and took the binding back from her.

"But...I..." she couldn't find the words. Finally she turned around and pulled up her shirt.

"Just tell me what to do." He began unrolling some of the strip.

"You're certainly bold, aren't you?" She scolded and then sighed. "If you'll just hold the end against my back, then I would have an easier time starting the binding process. The end not being secured is the most difficult part."

He laid the end of it on her upper back, against her spine and held it in place with his fingers before handing her the roll. "Is here alright?"

255

He meant where he held the end.

"Yes, it will do fine." She took the roll and began to carefully bind herself, trying with great difficulty to not let it twist as she wrapped it around herself. It had to be even and flat against her body. Once she was sufficiently covered, Edmond took the roll from her and he finished binding her so it would go faster. Arabella wanted to protest again, but she saw the determined look in his eyes as he came around in front of her and she almost felt sorry for him. For four days he lived on turnips and he had been looking forward to a real meal after not eating all day. She couldn't blame him for feeling grumpy and impatient. Finally he gave her the end to tuck in and then she set about tucking her shirt back into her pants, as he gathered their cloaks.

Edmond put his on and once she had finished tucking in her shirt, he helped her put hers on as well. "I already set our boots outside. We can put them on out there."

"Alright." She replied softly and then took his arm. "Are you angry with me?"

"Why would I be?"

"I haven't exactly been nice to you today. I'm feeling rather nervous about all of this." She wasn't sure what to say to him. "Please have some patience with me."

"I understand. I'm just can't stopped forgetting about the fact that we will only have two weeks before our lives go in different directions. I want for us to have everything that we can get before it's over. I don't want to have any regrets and always be asking myself if we only had more time."

"Then I will do my best not to make you unhappy with me again. Just tell me what to do and I'll do it. After all I did promise you I would give you your one request without reservation and I know I haven't done well on that promise yet, but I will try to be more considerate of it from now on."

"Don't worry about it." He smiled and then put his arm about her waist. "Let's just go and get something hot to eat and then we should try and get a good night's sleep. After that we can worry about what comes next." He reached forward to unlatch the door.

"I think I can handle that." She smiled up at him.

Chapter 14

Arabella felt a little uneasy as the barmaids hung all over Edmond and her (because they were under the impression that she was a boy named Aram). They flirted without care and leaned over to give a more then adequate view of what lay under their dress if the wealthy noblemen fancied it. "Are you not just the cutest young man?" One woman with red hair and a semi plump body said as she pinched Aram's cheek. "I'll bet you haven't had the pleasure of learning the ways of what a woman can do for you yet, have you, my love?" She grinned.

"Um…" Aram blushed and wasn't sure how to respond. This only encouraged her.

"And isn't this one simply to die for." A thinner blond woman smiled at Edmond. "There's nothing like a nobleman's hands, their so smooth and nimble." This set off all of the girls as they giggled in response.

"Ladies please…" The barman scolded. "Allow these gentlemen their meals before you silicate your services." This only set the women off again but they did back off some. "I'm sorry, it's been a while since two young men have come through here and stayed. Mostly the girls only receive tired farm hands and old men. Rarely do they have the pleasure of two young nobles."

"I'm sure this will disappoint them, but we won't be seeking their services while we're here." Edmond informed him. "We came to have a break from our responsibilities before we will be forced into marriages of our parents choosing."

"Ah, yes. I can see how that would be troublesome." The man of about forty agreed. "Well if you change your mind, I'm sure these girls of mine can give you some experience and guidelines to pleasing your wives in bed."

Aram choked on his soup. "No." He gasped for air. "No, I'm sure we'll figure it out just fine on our own. Thank you."

The bar tender laughed. "Your loss. These lass's have much to offer

JM Howard

to young men such as yourselves." He then left to tend to another customer.

"Are you alright?" Edmond laughed softly.

"Oh, shut up." Aram glared at him. "From now on, I'll figure out how to cook." This only made Edmond laugh more. "Just finish eating so we can get out of here."

"Alright, alright." Edmond continued to laugh.

When they had finished, Edmond paid the tab. They were about to leave when the two women from before came up to them. The redhead spoke, "Would you think about reconsidering if we gave you this night for free? It isn't often that we are given a chance to entertain young men like yourselves."

"Yes, please let us." The blond agreed.

Edmond sighed and then said, "If I desire entertainment, then I'll get it from here." He turned to Aram and placed one hand on his shoulder and used the fingers of his other hand to lift Aram's face up. Then he leaned down and kissed her. Both women gasped in a horrified realization of what he meant. Arabella was caught off guard but she received his kiss graciously. She could feel the heat rise to her face as she closed her eyes. Her heart's pace sped up as he cupped one side of her face with his large hand. His thumb gently caressed her cheek and she was a captive under his spell. When he was finished he pulled back only just enough to looking lovingly down into her hazel eyes. A small smirk made its way to her lips. He smiled back down at her before returning his attention back to the two women. "Have I made myself clear now?"

"Yes." The two barmaids answered and were nearly white with shock.

"Good." Edmond smiled and then he put his arm about Aram to escort him out. "We won't be coming back but thank you for the service."

"And just so you know," Aram couldn't help adding this last tidbit using her male Arminian voice, "I prefer men. I have no desire to be with a woman." She had to do all she could to keep from laughing and she could feel Edmond squeeze her shoulder.

"Let's go." Edmond told her and then they left the tavern. He kept a straight face but he knew he wouldn't be able to keep his laughter at

Beautiful Pretender

bay much longer. If things kept going like this, he really was going to enjoy these next two weeks. It was nice to see that Aram's personality was very much part of Arabella's. He squeezed her shoulder and she laid her head against his shoulder. "I love you." There was no one around but them now to hear their conversation as they made their way back to the little house on the rutted dirt road. "Thanks for playing along."

Arabella was slightly embarrassed by it. After all, everyone thought they were both men, even though they weren't. Edmond wasn't taking anytime about 'raising some eyebrows' as he had indicated he would when they were in the forest and she wasn't doing much better herself. "You're awful." She scolded in a whisper and then she started to laugh, she simply couldn't keep it to herself any longer. "They'll probably kick us out of this town before our two weeks are up at this rate."

"Probably." He agreed with a grin. "However, I didn't want those ladies to keep pestering us. It just seemed like the best way to nip the problem in the bud."

"I suppose." She kept laughing. "Those poor things looked like they were about to die from shock." Edmond was laughing as well. "I can just hear the rumors..."

"This should be fun." He agreed. "The looks on their faces were priceless."

"Yes, but let's just hope they don't discover who you really are. Can you imagine what would happen? Not just with your future wife but also if you end up having to take the throne. It would cause quite a scandal."

"I'm not too worried about it. It's unlikely that I'll need to ever assume the throne. As for my future wife, I really couldn't care less. It's not like we love each other, not to mention the fact that we haven't even ever met. Why should I care?"

"I care." She looked up at him in the night's shadows. "You may come to love her one day and you really should be considerate of her feelings."

"Didn't we agree not to mention anything of our futures outside of these two weeks?" He reminded her.

"Yes." She looked away from him. Their conversation was more serious now. "I just couldn't help myself."

"You are my only concern right now. You exist for me alone and I for you."

"Alright." She laid her head back down on his shoulder. "I'll exist only for you. I'll think only about how to make you the happiest I can."

"Good." He stopped walking. "Get on."

She looked back up at him with some confusion, "Huh?"

"I want to carry you home." He squatted down so she could get on his back.

"You're crazy." She laughed and then climbed on. "I love you." She sighed as she snuggled into him when he was standing back up. "Just promise not to drop me again. That really hurt."

"I promise." He felt her kiss his neck and it made him smile. "What should we do tomorrow?"

"Well…." She felt a bit embarrassed, "I thought maybe I should learn how to cook for you. At least I should learn a few simple dishes."

"Sounds good. I'll buy us bread from the baker. I hear it can be kind of hard to make if you've never done it before." He then changed the subject of conversation. "Will it bother you if I sleep with you on the bed? I know we've slept next to each other before but this is a little different."

"I told you that I would do anything you asked of me, didn't I? If you want to sleep by me, then sleep by me. To be honest, I like it when you do."

"I just wanted to make sure. I want to make sure that anything we do is what you want to do as well."

"I understand." She whispered as she snuggled him. "I want to do whatever you ask. I only want to make you happy."

He wasn't sure what to say next to her. It wouldn't be long before they arrived to the little house on the outskirts of Kinshek. The cool night air was already working its chilled fingers through their cloaks and clothing to tickle their skin with its icy breath. Even now the trees had lost many of their leaves as they prepared for their winter sleep and the fowl of the air had been exercising their skills daily in preparation for their yearly flight. However at the moment most of the creatures of the day had long ago made way to the creatures of the night. Even those creatures were starting to silence their songs as the weather grew

Beautiful Pretender

less friendly.

Edmond turned the latch on the door to their little home and carried Arabella inside. She hadn't spoken another word on the remainder of their short journey and he wondered if perhaps she had fallen asleep. It seemed that the sleepy Aram was also very much Arabella as well. The girl truly did like sleeping. "Are you awake?" He asked softly so he wouldn't startle her.

"Yes." She yawned. "You can let me down now." He did as she asked. "So what should we do now?"

"Go to sleep I guess." He was wondering what was going on in that little head of hers. "Come here."

"Hmm?" She asked sleepily.

He went over to her and turned her around. "It bothers me watching you sleep with this leather strapping in your hair." Edmond found the ends that she had tied and carefully worked the knot out. "Besides, your hair is much prettier when you let it down."

"Silly." She laughed. "Of course it does."

Once he finished he said, "Now that binding." He reached for her shirt but she stepped away before he could grab it.

"I can get it. Why don't you relight the fire? It has grown too cold in here."

"Very well." He almost sounded disappointed, but Arabella ignored it. "I think I'll heat up some water to drink before going to bed. Would you like some as well?"

"No thanks." She yawned as she continued to unwind the binding. Arabella did her best to do it with her shirt on and while having it hang down, as much as possible in order to keep her chest hidden. He wasn't looking but she wasn't sure if he might try. "I'm much too tired to drink anything."

"Very well." He struck the flint over the wood and kindling he just put in. Soon the fire took and grew in size. He listened as Arabella prepared for bed. It was obvious she wasn't comfortable with him being there. He knew that what he hoped for may never happen and he would have to except it. It was her innocence and it was hers to guard or give away. Still he wanted to be one with her but it was possible that it might not ever happen and he was determined to be alright with that possibility.

"Will you be long?" She asked.

"Not too long. I just need something warm to drink to drive the chill out." He filled one of the pots with the water he brought in earlier and placed its handle on the hook that hung over the fire. He felt her come up behind him as he squatted by the fire to absorb its warmth and then she got down on her knees beside him. He noticed she had dressed down to only her shirt which hung down to her knees.

"You should teach me how to make a fire. I felt so helpless tonight not knowing how to do anything."

"Sure." He poked at the fire with an iron rod to stir it up a bit. "You should probably go to bed so you can warm up."

Instead she laid her head on his shoulder and he put his arm about her. "I will in a moment. It just feels so nice here." She closed her eyes and took in the warmth of the fire and of the man beside her.

"Have you thought about your one request for me yet?" Edmond asked curiously.

"I'm still thinking. I don't want to ask for just anything. It has to be something really special and meaningful, like the one you asked from me."

"Another two weeks?" He suggested.

"It just seems so temporary." She sighed. "I want something that will last for the rest of my life, something that will keep my heart full."

"That is a pretty big request. I hope I will be able to fulfill it." He hugged her close. "The water is steaming already. It's probably hot enough to drink. Are you sure you don't want any?"

"I'm sure." She turned her face to kiss the shoulder she had been leaning against and then she got up off of the floor. "Don't take too long."

"I won't." He watched her as she walked over to the bed and got in. He loved the way her legs looked, seeing as how he never really had a chance to see them before. Even as Aram she never showed them. They were long, thin and delicate. In fact it was the first time he ever had such a privilege of seeing a woman's legs. No wonder they kept them hidden. The sight of them alone was enough to rouse desire in him. He wondered if she would complain should he touch them while they slept together. 'Get a hold of yourself, Edmond.' He scolded himself silently as the realization of how hard it would be not to touch

Beautiful Pretender

her in this situation might be. It would be stupid of him to think that he could stop at just touching her legs, even if she let him do it. He wanted all of her and there was just no other truth about it.

After Arabella was snuggly back in bed, she turned on her side so she could look at him and he could tell that sleep was already trying to claim her. He took down a mug and ladle from one of the shelves over the table and used the ladle to fill his cup with the hot steaming water. The drink felt good as it gently burned its way down his throat and then into his stomach. He then sat down and removed his boots and stockings and stretched out his ankles and feet. A content sigh escaped his lips as he leaned against the chairs back and watched the fire dance in the hearth.

Arabella watched as Edmond stretched out his arms and then he placed them behind his head. She knew he had to be a little sore from carrying her for so long on their journey home from the Tavern, not to mention the fact that he had to sleep on the hard cold earth for the last few days. She ached from that alone herself. Still he never complained. Right now he looked relaxed as he occasionally drank from the heated water that he had made for himself. She knew it was something that he enjoyed and he had often drunk it when they were out with the guys at night. 'I'll have to remember to make it for him at night.' She promised herself.

Already, even though things didn't go quite as he planned, they were making wonderful memories together and it had only just been one day. If things kept going like they were, he would have a treasure chest filled with memories to sustain him in the life that lay ahead. Every second with the woman he truly loved would be forever engraved into his heart, where he could often return to when he needed it most. He finished off the last of his water and then put his mug and ladle back on the shelf. After removing his pants he placed them in the cabinet, where Arabella had already put her things.

Arabella moved back closer to the wall so he could get in easier. She also pulled back the covers for him. "Don't worry, I was still awake."

"It's like you read my mind." He laughed softly as he got in, for he was just about to apologize for waking her up. Once he was in, she immediately she pulled the covers back up.

"It's still pretty cold." She told him as she snuggled close.

He gasped at what she did next. "What are you..." She was lifting up his shirt.

"Shhh. This is what you wanted, right?"

"Yeah, but..." He grabbed her wrists to stop her but she had already made it half way up his torso. "You don't have to do this."

Arabella released his shirt. "It's hard to do when you're lying down." She sat up. "I'll let you do your own." She worked her own shirt up from under her and then quickly took it off, tossing it on the floor near Edmond. She had never felt so nervous in her life but she did her best to hide this from him. It was the least she could do to thank him for everything he had done for her, including forgiving her for deceiving him.

He looked at her in the soft glow of the fire light. "But..."

"Go on and take yours off. If you wait too long, I'll lose my nerve and change my mind." She smiled sweetly. Arabella was doing her best to keep her nerves stilled. Even with trying her best she was shaking slightly.

As she had laid there and watch Edmond earlier, she had resolved that she would do this for him and it took everything she had to make it this far. Part of her felt like crying because she was afraid, not of Edmond hurting her or anything but of this act which was forbidden. However, part of her longed for his touch and had been longing for it for some time now.

He sat up and did as she asked. The blanket was still lying over their laps. "Are you sure that you're alright with this?"

"Just shut up." She whispered and reached out for him so she could pull him to her. "Doing it now will make the next two weeks much easier on both of us." She knew that giving into him would make it so she wouldn't have to be so timid around him anymore. If she could get this out of the way, it would help the days to come to be more bearable.

Edmond was unable to keep his feelings at bay anymore and he completely lost control. He allowed himself to give into her outpour of affection and passion. He wanted to savor every moment and every part of her. It was what he had hoped for, her complete and unshielded love. His hands and lips took in every portion of her body, bit by bit as she cried out in the pleasure that it brought her. "My beautiful wife."

Beautiful Pretender

He sighed when he finally began making love to her. He heard her cry but he knew it wasn't from sadness, pain or any other negative form because she kept pulling him to her. Her hands came up and brought his lips back to hers so she could kiss him over and over again.

"I love you." She whispered to him several times. "I love you so much." Her hands then glided along his chest to take in his masculine form which was firm and well defined for a man his age. "I don't want to let you go." She nearly sobbed.

"Where would I go?" He stopped and looked down into her tear streaked face.

"I'm not allowed to talk about it." She reminded him. "I just wish I could keep you with me forever."

Edmond felt the tears sting his eyes and then he brought his head down and kissed her passionately. He had promised himself not to badger her into letting him stay by her side because she couldn't live with the guilt of what it would do to him. She didn't want him to be cut off from his family because of her. Even though his mother adored her and had hoped she might be a prospective bride, because of the circumstances with the kings, this simply couldn't happen. It wasn't just because his mother was the older sister to both kings, it also had to do with an obligation to follow the decorum of the law and how things had to play out in order to avoid war. Edmond's mother was an Arminian just like her brother Kendrick, and Edmond was sure that Eric felt no obligation to his older sister. If she allowed this, it would be no different then if Kendrick decided to keep Arabella. Eric would see it as an opportunity to start a war. Edmond's only saving grace at the moment was in knowing that Eric was unaware that Edmond was his nephew. If he had known, things may have been even worse then what they were now.

This whole situation was killing him inside. It would be different if Arabella didn't want him to be with her because she didn't love him that way. However that wasn't the case. She wanted him as he wanted her, yet it would never be. If things hadn't gone so wrong with Arabella's family and she hadn't been promised to one of the two kings, his parents would have applauded his choice for a spouse. His mother, on more the one occasion, had mentioned that she wished Arabella had been available as a candidate, she even went so far as to put off Edmond's

JM Howard

engagement agreement to the countess in hopes of her brothers not choosing Arabella. "How can fate be so cruel?" He whispered.

"Edmond." Arabella called out softly to him. He carefully laid down on the top of her. He didn't notice that he had been crying and she cradled his head to her chest as she spoke words of comfort to him. "It's alright." She told him tenderly as she gently ran her fingers through his hair. "We'll be alright."

He held tightly onto her as his tears poured forth. "I don't think I'll know how to leave you when the time comes." He confessed. "Now more then ever, I just want to hold on to you and never let you go."

"Maybe we should go to sleep then." She tried her best to comfort him. "You may do whatever you want with me while we're here. I don't care what you want to do. I will gladly be your wife for these two weeks." She kissed the top of his head. "But for right now, you should rest. You're worn out, as am I."

He eased himself off of her but he brought his hand up to gently caress her. "I'm sorry for breaking down like this."

"I'm glad you did. It lets me know that I'm not alone in my grief." She kissed him gently before allowing herself to settle down for the night.

Arabella woke up long before Edmond did. It was obvious that he was more worn out then either of them had known. She really wanted to have hot water waiting for him, but she still hadn't learned how to light the fire. She went ahead and put her shirt back on and her stockings. A bath could wait until she could warm up some water. She was getting rather tired of taking baths in cold water. However she did use some of the water from the night before to wash her face.

The next task she set about doing was to find Edmond's dagger. She found it in the cabinet with their clothing and then set about using it to cut up the potatoes and onions. Once that was finished she set them aside in one of the cooking pots along with the dried meat she had brought up the evening before. She would have put water with them from the bucket, but she wasn't sure if Edmond would need to use it and it really didn't matter since she couldn't start cooking the stuff until he woke up to start the fire anyway. "What a disgrace I am." She whispered miserably to herself.

Beautiful Pretender

Edmond woke up and was slightly amused to see Arabella sawing away at the potatoes with his dagger. He would have preferred her not using it for that but she looked so cute and she was trying so hard to do this for him, that he simply couldn't scold her. He made a mental note to buy her a knife that she could use for doing such things. Perhaps when he went to market to buy bread, he could find one for her then. After she had finished, she did her best to clean and dry his dagger before putting it back where she had found it in the cabinet.

He finally resolved to get up. "Hey you." He smiled at her. "Why are you up so earlier?" It took more effort then he'd expected to sit up in the bed. The blanket slid down onto his lap, exposing his bared chest.

"I wasn't feeling too well and I couldn't sleep, so I thought I would get up and make myself useful for a change." She walked over and sat down by him. Then she leaned her head against his chest as he held her close.

"You feel warm." He lifted his hand to touch her forehead. "I think you might have a fever."

"I'm sure it will go away soon." Her voice wasn't too convincing. She sounded very tired. "I think I just over did it the last few days."

"Still, I think we should put a cool cloth on your head and try to bring the fever down." He assisted her to lie back down on the bed before getting out of it himself. Immediately he went to the cupboard and found a suitable cloth and then soaked it in the water from the bucket. Arabella loved looking at his unclothed body. For the first time she didn't have to shield her eyes from the beautiful sight. "This should help some." He smiled as he came back to her with the cold wet cloth. "It's better than nothing." Edmond laid it on her forehead.

"You don't have to fuss over me like this. I'm sure I'll be fine soon."

"Are you alright? About last night I mean." He gently smoothed her hair from her face as he looked tenderly into her eyes.

Arabella blushed as she remembered the intimate relation they shared. "Yeah." Her voice was near a whisper. "It was kind of fun actually." This made him laugh softly. "I was a little scared at first but then it was alright."

"To be honest, I was a bit unsettled as well. However, it's nice that we have that out of the way. Now I can play with you all I want, without worrying that I might offend you." He leaned over and kissed her as he placed his hand on a former forbidden place. It still amazed him at how she could bind her chest to the point that it made her look like a boy for she really wasn't all that flat, in fact she was very nicely formed.

"Yeah." She smiled. "That goes two ways you know." Arabella laid her hand on his hip which was still bare since he hadn't put on any clothing yet. "I like looking at you like this. It's kind of comforting."

"Comforting, huh?" He wasn't quite sure of what to make of that comment. If she were naked he would feel excitement over comfort. Perhaps things would settle down in time. "Time..." He thought out loud in a whisper.

"Time?"

"Sorry... I just was thinking about something." He brought his hand up from her chest and removed the cloth from her forehead, for it was growing warm from her fever. Then he took it to the bucket to refresh the water on it. Once it had cooled back down, he took it back over to her and placed it back on her head. "I'm going to start the fire and get more water. Will you be alright for a while?" Concern was evident his voice.

"Of course silly." She laughed softly, "I'm sure I'll be just fine. I'll start the food as soon as you bring in the water. Perhaps you should go to the market while our food is cooking."

Edmond was waiting for the baker to get to him, currently he had other customers. A sudden chill went down his spine, almost as if someone were watching him. He casually looked around and spotted two soldiers who looked like they were from Eldardesh. 'That didn't take long.' He thought to himself as he pulled up the hood from his cloak to cover his head and hide his face. They came his way but went by him to a man who was only just a few feet away.

One of the soldiers spoke, "We're looking for a young man and woman who may have come to your town. Have you had any travelers through here in the last few days?" The soldier's Eldardesh accent was unmistakable.

Beautiful Pretender

The older man, a villager of about fifty with short grey hair and blazing blue eyes, placed his hand to his bearded chin and rubbed it with his thumb and forefinger. "Hmm." He thought for a moment. "We haven't seen a young man with a woman but we do have two young men staying with us, their renting a house not far from here. Though I doubt they're the ones that you're looking for. They seem like nice boys, though a little odd and they come from prestigious families or at least that is what I've been told."

The two guards took a moment to talk about it in private. Then the soldier asked, "Where is this house? We'd like to go and check things out."

Edmond thought his heart was about to stop. If he ran for the house, the soldiers were sure to know that he was one of the two people they were looking for, but if he did nothing, they would catch Arabella off guard. Casually he turned and began to walk away. He figured he could find another way to get there before the soldiers did, but without using the main road. Unfortunately it would take longer doing it this way so he would have to run and run hard if he were to make it in time for it to do any good.

As the morning progressed, Arabella felt even worse then she had before. However, she didn't want to disappoint Edmond or be a burden on him, so she forced herself to get up out of bed and she started the meal she had promised him earlier. She didn't want to do anything to spoil these two weeks that meant so much to him.

Her body ached and her face felt like it was on fire. Her body shook because she was cold, even though she had put her cloak and pants on. Even pulling up its hood did little to keep her warm. Thankfully Edmond had the fire going, though it needed some more wood. That much she was at least able to do on her own without his help.

She tried washing her face again to cool it off, but it did little good. Her vision began to become hazy and she felt light headed and she swore she could hear horses outside. "Edmond?" She whispered as she tried to walk towards the door and then everything went dark.

Edmond wasn't fast enough and he saw the soldiers arrive at the little house only moments before he could. He hid behind the barn and peaked around as he watched them go to the door of his and Arabella's temporary home. "Damn it." He swore under his breath. "Now what do I do?" He was furious with himself for not making it on time. Also, he had to find a way to get to Arabella so she wouldn't fall into the hands of Eldardesh's Soldiers. He listened as they banged on the door several times. "Perhaps she heard them and hid." Edmond tried to assure himself that everything would be alright.

"Open it." One of the soldiers told the other.

"Yes sir." The soldier opened the door and they both went in. It was only seconds before the soldier that had opened the door ran out and mounted his horse, heading it back into town at its fastest speed.

"I wonder what's going on." Edmond whispered to himself. "It doesn't matter. There's only one soldier now. I should be able to handle him." He used quick and silent steps to make his way to the house. Taking the soldier by surprise was his best bet at having the upper hand since he was unarmed. If he would have had his sword on him, the soldiers would have been easy to take down, even if there were two of them. When he arrived to the house he carefully walked along side its wall and peaked in through the open door. What he saw surprised him. The soldier was kneeling down next to Arabella, holding a dampened cloth to her head.

"Milady, please wake up." He nearly begged her. "The king will have my head if something happens to you."

Fear struck Edmond's heart and he lost control of his senses. Instead of making war on the lone soldier with blondish brown hair, he instead went in to tend to his beloved. "Arabella!" He ran in and fell down on the floor next to her.

"I take it you're the one who took her from our king." The man had a look of suspicion in his light brown eyes. "You fit the description."

"Arabella is my wife and I wasn't about to let another man touch her." Edmond countered.

"Your wife, huh?" The soldier didn't believe him.

"I don't care if you don't believe me. I know in my heart that it is true, as does she. It is my right to protect her from people who mean her harm, including ill intent from your king."

The soldier sighed and looked down on Arabella as she slept in her fevered slumber. "I found her like this on the floor." His tone had

Beautiful Pretender

changed to one of concern. "How long has she been ill?"

"Since this morning, however it seems to have grown worse since then." Edmond reached over to feel her sweat dampened cheek. It was blazing hot. "Much worse."

"We should get her back to bed." The soldier of around twenty-five suggested. "It won't do her any good to continue to lie on the floor like this." He unlatched the toggle that held the cloak together at her throat so he could take it off. "It would be best if she had on as few things as possible so that the cool air can have a chance to do some good. All this clothing is only going to make things worse."

"How do you know all this?" Edmond asked curiously as they both lifted Arabella to carry her to the bed.

"I have a little sister who was always sick with fevers. This is how we brought them down." They carefully laid her out on the bed. "Well, I'll have to take your word for it about you being her husband. Undress her and lay the thinnest possible cover over her to provide her with some privacy and to keep off the drafts. I'm going to stand guard over her until I know for sure what the situation is."

"Where did the other soldier go?"

"He left to find this town's physician. He shouldn't be long." He turned around to face away from Edmond and Arabella. "I hope you don't mind, but I will stay here, just incase you try to escape. I wouldn't want to have to hunt you down, it's much too troublesome." He heard Edmond sigh with annoyance, "Rest assured, I will advert my eyes while you tend to her. However, I wouldn't take too long going about it since my man will be arriving shortly."

"I suppose that I don't have any choice then, do I?" He began removing her clothing.

"No, you don't."

"May I be so bold as to ask who you are?" Edmond said as he tended to Arabella.

"My name is Lord Peter Evanston III, first cousin to his majesty King Eric. His mother was my mother's sister, her name was Princess Anna. I am currently serving as a captain in his majesties army."

"I see." Edmond knew that this situation seemed hopeless for not only Arabella but for himself as well. He had hoped to maybe convince the soldier to let them go but being so closely related to Eric, this soldier would most likely not waver in his devotion to the king.

"The king has asked for your head, I do hope you realize what this means."

"I am to be killed." Edmond knew very well what it meant. His only hope now was that they didn't discover his sword hidden in the cupboard and that they would give him a chance to retrieve it. It was his and Arabella's last hope at escaping this madness.

"Your head is to be mounted on a pole and it will be displayed in front of the palace as a warning to others who dare to defy our king. However, there is one small problem."

"And that is?" Edmond pulled the lightest blanket up over Arabella's exposed body to hide it before getting up to sit beside her on the bed.

"Your death will have to wait until we are on Eldardesh's soil. Seeing as how you are an Arminian and it would be a crime to kill you here. I have no choice but to keep you alive until we reach Eldardesh. Once we cross the border you will be executed as our king instructed."

"I see. How incredibly civil it is of you to follow the code of conduct when it comes time to administer my punishment for saving my wife from that barbarian king of yours." Edmond sighed in frustration. The only good thing about this was that he knew he was safe for the moment. "What about Arabella? Obviously she also will also be punished because she chose to go with me."

"Yes, he will punish her as well, but death isn't one of the punishments." Peter didn't necessarily agree with Eric on many things but he was undoubtedly loyal to his cousin. He also had grown up with Eric and remembered Arabella from when they were children. When he found her unconscious on the floor, he knew without a doubt that it was indeed her. In the five years she had been gone she had blossomed into a very beautiful woman.

He was eight years older then her, his mother, though younger then Eric's mother, had given birth to him when she was young. She had an affair with a nobleman, Lord Steven Evanston, who at the time was married. His wife had been dying for sometime and he promised to marry Peter's mother when his wife passed. It wasn't until three years after Peter was born, that the duchess had finally passed on and then his mother married Peter's father. Though it brought a great deal of embarrassment to her older sister who was then the queen of both

Arminia and Eldardesh at the time, she still loved her sister very much and received Peter and his father with open arms.

Although they were only cousins, Peter and Eric were really close, more like brothers. Eric trusted him without reservation and Peter was the first one he turned to when it came to matters of the utmost importance. Not only that, but Peter was named Eric's successor until a son of Eric's could assume the throne. Already Eric had possibly one son, for his wife was pregnant and it was quite possible that more would be on the way in the near future.

The condition that was set on Peter's succession was that his own offspring couldn't assume the throne if Eric had one or more sons of his own. It was only a temporary kingship should anything happen to Eric before one of his sons could come of an age that was adequate for such a role. Peter decided that he should clarify a matter to Edmond. "Arabella is my second cousin, her father is my first cousin, and we grew up together while she lived in Eldardesh. I thought you should know so you won't be surprised when she sees me and knows me. Even though I love her like a little sister, I will not allow her to escape her duties to my king."

"I don't know what you see in that kid. Arabella hadn't been with him for very long before he began to mistreat her. I had to do something to take her away from him." Edmond looked over at Arabella. She shivered from being cold as she slept. "She's more precious to me then my own life. She also happens to be my cousin as well." He thought he would continue that conversation. "Though in our case her father is the son of the queen's sister and mine is from the king's sister…" (This also was true for his father was his mother's first cousin. Being able to use this avenue proved useful to hide his identity of also being the son of the king's sister.) Peter didn't allow him to finish.

"Yes, I know of Princess Cornelia, Baron Cordell's mother and elder sister to the queen. She married when their brother was still living and they hadn't known he would pass away like he did. He was born in between the times that Princess Cornelia was born and the time our late queen was born. When he passed, the late queen's engagement was called off while they searched for a prince to marry her." Peter thought it was necessary to make sure that Edmond knew that he was well aware of the history of the family.

"Our late queen had married the Arminian prince and soon he became king of both kingdoms. The plan was to join the two into one. However, they ended up having the two sons and decided to let each one have his own kingdom and our late queen brought Eric back to Eldardesh with her to one day rule it as king.

"Princess Cornelia had lived in Arminia with her sister but then she decided to come back to Eldardesh when the queen did for they were very close to each other and couldn't bear to live apart from each other. She passed away not long ago. If I remember correctly the queen and his mother had a very close relationship with each other." He thought for a moment, "So your father's mother had to have been Princess Sara, the late king's elder sister, if I'm not mistaken. Apparently there were a few children in-between them but a plague had come to the kingdom and killed them." He was pretty sure that was correct. He was more familiar with the Eldardesh side of the family and not the Arminian side.

"Indeed she was the eldest sister to the late king." Edmond remembered his grandmother fondly.

"If the Baron had not been an Eldardesh citizen he would have most likely succeeded you in the line up for the Arminian throne, true?"

"Possibly, though my father would still be closer to him since he is the king's cousin and Baron Wallace is the queen's." Edmond continued to talk about his lineage without thinking because he was trying to explain why he would exceed Arabella's father to the throne. For some reason he was unaware of what he was now doing. "However, my mother is the late king's eldest daughter from his first marriage. His first wife had died shortly after the plague and it had been a while before he took the princess from Eldardesh as his queen. My mother is Kendrick and Eric's older half sister, which makes me the nephew to both of the kings as well." Edmond stopped talking for a moment as he realized what he just said. He was trying to avoid giving away this information but it was too late now. He sighed before he continued. "The fact that she is Kendrick's and Eric's eldest sister is not widely known because she took on the title of baroness when she married my father. Eric didn't really have a chance to know much about his older half sister so it's possible that he may have forgotten about her. Our late king and your late queen felt it was best to allow things to be this

Beautiful Pretender

way with my mother and father. It is mostly for that reason and also because of my relationship with Kendrick that I am closer in line to the Arminian throne then Baron Cordell is."

"Very interesting." Talking with this man seemed to be very beneficial to Peter. He was learning things that might be of some interest to his king. He decided to try and see what other information this tired and distraught man might give. He just had to play his cards right. "You would make a fine catch for any noble woman indeed." The soldier turned and looked at Edmond. "Have your parents selected a bride for you yet?"

"Unfortunately the have." He had forgotten temporarily that he was supposed to be Arabella's husband. It seemed that he had other things on his mind, more important than this conversation and it was causing him to take leave of his senses. "She comes from a very wealthy family and is their only child, so I would stand to inherit her father's entire fortune upon his death should we marry. He felt it was a small price to pay to have grandchildren who would have a grandmother who is a princess, though she chose not to retain the title. Also my status to the succession of the throne doesn't hurt either. Should Kendrick die, my father is first inline and then I am after that."

"Hmm." Peter smiled, 'caught him'. "Are you planning on marrying her then?"

"I'm not sure I'll have a choice...." He just realized his mistake. "Damn it all." He slammed his fist on his knee as he heard Peter laugh quietly. "I guess you outsmarted me." He sighed as he stood up. "I'm going to heat up some water to drink, do you want any?"

"Sure. No tea?"

"I'm afraid not. I only brought so much money with me. When I left home I had no idea I would be gone for weeks. Arabella and I will get by for now but the money won't last forever."

"You should live it up." Peter walked over to one of the two vacant chairs near the table and took a seat. "You'll be dead soon, anyway."

"We'll see about that. I don't plan to go down without a fight."

Their conversation was amazingly casual. "We'll see, we'll see." Peter laughed softly again. They kept their voices down so Arabella could rest. "For now you have nothing to worry about. I don't plan to move her or report her whereabouts until after she is well. Eric will be mad at me if I bring her to him in the condition she's in."

Edmond took the other seat by the table and sat down. He stretched his arms over his head before bringing them behind it so he could rest his head back on them. "It hasn't been easy for her these last few days. Eric pretty much left her with almost nothing to wear and with the weather turning and how far we were away from town…" He sighed before continuing, "She really wasn't able to protect herself from the elements. I did my best to protect her but to be honest we were sort of lost in the woods temporarily. It was only by chance that I found Kinshek."

"I'm sure she'll be doing fine in a few days." Peter looked to the door, as did Edmond. It had been left open so Peter could better monitor the activities outside the cabin. "Ah, the physician is finally here." He got up to meet them at the door. He stationed the other soldier outside the cabin and escorted the physician in to examine Arabella.

Peter left the cabin and closed the door behind him. He knew there was no way Edmond would be able to escape and he was sure he wouldn't try to unless he could take Arabella with him. "Are they the ones we're looking for?" the other soldier asked.

"I'm not sure." Peter answered, even though he did know for sure. He wasn't sure why he lied to his fellow officer but what was done was done.

"I thought you knew the princess personally, to the point that you regarded her as your younger sister."

"I do, but it has been many years since I last saw her. That woman in there may be the child I knew from long ago. The only way I'll know for sure is when she wakes up and I can talk to her. I'm not saying that she isn't who we're looking for but the man claims that she is the woman who comes to clean his cabin and the town's people did tell us that two men lived here, not a man and a woman."

"I suppose you have a point."

"I wouldn't worry too much about it. We'll finish things up here one way or another and be on our way shortly." Why don't you take some time off and go to the pub. We've been working nonstop for several days and I'm sure you could use the break."

"You don't mind if I go to the one with the brothel do you?"

"Not at all. Enjoy yourself for both of us." Peter smiled and then

Beautiful Pretender

reached into his coin purse to produce some silver farthings. "Here, it's on me."

His subordinate greedily took the coins, "Thanks captain. With this I can have twice the fun." He was referring to two women instead of one.

"Make sure to report to me tomorrow but only after you sober up." Peter laughed.

"Will do." He promised and then headed for his horse. "Don't work too hard." He called back and then mounted the stead.

"Don't be a smart ass or you'll find yourself working." Peter called back to him just before the soldier rode away with a farewell wave. "Well that solves that problem for now." He sighed and wondered why he was hesitating about letting on that he had indeed found Arabella and the man she had escaped from Eric with. It made no sense to him but he decided to just go with the flow and see where fate led him next. At the moment his greatest concern was over Arabella's well being. She seemed to be in pretty bad shape and he needed to know what was wrong with her before he decided what his next move would be.

Indeed she was the younger sister he told Edmond about earlier. Even though it wasn't by blood, he had always adored Arabella. It seemed that her childhood weakness followed her into adulthood. There was much about her that was strong but her body didn't do well when it came to illnesses. She seemed to contract everything that came around and she seemed to suffer greatly. Where a child might have only had a head cold, Arabella would be laid up with a fever for days at a time. He remembered her father had a friend who was a physician. Together they went to Arminia because Arabella was always in need of his care. If he remembered correctly the man's name was Joseph.

Kinshek's physician carefully examined Arabella as Edmond stood off to one side of the room. He couldn't help but to watch as the physician examined her. Finally the man spoke, "Well, I am a little surprised that your friend here ended up being a woman, although I had my suspicions when I saw you two in town last night. Why does she feel it necessary to be passing herself off as a man?" The physician had also been at the tavern, although the two hadn't noticed him or who he was. To them he was just another customer.

JM Howard

"We were trying to avoid the trouble that seems to have made its way to our door this morning, despite our efforts." He was referring to the soldiers.

"Those solders are from Eldardesh, are they not?" The physician asked curiously.

"Yes, they are, unfortunately."

"Are you two in trouble?" He looked back at Edmond for a moment while he waited for an answer.

"I'm afraid we are, though I'd rather not discuss it."

"Did you murder someone?" The physician returned to what he had been doing.

"No, it's nothing like that. We just ticked off their king a little, that's all."

"Ah yes, that foolish child." The older physician laughed softly. "It doesn't seem to take much to ruffle his feathers." He pulled the blanket back up over Arabella before standing up. "Well, she is pretty sick but I don't think its life threatening. She seems to be more worn out more than anything and her prolonged exposure to the elements didn't help much. I'll leave you some herbs to brew into tea for her. Have her drink it four times a day. I'll give you the specifics before I leave. Make sure she drinks plenty of water and keep the cabin warm, but make sure you continue to apply the cool cloths to her head and neck until her fever breaks. Don't hesitate to send for me if she should become any worse. I'm sure that she'll feel fine if she can take some time to rest. After she wakes up from this fevered sleep, I would recommend that she should take a least one slightly cool bath per day to help keep her body temperature lowered. The water should help to cool her off and it should also make her feel better. Keeping her in good spirits should also help the healing process, in other words don't do anything to make her worry too much."

"That might be hard to do considering our friends outside." He looked towards the front door that blocked their view of the two soldiers. Edmond was unaware that Peter had sent the other soldier back to town.

"I'm not sure what to say about that, but I will talk with them about the serious nature of this situation. Worrying her won't help her to get better."

Beautiful Pretender

"I'd appreciate that." He stood when the doctor indicated that he was about to leave.

"I'll come back and check on her in a couple of days." He smiled warmly. "Make sure she drinks some warm broth and that she drinks plenty of fluids. All these things should help her to heal faster."

"Yes sir and thank you."

"You certainly are a lucky man to have such a fine lass as your wife."

"Indeed I am." He smiled warmly as he agreed. "I couldn't have hoped to ever find a woman such as her. I am convinced that she is an angel from heaven, sent just for me to love." This made the doctor laugh softly, for Edmond's words had touched him. "Oh, sir, please don't let on that you know our secret, I mean that she is actually a woman. We still have our reasons for hiding her gender."

"Though I don't really understand why you wish for this, I promise I will not breathe a word about her true nature. Though I must say it would calm some of the questionable gossip that is spreading about the two of you. I do say that the things many of the people are saying are quite startling." He was referring to the fact that the people thought they were two male lovers.

"We're sort of doing that on purpose." He laughed as the doctor placed several packets on the table. They contained the medicinal herbs Edmond would need to give to Arabella. "It's one of the few pleasures we are being afforded during our short stay here."

"Again, I don't understand why you choose to do this, but your secret is safe with me. Farewell friend." He allowed Edmond to open the door for him and they were immediately greeted by Peter. "Ah, young man, I need to speak with you." The physician addressed Peter. His voice faded away as Edmond closed the door behind him. He chose to stay in the cabin with Arabella.

"At least it's not too serious." He sighed in relief as he walked towards her. "So much for our two weeks alone together, my adorable little mousy, still…" he leaned down and kissed her warm dry lips. "For now we have no worries. We can stay here and rest for as long as you need to, despite the undesirable company." The opening of the cabin's door drew his attention.

"The physician filled me in on her condition." Peter closed the door once he was inside. "Our first priority is to get her back into good health. Once that is accomplished, I'll decide what to do next." He went back to the seat he had occupied earlier. "Is that stew cooking in the pot over the fire?"

Edmond looked over to the fire, "Yes, she had started it shortly before we came. I don't think that it's had enough time to finish but you're welcome to have some when you're ready to eat. There's also a cellar you can find food from as well. I had planned on buying some bread in town this morning but your arrival made it impossible."

"I can wait for the stew to finish cooking. Why don't you go ahead and go back to town for the bread. If Arabella wakes up she might be hungry and the broth from the stew and some bread, they'll probably be the two things that she will be able to stomach the best."

"Are you not concerned that I might try to escape?" Edmond asked as he stood up to fetch his cloak.

"Not hardly. I have my doubts about you leaving her behind so easily. But…" He said in a sigh as he lounged back in the chair, "If you do, I'm sure Eric would be happy enough that I found her."

"Yes, that's true but there is a price on my head." He reminded the soldier.

"I have confidence that you'll be back. Here," He reached into his pocket and pulled out some more coins, "use these to buy whatever we need. We'll let Eric pay for everything."

"I have no problem with that." Edmond didn't mind the free funds. There was no sense in dwelling on pride at times like these. Arabella's health came first and he would steal or even kill for her should it ever need to go that far, despite his beliefs in not killing others. Taking funds from the one who was responsible for this mess they were in the first place was not a problem, as far as he was concerned. In his mind Eric owed it to them. "I shouldn't be too long. What should I do if I run into any more of your friends?"

"There were only two of us assigned to this village, so you shouldn't have any problems. Just steer clear of the brothel, that's where my partner is for the time being."

"I was wondering about him. The women there are bound to show him the time of his life." Edmond remembered all too well the hospitality the women at the tavern had shown him and Aram the

Beautiful Pretender

night before. They were aching for some fresh meat in there. He noticed a humored smile on Peter's lips. "Take care of her for me."

"Don't worry, I plan to. Remember I do care about her as if she were a little sister, time hasn't changed that."

"Thank you, Lord Evanston." Edmond told him honestly. "Thank you for putting her health before your duty, even if it's just temporary."

Chapter 15

Arabella had slept soundly for two days straight. They could barely get her to wake up enough to use the chamber pot (Edmond had her to wearing one of the chemise gowns he had bought for her, so he could give her privacy as much as possible as they helped her in and out of bed). They also did all they could to get her to take some water. However, despite their efforts to get her up and about, she was not herself and mumbled senseless words to no one in a half sleep. Peter had bought suitable bedding for both him and Edmond to use on the floor. Arabella had a bad habit of snuggling into someone when she slept and it only made her temperature rise because of the added body heat. They were able to keep it lowered, though it didn't go completely down, even when she slept alone. The other soldier was not allowed admittance into the cabin. He would instead guard it during the night while the men inside slept and during the day he was allowed to visit the brothel and taverns. Needless to say, he didn't complain at all about the arrangement.

Every morning Edmond left for town to buy fresh bread and any other supplies they needed, of course these expenses were 'generously' funded by Eric, unbeknown to him of course. Thankfully because of the family connection Peter had with the king, he was bestowed higher favors then most military men were which included a rather large purse. Peter wasn't shy about spending the money either. This mission was not isolated in that habit. Eric encouraged him to use it liberally.

Currently Edmond was off to the village market to get their daily provisions that included bread, milk and other things that had to be renewed every day. Peter was kneeling near Arabella. He gently brushed the hair off her forehead so he could kiss it to see how her fever was doing. It was the way his mother had done it to him, although when Edmond was there he used his hand. He seemed relieved that it was nearly gone. She was still slightly warm but after three days of it being much higher, he was happy to find that it was nearly over.

He continued to kneel next to her as he watched her sleep. Her sleep seemed to be more peaceful then it had been the last couple of days. She was lying on her side facing him and he couldn't get over how adorable she looked while she slept. Carefully he leaned forward and kissed her, this time on her lips. This hadn't been their first kiss, for he had kissed her many years back. It was much like this time. He had stayed at the palace with her and Eric on many occasions.

One night he had stole into the room she had used and he went to her bedside. He only meant to check on her because he had a bad dream about her being hurt. However, the way she was lying there in her sleep touched him and he leaned down to give her a kiss, her first kiss. He knew at the time that she was, more likely then not, going to marry Eric, but he simply couldn't help himself, much like he couldn't now. He had thought those feelings didn't exist for her any longer, however it was apparent that he had been mistaken. "Arabella..." he whispered softly. "I don't think I ever did stop loving you." He heard her moan softly. "Arabella?" Her soft moan had surprised him because it was the first time she responded to someone without them forcing her to wake up.

"Edmond." She said softly in her sleep. "Don't leave me."

"You really love him, don't you?" He touched her cheek gently and listened to her as she continued to softly talk in her sleep.

"I love you so much. Don't leave me." It was obvious that the things she denied herself to say when she was awake, though Peter didn't know this, she said while she slept. In her sleep, her heart could express its true feelings. "I really do want to be your wife." A tear crept from one of her closed eyes and trickled down her nose. Peter reached forward to carefully wipe it off her. "I want to stay by your side." Her voice was barely audible now.

"Dearest cousin." Peter thought his heart just might break over the sound of the sadness in her voice. Suddenly she reached forward and grabbed the front of his shirt and pulled him to her. He quickly braced his hands on the side of the bed to catch himself so he wouldn't fall on her.

"Don't go." These were her final words before she snuggled close to him.

"Now what do I do?" He whispered to himself. Though awkward, he liked having her near him like this, depending on him, whether or not she was aware of whom it really was. He folded his arms up on the bed and laid down on them as best he could. It wasn't much longer after this that Edmond came back.

This first thing he did was laugh, which surprised Peter for he had expected Edmond to be cross. "She must be feeling better. It looks like she got you." He walked over to the table and laid his purchases down.

"Is this something she often does?" Peter asked him.

"She's very clingy when it comes to someone sleeping next to her. It's almost as if she's afraid of being alone." His smile was one that betrayed the humor he saw in Peter's uncomfortable situation. "I'll trade with you, if you want." He walked over and loosened Arabella's grip on Peter. Soon he was lying next to her and she immediately clung onto him as she snuggled her face into his chest. "It seems that her temperature is nearly gone now."

"I noticed that too." Peter sliced off a few pieces of the bread. He had warmed up the broth that they had made the day before. "We should see if maybe we can wake her so she can eat something."

"Arabella." Edmond said gently as he tenderly squeezed her shoulder. "Try to wake up dearest."

"Edmond, don't leave." Arabella moaned in her sleep.

"Come on, you need to wake up now, you've been sleeping long enough." He felt her grip loosen on his shirt and soon her hand made its way up to her eyes and she used her fist to rub the sleep from them. "We made you some broth and we have fresh bread to eat as well. You really should eat something."

Arabella looked up at him as best as she could. "What?" She asked in confusion. "I made stew..."

"That was three days ago, my love." He smiled tenderly. "You've been really sick."

"Sick?" Even though they had tried to wake her up to force her to drink and take care of certain needs, she had never truly woke up enough to be aware of what was happening around her.

"So she's finally awake, huh?" Peter got up to come look at her. "So, how do you feel?"

Arabella looked carefully at the man that stood above her and Edmond and was presently looking down at her. "I know you..." it took her a moment to remember exactly who it was looking down on her, after all it had been five years since they last saw each other, and they were just kids then. "Peter?"

"Indeed." He grinned making the light dusting of the blondish brown facial hair on his lip and chin bring out a slight sexiness to his already alluring charm. "Hello cousin."

Only for a moment did she forget that Edmond was lying next to her, "Peter, is that really you?" She smiled and then she tried to get up but was met with an instant headache which forced her to lie back down.

"Dearest you should take things a little slower." Edmond said tenderly. "You're still not completely better yet."

Arabella looked at him, "That is my cousin..."

"Yes, we've met." He smiled.

She looked back up at Peter, however now she realized that he wore the uniform of an Eldardesh soldier and she also remember that he was an extremely loyal subject to their cousin Eric. "Oh God." Her hand came up to her mouth as she realized what this meant. "You came to take me back, haven't you?"

"I'm afraid so."

Arabella threw her body against Edmond's to try and shield herself from the awful truth. They had been found. "I don't want to go back." She cried. "I don't want to marry Eric."

"He does love you, Arabella." Peter tried to assure her. "He's been looking forward to your arrival..."

"No, I don't want to go." She pleaded. "He was so mean to me."

Peter sighed. The truth was, Eric was mean to everyone if they displeased him. He could argue with her on that point, especially since Eric had ordered Edmond's death and he knew that Arabella too would receive punishment for her actions. However he did have some words of comfort for her, at least he hoped they were. "I don't plan to report that I've found you yet. The village physician had asked that we keep you calm and rested until you're feeling better again."

Arabella looked up at him, "Please don't make me go back, Peter."

"What would you do if I didn't?" He was curious to see how she would answer.

"I have my plans but I'm not sure if I can trust you with them." She replied honestly. "Edmond is supposed to return to Celendra Desh to marry the woman his parents made arrangements with and I... well I know where I liked to go as well. Please, show me mercy dearest cousin and don't take me back to Eric." She looked over at Edmond, "I am well aware that Eric wants Edmond dead. To assume otherwise would be foolish."

Peter sighed heavily and left to go sit in the chair near the table that he had unofficially claimed as his own. How could he answer her pleas? On one hand he was a proud and loyal Eldardesh soldier who always followed Eric's instructions with flawless execution. On the other hand he had before him the girl who had captured his heart and affections many years ago, begging him to disregard his duty to his king. She was literally asking him to risk his own life to save hers and Edmond's from Eric's wrath. He listened as she cried in Edmond's embrace.

"You must calm down dearest. All this fuss will only make you ill again." Edmond did his best to try and comfort her.

"No..." she cried, "Why did they have to find us, we didn't even get our two weeks..."

"I know, but for now we can stay. Let's be thankful for this time we do have." Their voices were lowered but Peter could still easily make out their words.

"How can I possibly be thankful when I know what awaits the both of us, Edmond?"

Peter cleared his throat, "I think I will head into town for awhile. I trust you two will stay put until I return." He stood up and gathered his few things. "It would be best for you both if you didn't try to escape."

"You place before us a big temptation." Edmond cautioned him.

"If you try to leave now with her, you'd only place her life back into danger. I'm positive that you wouldn't do something so foolish."

"It seems you know me well sir."

Beautiful Pretender

"As you do me, sir, although you haven't let on. It seems we have come to a pass of mutual understanding then."

"It does seem that way." Edmond responded. "We will do as you ask then."

"Very well." Peter walked over to the door without another word and left the cabin.

"Edmond..." Arabella sounded desperate.

"Let's get you up so you can eat something. You'll probably like a warm bath as well." He helped her to sit up.

"There's no time for that, we should escape while we have this chance."

"There's no need for that now." He smiled tenderly. "We have all the time in the world."

"What are you talking about? Eric is going to kill you." She pleaded desperately with him.

"No, he's not. Peter won't be coming back."

"What do you mean?" She looked towards the door in confusion. "He said he was."

"He left us unattended. He asked us not to go. Arabella, he has heard your pleas and he has decided to let us go. Our secret is safe for now."

"But..." she had no idea what he was talking about because that wasn't the impression that she got.

"Just trust me." He leaned over to kiss her. "It would be best if you stay indoors today until we are sure that they're gone. Peter made it a point to not let the other soldier know for certain that we were the ones they were looking for. I think all along he knew that he wouldn't be able to hand you over to Eric. He only just had to make sure that he was doing the right thing." He stood up and helped her to her feet, "Come sit down by the table and let's see if we can get you to stomach some food." His smile was unmistakable and she knew that his words to her were the truth. Though she didn't really understand all that had happened, she trusted Edmond's words.

Peter felt nervous as he went to the brothel to retrieve the other soldier. There was sure to be some suspicion when he would tell him that the people they were looking for were not the ones they found.

All he could do was to hope that he could make a convincing case and then they could set off as soon as possible. Once he marked the town as not being a place where they would be found, it was unlikely that the soldiers would return to look there again for quite some time. He would simply report that there was a couple that seemed suspicious and he stayed to make sure they weren't the ones they were looking for. It really was all that he could do. So far no one dared to question his word about anything, though he had never attempted to deceive anyone before.

However he knew now that he couldn't bring Arabella back to Eric. He simply couldn't do something so cruel to her. Not that he liked seeing her with that man, for it made him jealous, however Edmond seemed to be a good man and there was no doubt that she loved him dearly. Peter knew that they planned to part ways and he wished he knew her destination for the future so he could contact her. However, she was wise not to tell for he was tempted to go and look for her, not for Eric, but for himself. This certainly wouldn't be the best thing for her, for Eric knew his whereabouts for the most part, seeing as how he was the next in line, for the time being, to Eric's throne.

Peter now realized that there was only one person in the world who could make him weak enough to disobey his king's orders. If she hadn't been so ill when he found her, he might have not had the time to remember how dear she was to him. However, since she had needed his care and he had time to learn of the depth of love she had for Edmond, what little strength he had to obey Eric on this matter, slipped away.

Within a few days Arabella was back to her old self again. Every time she thought about Peter she couldn't help smiling. The memories of their childhood together came flooding back. One of those memories being how much he adored her and how he was always there to protect her. However unstable Eric had made her life, Peter had made it livable again. How could she forget how attentive he had been to her and how much he cared for her? She felt pangs of guilt over how she had mistrusted him and she wished that she had taken time to visit with him. Their reunion was so short lived and it made her sad.

"What's on your mind my little mousy?" Edmond asked as he poked at the fire. He noticed she had been lost in thought for some time.

"Nothing really." She smiled warmly. "It's just that seeing Peter brought back memories I had forgotten. I suppose all the time I spent with him and Eric could be the part of the reason why I liked playing with boys so much. I never really had a chance to play with girls when I was young."

"Speaking of that, I have been wondering how you came up with the name Aram."

Arabella laughed softly. "Simple really, the Ara of Aram is from Arabella and the m is from my middle name, Mina. Really it was just a play on words when we came up with it."

"It could have been a dead give away too if one took the time to think about it, how interesting." He placed the poker back up against the hearth before standing up. "Are you warm enough?"

"Yes." She reached up and he immediately came to her. "I can think of a great way to warm us up even more." They both laughed softly and he picked her up off the chair to take her to bed. "I plan to thoroughly enjoy the rest of these two weeks with you." She grinned.

"We should extend it since you were so sick for most of the first week. I feel like I was robbed of some of my time with you." He had hoped to make this last for the rest of their lives.

Arabella sighed, "Let's not talk about it right now." She laid her head on his chest. Honestly she wanted it to last forever but she couldn't bear the thought of what he stood to lose if she asked him to stay. Part of her also feared that he felt obligated to stay with her and it was something that her conscience couldn't live with. If he gave up everything to fulfill her selfish desires, it would certainly make them miserable in the years to come. She could live in the misery of being without him. After all she had already lost everything. This short time with him would be what she would use to sustain her for the years to come, knowing that she had loved and been loved. Not many women would ever know a love like this and for her to have a brief taste of it made her feel very fortunate. She never doubted that he truly did love her, but she did doubt the fact that this love would be worth all he stood to lose.

As the end of the two week period drew to a close, they had yet to discuss any extensions. In fact, the concept of them parting ways never came up again. They simply took time to be with one another without holding back. Finally, only just two days before the end of the two weeks, Edmond spoke of their future as they were lying in bed, facing one another. "There's an apprentice opening at the blacksmith's. I was thinking of taking it. It doesn't pay much but we could use the extra funds."

"Hmm." She sighed.

"You disapprove?"

"I don't think being a blacksmith would suit you, though you could fix your own armor and swords after tournaments." She laughed softly at the jest.

"Only nobles can do that you know. If I'm to leave that life behind, then I will no longer be able to compete." He reminded her.

"So instead of being a noble you intend to serve them." She huffed in frustration, "Really Edmond, I was looking forward to seeing you compete in the king's tournament this year. Besides, even if you left your noble life behind, you still have it in your blood, as do I. It's not like it just disappears. You are the son of a princess after all and you can't get any closer to being a noble then that. Don't forget that you are Kendrick's nephew as well. Do you think he is just going to let that slide?"

"I suppose you have a point." He rolled over onto his back and brought his arms up under his head.

Arabella decided to change the subject but only slightly. "I wonder how they're all doing. I'm sure our friends are worried about us."

"Probably. I'm guessing they might have an idea about me since the king's army is searching Arminia for us, but as for you they wouldn't have a clue unless someone revealed that you were Aram as well. Won't that surprise everyone?" He found this amusing as he thought of how their friends would react to the news. "I know I was floored when I discovered that my best friend was actually a woman."

"Floored...More like pissed if you ask me." Her soft feminine laughter rang sweetly in his ears and she brought her hand up onto his chest. "Thank you again for forgiving me for that."

He gathered her closer to him. "How could I not? You're too adorable for your own good."

"I told you, I'm not even close to being adorable." She kissed his

Beautiful Pretender

chest as she snuggled closer.

"Speaking of that, you sure don't seem to have too high of an opinion about yourself, you seemed to counter every positive opinion I had about you. As Aram you had the chance to play up how wonderful you are but instead you criticized everything that I find precious about you. Why?"

"Oh Edmond, please don't start this with me. I just don't feel like talking about it." She tried to roll away from him but he wouldn't let her. Instead he held her tighter to him.

"You are still planning on us going our separate ways when this two week period is over, aren't you?"

"I'm tired, let's go to sleep and talk about this later." She closed her eyes and tried to relax enough for sleep to claim her so she could escape this unavoidable conversation.

Edmond reached up with his free hand and wiped a tear that had escaped from his eye. He didn't know how to convince her that he was fine with leaving his old life behind to live out his remaining days with her. "I want to stay with you. I know you think I'll regret it but I'll regret not having you by my side even more."

"Go to sleep, Edmond. You promised we wouldn't talk about these things during our two weeks, yet you keep bringing it up."

"I can't help but worry that you won't let me stay with you. Lately I can't even sleep because I'm worried you won't be there when I wake up and that this has all been just a sweet dream."

"A very sweet dream indeed. I promise you won't have to watch me leave." She whispered sleepily to him. "Good night."

"You sure are a stubborn woman, Arabella." He sighed miserably. "If you weren't for you being so damn adorable, you're stubborn side would really annoy me." This made her laugh softly.

"I love you." She said through that soft laughter.

"I love you too." His hand gently caressed her arm as he closed his eyes to allow sleep to come to him as he continued to hold her snuggly to him. He wouldn't put it past her to sneak off in the night and he had no intention of letting her go without a fight. Her reservations about allowing him to stay with her were understandable but he was sure that he would never regret giving everything up for her.

The dawn of the end of their agreed time was coming and Edmond had been trying to think of ways to keep Arabella beside him. He racked his brains trying to come up with a scheme. The fact that it was sort of childish didn't matter to him. It was worth one last shot to try and convince her to let things stay as they were. "Hey." He said casually as they both brushed their horses in the barn where they kept them.

Arabella looked over her horse's back so she could look at him, "What?"

"I was thinking that perhaps..." he took a slow nervous breath, "perhaps you would agree to a challenge."

She laughed softly. "A challenge? For what?"

"I would let you pick anything you want for the challenge."

"And..."

"If I win, you must not leave me. If you win, I will no longer fight with you about going."

"I see." She said softly and walked over to place the brush she had been using on the shelf where it belonged. Without looking at him she said softly, "Swords."

"Why swords?" He asked confused. It was obvious he was a much better swordsman then her. "Maybe you should think of something else."

"What's the point?" She sighed miserably.

"What do you mean?" He stopped brushing his horse so he could concentrate on the conversation.

"You're better at everything then I am."

"Everything?"

"No matter what I chose, you are better at everything."

"Why swords? You know you can't win..." He walked over towards her.

She laughed softly. "It really makes no difference. Swords, cooking, starting fires...it's all the same. You're better at everything then I am. If I must do this, I at least want to do something that we'll both enjoy." She turned to look at him and she gave him her best smile. "Besides, we haven't had a good duel in a long time. It would be fun to cross swords with you again." In her mind she said, 'One last time.'

"I see." He brought his brush over to lay it next to hers. "I'll go to

Beautiful Pretender

town then and find a sword we can borrow or buy inexpensively. We'll set out match for tomorrow afternoon."

"I look forward to it." She leaned over to kiss his cheek. "This will be fun." Edmond was still baffled but he also couldn't help looking forward to their match. It would be the first time he would fight her knowing that she was a woman.

Arabella took her stance, of course she was dressed like Aram with her hair up but she left her chest unbound. Part of her wondered if it would affect her fighting style, whether good or bad. When bound it was uncomfortable and the bindings made it difficult for her to maneuver her torso when swinging her sword. Unbound gave her much more freedom but then she felt like her breasts were kind of in the way. Either way there were the good and bad points.

"Ready?" Edmond smiled. He figured he would try to play fair and not give it his all. This way their duel could last a while so she at least could find some satisfaction in the length of the competition. He also felt slightly different about fighting her now knowing that she was female. Despite this knowledge he was resolved to not let it influence him. Edmond wanted to win. He wanted her to stop pushing him away for these ideals of hers. This was his one last chance at convincing her not to leave.

Arabella raised her sword, with it slightly angled. "Will you make the first move?" She asked smiling her challenge.

He also raised his sword and took a step back with one leg to stabilize himself. "No."

"Very well then." She walked slowly towards him. "I won't go easy on you and I expect you to fight me without holding back."

"No more then usual, milady." He prepared his sword to received the blow that she was about to deliver as her pace quickened towards him. She swung her sword as hard as she could and it clashed against his with a deafening sound that echoed through the forest around their little home. She swung at his over and over, each time the metal ricocheted off of his.

Finally Arabella stopped and stepped back away from him. "Stop it." She scolded him.

"Stop what?" He asked, still in a defensive stance to receive her next swing.

"You're only defending. If this is to be any competition at all, you must fight back." She was only slightly out of breath but she still had a lot of vigor left in her. "Fight me!" She nearly yelled and charged at him again.

He blocked each blow she delivered, "Yes milady." He now granted her wish but within a controlled means. It amused him to watch her fight so hard. True, she was still a challenge but he had the strong upper hand. Anytime he wished he could start the process of ending this battle. However it wouldn't be as fun if it was over to quickly. Fighting with her was always fun, even now as a girl he still enjoyed the spirit and vitality in which she fought. He was sure that up against a person who was less skilled then himself, she would actually pose a threat.

The fighting went on longer then she expected it would and she knew it was because he was still holding back on her. Her breathing was quickened and slightly labored as she fought. Finally he pinned her blade to the ground. As he did he grabbed the handle and shoved the blade deeply into the earth, even as she still held it. He watched as she breathed hard, her head hung near his shoulder as they both hunched over the earth bound sword. "Well, you still managed to hold back on me." Her words came as she was able to talk in between breaths.

"Kiss me." He put his sword down so he could use his hand to lift her chin up so he could kiss her. He felt her hand brush against his leg as she stood upright to look up at him. Her eyes enchanted him with the pleasure she had found in this competition.

"Do you honestly think that you've won, milord?" She smiled sweetly.

"Of course, your sword is…." His words were silenced as she quickly brought the blade of his dagger up to his throat. "Ah, it seems I might have been mistaking." He laughed nervously. "When did you get my dagger?"

"Only just now." She told him proudly.

"That's cheating."

"No. Just declare me the winner and I'll set you free."

He laughed softly. "Winner." His head lowered as he whispered the words to her and he ended it with a kiss, despite the blade at his throat.

Beautiful Pretender

Technically she didn't win because this was a sword fight. It was only dumb luck that he had his dagger on him for her to confiscate. "Shall we go back inside?"

"Yes, but I order you as the loser to prepare the winner a bath."

"A bath?" He felt her remove the blade and she handed the dagger to him.

"Make it a really hot one too. My muscles are really going to hurt after doing this."

"May I join you?" He winked at her.

"You pervert!" She yelled and smacked his arm.

"Ouch." He complained. "Why did you hit me?"

Arabella could feel her face turning red, mostly from embarrassment. Sure they were mostly behaving like any husband and wife but to do something like this almost seemed like he was asking just a bit too much. Even with their time growing short, she didn't have enough courage yet to do something like that with him. "Just be quiet and do as you're told." She huffed and walked back to the house.

Edmond pulled her sword from the earth and followed her back to their little home. "Yes milady."

The last day of the agreed allotment of time was upon them and Edmond felt exceedingly uneasy all day. Arabella went about her normal routine as if nothing was going to change, yet he couldn't help but wonder if she was really going to leave or not. He had to prepare his heart for the fact that she might indeed go. It wasn't a question of whether or not she loved him, for he knew that she loved him very much. Nor did he question whether or not she wanted to truly be his wife because she confessed her true feelings when she slept. He liked it that she talked in her sleep because everything she kept secret from him about her feelings would be confessed. He never told her about it because those moments were sacred to him. However, he never found out what it was she was planning to do only that she really didn't want to leave his side.

"I haven't been to the village since we first came. Would it be alright if I went with you today?"

"I'd love to take you with me." He smiled. "I didn't realize you wanted to go or I would have taken you before."

"I didn't mind, it gave me time to do the chores around here so that I could spend the rest of the time with you when you were home. However today, I really feel like going." Edmond got up from the chair he had been sitting in and went to get their cloaks. Arabella still dressed in men's clothing because that was all he had bought for her, though she did have a couple of chemise gowns for sleeping in.

"Why don't you leave your hair down this time." He suggested.

"I'll look too much like a woman when I do." She smiled.

"Don't bind your chest either."

She placed the last cup she had been washing onto the shelf. "You want me to go as a woman?" Her voice was laced with curiosity.

"Yes. I know your clothing isn't feminine but I want to village to know that you are my woman."

"Very well then." She smiled and came to him. Edmond assisted her with putting her cloak on. "If it's what you really want, I suppose it can't be helped. Though I did enjoy the way we upset this town with our little show of affection. I'll never forget the looks on the villagers' faces when they thought we were both guys making out. It really was too funny." She laughed.

"Indeed it was." He kissed her before putting on his own cloak. "Shall we?"

She took the arm he offered her, "Do they serve hot foods in Kinshek or do they just sell produce?"

"Mainly produce but one man does sell cooked meat and he also has hot wine. Does that tempt you at all?"

"It sounds divine." She smiled. "Though we should be careful how much we spend. There isn't much left, is there?"

"My funds are running low, but I'm sure we can do that one thing today."

Arabella reflected on the day she had spent with Edmond, it truly was a perfect day. The bewildered faces of the villagers who learned that she was in fact a woman, was priceless. It was obvious they felt her taste in clothing was questionable, a noble woman, or so they assumed, walking around in men's clothing was even more taboo then the notion of two noble men having a love affair. The latter of which wasn't really that unheard of but for a noble woman to dress as a man

Beautiful Pretender

was unthinkable. Thinking about it brought an amused smile to her face every time and she wondered if Edmond's suggestion was actually his way of raising even more eyebrows, as he liked to put it. It seemed to amuse him to shock the people of this little town that was on the brink of no longer being a village.

She watched as he laid more wood in the hearth for the fire. The days were growing colder as winter approached. The farmers had finished the last of the harvests quite some time ago and it seemed everyone was settling in for a nice long winter. She actually enjoyed watching the people from the window of her cabin as the passed by. It had never dawned on her just how much work the common man had to do to just get by from day to day. Her previous life as the daughter of a high ranking nobleman had robbed her of this reality of the people of lesser means. Even now she and Edmond didn't have much to do because he had a rather large purse on him. Not only the funds he brought with him, but also the coin purse that Peter had left behind. They found where he had stashed it for them about two days after he had left. It was placed in one of Arabella's boots.

They really didn't do too much when they were in town, other then getting the daily provision and stopping to get the meat and wine that Edmond had mentioned. He took her to a few of the street venders to look at their wares. Mostly they just enjoyed walking together hand in hand as they talked about the things they saw in town and the people as well.

"Well that should get us through at least half of the night." Edmond proclaimed as he poked at the fire one last time.

"Would you like me to heat up some water for you?" Arabella asked him.

"I'd love it." He walked over towards their bed to undress. "It sure is getting cold."

"Yes it is." She brought down the small pot from the shelf and filled it with water from the bucket he had filled before the darkness of night hid the well. Then she placed it on the hook over the fire so it could heat up the water. She then sat down on a chair near the table and reached for the sewing box he had bought for her a few days earlier. A pair of Edmond's pants needed some mending. It wasn't something she was very good at doing, for she had only learned how to embroider and not mend, but she was willing to give it a shot, after all she had done well with his cloak that day he first met her as Arabella.

Edmond got into bed and laid down so he could watch her by the fire's light. She didn't seem to be in any hurry to prepare her things and gave no indication that she was planning on leaving. He just wished she would give him a definite indication of her intensions so he knew what to expect. However, she had made it clear that she didn't want to talk about it during the remainder of their two weeks together. He was hoping that it was because she needed time to think about what she should do.

Although he fought it, he fell asleep long before the water she heated for him came to a boil. They had done many things together that day and it had worn him out. Arabella finished mending his pants and then she neatly folded them and placed them in the cabinet. She then ladled herself a mug of the hot water and sat down to enjoy its warmth. Her eyes took in the sight of her beloved as he slept soundly in their bed. "I'll miss you." She whispered and took enough time to finish her water.

When she finished she rinsed out her cup and placed it back on the shelf beside Edmond's. Then she went to the cabinet and gathered her few belongings that fit in the satchel she whipped together out of her old smock, the one she escaped Eric in. Most of her things were packed, except her clothing. It would have been too obvious that she was planning on leaving if she'd have packed those. It was important to her to make this last day special for Edmond and she was sure that in time he would forgive her for leaving when he realized that it was done in his best interest.

Her movements were as silent as possible as she finished putting on her boots and cloak. She had never saddled a horse before but she was sure that she could manage it somehow. I wouldn't have been fair of her to ask Edmond to do it. This would be hard enough on him as it was. One thing did comfort her and that was that he knew where she was going. If he truly felt sure about leaving everything behind, he could come and look for her. Her grandfather wasn't too hard to find and he knew his name, which was all he needed to find her. "Farewell my beloved." She whispered before leaving the cabin as silently as possible.

Beautiful Pretender

When she opened the door she was greeted by the instant cold chill of the night's air. Quickly she went out the door and closed it behind her with the hope that it hadn't woke up Edmond. She had to wait a moment before heading to the barn until her eyes could adjust to the night's darkness. When it was to a point that was tolerable, she carefully made her way towards the barn. Over the last several days when Edmond had gone to the market, she practiced walking there, memorizing every obstacle along the way. This included memorizing where he kept everything in the barn where the horses were.

She had wanted desperately to figure out how to do the saddle during this time as well, but he would probably notice that things were moved so she didn't dare touch anything. She had seen Edmond and the men at her father's stables do it in the past and she was sure she could figure it out, even in the dark. She carefully placed her things down just inside the doorway and she then carefully made her way towards where he kept her saddle. Her hands searched for it, but it wasn't there. "Did he move it?" She wondered out loud in a whisper. Her horse whinnied and she went over to try and calm it down. It was apparent that her presence had startled it.

"It's alright little one." Her gentle voice to assure it and she reached in to pat its side. What she felt surprised her. "You're already saddled." Then she understood why she couldn't find her saddle and the thought brought a sad burden to her heart. He knew. Without a doubt he knew she was going to sneak off like this in the middle of the night without telling him. The tears which she had so far been successful in hiding poured forth and she quietly cried as she led the horse from its stall. As much as he had protested her leaving, he knew she would leave anyways and this was his last loving gesture to her. After gathering her things and tied them to the horse's saddle, she mounted it and began her journey back to Eldardesh. One other thing didn't escape her notice. Tied to the saddle's horn was the purse of coins that Peter had left behind for them. As far as she could tell, Edmond hadn't used any of the money that had been left. He instead saved it for her to use, should she choose this path in which she now traveled. Fighting her tears was no longer an option and she cried openly in the privacy of the night as she traveled towards her new future. A life without the man she loved.

Edmond had snuck outside once he was sure she was in the barn. He had to see with his own eyes, what it was she was doing, though he was sure to keep his presence hidden. The sounds of her tears informed him that this was just as hard on her as it was on him, perhaps even harder since she took it upon herself to do what he couldn't. "You lied." He whispered as she rode away. "My last memory of you, is watching you leave me." His hand came up to wipe at the tears that fell. "I had hoped that you would change your mind, with all my heart I prayed for it. However, it wasn't meant to be. I will do as you want and go back home, but I will never love another woman as I have loved you. Farewell, my beloved Little Mousy." Long after she disappeared into the darkness he finally found the courage to go back into the little empty dwelling on his own. Tomorrow he would gather his things and return to Celendra Desh and to his former life, which would now be empty of the love and friendship which had sustained him over the last five years.

Chapter 16

Arabella's horse came to a stop in front of her grandfather's home. She had only been there a few times but she still remembered it. He was an extremely wealthy man and his lands were vast. However he was also a very good man and the people who served under him were glad that he was the one who watched over them. The house was four stories high and was made of wood and stone. It had beautifully sculpted trees surrounding it. Actually the entire landscape around it was beautifully sculpted and immaculate. She smiled as she inhaled the cold October air. Earlier in the morning it was cold enough to produce a very light snow. It melted once it touched the ground but it was a nice distraction on her last morning of traveling.

She dismounted and walked up the few stairs that led to the front entry. "I do hope that mother also came here." She whispered before taking the large circular iron knocker to pound it on the door. Quickly she made sure that her hair and clothing were in order. Due to the risk it would pose to her to look like a girl, even at her grandfather's house, she was still forced to masquerade as Aram. She only had to wait a short moment before the servant answered it.

It was a graying woman of around fifty who was short and slightly plumb. "May I help you sir?"

Arabella used Aram's voice to answer. "I'm looking for the Baroness Cordell."

"May I ask who is calling?"

"Tell her it is Aram, the son of Joseph Aldonmire. He was the Baroness's family physician in Arminia." Arabella didn't want to take any chances, so she thought it best to hide her identity until she knew for sure that her mother was there. Not only that but she wasn't sure

301

who else might be there, so she didn't want to risk her security by accidentally informing the wrong Eldardeshian that she was there. She was in no hurry for Eric to find her.

"Baroness…" The servant looked over to where her mistress and her parents were having tea.

"Yes?"

"There is a young gentleman here to see you. An Arminian boy going by the name Aram, he said he was the son of…"

"Aram?" Jocelyn's face lit up. "Aram Aldonmire?"

"Yes mam."

Jocelyn quickly placed her cup down and stood up. "Hurry, take me to him." She grinned.

"What is it daughter?" Her father asked in confusion as he too put down his cup.

"You'll know in a moment." She beamed and then quickly left the room to follow the servant to the door.

Arabella looked around as she waited by the door. A stableman had come to take her horse back to the family's stables and care for it. She was glad because the poor thing had been traveling for days in this harsh weather and since she was unsure about how to put on its saddle and other things properly, she had left them on during the entire journey. She felt bad for the creamy brown mare but she really had no choice.

Her attention was drawn back to the door as it opened. "Child, it really is you!" Her mother beamed and grabbed Arabella up into her arms. "I was so worried." She began crying as she talked. "They said you had been kidnapped and you were missing for so long."

"Mother." Arabella said in her normal voice. "I wasn't kidnapped, not really. I actually ran away from Eric.'

"It no longer matters, as long as you're home." She backed away so she could look down into her daughter's eyes. "Where have you been all this time?"

"To be honest, it's a long story." She took her mother's arm to indicate that they should go inside.

This was Jocelyn's queue, "Go prepare a room for my daughter at

Beautiful Pretender

once." She told the woman who had been attending them.

"Daughter?" The servant asked confused.

Arabella laughed softly and then she spoke in her normal voice to the older woman. "Please forgive me for earlier." She smiled. "My name is actually Arabella."

The woman's faced paled, "You mean your Princess Arabella Mina Cordell?"

"Pleased to meet you." Arabella smiled at her.

"A royal guest? We're not prepared for a royal guest." The woman began to panic.

"Please don't fret over me." Arabella laughed softly.

"Who's there?" An older man's voice called. Soon his tall lean frame came into view and he looked at Arabella curiously. "Well I'll be... it's my little girl." He grinned. "So you've finally come home."

"Hello grandfather." She let go of her mother's arm so she could embrace the old man.

"Your disguise couldn't fool me." He told her as he held her firmly to him. "How I have missed you my little princess."

"I missed you too, grandfather." She smiled up at him when he released her.

"Your grandmother will be pleased to see you, child." He bent down to kiss her forehead. "Come on in, my dear and let's get you rested up and looking like a young lady again. You look like you've had a long and difficult journey."

"I have."

"Will you be willing to tell us about it?" He asked.

"Yes, but first I need to rest and it would be nice to get something to eat as well."

"Daughter," Her mother asked hesitantly. "You're not hurt at all are you?"

"I'm fine, really. I won't say this last month was easy but I don't regret any part of it. I plan to tell you everything that happened but some of it might upset you." She was thinking about the relation that she shared with Edmond. The fact that she was no longer a maiden would be hard for her mother to deal with.

"All that matters is that you're safe and that you are home with us now. Everything else can't compare to this."

"Thank you." Arabella smiled. She truly hoped that her mother and grandparents could allow her to maintain the joy she had found in those two heavenly weeks with Edmond, despite what it meant. Now that she was no longer a maiden, it would be harder for them to find a suitable husband for her, not that it mattered to her in the slightest. For as far as she was concerned, she never wanted anyone but Edmond, even if it meant that she couldn't have him. It wasn't a matter of her not wanting to do what her family asked of her, because if they wanted her to marry she would do it to honor them. However, if it could be avoided she would prefer it. Already she knew that her actions would probably upset them with the shame it brought. For a young woman, especially a princess, to give away such sanctity to a man who wasn't her real husband, was the highest degree of shame that a young woman could bring upon her family.

Though Arabella was going to tell her family all that happened but that day it didn't happen because she had laid down to sleep and didn't wake again. She continued to sleep except to meet her daily needs, for nearly four days. Between stress, the elements and the past month in general she had worn herself to complete exhaustion.

Her grandfather, Augustus, sat and watched over her as she slept soundly. He could tell that even in her sleep she had experienced things that were still haunting her. At times she would cry softly and at times she would whisper the name of someone called Edmond. He wasn't sure who Edmond was exactly but he knew that this person was someone she cared very deeply about by the way she said his name. Jocelyn had filled Arabella's room with the late fall's wild chrysanthemums in their gold, red and purple bouquets. It left a slightly bitter floral smell that gave an unusual romantic essence to the stone and wood built room.

His wife and daughter had found things to make the room feel more feminine. Many of these, blankets, pillows, rugs and so forth were from when Jocelyn was a child. Since he had his servants store these well, they stood the test of time and they almost looked like new. Obviously they needed to be washed well before they could be brought in for her use or they would cover her in the dust they managed to collect over the twenty or more years.

Augustus was snapped out of his thoughts as Arabella moaned softly. "Are you awake?" He asked cautiously, for he didn't want to startle her.

Arabella opened her eyes and looked up at her grandfather who seemed deeply concerned. "Yes." She yawned after speaking. "Where's mother?"

"She and your grandmother are in town looking at clothing for you. It seems that all you had with you were men's clothing." He was hinting for her to tell him why she was dressed that way.

"It was safer to travel that way since Eric's men are looking for a young woman." She hesitated before continuing. "Grandfather, will I bring you trouble by being here? I really wasn't sure where else to go." She eased herself up into a sitting position as she talked.

"My servants are carefully chosen before I hire them. No doubt you already know that I'm not fond of our young king and the last thing I need is someone reporting my disloyalty to him. You are safe here, my child."

"Still, I don't want to cause you and grandmother any grief, if there is even the slightest chance that my being here will cause you any trouble..."

He stopped her by placing the tips of his fingers on her lips, "Don't fret about it, precious girl. You are where you need to be. If you don't want to marry Eric, we are fine with that. You're mother had already told us about what happened with your father on the day Kendrick had come to ask for your hand. I'm truly sorry things had turned out as they did."

She waited until he removed his fingers before speaking again. "Thank you." Arabella reached out to take the dear old man into her embrace. "Thank you for protecting me."

"If you don't mind my asking, who is Edmond?"

"Edmond?"

"Yes, you had called out his name many times while you slept."

"Oh," she blushed with embarrassment. "I have a very bad habit of talking in my sleep. In fact, if you want the truth from me about anything, just ask me about it when I'm sleeping. Apparently I confess everything from my heart and talk about my greatest concerns."

He laughed softly, "Is that so?"

"Edmond liked to take advantage of it sometimes. He told me once that he wanted to know how I truly felt about some things and because I wouldn't tell him, he asked while I was sleeping. It was very embarrassing."

"Is he someone that you love?"

"Very much." She smiled sadly. "I'm not sure that I could ever give my heart to another after loving someone like him."

"What happened? Surely if you loved him that much he also loved you."

"Yes, he loves me just as I love him." She sighed, "However circumstances make it so that we can't be together."

"Why's that? Is he a commoner?"

"He's anything but common. He is the son of Baron and Baroness Wallace and also nephew to Kendrick and Eric."

Augustus sat back in his chair and gently rubbed at his short grey beard as he thought. "I see, so he is the princess's son. Now I understand why you can't be with him. If you two were together while Eric was still pursuing you then it could cause him to declare war on Arminia because Edmond is an Arminian and loyal to Kendrick. It would be no different then if Kendrick had taken you himself."

"Not only that, but Edmond would also stand to lose everything dear to him for that reason. His wealth, his family and his home could be denied to him in order to prevent the war. I couldn't do that to him."

"Where did he stand on all of this?"

Arabella sighed and laid back against the wall behind her, "He didn't care if he lost it all. He was willing to give up everything to stay by my side."

"That would take an incredible amount of courage for him to do. When someone like him is raised with wealth, title and security, it would be hard to lose it all for the sake of love."

"I was afraid that in time he would grow to resent me if I was selfish and granted his request. I think him resenting me would be a thousand times worse then losing him while he still loved me. I know he believes it would never happen but it could. I told him where I was going and if he truly feels as he does and he really is able to leave his life behind...."

"Then he will come here to find you." Her grandfather finished. "It's risky, but I believe you did the right thing."

Beautiful Pretender

She looked over at her grandfather's loving face, "If by chance he does come one day, would you take him in and treat him as your grandson?"

Augustus smiled as he reached over to lovingly cup her cheek. "With all of my heart, little one. If you have found him to be a suitable partner that you wish to spend your life with, then so do I. He is still the son of royalty which is enough in the eyes of society. You stand to inherit everything I have, seeing as how you are my only heir. So you will never want for anything."

"What if he doesn't come? Are you and grandmother going to arrange a marriage for me?"

"It would be best. Obviously we'd have to be careful who we chose but I couldn't bear it if you lived your entire life alone. Also, it must happen before I die because in Eldardesh, an inheritance can only go to a son or son in law. If neither is available, it may end up in the king's hands."

"Yes and I am sure that Eric is well aware of this. If he married me, he would get both your fortune and my fathers." Her face screwed up in discuss as she said the word father.

"I know your father has wounded you deeply, but you must learn to forgive him and let go of your anger someday. It's the only way you will find peace in that part of your heart."

"I'm not sure I can forgive him. I still love him, even though I don't want to…"

"Why don't you get up and come downstairs. I'll have the servants fix you a wonderful meal."

"Have them fix me a bath first. I feel just awful. I haven't had a decent bath since the day I left home."

"Of course." He smiled. "Anything for my little princess."

Arabella watched as her grandfather got up to leave. "I'm glad that I came here."

"As am I."

Arabella laughed at her grandfather's goofy gesture. He had been so pleased that she had come home to him, just as her mother had decided to do just weeks before Arabella had come home. Arabella had been living with them for over four months now and she was settling in quite splendidly. Her thoughts often returned to Edmond and she wondered how he was doing and when he would be marrying the Countess. It made her sad to think of him being with another woman but there really was nothing she could do about it. Her family knew that it was better to not tell her about the latest news of Arminia. Happy or sad, they were all well aware of what she had been through during the time the two kids were missing because she had confided in them about everything.

Jocelyn, Arabella's mother, was sad that her daughter wouldn't become a queen and was sadder still that her daughter was no longer a maiden but she decided that she would have to learn to live with this situation, they all would. Thankfully Jocelyn's father was a man of considerable means and influence, not only in Eldardesh but in the surrounding kingdom's as well. There was still a good chance that they could find someone of noble blood for Arabella to marry, perhaps not in Eldardesh or Arminia but hopefully in one of the surrounding kingdoms.

"Grandfather…" Arabella laughed uncontrollably. The thin elderly man of average height was currently making armpit farts to one of his favorite tunes. "That's absolutely disgusting."

"I thought you liked being around guys and doing guy things. Didn't your friends do things like this?" He continued his little tune as he grinned through his white neatly trimmed beard and mustache.

Still laughing, "Yes, but it was different."

"Oh, you mean something like this." He changed the tune.

"No, oh never mind. Grandmother! Grandfather's being vulgar again." She called in her fits of laughter.

"Augustus, stop torturing that poor girl." She said as she came into the room. "You should be ashamed of yourself behaving in such a crude manner in front of a princess. Not only that but you are a man of considerable reputation and influence, how on earth would society….."

"Mother, you need to stop fretting so much. Can't you tell that she actually likes it but she can't admit it because of social protocol?" He laughed and then he brought his hand out of his shirt.

"A protocol which you also should abide by, you old fart." The slightly plump woman of sixty-two scolded. Her words set both her husband

Beautiful Pretender

and granddaughter into even more fits of laughter. "Oh, you two will be the death of me." She turned abruptly and left the room, just in time to hide her smile. It was nice to see that her husband could help their granddaughter find her smile again. She had been so depressed when she first came home to them. Augustus had immediately taken to her and coddled the young woman, spoiling her with his finances and affections. She was their only grandchild from their only daughter. Like herself, Jocelyn had a difficult time conceiving and both had suffered numeral miscarriages. Her one saving grace was that Arabella seemed to be built much better then either of them had and she hoped that this would allow her granddaughter to be more successful at producing heirs.

Rachel and her husband, crowned the Duke of Searak (Searak is the town in which they live) were feeling blessed that both Jocelyn and her daughter were living with them. It was something that they had never expected to happen. It was almost as if fate heard the cries of their lonely hearts and it came to fill them once again. Both Rachel and her husband were glad that Arabella wouldn't be marrying Eric. Neither of them was very fond of their young king. King Eric's grandfather was her husband's uncle and he had bestowed her husband's title upon him. Rachel was the last of her clan from a distant kingdom. Her father had brought her west in the hope of finding someone worthy of her hand. Though she came from a simple clan of people, she was considered a princess. Unfortunately their land and people suffered from the Great Pestilence (Later known as the Black Death) and barely anyone survived. Though she came with little into the marriage, her status, though foreign, was enough to win her husband's parents approval.

Jocelyn made her way to the town's market about once per week to see what new things from the foreign lands had made their way there. She loved to shop, that was no secret to anyone and she had her favorite places to look for her newest treasures. Searak was a large town that was in a central location that lay between Brie-Ancou (Eldardesh's Capital where the king's palace was) and Celendra Desh (Arminia's capital). It also sat on the main roads that led from the two seaports of Scendell (Eldardesh) and Hyrush (Arminia). Both ports would take the roads that led through Searak on their way to delivering goods to the kingdoms east of Eldardesh and Arminia. Thanks to this, she was able to see and experience many wonderful treasures that were imported from foreign countries.

She was so busy looking over the newest import of jewelry being sold by one of the merchants that she hadn't noticed the tall young man standing beside her. "Good afternoon, mam." He said casually.

Jocelyn looked up at the young man next to her. "Do I know you? You look familiar somehow." She smiled sweetly at him.

"You really don't recognize me?" He grinned.

Suddenly the memory of the young man came back to her and she covered her mouth with her hand as she laughed in delight. "Peter? Dearest Peter, is that you?"

"Yes, it is." He continued to grin.

"Why... just look at you." She reached forward and took his upper arms into her hands as she held him back enough to look him over. "What a fine young man you've turned out to be and so handsome..." Then she suddenly brought him into her embrace. "I'm so glad we ran into each other. Seeing you brings back a flood of wonderful memories."

He embraced her in return. "I'm glad you're happy to see me." Peter waited to talk more to her until she released him. "Have you had any word from Arabella recently? I've been terribly worried about her."

"Oh, yes...that." Her demeanor instantly changed. Even though he had helped her daughter out in Kinshek, she still wasn't sure just how much she could trust him with their secret. "I'm afraid I can't say anything about that."

"I understand your reservations but I assure you, I intend your daughter no harm. I didn't turn her in before and I have no intention on doing so now. However, my concern for her hasn't lessened any."

"She's safe and is doing well." Jocelyn and Peter were walking now so they would be less likely to be overheard.

"Did she marry that young man yet or did they part ways?"

"No, they parted ways."

He stopped them both from walking, "How is that possible? They were both so much in love with each other that such a notion would have seemed impossible."

"It was what they had agreed upon before spending their time in

Beautiful Pretender

Kinshek. They would live like husband and wife for two weeks to allow themselves time to love one another and then she would release him to go back to his family and marry the woman that they had chosen for him."

"So he actually let her go. What a fool." He sighed. "I wouldn't have done it."

"What do you mean?" She asked with curiosity.

He cleared his throat, "Nothing, it's just that if it were me, I would have held tightly to her and kept her with me."

Jocelyn smiled, "You always were protective of her."

"Do you know where she is now?"

"Perhaps I do, why?"

"I'd like to see her again, if it is at all possible."

Jocelyn could tell that he was being earnest with her. "Come by and visit me sometime. I'd like to spend more time with you."

"Would today work?" He asked.

"Perhaps but only if you help me carry home my purchases."

"It would be my pleasure." He smiled warmly at her. Perhaps he was being given the chance he could have never dreamed of hoping for before, a chance that could bring him closer to the girl he had loved since childhood. It had been some time since he assisted a woman with her shopping and he quickly found himself growing bored as they went from merchant to merchant, though he would die before admitting it to her. She examined and bartered with, what seemed like every seller in town and most of the time she ended up buying nothing. He was sure that she came more for the excitement of the game more than for the merchandise itself. Still he ended up with quite an arm load of things wrapped in cloth or placed in wooden boxes of various sizes.

"Don't fret," she assured him, "I did bring the carriage."

"I must admit that I'm relieved to hear it." He heard her laugh softly.

"Would you like to ride home with me or would you rather come by your own means?"

"I'll ride my horse there. He's tethered not far from here." He walked with her to her carriage and gratefully accepted the help from its driver and footman when it came to unloading the packages from his person. "I know where your father resides and I will meet you there shortly."

"Please plan to join us for our evening meal." She smiled warmly. "You may even stay over if you wish. We have plenty of rooms to spare."

"I'd appreciate that mam." He bowed humbly before turning to leave. "I'll run home first to get a change of clothing. My place isn't too far from here." Jocelyn already knew that he must live locally since Searak was at least a three day ride by horse from Brie-Ancou. She figured that Peter must be stationed here for the time being because his family lived near the palace.

"Oh mother." Arabella sighed with frustration when she saw all the packages from the latest purchases come in. "Do you really need all that stuff?"

Jocelyn looked over everything, "No, not really but there were so many lovely things I just couldn't help myself. Besides, I bought some wonderful things for you too and..." she came closer to Arabella, "I have a surprise for you later as well. It hasn't arrived yet." She seemed to be brimming with excitement.

"Oh?" This seemed to spark Arabella's interest, "I do hope you didn't spend a fortune on it. Do you realize that there are many families in this town alone that have to struggle just to have enough to eat, just enough to survive?"

Jocelyn laughed, "Your short term life in poverty sure has changed the way you see money." She hugged Arabella not realizing that her daughter was one of the Black Bandits and she had always been this way. "Actually this one only cost me a meal, it was a real bargain."

"Very well then." She knew her mother was a hopeless case.

"Oh, though you must promise that you will wear the outfit I purchased for you today as well as some of the jewelry and shoes..." She continued to prattle on as she began rummaging through her purchases to find what she had bought for her daughter. It bothered her that Arabella almost exclusively dressed in men's clothing now. This was mostly because when she left the house, even to walk the grounds of her grandfather's estate, she pretended to be a young man. This was because it was possible that someone looking for her on Eric's behalf could stop by at any time.

Jocelyn purposefully didn't tell either of the children about the other. She first wanted to be sure that Peter came alone. However, she had a feeling that his devotion to Arabella was greater then his loyalty to Eric. It still wasn't confirmed but she had a comforting feeling about him. This held true when he finally arrived. He was dressed formally and his things were retrieved for him by one of her father's servants and were brought up to the room he would be using since he would be staying with them for a few days.

"Baroness." He greeted her in a formal and gentile voice. So far she was the only one aware of his arrival, with the exception of a few servants.

"Lord Evanston." She curtsied. "I haven't told anyone that you were coming yet, I wanted it to be a surprise."

"Oh…" He responded nervously. "Is it all right that I came?"

"Of course it is dear." She reached out and took his arm so he could escort her, though technically it was the other way around since she was leading him to where they need to go. "How long will you be stationed here?"

"I'm to spend the next year here observing things on the king's behalf. This town is his greatest source of revenue and he wanted someone he could trust to over see a few things."

"He always did depend on you, didn't he? He trusts you more then any other person, including that horrid man I married."

Peter looked at her sadly, "Your husband misses you dreadfully, milady."

"That's for him to be concerned about. I'm more than angry with him for what he did to our little girl. It's simply unforgivable."

"Though I value my king's happiness, I agree that it was unkind to force Arabella to marry him in the manner in which he went about it. Eric does have a reputation of having an ill temper with those he can't control. His wife is a very gentle woman who lives to please him, so they get along fairly well for the most part. However, it is clear that Arabella is much too independent for a man like him. It would be very unwise to put her in his care."

"I'm glad you agree with me on that." She patted his arm with her free hand as they turned to enter her father's sitting room. There her parents sat and talked quietly with each other near the hearth.

"Father, mother, we have a guest." Her grin couldn't be more obvious or proud.

Her parents stood up to greet their guest. Her father was the first to speak, for he knew instantly who this man his daughter brought home was. "What are you doing here, loyal servant of our king?" His demeanor was far from friendly.

"Oh father, don't be so rude. It's just Peter." She brought her arm about him to give Peter a motherly embrace.

"Yes, and he's also Eric's right hand man." He warned his daughter.

Arabella came down the stairs and went to the room where she heard all of the commotion, unaware of the guest that there was in their midst. She was wearing a gown of green velvet that conformed to her figure. It was the one that her mother had purchased for her that day. It was very befitting to the times with its flared sleeves and low bust line. A gold rope crossed over her torso and tied at her waist in the front. The gown itself was trimmed in gold. Her earrings, bracelets and tiara were also made of gold and were delicate to compliment the dress.

"Oh." She gasped in surprise when she saw the back view of their guest. This caught everyone's attention and soon all eyes were upon her. When she realized that Peter was there before her, fear struck up in her heart and she began to back away from him.

He reached out towards her, "No, wait. You have nothing to fear."

Arabella looked up at her mother but Jocelyn agreed, "Don't be frightened daughter."

"Mother, how could you?" Arabella couldn't stand still any longer and she quickly lifted her dress high enough that she could run freely without it confining her.

"Wait." Peter called and then quickly said to Jocelyn, "Don't be concerned, I'll bring her back to you." Immediately he took off after his childhood friend.

"What were you thinking daughter by bringing the enemy into our home. Don't you know that child was seeking our shelter and protection from his kind?"

"Father..." Jocelyn turned so she could look into his eyes, "You don't know Peter like I do. He would never do anything to hurt her. The only thing more important to him then Eric is protecting my

Beautiful Pretender

daughter."

"You don't know that for sure. Just because he didn't do anything when they were in Kinshek, doesn't mean he'll bestow that favor again."

"Well I guess only time will tell what will happen from this point on." Her mother Rachel finalized the argument. "It's too late to change what has happened." She turned to one of the servants. "Have another place set at the table for our guest, Nola."

"Yes, milady." The middle aged servant with graying black hair answered with a bow. Immediately she left to do as bidden.

"Arabella, please wait." Peter called after her. "I promise I won't breathe a word to another living soul that you're staying here. You must trust me."

She knew there was no use in running any further. The dress was much too cumbersome for running in and the shoes she wore were hurting her feet for they hadn't been used before. Finally she stopped near a tree and reached forward with one hand to lean against it to catch her breath. "I can't believe how daft mother can be sometimes." Her breath was labored as was her complaint. Peter came up along side her. "I suppose there is no use in trying to escape."

Peter reached forward and took the hand that hung down by her side. "I swear on all that is holy, that I will keep your secret safe, Arabella."

She looked up at him in the semi darkness. "I really don't have a choice but to take your word for it. However, I swear that if you ever betray me, I will never forgive you. No matter what we meant to each other in the past, I could never hold anything but hate towards you if you hand me over to Eric."

"I promise," He laid his hand on his heart, "I won't betray your trust. I will stay by your side and guard you from harm as long as it is humanly possible and as long as you want me there with you. I make this vow to you and if I should ever break it may our Lord God strike me dead."

"Alright then..." She sighed in defeat. "I will trust you as I have in the past. After all you did keep our secret safe in Kinshek, so there is no reason for me to doubt your word now."

315

JM Howard

"Thank you. However you must promise to keep mine safe as well. If Eric should learn that I have known your whereabouts and didn't report it, he may very well take my life as a consequence. To be honest, I am in no hurry to experience his wrath."

"That makes two of us." She took the arm he offered her and she allowed him to escort her back to the house. "Ouch." Her steps betrayed a limp.

"Did you hurt yourself?" There was no mistaking the concern in his voice.

"I think I might have twisted my ankle." Instantly her thoughts went back to the time when she had used that excuse to avoid seeing Edmond, the same day that he gave her the nickname of Little Mousy. The thought pulled at the strings that he still held on her heart.

"Would you like me to carry you?" He stopped walking.

Arabella suddenly felt embarrassed, "No, I'm sure that if I slow down my pace, I'll make it just fine."

"Are you sure?" He had a feeling she was just being stubborn.

"Yes, I'm sure." She continued to limp as they walked.

Peter sighed, "That's all I can take. Please forgive me for acting on my own accord." He quickly grabbed her up into his arms so that he could carry her the rest of the way to the house. Arabella had led them quite a ways away from it and he could tell that she was in a lot of pain as she walked.

"Put me down." She protested and hit him on the chest.

"Be still." Peter scolded her. "You will find that I'm not one to take orders when they're not in your best interest."

Arabella had forgotten how forthright Peter was. The way he dealt with her really hadn't changed that much from what it had been in the past. When they were children, he seemed to be the only one who could break through her stubborn streak when it was needed. She wasn't sure how he did it but she had a tendency to allow him to lead her. "Thank you." Her voice was timid.

He looked down at her, "For what?"

"Not telling Eric that I was in Kinshek. Not only did you help me but you saved Edmond's life as well."

"I don't understand why you left him. He's a very good man, Arabella, one who was willing to do anything just to be by your side."

Beautiful Pretender

"It is better if I don't talk about it. It just makes me sad when I think of him being with another woman. However I know he is better off at her side. I have nothing to give him but the troubles that plague me."

"I'm not sure that is so true…"

"Please Peter, I beg of you to let this go."

"Very well." He ascended the stairway that led back into the large mansion. "You're mother received quite a scolding for bringing me here, let's try to easy your grandfather's concerns, shall we?"

"Alright." She looked into the corridor of the home as a servant opened the door for them. Peter was still carrying her.

"Oh thank God." Jocelyn sighed in relief, "You found her."

"Yes Baroness, however she has managed to twist her ankle."

Immediately servants went to fetch the necessary supplies to bring comfort to their young mistress's injury as Jocelyn came to inspect it for herself. "How bad is it dear?" She asked her daughter.

"Stop fussing so much about it mother, it will be fine in a day or two." Arabella tried to shoo her mother away.

"Don't disrupt her, Arabella. She's just worried, let her look at it and stop acting like a child about it." Peter scolded her.

"But…" she looked up into his eyes and could see that he was serious about what he said. "Oh, very well." Arabella watched as her mother carefully removed her shoe and then let it drop to the ground.

"Perhaps you should take her upstairs to lie down. She can have her dinner up there, you too if you wish." Jocelyn offered.

"Mother!" Arabella scolded.

"I'm sure that would be fine, milady." He looked down at Arabella, "You'll have to show me which room is yours." She sighed in response and then he headed for the stairway. "You have an ornery streak about you, don't you?"

"Oh shut up." She countered.

"Lord help you should you ever fall into Eric's hands." He groaned in despair.

Arabella looked up at him with concern, "You don't think he will find me, do you?"

"Not by me, he won't." He promised, "But I'm not the only one who is loyal to Eric that lives in these parts. It just happens that I am more sympathetic to your plight. Eric is offering a large reward to anyone who finds you and brings you back to him."

"You're not serious are you?" Fear now haunted her as she realized the danger she was in.

"I only wish I wasn't. Eric is determined to find you and he is desperate to do so as soon as possible. He fears the longer you are away, the further you fall from his grasp."

She laid her head down on his chest and pointed to a doorway, "It's that room, there."

"Alright."

"What will I do if he does find me?"

"I will ask to be your servant."

"Servant?"

"Who better to guard the queen then Eric's most trusted man? I couldn't completely protect you from him but I can be there to comfort you when you need a friend." He knew that there would be a heavy price to pay should this happen but he didn't let on to her about it. "I wouldn't worry about it, though I will speak to your mother about trusting people so easily." He waited for her to open the door for him and then he brought her in and gently laid her down on her bed. "The servants should be here shortly to tend to your ankle. I'd like to take a few moments to freshen up before our meal arrives."

"I'm glad we've had a chance to meet again. I felt bad that you left so suddenly after our last encounter. I wasn't very polite and there was so much I had wished I had asked you. I really missed you during those five years. I know it probably didn't seem like it but you were the brother I never had and I really loved you." She meant this in the way that one sibling would love another.

"I'm glad that I found you again, milady. I will return shortly."

"Thank you." She smiled up at him. Peter just smiled back and nodded in return before leaving her room. After he returned to her room, they ended up spending a great deal of the evening in idle chitchat as they reminisced about the happier times of their childhood. As much as possible, Eric was not a part of it. Peter could tell that she preferred to not talk about anything dealing with him.

Even though she kept a smile on her face as they spoke, he could see an incredible amount of sorrow in her eyes. He could almost tell when her thoughts were with Edmond, she took on this distant forlorn look,

Beautiful Pretender

one that seemed lost in time and space. He did his best to guide the conversation as far from both Eric and Edmond as he could, but every now and again he could see that he lost her to the one she loved most.

Chapter 17

"Lord Edmond Wallace, we'd like to introduce you to our daughter, Countess Alicia D'Winter." Her father said formally.

Edmond bowed humbly before the woman he was expected to marry, "Milady."

The young pale blond girl curtsied in return. "Lord Wallace it is an honor to meet you at last."

He stood back up and looked his prospective bride of seventeen over. "I must apologize for my delay in our introductions." This was killing him. Alicia was indeed a very beautiful young woman, but she couldn't hold a candle to Arabella. Still he was determined to be the man that Arabella hoped he would be, so despite the pain this moment brought, he was resolved to go through with it because it was what Arabella wanted him to do.

"We are to blame for not coming to Celendra Desh sooner." The Countess's husky yet well trimmed father spoke on her behalf. "We thought we would do well to come and become acquainted with the place that will be our daughter's new home. I'm sure there are plenty of people who are anxious to meet her."

Baroness Wallace spoke up, "Indeed there is. Everyone has been talking endlessly about your visit. We even have a gathering of Nobles to celebrate this festive event, that being the formal announcement of Edmond and Alicia's betrothal. The king himself has decided to come so he can become acquainted with Edmond's prospective bride. That in itself is quite an honor."

"He is your brother, correct?"

"He is my half brother, yes. However we tend to not talk about that in public. My mother passed away when I was little and it had been several years before my father married again. Kendrick's mother and I were nearly the same age and it made things rather awkward socially."

"Still it is an honor to meet the daughter of our late king and even more so that she has chosen our daughter to be her son's bride." He reached forward to take the Baroness's hand so that he could kiss it.

"There's nothing like being in the presence of a beautiful princess, is there." Edmond smiled though he wasn't referring to his mother but instead Arabella, however no one was aware of that.

"Indeed not." Alicia's father agreed. "We are looking forward to watching you compete in the King's tournament. It's in a few more months if I'm not mistaken."

"Indeed it is, approximately three months from now in July." It had been five months since he and Arabella had parted. Due to matters of the kingdom, Kendrick was forced to postpone the tournament until the following year. More than once Edmond had wished to go and see Arabella at her grandfather's house but he knew if he did, he would never return to Arminia, even if she denied him her love. He would rather welcome the sweet abyss of death rather then havening to watch her leave him again. His heart simply couldn't stand being broken like that again.

"Are you only competing in swords?"

"Yes, I really haven't had a chance to brush up on any of the other categories though I do enjoy archery and axes."

"Axes, that's rather barbaric." He laughed. "I preferred the lance myself, but as you can see, time has robbed me of the strength and talent that allows one to participate in such amusing pastimes."

"This will probably be my last year as well. Many men do this as a profession but for me it was just a game. I've already lost one of my most talented partners and the other two are coming of age to begin homes of their own as well. Needless to say we are ready to join those who watch the tournaments instead of those who participate in them."

"Quite right." He agreed in an understanding tone. "I'm sure it will set my daughter at ease to know that you won't be participating in such a potentially dangerous sport."

"It's not all that dangerous if you know what you're doing. However I do understand where there could be reservations." He turned his attention to Alicia, "Would you care to take a stroll through my mother's gardens? The spring has been kind to her flower gardens due to its unusual warmth and moderate rains."

She smiled sweetly, "I would be delighted to do so, my lord." She waited for him to come to her and then she took his arm. One big difference he noticed between Alicia and Arabella was not only their outward appearance but also their personality. Alicia was very delicate and had impeccable manners. She spoke softly and there was not one ounce of her that wasn't feminine. He could tell already that she was a compliant girl and not stubborn like Arabella was. However all the things Alicia lacked were the very things that he loved about Arabella.

She was the only woman he knew that loved to sword fight and compete with him in archery, though when he had done those things with her, he was led to believe that she was male and not female. As boyish as Arabella could be, she could be equally as feminine when the time called for it. Her ability to read his thoughts and emotions was unparalleled. 'I must stop thinking about her and comparing Alicia with her.' He scolded himself. Even now as he walked with his future bride, he remembered the beautiful woman who had fully given herself to him. The many times that he had made love to her and the sounds of her voice as she reacted to his every touch were still very fresh in his mind even though so much time had passed. Even the feel of her hair as he let it slipped between his fingers, was enough to drive him mad with the desire to hold her in his arms again. He sighed in frustration and shook his head to try and stop these useless longings for a woman he could never embrace again.

Alicia looked up at Edmond, "Is something troubling you, my lord?"

"It's nothing that can't be resolved with time. Be assured that it is nothing to be concerned over." He smiled down at her. "May I ask a personal question of you?"

"Certainly, ask anything you want." Her angelic face had a hint of a smile on it.

"Was there someone that you cared for before coming here?"

"My, you didn't waste much time asking that." She laughed softly. "I had many admirers but I hadn't set my sights on anyone in particular. I simply let them dote on me. It was rather fun to be admired by so many gentlemen, noble and common alike."

"I can see why they felt that way, you are quite becoming." He noticed her blush under his praise.

"I'm glad you approve, my lord." She stopped to admire a rose bush that had the garden's first bud that was beginning to open. Its red blossom was slowly fighting its way out to show that world the beauty that lay within. "How lovely... Promise you will give me a rose garden like this once we're married and in our own home." She looked up at him with a charming smile.

"You're welcome to have whatever you desire." He smiled in return. This woman was acting as if they had known each other for a long time, yet he had only just met her. It was awkward behaving this way with a total stranger. However he didn't have much choice but to try and create a bond with her. By this time next year she would be his bride and there wasn't anything that he could do about it now. His heart was numb, no matter how long they waited, he was sure that it would be impossible for him to love her even half as much as he loved Arabella. 'I wonder what she's doing right now.' He thought quietly to himself. It was a question he asked himself probably a hundred times a day. That and also he wondered if she had anyone in her life to take his place.

Arabella worked in the small garden that she and her mother had created together. They had already planted carrots, turnips and some other root vegetables. Soon they could plant the seeds for the vegetables that would grow above ground. It really wasn't very big. It was more of a way for them to pass the time. Currently she was removing the small weeds that were trying to find a home in the fertilized soil. She heard someone approach from behind her. "Good morning beautiful."

She turned to look behind her, from her kneeling position. "Good morning, Peter." She smiled happily at him. "Are you off duty today or just stopping by?" He had managed to keep her secret for a couple months now and her grandfather finally had to admit that Peter could be trusted to protect Arabella's secret.

"I'm all yours today." He grinned.

"Good, get down here and help me finish removing these weeds." She laughed.

"Umm, I think I hear my mother calling." He turned to leave. It was one of the many ways he teased her.

"Peter..." She used her warning voice, though she too was just playing along.

He put his hands up in the air, "I surrender." Immediately he began laughing and walked over to kneel down beside her. His finger quickly went to work as he helped her to remove the weeds. "I was wondering if perhaps you would like to go for a ride on my horse with me later today. The weather seems to be cooperating for doing such a thing."

"Both of us on your horse?" She asked with confusion.

"Why not?"

"I do have my own horse you know. There's no need to tire your horse out with two riders."

"She can handle it well enough." He assured her. "I won't push her hard, so you need not worry about her condition."

"I don't know if I should..."

He immediately stopped her protest, "Don't read too much into it. I just thought it would be nice change for us." Honestly he had hoped to take Edmond's place in her heart but she had put up a wall that only Edmond could knew how to climb. For now, Peter was determined to bide his time. His new goal was to find a way that went either around this invisible wall or over it even thought it seemed too high to climb. He would do whatever it took to get past this unseen wall that blocked the way to her heart so that he too would have a chance at winning it over to himself. However he didn't want to push her too hard. He knew she was still hurting over the loss of the man she loved.

"Well," she wiped her dirty hands on her apron. "I suppose it wouldn't be such a bad idea. I actually do feel up for a ride today. The only thing I need to do is to dress as Aram, in case we come across anyone who might be looking for me."

"Then I'll wait out here for you." He stood up and looked at his mud caked hand. "I should probably deal with this problem first." Quickly he grabbed her apron so he could wipe his hands on it as well.

"Hey!" She laughed in surprise. He only grinned in response. "Alright, I'll be back down as soon as I can."

"Why don't you tell the cook to make us a small meal to take? We could stop to eat on our outing." He asked her and she waved as her affirmative response. There was more then one reason why he wanted to spend time with her alone. He just received notice that Eric wanted him to check out an estate just east of Searak and he would have to be gone for nearly a week. However, upon his return he had hoped to broach a subject with her that would be more serious and risky on his part. He was hoping that perhaps she would allow him to begin courting her, officially. Already he was doing it unofficially by coming to see her on a near daily basis.

Peter reached down and brushed off as much soil from his pants as he could. There really was only just a small amount on his knees and the fabric was slightly damp. He felt nervous for some strange reason and he looked up to the window that belonged to her room. 'Will she let me get close to her, I wonder? Will she see me as something more then an older brother? It's not like we're related by blood, well not in that fashion.' He could feel his cheeks growing warm as he began hoping that she would be willing to let him develop a more personal relationship with her.

"Has Aram contacted you yet at all?" Silas asked Edmond as they prepared to practice in the sword ring again.

"Yeah, I have been worried about him too and I really miss him..." Then Eustace added somewhat quickly, "...especially in the sword ring. Without him, you beat us in half the time." He joked and made the others laugh despite the empty feeling that they were all feeling. It was true that they all felt like something important had been torn from them and they wished he could have at least taken the time to say goodbye before he left.

"He apparently was sent to his cousin's home, you know the one his parents wanted for him to marry. I guess they're keeping him pretty busy." It was all Edmond could think to say.

"I hope he at least makes it out for the king's tournament." Silas said as he entered the sword ring. "It just wouldn't be the same without him here, especially since this will be our last year."

"It would be nice, but I wouldn't get your hopes up." Edmond had decided not to tell them about Aram actually being Arabella. For some reason it seemed important for his friends to remember her as being a boy. They all shared so many memories together that if they knew the truth it could cloud over those sunny and cherished childhood times they had all shared. He personally had come to terms with it but only after dealing with the sense of betrayal that he felt when he first discovered the truth. Now when he looked back those days seemed even more precious to him. "Well gentlemen," he smiled, "let's begin." He raised his sword and soon he was battling the other two. The combat with his friends grow more and more intense as he prepared for the day of the big tournament.

He also spent more time in training as well. Part of it was to prepare but part of it was an excuse for him to not be with Alicia more then necessary. He still wasn't all that fond of her. It wasn't that she was a bad person or anything but her sweet and innocent ways were sort of annoying and the fact that she agreed with everything he did or said got on his nerves as well. He also kept getting the feeling that she was hiding something from him too, perhaps a part of her that he probably wouldn't approve of.

Baron Cordell came before Eric and bowed humbly before him. "You're overdue." Eric told him in a rather formal voice.

"Please pardon me, milord. However I may have some news that will have been worth the wait."

"Oh?" Eric's interest peeked at this change of topic. "Do carry on."

The Baron stood up and took a seat across from Eric, "First of all, I'm sure you're aware that the Arminian 'King's Tournament' is only three months away."

"Yes, I'm aware. Ours is only two weeks before that one." Eric's interest was fading, so the baron moved onto another subject.

"Also your brother has other affairs of state that you might be interested in but I think those can wait because I have some news that will make you overjoyed."

"And that is?" Eric's patience was growing thin. He listened carefully to all the Baron had to say. "Are you sure about this?" It was indeed the most interesting news so far.

"Who would know better then I sire?" He smiled.

"This is good news indeed." Eric stood up and clapped his hands. "Prepare my men at once. We shall leave immediately." His grin couldn't have been more proud. "I finally figured out a way to break

Kendrick's resolve. I just have to act fast and work hard to be ready on time. These events couldn't have worked better in my favor." He was nearly drooling with the anticipation. "Send my brother word that we will be attending his tournament and that I expect him to reserve my mother's wing in the castle for my exclusive use."

"As you wish, sire." He was glad that he could make his king happy, though he had to betray others to do so, yet he still held a glimmer of hope that one day Eric could become a great king that far surpassed all of those before him. If these little sacrifices could produce that sort of king for Eldardesh then they were worth the cost.

Arabella was doing the finishing touches on her hair. She had mastered 'Aram's' hair style on her own, since she no longer had a chambermaid to assist her with it, this was by choice. Her grandfather had offered to hire one for her but she didn't feel that it was right to replace Ida. She still had hoped that someday she would find her faithful friend and servant and re-employ her if she still wished to work with Arabella. However, she hadn't really had the opportunity to look for Ida yet.

She took one last look in the mirror. Everything looked like Aram except the chest. She didn't want to bind it until later on that day, just before Peter came. They were planning on going to town to look at the most recent shipment of horses that came in the day before. The bindings were becoming more and more uncomfortable so she only wore them when she absolutely had to. "It won't be much longer before I turn eighteen." She reflected out loud, "Just five more months." Arabella was well aware of her mother's concerns about her age.

Most girls her age were married by now with babies of their own. She thought about Eric's wife, Miriam. There was no doubt that if her pregnancy and delivery went well that Eric now had his first off spring. She couldn't help but to wonder if it was a boy or a girl. Since her mother and grandparents never spoke to her about either of the kingdoms' monarchies or other matters of the social elite, she was ignorant of the latest news. If she was honest with herself she would have to admit that she was happy living in this ignorance. Not knowing anything meant that she didn't have to deal with anything unpleasant.

Arabella was happy that Peter was coming. He had originally

promised to come directly to her when he got back from dealing with that matter at the estate but unfortunately his visit was delayed by a day and he sent word that he would come for her the following day. He had mentioned that he left over a week earlier that he had something important to discuss with her and her grandfather suggested that Peter was probably going to ask her to allow him to begin his courtship. At first she was rather shocked at the idea of this person she had always seen as an older brother wanting to pursue her. After a few days had passed she realized that if it was truly what Peter wanted then perhaps she should allow him to do so. It wasn't that she cared for him in this manner but she had a great deal of trust and respect for him. Already her grandfather was thinking of a way to make a marriage possible. One of those plans was that they would have to move from Eldardesh to one of the eastern kingdoms. Obviously Arminia was out of the question because Eric was looking for any excuse to declare war on his brother's kingdom.

It was already the early afternoon and she was famished. After checking her appearance in the mirror one last time, she decided that she could still pass herself off as a boy and it pleased her. "Now for food." She grinned in anticipation. "I wonder what cook made for us. The entire house seems to smell of roasted meat and newly baked bread." Lately the cook had taken it upon himself to prepare food for Peter to take home with him, since he adored the cooks many dishes. Peter personally took time to chat with the older man and he loved sampling all of the latest dishes. Needless to say, Peter was starting to show signs of this healthy appetite. Thankfully, it wasn't showing too badly yet. He simply was looking like a well fed man, which more then fit his social status.

Arabella was smiling from ear to ear as she thought of the activities of the day ahead of her. Her grandfather was giving her money to buy another horse for her to use as well as funds to buy herself a new carriage. The one she had been using was nearly fifty years old and it was more than ready to retire. Thankfully a merchant handling these was also in town. He seemed to sell more carriages when he worked along side the men who sold the horses.

She was rather surprised to hear a number of voices coming from just outside the front of her grandfather's house and she took it upon herself to investigate. The door was left partially ajar and she looked out to see who had come to visit her grandfather. She had hoped it was Peter and that he came earlier then expected, however when she opened the door she was greeted by the most undesirable surprise. Her breath caught in her throat and she stood frozen at the scene before her and all eyes looked her way.

"Hello Arabella." Eric grinned. "At last I have finally found you."

"Daughter." Her father greeted her with a smile.

"Oh no." She whispered.

"Men, seize her." Eric ordered casually with a grin. Immediately Arabella turned to run. She had hoped to weave her way through her grandfather's house and out the back door. As far as where she hoped to hide from these men, she still wasn't completely sure. All she knew was that if she didn't get away, her worst nightmare would come true.

"Please God help me." She cried as she ran. "What should I do?" Finally the back door was in sight and she threw it open, however a pair of strong arms grabbed her as she ran out the door. A soldier apparently had been placed there to stop her should she try to escape. "Let me go!" She cried out.

"I'm sorry, your highness, but I can't do that." The man with a deep voice told her. She didn't even bother looking at him. Instead she fought with all of her might to break free from him. "Please, princess, you're only making this harder on yourself."

Her body fell limp in his arms as she cried, "Please....let me go." She had lost her will to fight, for she simply hadn't the strength to break free from his grip.

"Good work soldier." Another man said. Apparently he had been one of the men pursuing her through the house for he was out of breath. "Bring her back through the house and out to his majesty. He has given us permission to tie her up if she doesn't cooperate."

"Yes general." The soldier replied. He, along with one other man, each took one of her arms and escorted her back through the house to where Eric waited for her. Once they were back out front with her they awaited Eric's further instructions.

"She'll come with me in my carriage. First you will bind her hands and feet so she can't escape." He instructed them.

"Yes sire." The men answered and set about fulfilling his order.

Eric laughed with a near wicked laugh, "So you like to pretend you're a boy, huh? Did you honestly believe I would never find out?" He waited for her to answer but she remained silent. "It doesn't matter. You are mine now and I know for a fact that your beloved Lord Wallace won't be coming to rescue you this time. To think that my future wife was stolen by my own nephew, I must admit that I find that rather amusing." He snickered. "If it wasn't so funny, I might not be so merciful. My men have been watching him closely and it seems he has forgotten all about you my dear. He has found himself a very beautiful young woman to warm him in his bed at night and to take the place of his 'wife'. I dare say that he probably is so taken with her that he no longer even remembers that you exist."

Arabella bit her tongue and could taste the blood that her teeth drew. She wished she could cup her ears with her hands to block out his cruel words but instead all she could do was to keep herself from administering to him a well deserved tongue lashing. "Arabella," her mother said through her tears, "I'm so sorry child. I had no idea that your father was coming here from time to time to check on me. He saw you dressed as Aram and recognized you…"

"I have no father." She said through clenched teeth and she could hear his sad sigh in response though it meant nothing to her. "That man is my enemy, not my family."

"I see." Her mother responded. "You may see him in whatever way you see fit." The soldiers helped Arabella to stand back up and then one of them lifted her up into his arms so he could carry her to the carriage.

Another rider came up on horse back just as the soldier made it to the carriage with Arabella. "What is the meaning of this visit, your majesty?" Peter asked in confusion. It was best if he acted like he had no clue that this young woman was Arabella. "I had no idea you were coming out this way." He dismounted and then took a moment to bow before his king. His glance stole towards where Arabella who was currently being loaded into the king's carriage.

"To think that she was right under your nose this whole time and

Beautiful Pretender

you didn't even notice." Eric sighed in frustration.

"You mean the princess?" He acted surprised. "Here?"

"Indeed." He looked over to her carriage. "I want you to return to Eldardesh with me. I'll assign another man to take your post here. There are other duties I have for you to do now that the princess has been found."

"As you wish, sire. Please afford me the time to gather my belongings before I leave."

"Make haste and do so at once. I want you in Brie-Ancou when I get there."

Peter bowed humbly again, "As you wish, my king." He quickly made his way to his horse as he did his best to not seem too concerned over Arabella. If Eric knew that he was aware of her being there all this time, it could most certainly mean his death, especially since he was trying to court her. Now all he could do was to hope that Eric would assign him the task of watching over her.

"Edmond..." A woman's voice whispered.

"Arabella." Edmond answered in his sleep for he had recognized who the voice belonged to. From the darkness of his dreams came a faint glow and soon Arabella's beautiful figure came into view much like an angel. She had her hair down in its soft waist length waves that he adored so much. She wore a long white gown that conformed to her body with a low bust line and flared sleeves. A golden circlet sat delicately upon her head and about her neck was a simple white ribbon that was tied in the back.

"Come to me, I miss you." Even though she seemed to be standing right before him, her voice sounded so distant. *"I want you."* She reached her arms out to him.

"Arabella." He whispered again and in his dream he reached out for her but she was always just out of his grasp. "Come back to me, please." He begged. "Don't leave me."

She smiled lovingly at him. "*I need you with me Edmond. I'm so lonely without you.*"

"I need you too, please come to me." He walked towards her but she always stayed just out of his reach. Suddenly her smile disappeared as her arms slowly dropped down to her side as she backed away from him with a look of horror on her face. Slowly she raised her hand and her finger pointed to something behind him. "What is it?" He asked in fear.

"*No!*" Her frightened voice said. "*He has come.*" She turned and ran from him as her image slowly began to fade away. "*Edmond, please help me.*" Her crying voice faded to nothing as did her image until she was no more, not even a speck of light in the distance.

"Arabella." He desperately called out to her. His real voice mumbled her name in his fitful sleep.

"*EDMOND!*" A deep ghastly and ghost like male voice whispered angrily in his ear. "*SHE'S MINE NOW!*" Edmond bolted up out of his sleep to the moon lit room of his childhood. He could still hear the evil laughter ringing in his ears. "Uh!" He cried out, throwing his hands over his ears in an attempt to block the sound from his dreams. He found himself struggling for each breath. His heart raced and fear was nearly consuming him.

"Arabella." He whispered in a frightened voice. "Are you in trouble or was it just a bad dream?" Edmond brought down his hands from his ears and laid one hand over his heart as he fought to gain control over his emotions. "Is this the result of obsessing over you every moment of the day?" His free hand came up to wipe the tears that fell from his eyes. Edmond got out of bed and walked over to the window in his room and opened it so he could get some fresh air. High above him hung the full moon shining down on his parents' estate in its whites and grays.

He reached over to the table near him and picked up the handkerchief Arabella had embroidered for him that also held the broach, neatly tucked away in its delicate folds. He carefully unwrapped the cloth to reveal the broach and then he held it up to the moon light so he could

Beautiful Pretender

look at it. His other hand gently fingered the delicate embroidery of the handkerchief as he held it. "Where are you?" He whispered as he looked back up at the moon. "Please come home to me. It's not too late yet…"

"*Edmond.*" He could still hear her beautiful voice calling his name. "*I love you.*"

"I need you to come back to me." He whispered into the night. "Where are you, my wife? What's happening to you?" Edmond leaned his head gently against the window frame. It was rare that a dream could have such a powerful effect on him. "I love you too."

… To be continued
End of Book 1

The King's Concubine

Book 2 of Edmond and Arabella's Story

Trapped in a world of a corrupted and cruel king, Arabella is forced to endure his wrath and manipulation. Lord Peter Evanston has given up everything to do all he can to be of some comfort to her during this dark time in her life, while keeping King Eric from killing her with his fits of anger.

Meanwhile, Edmond has returned home to Arminia and has done as Arabella wanted. He is now engaged to the Countess D'Winter, even though the only one he can ever love is the one woman he can never have. Yet he loves her so much that he is willing to do this to make her happy, despite the misery it leaves in his heart.

However a small glimmer of hope comes when King Eric brings her back to Arminia for the King's Tournament. It is the hope of helping her to leave such a cruel and dark world behind. But can he do this when she is so well guarded and now that she is too afraid to leave the prison of malice that Eric has her in behind? Or will King Eric succeed in using Arabella to bring down King Kendrick and Edmond both by using her to seduce them into his plans?

Look forward to the continuing journey that will leave you spellbound and breathless.

Printed in the United States
118178LV00003B/19/P